SAM REAVES

Other Avon Books by
Sam Reaves

FEAR WILL DO IT
A LONG COLD FALL

Bury it Deep

SAM REAVES

AVON BOOKS ◆ NEW YORK

AVON BOOKS
A division of
The Hearst Corporation
1350 Avenue of the Americas
New York, New York 10019

Copyright © 1993 by Sam Reaves
Published by arrangement with G. P. Putnam's Sons
Library of Congress Catalog Card Number: 93-3242
ISBN: 0-380-72266-6

First Avon Books Printing: December 1994

AVON TRADEMARK REG. U.S. PAT. OFF. AND IN OTHER COUNTRIES, MARCA REGISTRADA, HECHO EN U.S.A.

Printed in U.S.A.

RA 10 9 8 7 6 5 4 3 2 1

With the exception of a few public figures such as Mayor Richard M. Daley of Chicago (whose probity the author has no reason to doubt), every person mentioned or depicted in this story is entirely fictional. The author claims only a superficial acquaintance with Chicago's political culture; it will be evident to readers familiar with that culture that this is no false modesty. The author's intention is merely to entertain. No denigration of any actual person or institution is intended.

Thanks are due to Bob Freed and Jim Quinlan, who educated the author in the ways and means of big-city journalism; they are not responsible for any errors or for any unfavorable impression the author might inadvertently give of the honest profession of journalism.

1 Tie askew, hair in disarray, and breath whistling faintly as he climbed, the newspaperman made it up the stairs. A look of weary irritation passed over his face as he struggled, panting, to wrestle his keys from a pocket in pants that were growing too tight. He tugged the heavy ring free and it leapt from his grasp onto the mat before the door.

"Aah fer . . ." He bent to retrieve the keys, not finding the energy or the concentration to finish the curse. Carefully, he found the right key and inserted it in the lock. The door swung open onto a dark hall and the ripe full odor of unemptied cat box welled gently into his face. The newspaperman swore under his breath, closed the door behind him, and felt for the light switch. A bulb in an ancient frosted globe above his head went on, weakly illuminating the little entranceway with its coats piled on hooks, boots and shoes in a jumble at his feet.

"Honey, I'm home," the newspaperman mumbled. He moved into the dark living room and careened softly into the end of a couch. Steadying, he bent to find the switch on the stem of a lamp, cursing again because as always the switch was in just the wrong place. The lamp went on at last and the small living room was revealed, the ancient swollen couch and blanket-draped armchairs facing the dim reflection of the fat man in the unshaded windows.

The newspaperman pulled the shades quickly to shut out his image, the sparse hair on top springing up from the shiny dome as if to call attention to its sparseness, the paunch spilling over the belt and spreading the wings of the sport jacket. Shades down, he nerved himself up to a struggle with the jacket, wriggled free of it, and retreated to the couch to collapse with a sigh.

He gave one ineffectual tug at his tie and looked around his living room, the alcoholic numbness in his head asserting itself with his immobility. Magazines sprawled across the hardwood floor; abandoned coffee mugs stood like Easter Island monoliths, left scattered inexplicably by a vanished race; stuffing peeked from an armchair where feline claws had torn the fabic. The newspaperman closed his eyes.

When the telephone rang he realized he had dozed off sitting up. Heart fluttering, he leaned to drag the receiver off its cradle toward him, losing his grip and nearly sending it clattering to the floor. He managed to get it to his ear. "Yeah," he said.

"So how do you like it?" a voice said: distant, male, unhurried.

"Huh? Like what?" The newspaperman had righted himself, supporting himself with one beefy hand on the cushions.

"You didn't go back in the kitchen yet, huh?" The voice was quiet, perhaps amused.

The newspaperman sat in silence for a considerable time, waiting to wake up, waiting to catch on, waiting for a click in his ear. The telephone hissed at him quietly. "Well, go ahead," said the voice. "I'll wait."

The newspaperman opened his mouth but then paused and closed it without saying anything. He set the receiver down on the cushion and rose laboriously to his feet. He stepped carefully around the couch and made his way down a short hallway. He stopped at the door to the kitchen and reached in to switch on the light. He felt no alarm, only confusion.

The gray and black striped tabby hung at eye level, its body elongated by the pull of gravity, hind legs and tail dangling, front paws permanently to the fore, reaching for something to scratch. The ring at the end of the skewer was flush with the cat's chest, the rest of the skewer behind it driven into the frame of the door to the pantry, bent slightly from the force of the thrust. The cat's eyes were open but glazed, a little blood showing in its open mouth. The cat was very still.

The newspaperman stalked back to the living room. "Who the hell are you?" he said into the phone.

"Like it, do you?" the voice said. "I call it cat-kebab."

"I said who are you?"

"I'm the guy that's gonna do to you what I did to the cat." The tone was suddenly very flat. "If you don't keep out of things that ain't none of your fuckin' business."

"What the . . ."

" 'Cause you know what they say about curiosity and cats, don't you?"

The newspaperman rallied. "I'm a reporter. It's . . ."

"Yeah, I know you're a reporter. That's the whole point. There are some things you better not report."

"Look, I don't even know what you're talking about."

"One question."

"Huh?"

"A question. How many of those skewer things did you have?"

"What?"

"Do you know how many were in the set?"

"Jesus, I . . ."

"Maybe you should count them. There might be one missing." The click in the ear came abruptly, and the newspaperman stood with the receiver to his ear, listening to outer space.

After a moment he hung up the phone and went very slowly back to the kitchen. He stood in the doorway looking at the cat, wheezing faintly. After a while he squeezed his eyes shut, kneaded his brows, and beat a retreat. He made for the bedroom, thinking perhaps the cat would not be there in the morning.

■ ■ ■

The lake was a litter of ice close in, with hard dark open water beyond, under a wash of palest blue. The wind was cold but feckless, probing fitfully across the beach, dying away. Cooper and Diana labored a little, trudging over mingled sand and snow. Going south, they squinted into the harsh light from a cool winter sun, bouncing off ice.

Breaking a long silence, Diana said, "I don't want to turn on the TV some night, see them dusting your cab for fingerprints, blood all over the seat. Every time I hear a cab driver gets shot, my heart stops."

Cooper marched with his eyes on the ground, knowing she was right but hating to admit it. "I don't drive much at night any more, and I'm careful about who I pick up."

"You drove till midnight last Thursday. And it only takes one mistake."

Cooper raised his eyes to the clean distinct skyline stretching down the shore and sighed. "What else would I do that would pay the rent and let me work when I want?"

"You don't need the damn money," Diana said, snarling just a bit. "All that money that fell into your lap when that stuff with Tommy happened would put you through school any time you want."

"I told you, the money's for you. You're the one with ambitions. Besides, after talking to that guy at Loyola I'm not sure any school would take me."

"Oh, for God's sake. You talk to one professor with different politics and you think there's a conspiracy against you."

"You know what he said? He said it looked like I'd been seduced by some extremist thinkers. Nozick, Hayek. Popper, for Christ's sake! The guy dismisses some of the greatest minds of the century as extremists."

"He also said those notebooks of yours contained, if I remember correctly, the seeds of three good master's theses and maybe a couple of doctorates."

Cooper shook his head. "I still don't know whether I'd go back in history or philosophy. And anyway, I won't be able to jump through the hoops."

Diana stopped and spun him around with a hand on his arm. "Cooper. Stop bullshitting me."

He could take that dark Iberian gaze for only a second before his eyes went away, far out over the lake.

"You know what your problem is?" Diana said. "Fear."

"Yeah." Cooper turned slowly, taking in the whole long sweep of shoreline, winding up with his back to her, looking into the park, trees stripped of leaves with the dark jumble of the city beyond. "Fear of change. You're right." He felt her step to his side, slip her arm through his. A breath of wind kicked up snow around their feet. "I like the way I live. Kicking around the neighborhood, driving a couple or three times a week, shooting pool, coming out here to get away from things. I like reading what I want, when I want. Writing if I've got something to say. That'll all change if I go back to school. Somebody else sets the agenda then."

"A bit of a challenge wouldn't hurt you."

He found nothing to say and they resumed walking, arm in arm. When they reached the pier they ducked through the cables and walked out to the end, where they could look south and see distant skyscrapers rigid in the chill. They were a million miles from human life, on a vast sea of ice. Diana put her arms around Cooper's waist and buried her face in the scarf at his neck, fleeing the wind. Cooper held her and said, "There's enough money for one of us to go to school, right now. It should be you. You've got the plan, the program. I'm happy this way."

They listened to the faint creaking of the ice. Diana raised her face to his and said, "If I take your money, go back to school now, will you do one thing for me?"

Cooper nodded, knowing what it was. "Get out of the cab," he said.

"Yeah. Get out of the cab. There's a million things you could do that won't get you shot. Pick one."

Cooper looked out over the frozen lake, feeling suddenly old and sad. At the same time, distantly, he felt relief. He felt he might like a world where the fear of getting shot wasn't a constant, muted presence. "OK," he said. "I'll get out of the cab." He felt her arms tighten; that was her only response. He still felt old but just as suddenly he didn't feel sad any more.

They walked back north through the park, in silence. As they left the park, heading for the coffee shop, Cooper said, "It may take me a while. I'm starting at zero here. I can't really picture doing anything besides driving."

"Everybody needs a mid-life crisis."

"Mid-life, hell. I'm the world's oldest adolescent."

Sitting in the window-fogging warmth of the coffee house, Diana said, "Speaking of adolescents, your friend Mel called. I forgot to tell you."

"Moreland? What the hell's he want?"

"He invited us to a party. Saturday, I think."

"Both of us? Not just a bachelor outing?"

"Not this time, I guess. Maybe he has a date. Or maybe he was just being polite."

Cooper smiled at her. "You don't like him too much, do you?"

Diana shrugged. "He talks too loud, he drinks a lot, and he fancies himself a womanizer. Other than that, he's OK."

Cooper downed his coffee and shrugged. "On the first two counts, he has to. He's a reporter. As for the third, it's funny because he's so bad at it."

"I'll let you two go by yourselves. I'll trust you to stay out of trouble."

"I know, Mel's the kind of guy women hate to see their men hang around with." Cooper was grinning. "But he has his uses."

"Such as?"

"He shoots a good game of pool. He knows everybody in town. And . . ."

"And?" Diana was smiling now.

"And he's always good for a few laughs."

■ ■ ■

The party was on the North Shore, in a big rambling house hidden by trees at the end of a lane that snaked up from Sheridan Road at the point where it wandered through a deep wooded ravine. Moreland drove fast and with reasonable skill, sketching to Cooper the wonders that awaited them. The house belonged to a developer Cooper had never heard of who Moreland said was politically connected and loaded with a capital L. "The cream of the cream, MacLeish. Money and power. Beautiful women, by all accounts. And us."

Moreland's editor, who knew the host, had invited him, telling him to bring a guest. "And in the absence of appropriate female company in my life right now, old buddy, I thought of you. I thought a Hoosier like you might appreciate seeing how the elite lives."

"You're going to start a rumor, bringing me."

"It's not a god damn office party, MacLeish. Nobody's going to know either of us. We're doing sociological research here. I thought you'd get a kick out of it."

The sign at the entrance to the lane said *Private—No Trespassing*. Moreland went up the drive as if calling on millionaires was something he did every weekend. The house was an impressive piece of work, decorated with a good deal of money and what Cooper supposed was taste. They entered by a front door flanked by columns, apparently passing the inspection of a sturdy-looking white-haired man with a florid face who was lounging just a shade too casually in the flagstoned entrance hall. They nodded at him, handed coats to a uniformed maid, and proceeded toward the noise.

Men with loud voices and women with painted faces dotted the expensive landscape. In an airy high-vaulted living room directing the eye to an arched window that by day would look out over the lake, Moreland collared a short plump man with dull blond hair, a round, over-nourished face, and nervously flicking eyes. "My editor, Jay Macy. Jay, my old friend Cooper MacLeish."

Cooper shook hands and saw the eyes going back and forth between him and Moreland like a pinball between posts. Cooper could see the man wondering. "Nice meeting you," Macy said, and slapped Moreland on the arm and fled. Cooper and Moreland found things to drink and stood at the edge of the living room, marginal to the proceedings.

"I do believe that's King Van Houten over there," said Moreland.

"Royalty? You should have told me. I'd have put on a tie."

"That's his name. But he's close to royalty. Or maybe even deity. He's a zoning lawyer, a very crafty one. Yes, definitely a minor deity."

"You mean the undersized gentleman with the obvious rug?"

"That's the one."

"And who's that he's talking to?"

"Nobody in particular." Cooper could tell by the tone of Moreland's voice that he had lost interest in the lawyer. "I don't know what it is, MacLeish. There's a certain type of woman that reduces me to incoherence." Moreland's eyes were tracking someone on the far side of the bright crowded room. Cooper looked over his shoulder and spotted her, a lithe blonde in glossy black pants sprayed onto trim rounded haunches. Her hair was artfully designed to give the impression she had just taken a few hundred amps through her system, and she transferred her long-stemmed champagne glass from one hand to the other with some slight difficulty because of the length of her blood-red nails. "See what I mean?" said Moreland.

"I see what you mean," said Cooper. He watched as the blonde tottered on spike heels toward a large man in a black suit and matching Stetson and spread her arms wide to receive his embrace, flashing him a smile that suggested his presence had made her life complete.

"What is it about that kind of woman? How would you describe that?" said Moreland, staring hauntedly over the rim of his tumbler.

"Cheap and tawdry?" Cooper suggested.

Moreland clutched his arm. "That's it. That's it exactly. You put your finger on it. That's the kind of woman I want." They watched for a moment as the blonde worked on the cowboy, and then Moreland pulled Cooper away. "Come on, before I start crying. Let's go celebrity hunting."

The house went on forever; Cooper had thought he'd had it scoped out only to be surprised by new rooms lurking around unsuspected corners. From the living room, they pushed gently through knots of people into a den crowded with serious drinkers four to a couch. "See the old gent over there about to fall off the sofa? That's Tucker, the guy they couldn't nail in Greylord. Nobody's sure if he's honest or just smart."

"Maybe he has a smart bailiff."

"Could be."

"Well, if he can maintain a judicial temperament with that much alcohol in him he gets my vote any day."

"So far so good—he managed not to miss the edge of the table with his glass. Oh my, there's our host and hostess together. That's a rare sight. Where's my photographer?" Moreland inclined his head in the direction of a huddle in the corner, dominated by a handsome couple standing shoulder-to-shouder. The man was tall, slender, gray-haired; he stood with one hand in a trouser pocket and the other wrapped around a tall drink. The woman was a frosted dark blonde, past the bloom of youth but expensively preserved. "Fill me in," said Cooper.

"Regis Swanson and his wife, *née* Astrid Huber. The big-time lawyer, you know? More money in that corner than you can shake a stick at."

"So what's unusual?"

"Word is, it's pretty much a *pro forma* marriage any more. Swanson's taste in mistresses is legendary and Astrid's too busy dabbling in politics to be a faithful boon companion. Macy told me the only thing that keeps them together is the high cost of divorce."

"Looks like a happy couple to me."

"They're rich, MacLeish. What do they have to be unhappy about?"

Moreland led Cooper through an archway into a quiet, dimly lighted temple, where a bar with a black marble top served as altar. Logs hissed and spat flames in a broad fireplace opposite the bar, a screen keeping sparks from flying onto a rug the color of very old port. Two young men in white jackets worked with wordless dispatch behind the bar; the six leather-upholstered bar stools were all occupied. Conversation was more muted in this room, and Moreland steered Cooper to a corner and murmured to him.

"There you go, MacLeish. We got the president of the Board of Appeals over there talking to two Cook County commissioners and the head of the Illinois Manufacturers Association. We got so much clout in this room I'm starting to feel faint."

"Better get another drink," said Cooper, who saw Moreland leaning in the direction of the bar.

"Quick thinking. I'm glad I brought you along."

Moreland sidled to the end of the bar and beamed at the occupants of the barstools, who ignored him. Cooper sipped beer and watched the politicos in the corner: middle-aged men with the easy smiles of people with favors to grant. Three were white, with nicely graying hair, and one was a tall broad black man with a round bald head and a bold stroke of a moustache.

Moreland was back at Cooper's elbow, resupplied. "I guess Mackey Hairston never gets tired of being the only black man at the party," he murmured, following Cooper's eyes. "He's no token, though. That's one of the half-dozen most powerful men in Cook County, and a good friend for Regis Swanson to have."

"I've heard the name," Cooper said.

Moreland raised his glass. "So what do you think, MacLeish? Could you live this way?"

"I'd have to spend more on clothes." Moreland had said casual, but Cooper had known that would have a different meaning here; he had put on the alligator cowboy boots bequeathed him by a dying Mexican gambler in L.A. to go with his tweed jacket and best jeans.

Moreland grinned at him, a balding cherub in a navy blue sport jacket over a pin-striped shirt without a tie. "Nah, you look terrific. You look like rough trade. Watch out for some of those decorator types out there or you'll have to use your judo to get out of here. It's those Marlboro Man looks of yours. Drives 'em wild."

Cooper looked at him with the faint smile he often wore in Moreland's company. "Mel, tell me again why we're here."

"To rub elbows with the rich and influential, my boy. To steal their women."

Cooper eyed the quartet in the corner. "I'll settle for their wallets."

"That's the spirit." Moreland spread his feet a little wider, puffed out his ample chest. "I told you, Jay knows our host. Jay's the world's biggest name-dropper, and Regis Swanson is a name he drops a lot. But he invited me out of guilt, I think."

"Guilt?"

"Yeah. See, Jay screwed me out of a good story last week. He was dodging me for days, couldn't look me in the eye. So the other day when I slid in next to him at the bar I guess he thought I was going to chew on him for it, and before I could say a word he says how would I like to come along to Swanson's big annual everyone-who's-anyone Christmas bash. He did it just to placate me."

Cooper shook his head, smiling. "OK, now why am I here?"

"Because I wanted to impress you, for Christ's sake." Moreland spread his arms wide, slopping vodka onto the rug. "Aren't you awed yet?"

"I'm working on it."

Moreland clinked glasses with him and sucked in some liquor. "Besides, I wanted to talk to you."

Cooper drank. "What, about something in particular?"

"Yeah. Let's go find a nook or a cranny." He steered Cooper out of the bar by a door on the far side and along a hallway with a gallery running above it. They found their way to a solarium at what Cooper calculated was the rear of the house, where a few other refugees had installed themselves on wicker furniture among tropical plants in fat earthen pots. Through the glass wall Cooper could see house lights shining on snowdrifts. The solarium was warm despite the acre of glass, and Cooper decided the wealthy were above worrying about heating bills.

Moreland had dragged one of the wicker chairs across the tile floor to the end of a sofa. The chair creaked as he sat on it, waving Cooper to the couch. "Park yourself there and get set for a story." Moreland's broad forehead and upper lip showed a faint sheen of sweat. A sprig of his remaining hair had sprung to attention on the top of his head. He leaned in close to Cooper. "Tell me something," he breathed. "You ever get a death threat?"

Cooper blinked a few times. "No. They usually skip that stage with me. Somebody been sending you notes with the letters cut out of the newspaper?"

"Nope. I got the creepy voice on the telephone. And the gruesome message in the kitchen."

Cooper drank beer. "How gruesome?"

"Somebody spitted my cat. The guy on the phone, I presume."

"Spitted it?"

"Ran a shish kebab skewer through it and stuck it in the wall. With a certain amount of force. I had a hell of a time getting the point out of the woodwork."

"Wow. Tough on the cat."

"Ah, he had it coming. I hated that cat, MacLeish. What bothered me was how easily the guy got in my apartment."

"What'd he do, come in the back?"

"Punched in the window, reached through. None of my deadbeat neighbors heard a thing."

"You report it?"

Moreland shrugged. "What do I tell the cops? Somebody hurt my kitty?"

"You tell 'em somebody threatened to kill you."

"Yeah, I probably should have. If you want to know the truth, I was kind of drunk when I got home and I just couldn't deal with it. The next morning, I tossed the cat in the garbage and said, 'Hey, he can't scare me.' But I got to thinking, and shit. The guy was watching, waiting for me to come home. He could have killed me instead."

"So what did he say on the phone?"

"He told me he was going to do to me what he did to the cat if I didn't stay out of things that weren't my business." Moreland drank deep, eyes flicking out over the room. "He didn't even say what particular business he was connected with."

"And you have no idea?"

"Oh, I think I know what he was talking about." Moreland cast a look down the hall toward the party noises, clutching the tumbler full of vodka for dear life. He frowned across the room at the four superbly coiffed middle-aged women who shared the solarium with them.

"Well, are you going to tell me or not?" said Cooper.

Moreland eased back on the chair, wicker groaning beneath him. "Last Monday I got a phone call at the office. I'd been out all morning, just got back to the desk. Phone rings and a guy says, 'Mr. Moreland, this is Vance Oyler,' like I should know who he is. I say, 'Give me a clue, Vance,' and he reminds me we met about three years ago when I was doing a story about the South Water Market. Weedy little guy. The guy works down there, I talked to him for ten minutes, now he thinks he's in my Rolodex. Christ, you know how many people I talk to in connection with stories every week?"

"So what did he have to say?"

"Well, he says first of all I got to keep him anonymous. I say OK, he says he's got a story for me. I say, 'In connection with what?' and he says, 'About a lying son of a bitch who's putting one over on the whole city.' I swear, that's the way the guy talks. So I say, 'Give me some particulars, Vance,' and he goes, 'How about we get together for lunch or something and I'll lay it all out for you.' I ask him why he can't tell me a little more over the phone and he says it's a face-to-face kind of deal. He says he's got something that will—what'd he say—he said it would sink some heavy cruisers.''

"Sink some heavy cruisers? What is the guy, a retired admiral?''

"That's what he said. So I say OK, we agree to meet at a tavern on Wabash at five o'clock, I hang up. I didn't give it too much thought, because guys with a story that will blow the lid off City Hall are a dime a dozen. But I think what the hell, I get a beer out of the deal, pretend to be interested, nothing comes of it, a day in the life. Five o'clock comes, I go over to the bar, nothing.'' Moreland polished off the drink at a gulp. "I wait for an hour, thinking I just haven't recognized the guy, because after all it's been three years and I barely noticed the son of a bitch when I talked to him, but nobody even close to the guy comes in, nobody approaches me and I'm sitting right by the door. I have three beers, piss 'em all out again, and go home. Another K on the scorecard. Just for fun, in an idle moment the next day I look at the phone book. Five Oylers, none of them Vance. I start calling them and it turns out I get his mother. She says yes, Vance lives with her but he's out, she doesn't know when he'll be back. Won't give me a work number. Doesn't sound cooperative. I try the other Oylers, I get one John Oyler on the phone, who admits to being Vance's brother. I identify myself, ask if he knows where his brother is, he says and I quote, 'I don't talk to fucking scumbag reporters,' and hangs up. I shrug in my lordly detached manner and get slightly curious about his reaction to reporters, but I don't think much of it until the next night I find the cat.''

Moreland stared into his empty glass, then looked longingly down the hall. To forestall a rush to the bar, Cooper said, "Would the guy on the phone that night have been John Oyler?''

"No. Different voice entirely. The guy who did the cat was older. Had kind of a growl to his voice.''

"And you're sure it was the Oyler business the guy on the phone was referring to.''

"Gotta be. You know what else I was working on that day? An

accident on the Ryan, an alleged miracle in a Guatemalan Pentecostal storefront church. And a feature on Cardinal Bernardin's wardrobe. No kidding. I'm the guy they call when a story is just too cold to handle. The only thing I've been within hailing distance of that smelled remotely like a story was the call from this Oyler creature. But there's more."

"The plot thickens, does it?"

"Unlike my hair, yes, it does."

"I got to give you credit, Mel, you haven't tried to hide it with a comb-over."

"I've been tempted. You don't know the trauma, MacLeish. But listen, this is serious."

"Oh yeah, the plot. It was thickening."

"Yeah. The day after I find the cat, I'm feeling brave and I call Oyler's ma again. He's out again, his mother says no, she doesn't know when he'll be in but he'll call me, yes sir. Fine. That afternoon at the office I come back, find a message in my box. Copy clerk took it, says the caller dictated it very carefully. The message says V.O. will meet me at a Streets and San garage on Ravenswood, in Uptown, on Sunday night. Gives the address but says come around back in the alley. That's tomorrow night. At midnight, for dramatic effect, I guess. And it says he will have the goods."

"Who, V.O.?"

"Yeah. The mysterious V.O. That's what he said, the goods."

Cooper nodded. "Why a Streets and San garage? Is that where the goods are?"

"That's what I presumed. I don't know."

Cooper wanted to set his empty beer glass on the coffee table, but the finish looked expensive and there were no coasters. He held the glass in both hands and said, "What do you want me to tell you? If you want the story, you better go."

"I don't want you to tell me anything, MacLeish. I want you to come with me."

Cooper met Moreland's earnest gaze with a faint smile. "How come?" he said.

Moreland leaned forward with a creaking of wicker and a slight exhalation and plunked his tumbler down on the table. "Because I'm scared, for Christ's sake." He sat back, eyes flicking to the women and back again. "The thought has crossed my mind that someone could have found out about Oyler's big mouth and be setting me up tomorrow night. I'm not sure Oyler would have left a message. He would have talked to me in person, I think. And anyone can leave a message in someone else's name."

"Well, then, don't go unless you talk to Oyler in person and confirm it."

"I tried. His ma says he's out of town till Sunday night."

Cooper shrugged. "So don't go. Sounds suspicious."

"It is suspicious. And it gives me the willies. I remember that voice and the way the fucking cat looked hanging up there on the wall and I get scared. But I want the story. If somebody thinks they have to threaten me, then there's something there. And I want it, because I'm tired of covering ethnic parades. So confirm or not confirm, I'm going. And you're coming with me."

"Why me?"

Moreland stared, then smiled and slapped Cooper on the shoulder. "Because you're the meanest motherfucker in the valley. I want you walking next to me."

Cooper set his glass next to Moreland's and shook his head. "I'm retired, Mel. I'm done with the rough stuff. If you think there's serious danger, hire a bodyguard. I promised Diana I was through getting shot at."

"All I want is a lookout. Just someone to watch my back. Drive over there with me, keep your eyes open, that kind of thing. I just need somebody with a little nerve, to bolster mine."

"So take another reporter."

"Another reporter? Uh-uh, this one's mine. Look, I figure there's a ninety percent chance there's no danger, just Oyler with some kind of story. I'll keep trying to reach the guy tomorrow and hopefully I'll get him. But even if I don't, I can't just let it slide. I gotta check it out. And I don't want to go alone."

"If you're worried about a setup, what you do is you go early. An hour early, and watch."

"Terrific advice. I still want you along."

"Mel, I'm a tired old man."

"And you're still the only guy I know who laughs at danger and eats red meat."

Cooper shook his head. "I've hung up my spurs."

Moreland cocked an eyebrow at him. "Aren't you curious?"

A silence ensued. With a flutter of laughter the women rose and left the solarium, leaving Cooper and Moreland alone with the distant party commotion. "No," said Cooper.

"Bullshit."

Cooper stared down the hall, trying to suppress a laugh. "I'll read about it in the paper."

"I'm asking you as a pal, MacLeish. You'll be in on a breaking news story, watching an ace reporter in action."

"I'll be home in bed while the ace reporter is freezing his ass off."

"You'll be sorry. You'll sit there at home feeling those adrenal glands starting to atrophy. I know you."

Cooper shook his head and smiled. He rose and picked up his empty glass. "I'm going to go find a bathroom. When I come out, I'll give you an answer."

"Check out the big one on the other side of the house," said Moreland, following him. "I thought I'd wandered into the YMCA by mistake."

The bathroom was tiled in black and white with a skylight above a whirlpool tub. It was large enough to play a fair game of handball in. Cooper dried his hands on a black towel that felt like velvet and hiked back to the door, emerging into the light and noise. Moreland had been heading for the bar but was gone by the time Cooper made his way back there. Cooper went on a tour, smiling at people, eavesdropping in a half-hearted way, waving off drinks from anxious waiters. He saw King Van Houten speaking into the ear of a man he thought he recognized as an alderman.

When he found Moreland in a thickly populated crimson-walled parlor he just stood watching for a moment, waiting for him to look up. Moreland was sunk into a deep armchair with a fresh drink in his right hand and his left hand around the waist of the blonde in the black pants. She was perched on one of his ample thighs, resting an elbow on his shoulder and laughing into his round beaming face. When Moreland finally looked up, the light of joyous dementia in his eyes, Cooper shook his head, thinking that if any adult he knew needed a keeper, it was Moreland. Cooper figured there were better ways of getting home than being driven by Melvin Moreland with a bellyful of drinks. "I'm taking off, Mel," he said. "I'll find a lackey to call me a cab."

"Don't leave yet, Coop." For an instant Moreland seemed on

the verge of panic, suddenly about to dump the blonde onto the floor. "What about tomorrow?"

"We're on. Who's driving, me or you?" Cooper said.

Moreland stared; the blonde was smiling emptily up at Cooper. "You're the pro," said Moreland, starting to grin. "You come by and get me."

"All right. If we're going to be there early, let's say ten-thirty. Should be enough time."

"I'll be ready. Thanks, Coop."

"Don't spill that drink," said Cooper. The blonde wiggled long-nailed fingers at him as he left.

 "I DIG YOUR THREADS, MAN," Cooper said as Dominic shrugged off the black woolen overcoat to reveal a black sport jacket over a black shirt buttoned to the neck beneath it. The boy froze and stared blankly at Cooper, an explorer greeted by a savage in an obscure tongue.

"Huh?" he said.

"The clothes, Jack. The threads."

Dominic shook his head in disgust. "You're like my grandma," he said. "You think I should dress like a golfer. Polyester plaids and those dorky haircuts."

"This from a man whose hair is cut to hang in his eyes. Hey, lighten up. I said I liked 'em. How is your grandma?"

"She's a pain in the ass, as usual."

"Well, it's not like you've done anything to make her worry recently. I mean, what eighteen-year-old kid hasn't run off with a carnival and wound up in Keokuk, Iowa, broke?"

"I'm nineteen. And I left her a note."

Cooper laughed in spite of himself. "You're a wastrel, you know that?"

"I guess I get it from you."

"Hey, have some respect for your father."

"I like froze my ass off walking over here," the boy said.

"Yeah, it's a mean one, ain't it? I think we got some hot chocolate back here."

Dominic followed him down the hall. "Cool place," he said.

"Yeah, we're starting to settle in. I wound up tossing most of my old stuff and just letting Diana arrange the place. She had all the nice things anyway."

Diana looked up from the dining room table as they entered. "Except for the desk, and the director's chair that John Huston supposedly once sat in. I didn't dare touch those."

"Hi. What's all this?" Dominic pointed at the sprawl of papers and reference books across the dining room table.

Diana smiled. "Work in progress. I've got the editor of a little review in North Carolina interested in some Spanish poetry I'm translating."

"Cool." Dominic came to rest by the table and stood still for a moment, staring down at the books. "Cooper says you're going back to school."

"Yeah. I finally decided to do it. There's a good program in comparative literature at U. of C. It'll mean a long commute, but it's what I want. That'll give me the depth I need. But I have to get in first."

"You'll get in," said Cooper from the kitchen. "The way you buzzsawed through those sample problems in the GRE booklet? Your waitressing days are numbered."

"The GRE's only a start," said Diana. "They'll want writing samples, an interview, all kinds of things."

Dominic picked up the volume that was spread in front of her. "What does . . . *salpicado* mean?"

"Spattered, sprinkled. In this context probably more like 'flecked.' "

Dominic put the book down. "Wow. That must be wild, having all those different words in your head like that."

Cooper found cocoa and put milk on to heat while he listened to Diana and his son, the stranger. He leaned on the counter and stared out the back window at the ice that had hardened on power lines and trees in the back yards across the alley. The radiator was hissing as it pumped out heat and Cooper was comforted by the sound: the sound of being warm inside on a winter day. At the same time he was prey to a mysterious sadness, staring out at a view that was not the old view, in a home that was not the old home and no longer exclusively his, listening to the future being planned, wishing he had one to plan. For a moment all he wanted was the past.

"Don't let the milk boil," Diana said from the doorway.

"I forgot to tell you," he said, pouring the milk into mugs. "I'm going out with Moreland again tonight."

She didn't answer immediately, having read his tone of voice perfectly. "You two are thick as thieves all of a sudden. What is it tonight, someone waiting to be fleeced at pool?"

Cooper smiled, concentrating on the pouring, wondering what to tell her. Deciding he couldn't lie to her, he said, "No. He wants me to come along on an interview with him."

"How come? You interested in journalism now?"

Cooper looked into those dark eyes under the auburn hair and had to tell her. "He thinks there might be some danger. He wanted a partner along."

Diana stared for a moment, betrayed, frozen. Then she turned and went back to the dining room table, arms folded. Dominic blinked at them both.

"It's at midnight," Cooper said, setting a mug beside her. "The guy he's talking to wants to keep it under wraps. Mel just wants somebody to watch for shadows. Nothing's going to happen."

"Fine. You're a big boy," Diana said, shuffling papers.

Cooper handed a mug to Dominic. "Come on, Karpov. Let's go set up the chessboard."

▪ ▪ ▪

"Where exactly did the message say to meet him?" Cooper eased off the gas and the old Valiant began to rumble as it rolled over bricks. On the left a weed-covered embankment sloped up to railroad tracks. On the right a procession of low brick façades with glass-block windows went past in the dim lamplight, low-tech workshops jammed shoulder-to-shoulder. Cooper read signs: Keough Glass, Dunlap Costume Co., For Sale By Owner.

"It gave the address and said 'in back.' In the alley, I guess." Moreland spoke in hushed tones, as if fearing someone outside the car would hear him.

"Where's the garage?"

"We passed it back there, in the middle of the block," Moreland said, in his husky whisper. "The gangs have it now, from the look of the graffiti all over it."

"What, you mean it's empty?"

"Yeah, this is an old garage. I looked it up. Streets and San got a new facility in this ward a few years ago but held on to this one. You know how it is with a city fiefdom. You don't just go giving property away."

"Yeah. So somebody's had his own little private garage back there. What do you think they've been doing in there?"

"Beats me. The more criminal the better, far as I'm concerned."

There were a few cars parked along the block, a scattering in the parking strip at the foot of the embankment, one or two along the curb. Cooper braked at the stop sign and looked up the side street. There were more cars there, parked under bare trees. "Not a happening neighborhood," he said. He put the Valiant in park and checked his mirrors. He didn't think any of the cars they'd passed had been occupied, but he wasn't sure. Across the railroad tracks, water tanks on the roofs of empty factories were black against the unhealthy yellow glow of the sky.

"Let's make a pass." Cooper put the car in gear and went south, past more workshops, and turned right onto a street full of shuttered storefronts. Just ahead, El tracks loomed above the street. They went under the tracks, past the station entrance on their right, and Cooper slowed abruptly and nosed the Valiant into the alley just beyond the tracks.

"Here's our alley, I bet." Moreland grunted in reply. Cooper drove slowly past the massive girders of the El tracks. The tracks ran just behind the buildings they had passed coming down the brick street; light bulbs illuminated overhead doors and peeling signs that said *Shipping and Receiving.* To the left were narrow dark yards and back stairs of apartment buildings. There were a few cars parked along the way; Cooper flashed his brights into them as he approached. They were empty.

He paused at the side street, watching in both directions for a moment, and then pushed on.

Moreland was silent as they rolled up the alley. After a moment he said, "It could be a setup, couldn't it?"

"Could be. On the other hand, it could be Oyler waiting with the story of a lifetime."

Cooper's headlight beams washed over the trash cans, tire-churned ice, piles of railroad ties stacked in the snow under the El tracks. "You're a big help, MacLeish," said Moreland. "I'd feel better if I'd talked to the guy. Maybe I should have waited for him to call back. His mother said she expected him late."

"And if we'd waited any longer we wouldn't have been able to come early and scout it out. Besides, this isn't the type of guy whose mother always knows what he's doing. Screw it, Mel. We're committed. Now, did you happen to notice how far down the block the place we want is?"

"Five from the north end. I counted."

"Good man. Here's the middle of the block. Would it be one of these?" Cooper slowed to a crawl, scanning the front, keeping an eye on the mirrors. The alley was deserted. Cooper switched off the car heater and rolled down the window, wanting to hear what there was to hear. The steady chug of the Valiant's engine and the grinding of tires over ice was all there was. Nothing moved in the shadows.

"I haven't seen another human being in half an hour," said Moreland.

Cooper wasn't inclined to believe that anyone was waiting to take a potshot at Moreland, but his heart had accelerated nonetheless. He looked hard into the shadows to his left, into the back yards and the sheltered stairways.

The buildings on their right ended and there was a broad open space beyond the tracks. Here there were a number of cars parked; Cooper scanned them and gave the Valiant a little gas, rolling quickly up to the next side street. "Looks pretty dead," he said.

"What now?" said Moreland.

Cooper had turned left, away from the industrial strip. "Nobody shot at us. But we're good and early. I'd say we park and watch."

"Pull over up here and let's think for a second."

With the Valiant idling at the curb, Cooper looked across the seat at Moreland and said, "What's to think about?"

"If it is a setup, we're sitting ducks just parked somewhere."

"Parked right by the garage, maybe. We park a block away and watch. They aren't expecting us to be early. If somebody does want to take a shot at you, we'll see him moving into position."

Moreland cocked his head, doubtfully. "I guess."

Cooper reached for the gear lever. "Let's make one more pass. I want to make sure I know what door we're watching." He reversed back to the mouth of the alley and turned into it from the north. "Keep your eyes open," he said.

Coming south down the alley, he noticed things he hadn't seen before: a cluster of fifty-gallon drums against a wall, a sunken loading ramp dug at a steep angle into the ground. The buildings were flush with one another and he had to go slowly to be sure which was the fifth building down. "Here we go," said Moreland, leaning across the seat to get a better look. "See anyone?"

Cooper saw no one. He saw wire mesh over begrimed windows, an overhead door with paint peeling, a smaller door beside it. Cooper looked hard as they rolled past.

"Well, that's interesting," he said.

"What?"

"The door's unlocked."

"Huh?"

"The smaller door. There was a hasp, with a padlock. The hasp was open and the padlock was hanging from its chain."

"Are you sure?"

"Mel, I'm not blind." They had reached the end of the block and Cooper turned onto the side street. He went for a hundred feet and double-parked. "You want to go in?" he said.

"Go in?"

"Mel, get a hold of yourself. I said, do you want to go in?"

Moreland looked out the windshield. Cooper could hear his teeth chattering. He rolled up the window and turned the heater back on. "I thought we were just going to wait," Moreland said.

"That was before we saw the door unlocked."

"What do you think's going on in there?"

"I don't know, Mel. That's what we're going to find out. You're a reporter, aren't you?"

Seconds passed. In the distance a siren swelled and faded. Moreland turned toward Cooper. "I don't know. I don't know that that's real wise. You know what I mean?"

Cooper nodded slowly. After a moment he said, "Reach under the seat and you'll find a flashlight." Moreland stared through the dark for a moment and then fumbled between his legs and extracted the two-foot steel-cased flashlight Cooper had acquired for emergencies of one sort or another. Cooper took the light from him and said, "Pull the car back in the alley and point it up toward the garage. Turn the lights off but keep it idling. If you see or hear any trouble, haul ass up and get me. If I find Oyler, I'll come out and wave to you." Cooper reached for the door handle.

"Wait a second." Moreland's eyes shone wide in the dark. "You sure you don't want me to come with you?"

Cooper gave it a moment's honest thought. "If somebody's laying for you, they may let me walk by. You better stay with the car."

Moreland nodded. "OK. Watch your step."

"Let me get into the alley before you bring the car around." Cooper pulled gloves and a navy-blue watch cap from the side pockets of his jacket and put them on. He stepped out into the chill. He slammed the door and made for the entrance to the alley, the heavy flashlight swinging at his side like a club. He hunched his shoulders against the cold, his breath trailing away behind him as he walked. Moreland had looked like the Michelin man in his down parka, but Cooper was used to spending winter nights in a heated taxicab, and had brought nothing heavier than the old leather bomber jacket. He turned into the alley, suppressing a shiver.

He looked ahead and saw no movement, just the frigid stasis of a back alley at midnight with the temperature ten degrees the wrong side of freezing. His feet crunched softly over ice. The alley was lighted by lamps on high poles; the space beneath the El tracks was in shadow but feebly illuminated at intervals by forlorn light-bulbs standing guard at the back of the workshops. Cooper looked hard into the shadows, not wanting surprises. Behind him he heard the Valiant creep into the alley.

A sign on the back of the garage said *City of Chicago Department of Streets and Sanitation—No Parking.* Cooper stepped into the shadows and put his back to a girder and stood still. He watched and waited for half a minute. The overhead door was still losing its paint; the hasp on the small door beside it was still open. There were no lights on inside the garage, none at least that he could detect through the filthy windows. The only sounds he heard came from far away: traffic sounds, night sounds.

Cooper figured there was no serious danger of him getting hurt; he figured Oyler was probably lying low inside the garage, waiting for Moreland to rap on the door. But Cooper had learned that what you figured could be wrong, and Moreland's story was just enough to make him want to go very carefully. He stepped away from the girder.

Cooper approached the door and put his hand on the knob

beneath the cylinder lock. He turned the knob and the latch clicked. He pushed the door open a few inches and listened. Through the gap he saw impenetrable darkness. He let go of the knob and reached out with the flashlight and rapped twice on the metal door, sending faint echoes through the interior of the garage. "Oyler?" he said, not too loudly.

The echoes died away. The garage remained dark and silent. Cooper looked both ways along the alley, watching for signs he'd aroused someone. The track supports blocked his view back down to where Moreland should be. He was on a deserted planet.

Go home, said one voice. Go in, said another. Cooper figured again; he figured whatever was happening, if there was a story it was inside the garage.

Cooper shoved the door wide open with his foot; it swung in slowly and bumped gently against the wall. He held the flashlight at arm's length and switched it on and swept it quickly over the interior, sheltering behind the doorframe. He saw a concrete floor, stacks of something made of wood, crates or skids, the rear of a truck. He switched the light off.

Cooper reached inside the door and felt for light switches. Too good to be true, he thought, finding nothing. He took a breath and plunged, slipping in quickly and grabbing the edge of the door and swinging it shut behind him. He put his back to the wall and slid down until he was squatting on the floor, waiting. Nothing stirred.

When he was almost certain he was alone he switched on the flashlight, holding it high and away from his body just in case. He took in the whole of the garage with one slow sweep. Looming ghostlike out of the darkness he saw the stack of wooden skids directly in front of him, an old battered pickup with the Streets and San seal on the side, its rear up on blocks and wheels missing. Shadows shifted as the light washed over unidentifiable dismantled machinery cluttering the floor. He swept further left and there was a shapeless barrier; as he steadied the light it became a tarp draped over something about the size of a car.

Cooper switched off the light and listened again. First he heard only his breathing, and then, holding it, nothing. I'm alone, he thought. He rose to his feet and flicked on the light. He paced over the floor toward the tarp-covered bulk, stepping carefully. He cast light left and right by turns as he went, still wary. Shapes appeared, the detritus of a once-functioning garage: a workbench, hanging chains, empty shelves.

He bent down to pull up a corner of the tarp. His light played over the rear fender of a dark blue automobile. Lifting the tarp a little more, he saw the round BMW logo above the fender. The license plate had been removed. He stepped around the end of the car, sweeping the light over the front wall of the garage. He saw the door that would lead to the street, closed tight.

On the other side of the car were other shapes, more tarps thrown over what might have been piles of boxes. There was also another door. The corner of the garage had been partitioned off to make a small office, perhaps ten feet square. Beside the door in the flimsy wall of the office was a window. Cooper shone the light through the window and saw pockmarked wallboard, an abandoned calendar from the middle eighties, a filing cabinet with drawers partly open and apparently empty. The door to the office was about half open.

If anybody's in here, Cooper thought, they're in that room. Behind the door, or below the window. He flashed the light through the doorway, seeing only a narrow slice of wall. Let sleeping dogs lie, he thought. You've seen enough. He lowered the light and through the partly open door he saw the sole of a shoe.

He saw the slightly worn sole, and the upper, and an ankle in an argyle sock. He saw a half-inch of pale calf between the sock and the leg of the trousers. He could see no more because the rest was blocked by the door. The leg lay very still on the concrete floor of the office. Cooper felt the Arctic inside him, spreading slowly.

His first reaction was to switch off the light. He stood in darkness, listening hard, listening for life. What he heard was the growing rumble of an approaching El train, coming north from the station. The distant hollow murmur grew slowly to a smothering roar as the building began to shake. Cooper was paralyzed by the noise, standing rigid as the train passed overhead, not wanting to deal with what the light had shown him.

The noise of the train had diminished and Cooper was feeling for the switch of the flashlight when, somewhere not too far from him in the dark, someone moved.

The noise was faint, but Cooper knew he had heard it and knew it had been made by a living creature. Rats, he thought. There would be rats in a place like this. Rats, however, move with frenetic unconcern, not the slow stealth that Cooper had heard. He stood very still, holding his breath, and heard it again: a rustle of clothing.

Against the background thumping of his heart Cooper strained to listen. And heard this time a faint scrape of shoe on the cold concrete. Someone had taken advantage of the passage of the train to come out of hiding.

Cooper's first panicked impulse was to switch on the light and find him; he stopped himself only by old reflexes that worked against giving his position away. His second impulse was to turn and sprint for the door; he remembered the minefield of scrap iron on the floor and remained still, his heart drumming. Another soft step sounded in the darkness.

And Cooper realized he was in victim mode. In victim mode people waited for bad things to happen to them. Again old circuits kicked in, and in an instant Cooper was shaking off victim mode and feeling grimly for combat mode. In night combat the man who is not afraid wins, he remembered an old top sergeant telling them, many years before.

Cooper stepped away from the office, making no attempt at quiet. Whoever was out there had known where he was all along. He felt his way to the end of the tarpaulined car and knelt to listen, the reassuring heft of the flashlight in his right hand. Seconds went by, and the soft brushing, the faint scraping came again.

Cooper snapped his head toward the windows that gave onto the alley. He knew sound could be deceptive, but this sound had come from his right. A very faint glow from outside came through the filthy windows.

Silence. Calmer now, Cooper knew nobody could get too close to him without his hearing; the flashlight at this point had more value as a weapon than as a reconnaissance tool. He waited.

And the soft rustle and scrape came again, resolving itself into footsteps. Soft, careful, and oddly asymmetrical. Scrape, step; scrape, step.

Something moved across the faint luminosity of the windows. A silhouette, dark on slightly less dark, unreadable. Cooper raised the flashlight. His thumb was on the switch, ready to shoot the beam down there, when he thought of firearms. The silhouette passed and Cooper had missed his chance.

Somebody was getting away. Cooper ducked back around the

end of the car, rising to his feet. The other feet were scuttling now, with their strange uneven tread, through the dark and toward the door by which Cooper had entered. Even with a limp, somebody was covering a lot of ground. Cooper raised the light, thumbing the switch, sending a wildly swinging beam out across the garage, managing to train it only on the side of the truck, which blocked his view of the door. He heard the door come open and someone making tracks outside.

He took off across the floor, shining the light ahead of him but catching his foot on something unyielding in the shadows at his feet. He went headlong onto the concrete, the flashlight taking a whack but not going out, his shoulder ramming something heavy and iron as he sprawled. He grunted in pain and rose to his hands and knees, taking stock. His shoulder pained him as he flexed it, but it was functional. He heard footsteps outside, fading. He made it to his feet and retrieved the flashlight, going more carefully but determined to get to that door.

By the time he got there the alley was empty. Nothing moved in the still cold air. Cooper listened, standing rigid in the doorway. He heard the nighttime sighing of the city, an unmuffled car engine growling a block or two away.

He went across the alley, Cooper thought. Into the gangway, between the houses and through to the street beyond. He glanced at the ground, but not enough snow had accumulated under the tracks to leave a record.

It was either across the alley or into a recess close at hand. Feeling exposed, Cooper stepped away from the door. His footsteps were loud on the frozen concrete. As if in response, something sounded in the gangway across the alley, a purposeful scrape-step moving away.

If he wanted to nail me, he could have already, Cooper thought. If he had a gun, he would have used it in there. Cooper was moving at a trot already, across the alley toward the dark mouth of the gangway, aware that there was no guarantee his reasoning was sound.

He halted at the mouth of the gangway between the high wall of an apartment building and a low garage and shone the light down the narrow passage, just in time to see a flimsy gate swing back against its post. Cooper flicked off the light.

Five years earlier, he might have gone down the gangway into the dark. Now the first thing that came to him was that there was no way he could ever justify that to Diana. Instead he stepped back into the alley and waved the light at the Valiant. The lights came on and the car started to roll. When Moreland skidded to a halt beside him, frantically cranking the window down, Cooper leaned close and said, "Did you see him?"

"See who?"

"The guy that just came out of here."

"I just saw something out of the corner of my eye. I wasn't looking up here." Moreland gaped at him.

Keeping his voice low, aware someone might be in earshot, Cooper said, "Go around to the street on the other side and look for a guy with a limp. Hurry."

Moreland blinked at him and said, "What do I do if I find him?"

"Get a look at him. See where he goes." Moreland nodded and spun the tires on the ice. When the Valiant disappeared, Cooper went back across the alley and into the garage. He was going to have to look into that office.

He put on the light again and stepped carefully across the cluttered floor toward the office, not anxious to look in there but unable to leave it. He shoved the door open with his foot, standing aside in case he was wrong about the absence of life, holding the light steady in the middle of the doorway. The door banged against the partition and bounced partway back and came to rest. Cooper gripped the light hard and tried to make sense out of the shapes it picked out of the darkness.

The man sat propped against the wall, legs splayed, one hand in his lap and the other trailing on the floor, head drooping to one side. The black-framed glasses had come off one ear but still held on the other, hanging crookedly across the partly open mouth. Cooper trained the light on the pale wax features fixed in an expression of apparent disgust, and then lowered the light to the torso.

The man looked like Saint Sebastian, like Custer after the fight or like grandma's pincushion. Cooper had to take a half-step into the office to get a fix on what had happened to him; there were five thin metal rods coming at odd angles out of his chest and stomach.

Cooper flashed the light quickly around the office, his skin prickling. Certain that he was alone with the dead man, his breathing under control but his heart going staccato, he leaned closer. He looked at the rods for a few seconds, then flashed the light back to the filing cabinet he'd seen through the window, understanding. The five empty drawers of the filing cabinet had had their aligning rods removed; the ferruled ends of the rods now jutted from the flannel shirt that showed between the open wings of the corduroy coat on the corpse in the corner.

Cooper took a deep breath and let it out; suddenly he wanted open sky above him and a clean wind in his face. He switched off the light so that he wouldn't have to look at the dead man. He decided that he'd done all the observing he could reasonably be expected to do; there was no useful thing he could do now except get back to the car and have Moreland take him to a telephone so he could talk with a policeman.

When he stepped into the alley he saw he wasn't going to need Moreland; the police were already there. The squad had come up the alley from the south and was creeping to a halt opposite the open door. Cooper stepped toward it as the cops emerged. He halted when he saw the one closest to him had his revolver out. It was held casually at his side but the look on the cop's face was not at all casual. "Drop the club," the cop said.

Cooper laid the flashlight on the ground. "You guys are about three minutes too late," he said.

"Looks to me like we're just in time," the cop said.

■ ■ ■

The homicide detective was black, placid-looking, and nattily dressed in a dark blue suit. His hairline had beaten a retreat from his forehead except for a tuft about the size of a silver dollar that was holding out like an island in a flood. He had a moustache and a deceptive sleepy-eyed look that never disappeared, even when he was asking questions in that tone of voice that says this cop is too smart to buy whatever answer comes out.

"If you're the reporter, why didn't you go in?" he was saying to Moreland.

Moreland opened his mouth and then closed it. He shifted on the chair. Cooper came to his rescue. "I told him to stay with the car," he said. "I didn't like the way things looked."

"I'm not talking to you," said the detective.

Moreland cleared his throat. "I was scared," he said. A few seconds passed. Moreland's mouth was set in a thin firm line.

The detective gave Moreland a long blank look and then nodded and turned to Cooper. "And you weren't?" he said.

"I was cautious," Cooper said. "I figured if there was any danger it was for Mel, not me. I figured I could walk in there without worrying too much."

The detective looked down at the notes he had scrawled across a sheet of paper. "How come you didn't see this fellow with the uh . . . limp, when he came out?" He looked up at Moreland.

"I told you. I was looking down at the dashboard fiddling with the damn heater and just saw movement out of the corner of my eye. When I looked up, Coop here was signaling me to come on up."

"And you never saw the guy when you went around the block."

"No. I didn't see anybody. I think he hid in a gangway or a back yard. The officers didn't look too hard for him, by the way."

"Yeah, well, they had other things to do, didn't they?" The detective was looking down at his notes again. "You don't work for the paper in any official capacity, do you, Mr. MacLeish?"

"No. I came along purely as a personal favor."

"Why did you ask him?" the detective said to Moreland, laying stress on the 'him.'

Moreland flicked a quick look at Cooper. "Because he's . . . he doesn't scare easy, I guess."

The look the detective gave Cooper was long and inscrutable under the heavy lids. "You don't scare easy, huh?"

"Everybody's got a different threshold," Cooper said.

The detective expelled a quick puff of air, in what might have been a laugh. "So you came along to handle the rough stuff."

"He came along to protect me, if protection was needed," Moreland put in. "Look, excuse me, but this is all irrelevant. You've checked my credentials. I'm a reporter, not a crook."

The detective gave Moreland a sleepy-eyed look that was utterly impassive and sat back on his chair. "Look at it from my point of view. The officers get a call from the lady across the alley about a burglary in progress, they pull up and find your partner here coming out of a building with a dead body inside, then you come tearing up in the car waving your press badge and saying he's your buddy. I'm sorry but I'm gonna have to take a long hard look at the thing."

Moreland, defeated, nodded and swept something invisible from the tabletop.

Cooper stirred and said, "Can I make a phone call? I have a feeling I'm going to catch hell when I get home tonight."

3

"I CAN GIVE YOU ABOUT a minute," said the detective, not breaking stride.

"That ought to do it," said Moreland. He was already five feet behind the detective and losing ground. The broad-shouldered black man was making for his car in a lot full of Buicks and Chevrolets behind the bleak brick fortress of Area Six at Belmont and Western. The detective had not deigned to close his overcoat and the tails flapped behind him in the chill morning air as he walked.

"So what do you want?" said the detective as Moreland drew even with him, trotting.

"I'd like to talk to you in a different capacity than last night," said Moreland. "As a reporter, not a suspect."

The detective shot him a sideways glance. "I never said you were a suspect."

"OK, maybe it was my guilty conscience. Can I ask you where your investigation stands?"

"Sure." The detective pulled up at the rear of a black Mercury Cougar and pulled car keys from a pocket.

"OK, where does it stand?"

"We just started." The detective jiggled the keys, making them ring.

"Let me write that down," said Moreland, opening his notebook. "That'll look good in the paper."

The detective stopped jiggling the keys and looked at Moreland with a sleepy-eyed look that looked anything but sleepy. "What do you want me to tell you?" he said.

Moreland was frowning at his notebook. "Let's try a few basics. Who identified the body?"

"The victim's brother."

"John Oyler?"

"That's right."

"Was it the stab wounds that killed Vance?"

"One of them."

"Oh? Which one?"

"The one that went into his brain."

Moreland looked up. "Into his brain? I thought he was stabbed in the torso. With those rod things from the filing cabinet."

"He was. But first somebody stuck him under the chin with something about the size of an icepick. Put it to his throat and shoved upwards. A nice piece of work. Quick and dirty."

"Ouch."

"He didn't even have time to say that, probably."

"So the rods were superfluous."

"The rods were for decoration. I'd bet the rods were for you." For the first time the detective smiled. It did not make him look more friendly.

"For me?"

"For your edification. Something for you to think about lying in bed at night."

Moreland stared at him, shrugged, and returned to the notebook. "So how did Oyler get in there? You find keys on him?"

The detective grunted. "Fresh copies."

"Interesting. What about the car that was sitting there? Have you ID'd it?"

"It was stolen out in Barrington a week ago."

"Unbelievable. They were running a chop shop in there?"

"You got about ten seconds left."

"I presume you've talked to the people over at Streets and San?"

"We have."

Moreland looked up. "And?"

"And we're still talking to them."

"Have you made an arrest?"

"Not for the murder."

"For the cars? You got the chop shop guys?"

"Let's say we found a guy with keys to the garage. He was kind of embarrassed to be caught with them."

"Name?"

The detective looked at Moreland the way a postman looks at a small dog. "Fisher. You want more, go back in there and wait.

He's in a room up there talking so fast my partner's having trouble keeping up."

"Did he kill Oyler?"

"We'll know before long." The detective turned to the door of the car and Moreland knew the interview was over. He wheeled and ran for the building, his breath trailing away in the morning light.

■ ■ ■

When Cooper arose Diana was on her way out, off on another mysterious errand connected with the stacks of applications on the dining room table. The freeze was still on, Cooper noted as she went past him like a breath of winter wind in the hall. He went into the kitchen and started the coffee going, ill-rested after six fitful hours in bed, at odds with Diana and himself, the world still slightly soured by a vision of death.

It was bright outside but the ice was still there, the ice and the need to re-invent himself. He heard Diana come back in and looked up to see her in the doorway, swathed in scarf and woolen cap, satchel slung over her shoulder. "My car won't start. Can I take yours?"

"Help yourself. I got no particular plans for today."

She stood there long enought to make the point silently: maybe you should make some.

"You got the spare key, right?" said Cooper.

"Yeah," she said. She looked at him for a moment longer and shook her head. "Do something boring today, will you?" She turned on her heel and went.

■ ■ ■

"You can't do this to me, Jay." Moreland grabbed a handful of camel hair jacket.

"The hell I can't." Jay Macy halted his turn and the quickly darting eyes stopped for a moment on Moreland's face. "Last time I checked you were still working for me."

"This story can't wait. Asses are being covered, stories cooked up, files burned, even as we speak."

"It'll keep for an hour. You got the basic facts already."

"The *story,* Jay. The real story. Not the schmuck in the garage. The whole thing. The crooks in the department, the blind eyes, and the shifty cousins on the payroll. People are cracking, Jay.

And I gotta be around to pick up the pieces. There's a fucking page-one exposé here.''

Macy wiped a droplet of Moreland's saliva from his cheek with a finger. "And there's a news conference in fifteen minutes at City Hall that I need a reporter for, and you're a reporter, or so you claim. Now get over there.''

"Kubiak's over there already, for God's sake.''

"He's busy on the Board of Appeals thing.''

"Listen, all Throop's going to do is trash the mayor. It's ritual, pure ritual.''

"It's the first shot in the mayoral campaign. It's news. It's starting in fourteen minutes. Get going.'' Macy tugged at the lapels of his camel hair jacket, his eyes dancing around the edges of Moreland's face, and stalked off. Moreland stared at his back for three seconds, groping for a line, then wheeled and dashed for the door.

Things were just getting started when Moreland, panting just a little, squeezed into the City Hall press room on the second floor. The customary jostling for place, clearing of throats, and tentative poking at microphones was underway. A tall handsome black man with a trim moustache was moving toward a podium at the front of the room. He wore a navy blue suit and a tie with decorous stripes of maroon and blue. "Breathe in, ladies and gentlemen, there's room for everybody,'' he said in a sonorous cultivated bass. A polite rumble of laughter stirred the multitude briefly.

"Excuse me,'' muttered Moreland, shoving his way around the back of the room, drawing glares. He saw his man against the far wall, a short, bespectacled man with a beard, who was craning to see the podium at the front of the room. "Move,'' growled Moreland at a broad back with the NBC peacock on it and a minicam perched on the shoulder. "Yes, you. How you doing? Just lemme get by here, will you?''

The man at the podium frowned with serene authority into the TV lights. "If we could get started here,'' he said. Behind him a small array of retainers, mostly black males with a couple of whites and a black woman thrown in, stood in watchful deference.

The man with the beard nodded when Moreland reached out to grab his arm. "Hey, Mel,'' he whispered. "Just in time for the show.''

"Blackie, you gotta do me a favor." Moreland fetched up against the wall and leaned close to the other man's ear.

"Here and now?" breathed Blackie, unfurling a notebook.

"Here and now. Name your price." A head or two turned at Moreland's urgent undertone.

"Ten grand," said Blackie.

"I'm serious. You got to help me out here."

"How?" Blackie was having trouble dividing his attention.

Moreland cooed into his ear. "I got a story going that I gotta jump on before it crawls away. Just tape this thing for me, will you?" Moreland slipped a small Japanese recorder from his pocket and into Blackie's hand.

Blackie looked at the recorder and then at Moreland, then shrugged. "Meet you where?"

"In the hall outside. How long's this supposed to take?"

"Who knows? If Throop gets going on the casino and the airport and the taxes all at once it could be a while."

"Meet me in an hour then. Right outside here."

"Sure." Blackie was intent on the podium again. Moreland didn't wait; he began pushing back the way he had come.

"We're here today to send a message," said the man at the podium in his beautiful voice. A hush fell as Moreland slipped out the door.

▪ ▪ ▪

Cooper spread the books in an array across the top of the old oak desk. Sowell's *Conflict of Visions*, Hayek's *The Constitution of Liberty*, Popper's *Conjectures and Refutations*. As an after-thought he added *The Strange Death of Liberal England*. He stared at the books for a few seconds, unable to choose, and finally swept them all into the knapsack along with the notebook.

He trudged up Sheridan Road in the cold, leaning into the sharp north wind. At Pratt he went east to the park and saw the horizon open out in front of him. The sky was clear and the ice piled at the edge of the lake gleamed immaculate under the winter sun. Cooper hiked out to the end of the pier and stood exposed, shoulders hunched in the inadequate jacket but enjoying the cleansing effect of the wind that came screaming unimpeded across the lake from Canada. He turned his back to it and looked south to the skyline.

I should be out driving, he thought. Marsh is out there, Skip is out there, there are a thousand drivers out there on the street, doing my work.

Driving had been Cooper's work, and like all laboring men he had often resented it but secretly cherished it. It had given him structure and discipline as well as cash for the rent each month. Cooper knew that a man had to whip something every day, had to take on something and beat it, if he wanted to stay with the living. When life got too easy, people lost their edge.

Now what, he thought. He turned square into the wind, looking for something to whip. Life had been too easy for a few months, and now it was all up for grabs.

The scrape of footsteps sounded behind him and he turned. Another man had made his way out along the pier and was skirting the base of the light to join Cooper at the end. Cooper nodded a greeting, taking in the wool overcoat with the collar turned up, the scarf obscuring half the face, the rheumy eyes under the black fur cap, the hands jammed in the pockets.

And the limp. Cooper watched as the man came toward him with a shuffle and a dragging leg, suddenly hearing the same scrape over the cold concrete floor of a garage in the dark. The man was looking at him with those rheumy eyes fixed on him, and Cooper was getting that rush of alarm, starting to move to his right, looking for room to dodge, to run, to kick. The right hand was coming out of the pocket.

The man raised the hand, empty, in greeting, and words came out from behind the scarf, in Russian. The man had halted, reacting to Cooper's alarm, and suddenly he was just an old Russian man with a bad leg.

Cooper nodded and smiled at him, alarm subsiding. The man gestured out over the lake, into the wind, and the old eyes were crinkled with humor. He said something else in Russian.

"Yeah," said Cooper, heading shoreward. "It's a great day for it."

■ ■ ■

"So who would actually keep the keys, then?" said Moreland.

The fat man behind the desk looked as if he wished someone, anyone, would come through the door and carry Moreland away, out of his sight. The fat man was conical in shape, widening inexorably from the point of his bald head to jowls that spilled over an unbuttoned collar and loosened tie, from there to a chest that was heaving very slightly and finally to a massive midsection that swelled the white shirt to the bursting point. Moreland imagined him continuing to widen beneath the desk, like a child's punching toy rocking on a weighted base.

"I would," said the fat man, a look of weary forbearance passing across his smooth round face. "I have a set right here in the office. But like I told you, the son of a bitch changed them on me, put in his own locks. The cops took mine over there and tried 'em already. That's my best proof I wasn't involved. My keys didn't work."

"And you never noticed."

"Why in the hell would I?" He flapped a stubby hand in exasperation. "The facility was closed. Why would I ever go over there? Fisher was in charge. He could pretty much do what he damn pleased in there. I should have checked, maybe. But for Christ's sake, I've known the guy for twenty years. Who's gonna think a guy they've worked with that long is a crook?"

Moreland scribbled on his notepad. "Tell me about Fisher's associates," he said.

"What the hell associates you talking about? The guys that worked for him? I didn't hire a one of 'em. The guys he hung around with? I don't even know where he drank. I don't check out the personal and private life of all my ward supervisors."

"I mean the associates he's named to the police. You don't know this Conley or this Montini?"

"Heard of 'em, yes. I know they used to work there at the ward. Know 'em? Hell, I thought I knew Fisher."

"Nothing against these guys previously that you know of?"

"Look, I'm not a priest. I don't confess these guys every week. You show me a law says I have to monitor the personal and private lives and criminal records of all Streets and San employees. Go on, show me."

Moreland flicked back a page or two, peered at his notes. "This Montini, I'm told, is a nephew of a fellow named Bart Cappellari."

"Yeah, so?"

"Well, Bart Cappellari is under Federal indictment downtown right now for an interesting variety of things. He also happens to be a cousin of the president of the union that represents most Streets and San employees."

Irritation creased the smooth face. "Look, I have work to do here and I don't really have the time to play guessing games with you. You got a point to make, make it."

"I'm just wondering if you'd care to comment on the alleged ties between certain union figures and organized crime."

The fat man looked as if something were paining him, somewhere deep inside the swollen torso. "Alleged is the word, you said it. I got nothing to say about the union. You can use words like 'allege' and 'organized crime' all you want, but that doesn't mean anybody's done anything wrong."

"Except for these guys stashing stolen vehicles on Streets and San premises."

"Allegedly. They been convicted already? That was fast."

"Allegedly. OK, can I ask you another question?"

"Make it fast. I don't have unlimited time here."

"Here's a quick one. When the facility was closed, back in 'eighty-seven, who would have been responsible for the disposal of the property?"

"What do you mean, disposal?"

"I mean the sale, the rental, the demolition of the property, maybe. What's supposed to happen to old city facilities?"

"You'd have to go ask somebody up on the ninth floor. I don't deal with stuff like that."

"Who does?"

"I don't know."

"You're the number three man in Streets and San and you don't know what happens to discontinued facilities?"

"No, I don't know. Now if you'll excuse me I have a lot of work to do here. There's three million people out there right now generating garbage and tearing up the streets." The fat man pulled a sheaf of papers toward him, grunting a bit with the effort.

Moreland flipped the notebook shut. "OK, thanks for your time. Maybe I will go look in on the folks upstairs."

He got a distinct impression as he left that the look of discomfort on the fat man's face was not entirely due to the stress of hauling around three hundred and fifty pounds.

■ ■ ■

When Cooper got home in the late afternoon, Diana kissed him with her arms around his neck, the freeze over. He kissed her back and held her. When she pulled away she said, "There was a thing on the radio about a murder in a city garage. I think it was yours."

"Mine?"

"You know what I mean."

"Did they mention my name?"

"No. All it said was the guy, I don't remember his name, was found in a city garage last night and the police were trying to figure out how he got there. No details."

"Good. I don't need the notoriety."

She stood with arms crossed in front of him. "They said he died of multiple stab wounds."

"Five by my quick count." Cooper shucked off his jacket and hung it on the closet doorknob.

"Last night I was too mad to think about the details," Diana said. "But I heard you tossing and turning. I guess it couldn't have been too pleasant for you."

Cooper shrugged. "At least it was nobody I knew."

"Do you ever get used to it?"

"What, looking at dead people?"

"Yeah."

"I haven't yet."

Diana shook her head, moving away down the hall. "Well, don't," she said. "There's a message from Mel on the answering machine."

Cooper punched the button and Moreland's voice came scratching out of the machine. "Mel here. I'm busy till six-thirty at least, but if you want to hear all the juicy details meet me at Spiro's at seven."

Cooper made a token effort with Diana. "Come on, we'll make an evening of it. We'll have a drink with Mel and then go out to dinner. We haven't done the town in a while."

She looked at him gravely for a moment and said, "No, thanks. I'm not sure I'm in the mood to listen to Mel brag."

Cooper shrugged and reached for his jacket.

Spiro's was a gloomy tavern on State Street near the newspaper building, full of framed celebrity pictures and drunken newspapermen. Moreland hailed Cooper from the end of the bar, where he sat perched on a high stool like St. Simeon Stylites.

"MacLeish. I knew you'd be here. You're a hell of a man. Jake, pull one for my sidekick here." Moreland had a good head start on him, Cooper judged; he was slightly flushed and the knot of his tie had been wrenched away from his throat. "Grab that stool before one of those sportswriter types gets it."

Cooper drank beer and said, "I hear the radio had the story this afternoon."

"They had a report on the body in the garage. And the TV will have it tonight. But that's not the story. That's just the crime report. The story comes out tomorrow. I got it all wrapped up and in the computer just a while ago."

"And what do you have ?"

Moreland thumped his stein down on the bar and leaned closer. His voice sank to a low murmur. "I got an only-in-Chicago type of story. But it's top secret till it hits the stands. Loose lips sink ships, MacLeish."

"So don't tell me if it's secret."

"Nah, I can trust you. You know that car you saw in there last night?"

"Yeah."

"Swiped out in Barrington last week. And they found plates from five other stolen vehicles in there." Moreland leaned back and groped for his beer.

Cooper smiled. "I was right, wasn't I? I told you last night."

"You called it. That was a chop shop in there. On city property. Can you beat that?"

"Who was running it?"

Again Moreland leaned close, breathing beer fumes. "Guy named Delbert Fisher, the ward boss. He's got an alibi for the killing but he caved in and admitted the scam. Two other guys were in it with him. Patrick Conley and Joseph Montini. Former city employees. And professional criminals with connections to the Outfit. That's the story, MacLeish. These guys get these jobs through connections and just plunder the fuckin' city. They'd still be at it if Oyler hadn't blown the whistle."

Cooper nodded. "That was Oyler, then?"

"Oh yeah. His brother identified him."

"So who killed him?"

"That's what they're working on. Fisher's talking but denying he had anything to do with the killing. And of course he wants to know who sold him out, who gave Oyler the keys."

"I wondered about that. He didn't break in."

"The keys were on his body. Fresh copies of all three locks. Fisher's accused the other two, they're screaming foul and accusing him back. Somebody's lying."

"Sounds like it. Do they know exactly what killed him?"

"You saw the guy. What do you think killed him?"

"It didn't look to me like there had been much of a struggle. And I know I'd struggle like hell if somebody was trying to ram those rods into me."

"You're sharp today, MacLeish. What killed him was a little prick under the chin. With something long and sharp. Right into the brain."

"Jesus."

"Yeah. Although there are probably slower ways to die."

"They find a weapon?"

"Not yet. My money's on Conley. He's got an assault or two on his record. Has an alibi for Sunday night but they're trying to break it. They'll charge him in a day or two."

Cooper shook his head. "You must have worked like hell to get all this put together."

"Tell me about it. I've had about five minutes of sleep since our little escapade. I spent the whole day running between Area Six and Streets and San or camped out on the telephone. But the story goes in tomorrow, under my byline."

"Nice work. I guess you can go home and get some sleep now."

"Not a chance."

"Why, what now?"

Moreland slapped Cooper on the shoulder, looking like the fox with the keys to the henhouse. "I got a hot date, MacLeish."

"No shit. Who's the lucky woman?"

"I'll give you a hint. She's cheap, and she's tawdry. She's everything a man could want."

Cooper froze with the beer halfway to his mouth. "No."

"Yes."

"Not the one who landed on your lap the other night."

"That one, yes."

Cooper set his glass on the bar and shook his head. "I guess she liked it there, huh?"

"She seemed to. I gotta say, I was glad you took off."

"Anything for a pal. So you got her phone number, huh?"

Moreland leaned closer, his hand on Cooper's arm. "Coop, you're behind the curve. I took the lady *home* that night."

Cooper's eyebrows rose. "Fast work, Mel. I'm impressed."

"I am, too. This is my finest hour since I bedded a redhead from the French consulate on Bastille Day in 1981."

"You didn't say anything last night."

"Hey, when I'm working it's all business. It wasn't the time or the place for bragging."

Cooper looked at him, a big round man with unruly thinning hair and a wide grin, and moved his glass over to clink against Moreland's. "Well, here's to fast work and fast women."

"Tonight will be our first real date. We got reservations at Eli's at eight and then we'll see what happens. I figure if necessary I can go another twenty-four hours before sleep really becomes an issue."

"Got a big evening planned, huh?"

"Hey, I'm playing it by ear. I'm just getting to know the lady."

"What's her name?"

"Cleo. Cleo Mix, like Tom Mix the cowboy star. She claims to be a great-niece of his. And I can believe it, the way she rode me the other night. The spur marks on my flanks are just starting to heal. You're giving me that skeptical smile again, MacLeish. The one you do so well."

"I'm just listening to you talk. You're better than TV."

"Hell, a loaded dryer at the Laundromat is better than TV. Listen, I owe you for your help last night."

"Forget it. I needed the fresh air. You want a word of advice about tonight?"

"I got it under control, Ace. I'm a love machine. But sure, you got any pointers?"

"Try for her place."

"How come?"

"I'm just thinking about your cat."

Moreland stared and then shook his head. "Nah. They're all in custody. We blew 'em wide open. It's too late, the story's written and going to press."

Cooper shrugged. "OK. Just a thought."

"They killed one guy and the story's out anyway. They'll forget all about me."

"I hope you're right."

"I'm right. Trust my instincts. I had an instinct about last night, didn't I? Well, my instinct now says it's over."

"All over, huh?"

"All except the shouting."

DIANA ANSWERED THE PHONE, and from the look on her face when she said, "It's for you," Cooper knew it was Moreland. He took the phone from her and stood looking out the window while he talked, his back to Diana on the sofa.

"Did you see the story?" Moreland said.

"Yeah. They gave it pretty good play, I'd say."

"That's the closest to page one I've been since Gus Savage called me a racist."

"So, you the toast of the town now?"

"Except over at Streets and San. They'll never talk to me again."

"Breaks of the game, I guess."

"Occupational hazard. People put you below lawyers and cannibals on the evolutionary scale. You get used to it."

Cooper looked out at exhaust rising from an idling car on the street below, whipped away by a darting wind. "They got a killer yet?"

"Not that I know of. I've called Area Six a few times, but they haven't gotten back to me. As you may have noticed the other night, I have trouble getting cops to talk to me."

"Why's that?"

"Long story. Old story. Once when I was young and ambitious I pressed real hard on a brutality allegation and got a couple of patrolmen suspended."

"I had no idea you were such a crusader."

"I'll tell you, if I'd had any idea how those bastards carry a grudge I wouldn't have written a word about it. Cops have long memories."

"Like the guy the other night?"

"Yeah. Detective M. Garvey Brown. I got a distinct impression he recognized my name. At least I don't think he still suspects us, though you never know. Cops love the obvious."

"Hard to blame them. Listen, there's a couple of things I don't understand."

"What's not to understand?"

"Start with how Oyler found out about it."

"We don't know yet. But the cops'll wring it out of somebody. Obviously, access to those keys was fairly limited. They'll figure out what happened before too long. Probably somebody had it in for Fisher and sold him out, like I said."

"Huh. Maybe. So why did Oyler get killed?"

"What do you mean? He blew the whistle, they had somebody whack him."

"How did they know he was blowing the whistle? You don't make a public announcement when you sell somebody out. You quietly set up a meeting with a reporter and the first thing the sellee knows about it is when the paper hits the stands. If Fisher or his partners sent somebody over to hit Oyler, how did they know he was going to be there?"

"I don't know. They suspected something maybe, tailed Oyler, saw him go in and went in after him. Or maybe it was just an accident. Somebody was over there fooling around when Oyler blundered in."

"Maybe. Do the cops know where Oyler was all weekend?"

"Apparently his mother says he went to Alton for the riverboat gambling. That's what he told her, anyway. Does it matter?"

"Maybe not. I'm just thinking it's a pity you couldn't contact him to confirm it was him who set up the meeting. Did his mother say who he went with?"

There was a brief silence. "What's on your mind?"

"Nothing in particular." Cooper turned from the window, glanced at Diana on the couch, deep in her book. "Three more questions, Mel."

"Shoot."

"One. Does this guy Fisher qualify as a heavy cruiser?"

There was a brief silence. "I don't know. I'll have to think about that."

"I mean even allowing for exaggeration on Oyler's part, does Fisher fit the profile? A lying son of a bitch who's putting one over on the whole city?"

"Why not?"

"I just thought it sounded a bit exalted for a Streets and San supervisor running a chop shop."

"I'll think about it." The response was a bit terse, Cooper thought. "Next question."

"Why was Oyler killed there at the garage? I mean if you're trying to keep something a secret, you don't leave a body on the premises where the secret is."

"We came early and interrupted them, before they could move the body."

"But why would they even think of hitting him there? They'd wait until he was miles away before they made a move on him. Killing him there is the surest way to call attention to the spot."

"They had no choice. They followed him, realized he was about to spill the frijoles, and took drastic measures."

"Maybe. Third question."

"Fire away."

"Are you watching your back?"

This time a considerable silence ensued. "I told you, I'm not worried. The story's out. Why would they do anything now?"

"I guess they wouldn't. Unless."

"Unless what?"

"Unless you decide that the Fisher story is just a play-action fake and keep digging for the real story."

After a moment Moreland said, "You have a very devious mind, you know that, MacLeish?"

"All I know I learned from you, Mel."

"I'm going to have to think about this."

"Do that. But step carefully. Remember your cat."

Cooper could hear Moreland breathing into the phone. "OK, listen. I still owe you for your help. And I want you and Diana to meet Cleo."

"Oh yeah. How'd it go?"

"Well, sleep finally became an issue, but not till around three in the morning. Listen, I'll get in touch when I'm a little less busy, we'll all have dinner."

"Sounds good. Keep me posted."

Diana looked up from her book when Cooper hung up the phone. "Is Mel in danger?"

Cooper scratched at the stubble on his neck. "I don't know. Probably not."

"How about you?" Diana's eyes were back on the book, frowning faintly.

"Me?" Cooper ambled away from the window. "Why would I be in danger?"

■ ■ ■

Days passed; no more snow fell but the temperature stayed below freezing. The old year expired and a new one arrived, bringing the millennium one year closer. Cooper split time between the old oak desk by the window and various warm places to drink. Almost every day now Cooper wanted badly to go hop in a cab and drive, but he'd promised Diana. There was no such thing as only driving by day; if you leased a cab for twenty-four hours, you had to drive at night to get your money's worth. For a long time, that had been Cooper's work week: three days a week he took out a cab and drove as long and hard as he could stand. If he needed a little more money for a vacation or Christmas or whatever, he upped it to five or six; if he felt lazy he only drove a day or two. He never saved a lot of money but he lived as he wanted, under a roof, with something to put on the table, enough ready cash to pay the tab. And time, lots of time. Time to read, shoot pool, walk along the lake, lie abed late with Diana. Cooper could have lived like that till he was past sixty-five.

Except for the stickups. Cooper had to admit Diana was right; the risks were getting too high for a man who had already survived his share of gunshot wounds. She was right about another thing, too: he wouldn't be able to drive forever, and there wouldn't be any pension checks. The VA would take care of his medical needs, but there wasn't going to be any condo in Florida unless he started doing something about it now. "You're forty-three years old and you have no assets," Diana had told him. "None."

Except your brains, she had added more charitably. Diana had what Cooper lacked: ambition and focus. And Cooper knew, in an obscure corner of his awareness, that he had to develop some or he was going to lose her, someday. She would have denied it, but he knew how those things worked.

Cooper sailed the jobs section of the Sunday paper across the table away from him. Computers, he thought. It's all computers now. The geek shall inherit the earth. There was an *Intro to Programming* course at Truman College; maybe it was time.

He heard Diana's key in the lock and went into the kitchen to turn on the gas under the percolator. He was whipping eggs around in a bowl when she came back to the kitchen, cheeks still red from the cold, auburn hair freshly brushed. "I didn't think you'd be up," she said.

"I couldn't get back to sleep after you left, and then Moreland called and I just said hell with it and got up to answer the phone." Cooper set down the fork and gathered her in. "Your nose is cold."

"It's freezing out there." She disengaged herself gently. "I'm sorry I woke you."

"It's OK." Cooper retrieved the fork and studied the tines. "You don't have to sneak around, you know, I've figured out where you go on Sunday mornings."

She wandered to the stove to look at the percolator. "I wasn't sneaking around. I just didn't want to . . . make a big deal of it."

"Any particular reason for it? Am I that hard to live with?"

She smiled. "I guess I finally decided that if there wasn't someone watching over me, I wouldn't have made it out of that guy's car trunk alive. So I decided it was time to pay a little attention."

Cooper nodded slowly, thinking with a twinge of jealousy that he'd had as much to do with getting her out of that car trunk as Providence had. "Well, I've seen so much bad stuff happen to people who were sure somebody was watching over them, I find it more comforting to think it's all a roll of the dice."

"That's comfort, huh?"

Cooper shrugged. "We all look into the same black hole, we all come up with different ways to deal with it. I'm glad if it makes you happier, that's the bottom line."

Diana stared at the bubbles just starting to pop in the glass knob of the percolator. "It doesn't always make me happier. Sometimes it's harder." After a moment she roused herself and turned off the percolator. "What did Moreland want? He have another murder for you?"

"No such luck. He wants to buy us dinner. Tomorrow night. At La Valenciana."

"La Valenciana? Where all the politicians eat?"

"I don't know. That kind of place is a bit out of my league."

"That's what I hear. It's the new in spot for wheeling and dealing."

"Then it ought to cost Moreland an arm and a leg. Should be fun."

"Do I have to hear all about the murder?"

"Probably not. He wants us to meet someone."

"I see. Female?"

"Yeah. I trust she will provide a civilizing influence."

Diana shrugged. "Sounds good. I could work up a taste for a good *cocido*." She came and put her arms around Cooper, the crown of her head fitting perfectly beneath his chin, pulling him hard against her.

Cooper squeezed back. "If you want to know the truth, I kind of like it when you go to Mass. You come home all thoughtful and serene and . . . well, like this."

They stood there for a time, just holding fast, and Cooper felt lucky again, the luckiest man on the face of the earth. Finally Diana raised her face to his. "Put the eggs back in the fridge," she said.

Later, skin to skin with Diana under flannel sheets, two blankets and a quilt, Cooper said, "Are you going to have to confess this?"

"I always do," she said.

▪ ▪ ▪

The lighting in La Valenciana was muted, as were the noises of the cars elbowing their way along Clark Street outside. The restaurant was a sizable rectangular room, with booths along the walls running back to a small but bustling bar at the rear, with a few tables down the middle. The dominant color was a restful shade of peach.

Cooper spotted them in the third booth back on the right, facing the door. Their heads were nearly touching, Moreland's round and shiny one next to the shock of golden hair. Cooper had not quite believed Moreland's story until this moment, but he had to believe it now; it was the cheap and tawdry blonde and she was looking into Moreland's eyes as if he were Valentino himself.

The grave Spanish maître d' saw where they were heading and waved them on. Moreland looked up and grinned as they came. "Ahoy," he called. "The fleet's in." As Cooper hove to, he looked into the woman's startling blue eyes and for a moment could only gawk.

"Hi," he said.

"It's the Marlboro Man," said the cheap and tawdry blonde, smiling.

"You two have met," said Moreland. "But I don't think names ever got exchanged. Cooper MacLeish, Cleo Mix."

"Hi, Cooper. Excuse me, that's how Mel described you the other night. The Marlboro Man." The voice was a touch husky, and playful.

"You should hear what I call him when he's not around."

"And this," said Moreland, "is Diana."

Diana's crooked smile was just showing as she shook hands.

"Hiiii." Cleo drew out the vowel to show the depth of her pleasure. She was dressed in a hot pink jacket over a black jewel neck blouse. Her lipstick was muted by comparison to the jacket but her eyes were electric. Contacts? thought Cooper. Tawdry or not, she was bright-eyed and blonde and a sight to behold.

Cooper and Diana slid into the booth opposite Moreland and Cleo. "And a happy New Year to you both," said Moreland. "May it be a prosperous one."

"So far so good. That's a pretty small glass for a man with your appetites," Cooper said, nodding at the glass of amber liquid in front of Moreland.

"MacLeish, you're a peasant. You don't gulp this stuff like beer. This is what the Spanish call a hair ace."

"A what?"

"A *jerez*," Diana said. "Sherry. *Un fino*, from the look of it. Dry."

"You really don't deserve this woman, you know that?" Moreland reached across the table and clapped Cooper on the shoulder.

"You speak Spanish?" said Cleo to Diana, wide-eyed.

"It's my first language."

"She speaks seven other languages, too," Moreland said.

"Two," said Diana.

"I think that's so wonderful." Cleo shook her head in admiration; Diana blinked back.

"MacLeish here, on the other hand, barely speaks English, being a Hoosier," Moreland said by way of rescuing her. "When I first met him he still thought the capital of the country was called Worshington."

Cooper was laughing in spite of himself. "I never said 'Worshington.' I'm one of those genteel Hoosiers. Like Cole Porter."

"Or that Quayle fellow. Yes, the great Genteel Hoosier tradition."

A waiter loomed; Moreland pressed sherry on Cooper, and Diana ordered a vermouth. Waiting for the drinks, Cooper looked from Moreland to Cleo and back. "Been to any good parties lately?" he said.

Moreland grinned. "She attacked me there that night. I haven't been able to pry her loose."

"Now wait a second." Cleo was brightly and quite artificially indignant. "You attacked me. I was just looking for a place to sit down."

"Baby, as long as I have a face . . ."

"STOP it." Cleo grabbed Moreland's wrist, feigning shock and looking sidelong at Cooper and Diana, who were staring. "My feet were killing me and all the chairs were taken. I asked if he minded if I sat on the arm of the chair and he said, 'Try the leg, it's more comfortable.' "

"Not my best line, perhaps," said Moreland modestly. "But it worked."

"Mel's got a million of 'em," said Cooper.

"The next thing I knew he was like psychoanalyzing me."

"All I said was she seemed to be an extroverted sort of personality. I thought that was a fairly easy call."

"And I started telling him how I used to be real shy, but I overcame it by doing comedy improv."

"And he no doubt told you about his operation," Cooper said.

Moreland laughed; Cleo stared, uncertain. Diana sipped her drink.

Cleo regained her footing. "He told me he was a reporter. And I just think that's so fascinating. So he started telling me stories, about famous people he'd interviewed and stuff. We talked for like an hour."

"Until my leg went to sleep," said Moreland.

"Good thing the rest of you stayed awake," said Cleo.

Moreland gave her and then Cooper the coy look, the eyebrows raised but the lids lowered.

"And the rest is history," Cooper prompted.

"I guess you could say we hit it off," said Moreland, grinning across the table. "Although I was a little distracted right at the start. Things were kind of scrambled there for a couple of days with the big story coming out."

"Did you see Mel's story? I think that's so exciting." Cleo trained the blue eyes on Cooper and Diana in turn.

"I saw it," said Cooper.

"He was there," said Diana coolly. "He found the body."

"Mel told me. That must have been awful." Cleo showed a lot of white teeth as she crinkled her face in distaste. Cooper was trying to estimate her age; she had already seen twenty-five, for sure, maybe thirty.

"I've seen bodies before," he said.

"Ick," said Cleo.

■ ■ ■

Cooper put himself in Diana's hands, and after a sizzling *gambas al ajillo* she recommended the *zarzuela de mariscos*. It turned out to be a fish stew that filled him to his toes. Diana passed up the *cocido Andaluz* in favor of a plump and neatly dispatched partridge, and they split a bottle of a crisp white Spanish wine. The getting-to-know-you talk danced gracefully over Cooper's checkered past, Diana's Puerto Rican girlhood, and Cleo's flight from small-town Ohio. Moreland beamed in the background. "And we all came to the big city to seek our fortunes," he said.

"Let me know if you see one lying around," said Cleo.

"Well, this is the place to look. There's probably a fortune or two being made right now in that booth over there. That's Jake Slazenger." Moreland cocked a thumb at a booth across the room in which an elderly gentleman with a bald and freckled pate leaned over the table in intense communion with a man with a graying beard.

"And who is this personage?" said Cooper.

"Such ignorance, MacLeish. You dismay me. Jake Slazenger is senior partner in Slazenger, Galey and Worth, only the best-connected law firm in the city. I don't know who that is with him, but I can tell from the reverent looks on their faces they're talking about money."

"That's Milt Sellers," said Cleo, startling them slightly. "He comes into King's office all the time. He's some kind of honcho guy with the city or something."

"A honcho guy with the city," said Moreland, grinning at her.

"Well, I don't know what he does, exactly."

"Hey, that's probably all the job description he needs to open doors."

"You work for King Van Houten?" said Cooper.

Cleo nodded. "I'm just a receptionist." She shrugged, a disarming gesture. "You don't have to be a rocket scientist."

"You're talking to a cab driver," Cooper said with a smile. "I don't think anybody at this table's going to pull rank on you. Except maybe Mr. Pulitzer there."

"The day I win a Pulitzer Prize is the day Jesse Helms joins the NAACP," Moreland said.

"I know I should know who that is," said Cleo. "A politician, right?"

"Right," said Moreland, beaming. "Hey, look who just walked in. No, don't crane like that for Christ's sake. You look like Hoosier tourists at Disneyland."

Cooper looked over his shoulder anyway and saw a tall man standing just inside the entrance with the casual but slightly impatient manner of a man who is not accustomed to waiting for a table. It took him a moment, but as the maître d' hastened to attend to the man, Cooper remembered where he'd seen him. "Your friend Swanson," he said, turning back to Moreland.

"Ol' Regis himself. My, we are privileged this evening."

Cooper turned back and watched Moreland watching Swanson as he came down the room; he wondered if he was imagining the slight touch of wariness in Moreland's look. When he glanced at Cleo he was sure; she had frozen with her wineglass in her hand and only her eyes were moving, following Swanson. Cooper exchanged looks with Diana; she had noticed it too. He heard soft greetings being called behind him; across the way the old bald man and the man with the gray beard interrupted their tête-à-tête long enough to nod at Swanson's passage. Then Moreland and Cleo were looking directly up at Swanson, who had halted at their booth.

He was close to six-four and had a long handsome face with gray eyes and a square jaw; his hair was pure silver. The eyes had laugh lines at the corners. He wore a double-breasted gray silk jacket with a tie of subdued red. He had his hands in his trouser pockets and he was smiling at Cleo. "Well," he said. "We seem to be seeing a lot of each other suddenly." His eyes flicked quickly over the others, locking with Cooper's for just a moment, perhaps wondering where he'd seen him.

"Hello, Regis," Cleo said, setting the wineglass down and smiling, though not with full wattage. "Great party the other night."

"We did have ourselves a time, didn't we?" Swanson looked at Diana and nodded a greeting, with just enough interest to trigger a reflex in Cooper. Cooper was neither particularly jealous by nature nor intimidated by wealth, but something in Swanson's look made him want to point out that the maître d' was waiting for him farther along.

Cleo made introductions, starting with Moreland, who grabbed Swanson's hand like a politician on the hustings. Cooper gave him a brief firm clasp, and Diana kept her hands in her lap and gave him a cool smile. Swanson put his hand back in his pocket and looked at Moreland. "You write for Jay Macy, don't you?"

Moreland grinned. "That's apparently what he thinks. Actually I write for the paper. Jay tries to tell me what to write, though."

"I've seen your byline," said Swanson. "You do good work."

Moreland gawked up at him for a moment before collecting himself. "Thanks, I appreciate that," he said.

Swanson was looking at Cleo again, a faint smile on his lips. Cooper looked at Cleo and saw her returning it.

"You're looking well, I must say," said Swanson.

"Thank you," she said. "I'm feeling pretty good these days, too."

Swanson's smile broadened. "That's good to hear. That's a lovely jacket you're wearing, by the way. Well, Enrique's waiting on me. I'll leave you to your dinner. A pleasure meeting you." He took them all in with the parting words and moved away, smoothly.

Moreland was smiling at Cleo with raised eyebrows; she looked steadily back at him and took a drink of wine. Over the glass she winked, actually winked, at Moreland. Cooper said, "OK, what's the joke?"

Moreland looked at him, grinning. "I'd bet Regis was the one who bought that jacket for her," he said.

"I see."

Cleo appeared vaguely disconcerted. She looked at Diana and said, "Ancient history."

Moreland said, "I told you Swanson's taste in mistresses was legendary."

Cleo hit him on the arm, spilling a dollop of his blood-red Rioja on the tablecloth. "I was not his mistress. We were friends. Good friends, OK?"

"I'm sorry. Here I am sullying your reputation, in front of people, too." Moreland did not look repentant. For that matter, Cleo did not look particularly embarrassed.

"He and Astrid were on the rocks anyway." Cleo addressed this remark to Diana, who gave a slightly bewildered and completely indecipherable murmur. "And anyway, Astrid's no saint. I could tell you tales about her." Cleo dipped into her wine again, looking momentarily vacant.

The silence that followed was awkward; Cooper was groping for a line when Moreland's eyes lit on the entrance again and he said, "Well, I'll be hornswaggled. Speak of the devil. The whole menage is here."

This time Cooper looked at Cleo first and saw her eyes narrow, infinitesimally, before she giggled, grasped Moreland's arm and said, "My God, it's like she knew we were talking about her."

Cooper looked at Moreland and said, "What now?"

"The redoubtable Mrs. Swanson. Astrid Huber. Don't look now."

Cooper didn't, figuring she would come into view soon enough. When she did, it was to stop at the booth opposite where Jake Slazenger and Milt Sellers came out of their huddle to smile and murmur at her. Astrid Huber was dressed in a subdued gray suit that made her look deadly serious while at the same time quietly outlining a figure that many younger women would envy. The frosted hair shone to great advantage in the lamplight and the soft curves of the face bespoke a maturity that had only gained in charm. She exchanged a few words with Slazenger, smiled at Sellers, and looked up. She saw Swanson in a booth at the back and gave him a brief wave, still listening to Slazenger. Her eyes continued to scan the restaurant until they lit on the booth where Moreland and his party were sitting. She catalogued the occupants of the booth with a single unhurried look and then nodded, apparently at Cleo.

Cleo waved, with a very cool smile. Moreland looked at her and murmured, "My God. I didn't know you were on speaking terms."

"I used to work for her," said Cleo, looking a bit shamefaced now.

"You'll have to tell me that whole story some time," said Moreland.

Astrid Huber took her leave of Slazenger and Sellers and moved toward the booth in the back where Swanson sat. "I don't believe it," breathed Moreland. "It looks like they're going to have dinner together. This is an event."

"What's the big deal? They're still married," said Cleo.

"Well, you'd know better than I what shape the marriage is in. But I've heard it described as a marriage of inconvenience now. If they're having dinner together, it's got to be money or politics or both."

"She's the county clerk or something, isn't she?" said Diana.

"Was. She was the great reform candidate a few years back. The wags say that's what led to her marital problems, since Regis is the consummate dealer. Now she's back in private practice but rumor has it she's got her eye on the County Board or the State Legislature. Shit, I'd give a week's salary to hear what comes out over the appetizers." Moreland was drumming fingers on the thick tablecloth.

"Oh, stop. You're off duty." Cleo tugged gently at his arm.

"A reporter's never off duty. But . . ." Moreland raised his glass. "We're occasionally out of position. So we just sit and watch and wonder, which is half the fun of eating in a place like this."

Cooper took a drink of his own wine and said, "It's kind of like a big Monopoly game, isn't it?"

Moreland smiled. "Yeah. Except the money's real. And if you're good, you never have to go to Jail."

▪ ▪ ▪

Over brandy Diana and Cleo became engaged in a lengthy discussion of waitressing, a trade Cleo also had plied. Cooper listened until Moreland leaned close and murmured, "About those questions you had."

"Uh-huh."

"I've been thinking."

"And what have you come up with?"

Moreland swirled brandy gently and expertly in his snifter, cupped in his hand. "A couple of things. The cops are still trying to run down all the thieves, the guys Conley and Montini gave them. Meanwhile, they're convinced now neither of them sold Fisher out. Why would they? They'd be slitting their own throats."

"Huh. So maybe Oyler found out about it from the other end, from the thieves' end of things."

"Yeah. Which sounds plausible, that they would kill him, I mean. If they found out he was going to blow the whistle on them or they walked in on him or something."

"OK, I'll buy that. Still . . ."

"Yeah. Still. The whole fucking thing was a setup, wasn't it?"

"You're the newshound. You tell me."

"I think it was a setup." Moreland glanced at the women, who had fallen silent. Diana was looking at Moreland warily; Cleo vacantly. Moreland warmed to his audience, putting down the snifter and parking his elbows on the stiff white tablecloth. "Look at it this way. Oyler didn't set up this meeting."

Cooper nodded slowly. "Who did?"

"Whoever killed him. Oyler was set up just like we were. And the setup was to squash whatever Oyler had—and to make me think that Fisher was the story."

Cooper looked over Moreland's shoulder at the bottles behind the bar, ranks of gleaming, well-ordered bottles. "A feint, like I said."

"Yeah. A red herring. A fish of a different color."

"So what's the real story?"

Moreland smiled at Cooper over the rim of his snifter, plump and content and full of mischief. "That's what I'm going to find out. And I think I'll start with Vance's ill-tempered brother John."

Cooper watched him drink, remembering Saint Sebastian and the late General George Armstrong Custer. "You've been warned off, Mel," he said.

Moreland set the glass down firmly on the thick linen tablecloth. "A lot of reporters have been warned off stories." His eyes rose to Cooper's. "If there's a story there, I'm gonna get it."

Cooper nodded slowly. "Did you share these thoughts with our friend Brown?"

"No."

"You should. Let the cops get the story, Mel."

"Uh-uh. When they get it, so does everybody else. I want to get it before the pretty faces get it."

"The pretty faces?"

"The TV people. From here on out, I'm on my own."

Cooper spun the stem of his glass slowly between thumb and

forefinger. "Think about this. It looks like the story here means finding the guy who stuck Oyler and having a nice heart-to-heart with him. You think you're better equipped than the police to do that?"

"The guy who stuck Oyler is not going to be the story. The story is going to be who told him to stick Oyler. And there's got to be a trail there."

"How do you follow it without coming to the attention of the guy with the nasty temper? He already knows where you live."

Moreland shrugged, a brief, macho dismissal. "I'll step carefully." He looked at the two women and smiled. "Besides," he said, "I got a hell of a bodyguard." He cocked a thumb at Cooper.

Cooper exchanged a look with Diana, a let's-talk-later look.

"I think this is so exciting," said Cleo.

■ ■ ■

"It's kind of nauseating, isn't it?" said Cooper. "I haven't seen that kind of thing since junior high school."

"Passion is always embarrassing to watch." Diana sounded sleepy, huddled on the passenger seat as Cooper cruised north through the spangled night on Lake Shore Drive.

"Having seen her work at the party, I would have thought she'd go for someone with a lot more looks or a lot more money," Cooper said.

"Mel's not ugly. Losing twenty or thirty pounds would help, but he's not hideous. I'm wondering what he sees in her."

"I would have thought that was obvious."

"You think she's beautiful?"

Cooper grinned in the dark. "I think I speak for all normal healthy males in saying the first thing she brings to my mind is vigorous sexual congress."

"What is it, the blond hair?"

"The exuberant style. The body. The air of enthusiastic availability."

"So that's all there is to it, for him."

Cooper shrugged. "Mel's been married and divorced. I don't know if he thinks in terms of stable relationships any more. I think he's having the time of his life."

Diana shifted on the seat. "He's not serious about this bodyguard business, I hope. Or you're not serious."

Cooper came down the curve at the end of the drive and braked to a stop at the red light. "What bothers me is, I'm not sure if he's completely serious about anything right now. To tell you the truth, I don't think Mel's scared enough about this thing. I guess it's . . . being in love or something. I don't think he quite has his feet on the ground right now. So . . ."

"So?"

"So I'm not going to go snooping again, 'cause I don't want to spend any more nights at the police station. But if he asks me to watch his back or something, I'll do it. I'm not sure the son of a bitch can take care of himself."

The silence lasted them all the way home. When Cooper parked, a half-block from their apartment, Diana pulled on the door handle and said, "If you want my prejudiced opinion, he's not worth it."

"Not worth what?" Cooper heard the ice in her voice.

"Not worth your getting hurt. Don't get involved." She was out of the car, slamming the door. Cooper followed, slowly.

Later, standing in the doorway to the bedroom, the light from the bathroom showing her dim outline under the blanket, Cooper said, "I won't do anything risky."

"Don't," said Diana. "Don't make promises you can't keep."

5

COOPER ANSWERED AN AD for a limo company that needed drivers. He was surprised he hadn't thought of it before; it was still driving, something he enjoyed and was good at, but it couldn't possibly be as dangerous as driving a taxi. Up-scale clientele, reasonable hours. Show up dressed presentably, give the suits in back a nice smooth ride, collect a check. Years before, he had chauffeured a Hollywood producer around L.A. until the man had drunk too much in his Jacuzzi one Sunday evening and drowned; it would be like old times.

The problem was money, of course; not much of the stiff fee the suits paid for their ride filtered down to the man behind the wheel. And there were, of course, no benefits, no future. Diana forbore from pointing this out, feeling she had pushed the nagging as far as it would go, but her silent nod when he told her about it spoke all that was necessary. Cooper's first job was to ferry a brace of newlyweds from their reception in the suburbs to a downtown hotel; the overwhelmed bride threw up champagne and wedding cake all over the back seat.

▪ ▪ ▪

"The next time any of these phones rings, rip the fucker out of the wall," said John Oyler. The woman with the white bouffant hairdo paused with her fingers on the typewriter keys and stared warily as Oyler rose from his desk. He shot a malevolent look through the window into the drivers' room and made for the door. Before he got the door open he could sense the surge of hostile truck drivers toward him.

"Johnny, how about takin' care of me here? I got a hundred bucks in toll tickets here."

"Get in line, bud. I been here longer'n you have." The drivers' room was filled with smoke and littered with Coke cans, coffee cups, and fatigued men in blue jeans and down vests.

Oyler flung the door shut behind him with a wall-shuddering slam. He had fixed his eyes resolutely on the door to the hallway, hoping to run the gantlet on sheer angry momentum, but these were veteran drivers and they were already edging into his path.

"I hear you, I hear you," he said. "Give me a minute, will you? I been in that office for six hours straight drinking coffee. You don't want piss on your shoes, you better let me get to the urinal." He ignored the snarls and dodged the shoulders and strode down the hallway, leaving the murmur of discontent behind. Through the glass doors at the end of the hall he could see a parking lot with piles of plowed snow at the edge, filthy gray snow.

John Oyler thought briefly of Florida, where it never snowed. He thought briefly and wistfully of long drives to Florida in a blue Rambler station wagon, with Ma and the old man up front and Deanna and little Vance playing in the back.

Fucking Vance. John Oyler shoved the restroom door open with such force that he nearly clipped a man just coming out. "Whoa there," said the man, scowling. Oyler pushed past him without a word and made for the urinal, clawing at his zipper.

Fucking Vance, he thought. Oyler stared at the tiles a foot from his face and thought of his little brother with the mixture of blistering rage and withering sadness that had possessed him since his wife Marie had taken the call from his distraught mother six days before. Since then John Oyler had moved in a ferment of rage, rage toward women and priests and most of all his dead little brother Vance, who had crowned all his betrayals of the family with the ultimate discourtesy of getting himself killed.

Leaving me to clean up the fucking mess, thought John Oyler, zipping up.

Knowing it would further anger the drivers awaiting him, Oyler stopped at the coffee machine in the hallway and rammed quarters into the slot. Waiting for the cup to fill, he looked up to see a man coming down the hallway from the drivers' room. This man was not a driver; under his open down jacket Oyler could see a thin blue tie descending over an ample stomach. Thinning hair stuck up from a round head. Oyler leveled his most poisonous look at the man.

"John Oyler?" the man said.

"Guilty. I plead guilty. Don't even bother reading the charges." He pulled the cup out of the receptacle, spilling hot coffee on his fingers. "Fuck," he said.

The man held a faint, uncertain smile in place as Oyler brushed past him. "My name's Melvin Moreland," he said, starting to come after Oyler.

"Who?"

"Melvin Moreland. I spoke to you a couple of weeks ago on the phone."

"Aw, Christ." Oyler stopped dead in his tracks and faced the man. "You're the reporter."

"That's correct. I was wondering if you had a moment to talk with me." The reporter's smile was gone, replaced by a grave lowering of brows.

"What did I tell you on the phone?"

"You weren't anxious to talk to me. I was hoping to persuade you to."

"You won't." Oyler spun and made tracks toward the blue haze in the drivers' room. He heard the reporter coming after him. A large bearded figure filled the doorway.

"John, you got a load going west for me? I ain't been home in a month."

Oyler squeezed through the door and waved off all supplicants. "Give me a minute, give me a minute." All he wanted was to make the safety of the office.

Behind him the reporter said, "If we could set up a time at your convenience . . ."

Oyler halted in the middle of the drivers' room, sloshing coffee on the floor. "Hey," he said.

That got the reporter's attention; he stood stock-still, hands in the pockets of the down jacket, a cautious frown on his face.

"What do you see here?" said John Oyler, waving his free hand at the surroundings.

After a second or two the reporter said, "You tell me."

"What you see here is what I have to deal with today. I got a dozen or so pissed-off truck drivers on my hands. They all got log books and bills of lading for me to look at and they want money from me and they want loads going west when all I got's going east and if they don't get it in two minutes they're gonna try and climb through that window there. And I'm not even safe in the office, 'cause I got phones in there that won't stop ringing because I got sixty drivers all trying to call in at once, not to mention customers with their hair on fire because a load hasn't been picked up because the driver overslept or got lost. Today I got a driver that quit and walked away and left a load sitting in a parking lot. I got the Ohio state police on the phone because a driver killed three people in a fucking Volkswagen. I got the driver in jail and a load sitting out on the highway that has to get picked up. I got drivers in New Jersey that can't find their way to fucking New York City. This is what I have to deal with today. Are you starting to get the picture?"

"I got the picture," said the reporter, flashing the little smile again, quickly. "I'm sorry I picked a bad time."

"For you, there is no good time. Good-bye."

"All I want's a statement," said the reporter.

Oyler halted yet again, feeling hot coffee splash on his wrist. "You want a statement? Here's a statement for you." John Oyler reached for the waistband of the reporter's pants, stuffing his fingers down behind the belt and tugging, holding tight against the reporter's belated defensive swipes, emptying the cup of coffee down the gap between the belt and the white shirtfront. The reporter yelped and jerked free and Oyler tossed the cup away, whirling toward the office door, shaking coffee from his hand; the sudden roar of laughter that filled the room was the first thing that had happened that day that relieved to the slightest degree John Oyler's misery.

When he slammed the door behind him the woman with the white bouffant hairdo looked up timorously and said, "There's three drivers on hold waiting to talk to you."

* * *

Cooper sat with his feet up on the windowsill in the front room and wished for spring. Diana was gone, away at work; the radiators hissed quietly and outside the window the snow drifted down in the dying light. During the afternoon the killer wind off the lake had died, the temperature had crept up, and the thick wet air had begun to disgorge clots of heavy flakes. When the telephone rang Cooper made for it at speed, hoping for relief.

"MacLeish, what's new?"

"Hey, Mel. Not a lot. Just watching the snow pile up."

"Good. I got a job for you."

"I'm not sure I like the sound of that."

"Hey now, where's your work ethic?"

"Since when does your kind of work involve ethics?"

"Low blow, MacLeish."

"What's the job pay?"

"All you can drink. Payable in the currency of your choice."

"Well, the price sounds right. But I'm not going down any more tunnels for you."

"Nah, this is easier. All I need you to do is lie a little bit."

Cooper laughed, forcing it a bit to show Moreland what he thought of his schemes, but knowing as he sank onto the sofa that he was going to listen to the rest of it. "I want you to explain your concept of journalism to me someday, Mel. So who's the mark?"

"The redoubtable John Oyler."

"Him again."

"His own self. The motherfucker."

"Fightin' words. What's going on?"

"I'm telling you, MacLeish, there are people out there who simply don't appreciate the value of the press in a free society."

"He won't talk to you."

"He is positively agitated about not talking to me. I bearded him in his lair this morning and he was discourteous in the extreme."

"What'd he do, take a swing at you?"

"He made free with a cup of coffee, if you must know."

"No shit. Cream and sugar?"

"I didn't notice. It was piping hot, that I can tell you."

"The man's a menace."

"He's an asshole, and he has something I want."

"What's that?"

"The son of a bitch knows something about Vance's murder."

"How do you know?"

"I know. I tried to see his mother this morning. She and Vance lived down in Bridgeport. I found the house, rang the bell. No answer. This after six or seven attempts to contact her by phone. I try the neighbor lady, show her my press card, tell her I'm doing a story on the families of murder victims. She blabs. Virginia's gone, off to Florida. The day after Vance got put in the ground, John came by and put the suitcases in the car and off they went. The neighbor says don't expect her back too soon. There's a vacation home down there or something. So I go try John."

"With disastrous results."

"Yeah. That's why I need your help."

"Look, why can't you ask the cops what John told them?"

"I told you, cops don't usually return my calls. But I gather through third parties he basically played dumb with them."

"And you don't think he's so dumb."

"I think he wouldn't be so anxious not to talk unless he had something he didn't want to say."

"That makes sense, I think. Where the hell do I come in?"

"You come in as one of Vance's creditors."

"What?"

"Oyler won't talk to reporters. Or cops. He might talk to somebody else who had a good reason to want to know about Vance's death. Like somebody Vance owed money to. And I don't mean the guy from the furniture store. I mean like if Vance had a problem with the ponies or something."

"What? Why would he tell a creditor anything?"

"Because a creditor shares his interests. He wants to find out who killed Vance and he wants to keep it quiet."

"No. All a creditor wants is his money."

"Yeah. But when you make clear that you're going to get it one way or another, John's going to want to deflect your kind attentions from him to the person who's responsible."

Cooper considered, crossing his outstretched legs on the coffee table. "I don't know, Mel. That sounds pretty thin to me."

"Look, it's worth a try, for Christ's sake. I'm stonewalled. The cops are freezing me out, now Oyler sees me three blocks away, his lips are sealed. I've got to find out what he knows. It's an easy part for you. All you do is work up a bit of a story and look tough."

"Mel, you got me typecast."

"What else are you doing with your life? Listen, I'm at Cleo's right now. Meet me down here, I'll drive. All you have to do is talk to him, I'll hang out of sight."

Cooper looked out the window at the lowering sky. "Last time I listened to you I walked in on a homicide. Somebody's playing hardball here, Mel. And I'm not sure you're scared enough."

"I'm through being scared. I'm too busy to be scared. Listen, there's a big fucking story here, and I'm asking you to help dig it out. If you don't do it, you know damn well you'll regret it."

"You going to include me in the byline?"

"I'll include you in my acceptance speech at the Pulitzer dinner. Come on, time's a-wastin'. Give me a yes or a no."

Cooper made him wait while he took his feet off the table, sat up, scratched the stubble on his neck. He could hear the ice in Diana's voice, see that distant disappointed look. But Diana was gone till at least midnight. "Where do we find the guy?" he said.

"He lives in Alsip."

"Alsip? That's the other end of the earth."

"For Christ's sake, I'm driving. Listen, get your butt down here. The guy'll be home from work by six."

Cooper was aware of two contending currents of feeling as he held the phone to his ear. One was a faint foreboding, a when-will-you-learn type of feeling. The other was the quiet thrill of the chase. "OK," he said. "Where's Cleo live?"

■ ■ ■

John Oyler pulled the big Olds over at the curb in front of the yellow brick house. He shoved the lever to park and gave it a burst of gas, just to hear the engine roar. Then he switched off the lights, the wipers, and finally the ignition. He sat for a moment in the dark car, watching snowflakes settle on the windshield, wishing he'd stayed at the bar for one more beer, wishing he'd gone home. He hadn't seen the boys in three or four days and he could probably be civil to Marie long enough to get a decent meal out of the deal.

John sighed as he heard Tammy Wynette singing "D-I-V-O-R-C-E" in his head again. Life's a bitch and then you marry one, he thought. And then it all goes to hell. He closed his eyes for a moment, not wanting to go inside the squalid little rented room at the top of the stairs around in back, not wanting to open another can of Campbell's soup, not even a Manhandler.

He opened his eyes and leaned to open the glove compartment. He reached in and took out the Ruger .38 and slipped it into the pocket of his jacket. He got out of the car and went down the gangway to the back, shuffling through the fresh snow.

Standing over the little stove under the fluorescent ring waiting for the bean with bacon soup to boil, John Oyler had never felt so alone. I could live with my boys, he thought. Just me and Jack and Richie. He gave the soup a stir, knowing it would never happen, knowing Marie would get them and that it was probably best that way, knowing they would grow apart from him over the years, his boys. He had seen the fear in their eyes already.

I never should have walloped her, he thought. John Oyler was not a man to admit mistakes easily, but he knew he should never have hit his wife, no matter what the provocation; that had been the beginning of the end.

Outside he heard footsteps. Someone was coming down the gangway, slowly. Oyler stirred the soup, steaming now, and listened. The footsteps reached the door at the bottom of the stairs and paused. Oyler put down the spoon and glanced toward his coat hanging over the back of the single kitchen chair, the revolver still in the pocket. The door opened and the footsteps mounted the stairs. Who the fuck, Oyler thought, wondering if he should be alarmed but listening to the footsteps and deciding not.

The footsteps came laboring up the rickety stairs, and John Oyler wondered why somebody with a limp was coming to see him.

■ ■ ■

Cleo lived in a coach house in Lincoln Park which had been converted at some expense to a cozy hideout at the end of a gangway between two well-kept houses that would go for half a million easily. The ground floor of the place had blank white walls, furniture that had been purchased new within the past couple of years, and lots of plants. A gleaming kitchenette nestled to the right of the door and a spiral staircase in a far corner led to upper regions.

Moreland answered the door, tie askew, and ushered him in. Cleo had apparently only recently arrived from work and stood behind the counter in the kitchenette, resplendent in a scarlet jacket with a black collar and shoulder pads worthy of Ray Nitschke. The golden hair framed a face with blood-red lips and the startling eyes. "Can I get you a drink?" she said, replacing the cap on a bottle of scotch and flashing the high-wattage smile.

It's a party, thought Cooper, a permanent party. "I thought we had to get going," he said to Moreland.

"Yeah we do, actually. Lemme just finish this." He downed the contents of a thick glass tumbler and set it on the counter. "I'm afraid you'll have to drink that by yourself," he said as Cleo held up a fresh drink. "We gotta roll."

"That's not very nice," Cleo said in a pouting tone.

"I can't be nice right now. I'm working." Moreland leaned across the counter angling for a kiss. Cleo smiled, touched lips briefly, and then assumed a look of disappointment. "I'll just have to sit here by myself, drinking alone. That's how people become alcoholics."

"The number of drinks you've had to put away sitting alone I can count on one hand, I bet," said Moreland. "We'll all hoist a few when Coop and I get back."

"You'll be careful, won't you?" Cleo said, looking at Cooper, as if he were responsible for Moreland.

"Don't worry. Mel will be there in case I get in trouble," said Cooper with his hand on the doorknob, needing fresh air.

Careening down the Dan Ryan Expressway through the leisurely snowfall, just a little too fast for conditions, Moreland said, "I'm telling you, MacLeish, it's been unreal. Nothing quite like her has ever happened to this old dog before."

Cooper had tried to talk about business but there was no way to get through to a man who was floating six inches off the ground. "She's not tough to look at."

"No. And the contents lives up to the packaging, let me tell you." Moreland waited in vain for a response, then went on. "She's not as dumb as she pretends to be, you know."

Cooper contented himself with saying, "Few people are."

"She's been around the block a few times. She may not have a lot of book learnin', but she's smart, MacLeish."

"I can tell," Cooper said, not looking at Moreland.

Alsip was the Great Southwest, where Chicago hemorrhages out onto the Illinois prairie, a limitless sprawl of subdivisions, truck depots, malls, and bewildered old towns caught in the flood. Moreland got off the expressway at 115th and went west past cemeteries and subdivisions to Pulaski, where he turned south. The snow had eased up and traffic was reasonably smooth. The address Moreland had for Oyler was not far off Pulaski, in a region of low brick ranch homes with push-up dormers and fiberglass awnings. "This is it, MacLeish," he said. "The American Dream. Live in a house just like your neighbor's."

"Beats living in a tenement." Cooper sat feeling his feet grow cold. The resolve Moreland had filled him with had evaporated on the long drive; the whole thing was starting to feel like a fool's errand. They cruised through the early darkness, looking for the address and seeing the first few hardy souls emerging with snow shovels.

When they found the house, Moreland pulled the Toyota over to the curb fifty yards past it. "Lights. Camera. Action." He slapped Cooper on the shoulder. "I'll turn around up there and be watching in case he runs you. With the motor going. You got the role down? You into the part?"

"I'm a bad liar," Cooper said.

"Just remember, you want your money and you're going to get it."

Cooper shook his head and got out of the car.

The doorbell was answered by a boy teetering on the brink of a turbulent adolescence: a face just starting to lengthen and harden under the first rush of testosterone, crowned by a dark blond crewcut with a tail in back, a black T-shirt with neon-bright lettering. "I'm looking for John Oyler," Cooper said.

The boy stared at him, affronted, and said, "He don't live here no more."

Cooper said, "I see," feeling relief. Aware of Moreland's eyes on his back, he said, "Where could I find him?"

The boy stepped back slowly, recoiling from Cooper or the cold air or both. He turned and shouted "Mom!" back into the house. "Just a minute," he said to Cooper, and disappeared, leaving the door open. Cooper took the liberty of knocking the snow off his boots and stepping inside and pulling the door shut. The living room was unlighted and undistinguished. The house had a warm, indeterminate odor of cooking. A woman came through a hallway from brightly lit back regions, drying her hands on a tea towel. She flicked a switch on the wall and a ceiling light went on.

She was small, brisk, and hardened by toil and strife. Dark curls and dark eyes set off a pale face that had retained its prettiness into the mid-thirties. She met Cooper with a look that said hit me with the worst. "Yes?" she said.

"I'm looking for John Oyler. Your boy said he doesn't live here any more."

She stopped short and her hands fell to her waist, holding the towel. "That's right. He moved out a month ago. They should have his address at the office." Her look was wary.

"Ah . . . I'm not from the office. I was wondering if you could tell me where to find him, maybe just give me a phone number?"

In the rear of the house children were fighting. Squealing voices rose, a chair scraped violently across a floor. The woman half-turned, lips tight, then rolled her eyes to heaven and flashed Cooper a brief smile. "Everybody wants him all of a sudden," she said. "Someone else called today wanting the address. Let me write it down for you." A thump sounded from the back of the house.

"House full of boys?" Cooper said.

"Two." She was scrabbling in a drawer. "More than I can handle." She jotted on a sheet of note paper and brought it to Cooper. There was a phone number and an address in Oak Lawn. "You have to go around to the back," she said. "The door at the top of the stairs."

"Thanks, I appreciate it," said Cooper. "Sounds like you better get back there and referee."

She returned his smile with a haunting glimpse of past happiness and opened the door for him. "They're out of control since *he* left," she said.

Cooper walked back to the car wishing he hadn't peeked into the Oyler household but glad that he wouldn't have to tell his lies in front of the family. "You gave up too easy," said Moreland when he climbed into the car.

"Relax. I got an address for him. I get the impression the marriage isn't in real good shape."

It wasn't a long drive up Pulaski, and in fifteen minutes they had found the right block. The address turned out to be a yellow brick box of a place on a block full of small solid houses. Moreland parked half a block beyond the house and Cooper walked back. There was a light on behind curtains in the front room, but nobody peered out at him as he tramped through the snow around the side of the house. He had managed to regain his focus, and as he walked down the gangway he ran over the outlines of his role.

At the back was a covered stairway leading up to a porch. There was a landing at the top illuminated by a dim light over the door, cluttered with boxes. Cooper located a doorbell and pressed it. He didn't hear any corresponding buzz or chime from inside and after a moment he pulled the screen door open to rap on the inner door.

There was a window in the door and through it Cooper could see an old Formica-topped kitchen table and a doorway beyond leading into a dark hall. He knocked on the pane of glass in the door, the blow muffled by his glove. He knocked harder.

Leaning left, he could see a patch of floor through the window, cheap hard-trodden linoleum. At the edge of his field of vision, he could see the legs of a chair lying on its side and something spilled across the floor, a smear of beans in a dull orange liquid.

Cooper stared at the spill; it bothered him. Go away, he told himself. Go away now, tell Moreland you couldn't find Oyler. Instead he tried the door. The knob turned; the door opened at his push.

The kitchen was small and warm, but coldly lit by the fluorescent light. The man lay on his back, legs splayed but crossed at the ankles, one arm thrown wide and resting on a black jacket dumped on the floor, the other bent at his side, the still hand hovering half-open as if looking for something to grasp. The face had taken most of the soup; Cooper knew the man was dead because the eyes were half-open and soup was congealing on the eyeballs. There was a small hole under the man's chin with a thin trickle of blood running down into the collar of the shirt.

Cooper leaned in the door taking in the sight and cursing silently—cursing himself, cursing Moreland, cursing the police he knew he would be spending the evening with. For a moment he considered simply pulling the door shut and walking down the stairs and away into the night, but he knew he could not get away with that.

There was a phone here; he could walk in and find it and wait for the police to come.

And find a man who limped waiting down the dark hallway? Cooper had no way of guessing how long ago someone had thrown that soup and punctured that throat, but he didn't think he had missed it by much.

Cooper pulled the door firmly shut and went down the steps, holding the bannister. He went back up the gangway, emerging into the glare of the streetlights with an irrational shiver of guilt. An old man leaning on a snow shovel in the gangway of the next house down watched him with suspicion.

Cooper stalked back to the car. "You know where the police station is in this town?" he said, sliding onto the seat and slamming the door.

Moreland stared at him. "What," he said. "What happened?"

"We're right behind the guy. About two steps behind him. Now find a phone or find the god damn police station." Cooper pointed ahead, still seeing the half-open eyes.

Moreland's eyes showed white all around. "He's up there?"

"He's up there. He's dead. He was stabbed. Turn on the ignition and roll." Cooper's arms were folded against the cold, clamped tight to his chest.

Moreland cast one frantic look over his shoulder, goggled at Cooper for a couple of seconds more, and then frowned out the windshield, processing. He turned the key, slowly. When the engine was running he said, "No cops this time."

"Huh?"

Moreland's voice was half an octave higher than normal and his words were nipping at each other's heels coming out. "Listen, we bring the cops in on this one, we'll never get free. They'll wrap us up so tight we won't be able to move. And that's if they're smart enough to realize we didn't do it." With a jerk Moreland put the car in gear and squealed away from the curb. "The only thing to do is drive. We were never here, you never saw that place back there."

Cooper waited until Moreland had to pull up at a stop sign, figuring that showed he was registering his surroundings again. "And I suppose we never visited Mrs. Oyler."

"That's right."

"I guess we'll have to go back and kill her then, her and the boys, so that she won't be able to give the cops a detailed description of me. And that old man back there, too. Jeez, we'll have to kill four people. We better get started."

Moreland swore a single vicious syllable and pulled the car over. He rammed it into neutral. "All right, what the fuck do we do? They'll crucify us."

"Number one, we act like normal human beings and we report the crime. Number two, you act like a big-time reporter instead of a pithed frog and you tell the police what you know about it. They'll appreciate it."

"They'll draw me and quarter me, and even if they decide I didn't kill the Oyler brothers, I'll never get to talk to a cop again. I'll be frozen so far out I'll have to read about it in the out-of-town papers. This is the end of my fucking career."

Cooper spoke through his teeth. "Would you fucking get a hold of yourself?" Alerted by his tone, Moreland subsided on the seat. Cooper proceeded. "What the cops will see is a reporter so good he's practically on top of a murder before it happens. They'll be suspicious because they have to be, but if we come clean they'll see we're just chasing things, not causing them. They'll catch the guy and you will get the story of your life." Cooper grabbed Moreland's arm and tugged, to make the reporter look at him. When the round pallid face turned to his, he said slowly, "That's the only way to play it, Mel."

Moreland blinked until his mouth firmed. He said, "I could have gone into the insurance business, you know that? I could have my own agency by now."

■ ■ ■

"Why did you want to see him?" the Oak Lawn detective said. The detective had a broad face with too much flesh, but the eyes betrayed no softness. He and Cooper were sitting on the front seat of a squad, in front of the yellow brick building. Moreland was in the back, chewing fingernails down to the knuckle. The heater was on full blast, but Cooper was still chilled. Another squad had pulled into the alley and a third, with lights flashing, sat across the street.

"We wanted to ask him some questions about his brother's death," Cooper said.

"His brother?"

"Yeah. His brother was murdered a few days ago."

"Hard luck family, huh?" The detective looked over his shoulder at Moreland.

Moreland said, "I don't think luck has a lot to do with it." He shot a quick look at Cooper, who merely stared back at him.

Moreland glared straight ahead, out the windshield. "I'm going to save you some time, officer. You need to get in touch with a Detective M. Garvey Brown at Area Six in the city. He'll tell you about Vance Oyler and he'll tell you about us."

The eyes narrowed. "What kind of things is he going to tell me about you?" His eyes flicked to Cooper.

Cooper said, "He'll tell you how I found Vance's body, too."

The detective was silent for a moment. "I think maybe we're going to have to ask you two to come over to the station for a while."

■ ■ ■

"But this isn't Russia," said Cleo, indignant in a pink plush velour robe, hair subdued in a ponytail and make-up free, a rather ordinary-looking woman at three in the morning. "How can they get away with keeping you there half the night?"

"They're the cops. They can do pretty much what they damn please," said Moreland. He leaned forward on the edge of the white saddlebag sofa, jacket off and tie loosened. Cleo's hand rested lightly on his shoulder.

"Mel and I seem to be finding a lot of dead people suddenly," said Cooper from the depths of the matching armchair. From where he sat he had a marvelous view of a bank of audio and video equipment that had cost more than he made in three months. "It sort of has to get their attention."

Moreland tossed off the last of his scotch and set the tumbler on the glass tabletop in front of him. "I'll tell you, third time's the charm. We find another body, they won't need evidence. They'll make some up, and we'll be spending nights at Twenty-sixth and California."

"They would do that?" Cleo's voice came close to squeaking.

"Who knows? They might," said Moreland.

Cooper rubbed at his temples, fighting a headache. "I don't think so. All I know is I don't want to follow the guy with the icepick around any more." Cleo slid both hands beneath Moreland's arm and shifted closer to him on the sofa.

"It's gotta be a monster," said Moreland. "Somebody wants this thing buried deep."

"It's creepy," Cleo said.

"It's creepy all right," said Moreland. "And I'm going to find the creep. They're not going to be able to keep the lid on it."

Cooper fixed him with a stare. "I'd forget it if I were you."

"Sure you would," said Moreland. "Like hell you would. This is gonna rescue my fuckin' career."

"Got your optimism back, huh?"

"I got my dander up is what I got. I'm gonna root it out, MacLeish."

"It's going to put you six feet down if you don't watch your step."

"I'm not worried. It's like I told you. I'm through being afraid."

Looking at Moreland across the room with Cleo hanging on to him, Cooper wondered which was a more treacherous source of courage, women or drink. "I've got to tell you, Mel, I can't see why. In your shoes I'd just be starting to get scared. The cat was just for laughs. The next time that guy slips into your place, it'll be to do what he did to the Oyler boys. Are you going to be ready?"

"I got bars put on the back door." He hesitated a beat, squeezing Cleo's knee. "I'm spending most nights over here anyway. I've kind of moved in, temporarily."

"Great. You get bars put around every alley you walk past, every restroom you walk into, every place you park your car, maybe you'll be ready."

"Look, I'm not a fuckin' war hero like you. But I'm not gonna let these people keep the lid on this. OK?"

"That's great, Mel. But let me tell you something about war heroes. There's not a one of 'em won't tell you how easy it is to get killed."

"So what do you want me to do? Give up? Say, OK fellas, we'll just forget about these two murders?"

"Let the police handle it. They're good at it. They have guns."

"And get in line behind their pet reporters for the story? No thanks. I'm going to get it first. You don't have to come along if you don't want to."

"Great. You can start finding the bodies for yourself, then."

Moreland nodded a small tight nod. "Look, I know I let you in for some hassles with all this. I appreciate your help."

"It's more than a hassle. It's kind of spoiled the last week or so, know what I mean? Violent death does not go well with dinner."

Moreland stared solemnly, upper lip sucked in between his teeth. "I hear you. Believe me, I'm not taking this lightly. Not after tonight."

Cooper climbed out of the chair. "It's time you got scared, pal. It doesn't get much more serious than puncture wounds in the throat."

Moreland rose and followed him to the door. "I'll watch my step. I'm gonna hit the South Water Market tomorrow, check out Vance's former colleagues. Whatever he got into, somebody had to know about it. We'll find it."

Cooper just stared. "What did you say? What was that pronoun?"

Moreland grinned at him. "Go home and get your rest. I'll let you know what happens."

"I don't get it. Am I working for you now?"

"You're not going to be able to stay out of this. I'm going to need your help again and you're not going to be able to say no. I know you."

"No, Mel. Capital *N*, capital *O*. Two murders is all I need to lose interest."

"Well, I'm a reporter, MacLeish. There's nothing that gets my attention faster than a couple of murders."

Cooper looked from Moreland to Cleo, wide-eyed on the sofa, and back. "Yeah. Well, let's just hope it stays at two."

 THE SUN HAD RISEN FROM the frozen lake a mile to the east and was casting a feeble light on the brick and concrete and shingleboard city. There would be no warmth from it. For a moment Moreland was tempted to forget Oyler, forget the story; all he wanted was to go climb back under the blankets.

The market had been hopping for several hours. Moreland felt a moment of fervent gratitude that he was not in the food business. The pre-dawn hours were for sleeping; in Moreland's estimation this came close to a moral imperative. The South Water Market was two blocks long and filled with creeping trucks and shouting men. Along the dock, stacks of cardboard boxes sat on skids or were being hauled along the platform on handlifts to waiting trucks and vans backed up to the dock. A smell of crushed vegetable matter pervaded the air. So much activity before breakfast filled Moreland with dread.

Halfway along the market on the south side of the street Moreland spotted the little diner where men on break retreated to wolf down rancid coffee and hot food. Setting his compass for it, Moreland crossed the street at mild peril to life and limb, peered through the misted window in the door, and pushed through into the steamy interior.

Men sat two or three to a table, hunched over trays of scrambled eggs and sausage or nursing mugs of coffee. The walls were dark with some kind of varnish or perhaps only grease. Moreland was momentarily intimidated but summoned his courage. In front of him was a broad back sporting a Teamster jacket with the mule-and-wheel emblem above the number of the local. Eyes rose to inspect him as he moved to the end of the table. "Morning," he said.

Rumbles of greeting came out past mouthfuls of food. The man in the Teamster jacket was huge, with a walrus moustache hiding the mouth. He and the two men with him looked Moreland up and down, classing him. Moreland gave his name and the name of the paper.

"Ha," said the Teamster. "Another feature."

"Try and get my name right this time," said the man across from him, a small and wiry specimen. The third man chewed silently, watching Moreland with mournful skepticism.

"I'm tired of talking to you newspaper guys," the Teamster said. "I want to know when that TV broad's coming back."

"Sorry to disappoint you, gentlemen," said Moreland. "Actually I'm not writing a feature this time. Mind if I join you?" Before anyone could do anything more than shrug, he slid onto the vacant chair across from the Teamster.

"Help yourself," said the Teamster.

"Thanks. Any of you guys know Vance Oyler?"

Grease sizzled back in the kitchen while eyes flicked back and forth. "Who?" said the wiry man at Moreland's elbow.

"Vance Oyler. He used to be a produce handler here. I met him three years ago when I did a story on the market."

The Teamster took a long pull on his coffee and looked down the table at the third man. "Vance Oyler. That name kind of rings a bell, don't it, Bob?"

The third man was young, red-faced, perhaps from the cold, with a moustache and dark blond hair under a Bears stocking cap. He blinked slowly at the large man and then looked at Moreland. "You mean the guy that got himself killed the other day," he said.

"That's the guy. I was hoping to find someone who knew him while he was here."

The blond man shrugged. "We all knew him."

Moreland waited in vain for elaboration. When none came he said, "Have the police been down here to talk to you?"

"Not to me." The blond man looked at the others. Heads were shaken.

"When was the last time you saw Vance?" Moreland directed the question to the blond man.

"Shit, I don't know. More'n a year ago."

"A year ago?"

"Around the time he was fired, I guess."

"He got fired?"

"Yeah."

"I didn't think that was possible." Moreland had meant it as a joke but it drew no smiles.

Looks were passed around the table. Across from Moreland the giant Teamster said, "It is if you're stealing."

"Ah." Moreland frowned. "Who was he stealing from?"

"Is it any of your business?" The big man watched Moreland over the rim of the mug as he drank.

"I'm a reporter. Everything's my business, if it'll sell papers." Moreland gave them his broadest, most cynical smile, hoping he'd judged the audience right. "Of course, you don't have to talk to me."

"No, we don't." The big man was staring, but he looked almost amused.

Moreland plunged ahead. "Here's the deal. Oyler called me a few days before he got killed and said he had a story for me. He set up a meeting but he was killed before I saw him. I want to find out what he had to say."

After a brief pause the big man said, "You're talking to the wrong people. That guy didn't have many friends around here and he never came around after he was canned. The stupid son of a bitch was stealing produce. Vance Oyler was a fucking weasel, and you can quote me on that."

Moreland nodded. "When was he fired? Do you remember?"

"Over a year ago. That guy's old news around here."

"Mm. Any idea who would be able to tell me more about him?"

More looks passed. The big man said, "I think he had a brother."

"Ah." I know something you don't know, thought Moreland with a thrill, realizing he was maybe a couple of hours ahead of the news. "Would that be John Oyler?" he said.

"You got me. All I know is he used to brag about his old man and his brother being high up in the union. Which is the only reason I can think of that he was working here, 'cause he sure was a fuck-up."

"I see. No other leads you could give me? Nobody he hung around with here who might have kept in touch?"

The man at Moreland's elbow snorted. "If he hung around with anybody here, I hope they canned his ass, too."

"There was a bar he went to," said the red-faced man. "He used to shoot off his mouth about winning bets and shit in there. I think it was over there in Bridgeport somewhere."

Moreland waited a beat and said, "He ever mention the name?"

"Yeah. I'm trying to remember. A guy's name. Mac's or Bud's or some shit like that, you know."

The giant in the Teamster jacket stirred. "Yeah, no, it was Mike's, that's it. It's on 35th, around Union or Lowe or someplace in there. I been in there. I remember thinking when he mentioned it to stay the hell out of there after that."

"Mike's, yeah, that was it. Try there. They might remember the guy."

"They probably threw a fuckin' party when he got killed."

"I get the impression Vance Oyler was not a popular man," said Moreland.

"I don't know how to tell you," said the big man. "He just had a way of getting on people's nerves. He was a weasel, like I said."

Moreland nodded, staring out through the misted window in the door, already leaving the market behind. He pushed away from the table. "Thanks. I appreciate your time, gentlemen."

"I'll tell you one thing about Vance Oyler," said the red-faced man.

"What's that?"

"Whoever killed him, he probably deserved it."

■ ■ ■

When the phone on his desk rang, Moreland reached for it with such alacrity that he sideswiped his mug and sent a dollop of coffee splashing out onto the wrack of papers on the desktop.

"Dammit. Moreland here," he said into the phone.

"That's a hell of a greeting for a man doing you the favor of returning a phone call."

"Buck, sorry. I just did an Exxon Valdez with my coffee here."

"Rough night?"

"If you only knew. How's business over there at Teamster City these days?"

"Dull. It's no fun around here now that we're squeaky clean."

"I bet. Did the Feds take away your Hawks tickets, too?"

"Nah, they let us keep those. Tell me when you want to go, I'll see if I can swing it."

"That's OK, that's not what I'm calling about. I need some infotainment from you today."

"Hold on. I'll get my prepared speech. 'The Teamsters Union Faces the Twenty-first Century.' "

"Spare me. I'll take it as read. What I really need this morning is gossip."

"Gossip? You got the wrong department here, pal. I'm a professional spin doctor."

"So spin me a yarn. Tell me about the Oyler family."

There was a pause. "The Oyler family. You mean as in John Oyler, no doubt."

"That's exactly what I mean."

"The late John Oyler."

"The late lamented. And his late lamented brother, Vance."

"Well, there are two schools of thought on Vance."

"I'm all ears, Buck."

"What the fuck you want me to tell you? I just heard about John when I got in this morning. That's pretty heavy, two brothers in two weeks."

"I'm just looking for background."

"Looking for dirt, you mean."

"Dirt? On the Teamsters? You shock me."

"Look, what the hell makes you think that any of this has anything to do with the union? You're the one who wrote the god damn story on Vance. He got himself killed playing with the wrong people. The little shit wasn't even in the union any more, hadn't been for a year."

"So I hear. I understand things stuck to his fingers."

"Well, you saw what happened to him. He probably tried to steal from the wrong people. As for John, who the fuck knows? If it's connected to Vance's murder, then it's got nothing to do with us."

"I guess not. But I hear they were a Teamster family, so what pops into my head? Just help me out a little. I hear his father used to work over there with you people."

In the ensuing silence Moreland could hear wheels turning, drawbridges creaking shut. "Yeah," said Buck, tentatively. "So what?"

Moreland leaned forward wishing he were talking face-to-face so he could bring his arsenal of disarming mannerisms into play. "So maybe nothing. I don't have any reason to believe there's any connection to the union. I just want to know a little more about 'em. Tell me about the father for a start."

Moreland could tell he wasn't talking to a pal any more; he was talking to the professional now. "He was on the Joint Council for a while. He died. Six or eight years back. In a hospital bed. That's all."

"So he was around back in the old days? The days when a Federal indictment was a prerequisite for union leadership?"

"That's the kind of insinuation we don't appreciate much around here, Mel."

"It's not an insinuation. I'm honest to God just looking for local color here. Did Gerald Oyler have any particular kind of reputation down there?"

"What kind of reputation you mean?"

"Any kind. Was he the type of Teamster who wouldn't be around now in the new squeaky clean union, if he had lived?"

"That's pure speculation. I'm not gonna speculate with you."

"OK, so he was pretty much a part of that old clique, was he? The bunch that gave organized labor a bad name in this town?"

"Gerald Oyler was never indicted for anything, if that's what you're angling for."

"I'll make a note of that. Fair enough. Tell me about John."

"John Oyler? What the hell you want? He was a good man. I think he was steward down there at one of the locals on the Southwest Side. Absolutely nothing against him."

"Never said there was. What happened to Vance? How come he turned out different?"

"You got me. All I know is he was a disappointment to the old man. Kind of a fuck-up. That business on the market last year was the last straw. We had a hell of a time keeping the son of a bitch out of jail, to tell you the truth."

"So you can still do that, can you? Keep people out of jail?"

"Mel, I'm trusting you here. You've always treated us right before."

"I'm just kidding, Buck. I don't believe the new improved Teamsters would exert undue influence to shield anyone from the law. Perish the thought."

"You know this town. There's a lot of people who ought to be in jail who aren't. Don't tell me about the Teamsters. We get real tired of hearing all the old myths."

"I don't deal in myths. Just the facts, ma'am."

"Well, you want the facts, here they are. The Oylers were pretty well regarded around here. Exept for Vance. And he was just a petty thief. Every family's got a black sheep."

"Tell me about it," said Moreland. "I don't even get invited home for Thanksgiving any more."

■ ■ ■

The office of the limousine company was a cubicle in the corner of a gloomy garage on Erie. Kress was on the phone when Cooper looked in the door; he waved Cooper to a chair and finished justifying his life to what sounded like a wife at the other end of the line. Kress was over fifty, overweight and overloud.

"You married?" Kress said after dropping the receiver back on the cradle.

"Not exactly," said Cooper.

"Well, take my advice, keep it fuzzy around the edges. Once they get the bit in your mouth they don't let go."

"I'll keep that in mind. What you got for me today?"

"You're picking up a Mr. Thomas Combs at O'Hare at two-forty. I got the flight number and everything here. You'll have to make one of those signs, you know, to hold up at the gate. You're taking him to the Four Seasons and then to 185 LaSalle Street. Where the hell's your tie?"

Cooper blinked across the desk at Kress. "In my pocket."

"Put the damn thing on. Is that the best jacket you have?"

"What's wrong with it?"

"You're not driving a hack now. In this business you dress as good as the clients or you lose them. Stop off somewhere and get yourself a decent-looking sport jacket, and the next time you come in I want to see you in a suit. Here." Kress shoved papers across the desk. "You got a nice Lincoln today. Solly's got the keys."

Cooper made no move to pick up the papers. After a second or two Kress fixed him with a glare and said, "What's the matter with you?"

"I don't wear suits," said Cooper.

For three seconds Kress looked blank. Then his eyebrows clamped down hard. "What is this, you didn't get this out of your system when you were a teenager? Grown-up men wear suits."

"Not this grown-up man."

"You'll wear a suit if you want to drive for me, I'll tell you that." Kress leveled a finger at him.

Cooper smiled. "The last time I got a lecture on clothing was in August 1976. I quit that job, too." He came up off the chair.

"Sit down, sit down. Listen to me for one minute, will you? Sit."

"Sit. Heel. Roll over. I don't do real well on any of them."

"Jesus, I got fucking James Dean in my office. You want a job or not? Times are that good, you can afford to walk off a job?"

Cooper turned in the doorway. "Times are never bad enough that I have to jump when you say jump."

"Look, I'm sorry, my manner was a little . . . blunt. I got a business to worry about, I got standards."

"Me too." Cooper took two slow steps to the desk and leaned over it, driving Kress back in his chair. He smiled again. "Look. Everybody wants a few luxuries in their life, right? Well, there's a couple of luxuries I decided long ago to permit myself. One is the luxury of never wearing a suit except when I want to, which is almost never. A tie is pushing it for me. And two is the luxury of never again taking lectures from anybody. Never. Nobody. It's cost me a little money, maybe, but then luxuries do. You getting the picture?"

Kress tapped the palm of his hand with a pen. "I think I'm getting the picture. You don't want a job bad enough."

"That's right. Not this one, anyway."

"You're going to die poor with an attitude like that."

Cooper straightened up and turned to the door again. "Maybe. But at least I won't die with that bit jammed between my teeth." He left the office, nearly sideswiping a man in the doorway.

On the street outside, Cooper scowled into a stiff wind. He felt the old sinking feeling, another bridge burned. He tried to ignore the chorus of voices telling him to walk back in there with his head down. Forty-three and jobless, a rebel without a clue. He dug in his jacket pocket for the tie and dropped it in the trash can on the corner.

Behind him someone called, "MacLeish." Cooper turned to see the man he'd nearly run into leaving the office, coming down the sidewalk after him. The man was gray-haired and medium height, medium everything, nondescript in every way except the forcefulness of his voice and his walk. What the hell, thought Cooper.

"Your boss is still swearing back there," the man said as he reached Cooper.

"Ex-boss," said Cooper. "What can I do for you?"

The eyes were forceful, too. "You can step into my car. I got some questions I'd like to ask." He produced a star from a pocket and flashed it at Cooper. "Officer Walsh, Violent Crimes. You talked to my partner last week."

Cooper nodded, the old sinking feeling returning. "You want to hear about last night, don't you?"

"All about it," said the cop, smiling.

■ ■ ■

"I want everything you have," said Detective M. Garvey Brown. "Every fucking thing."

Moreland opened his mouth to say something tough, something defiant, but couldn't come up with the line. He closed his mouth, reconsidered, and nodded. "It's not a whole lot," he said.

"Let's have it. Keep talking till I say stop." Brown leaned back on his chair with a creak. Behind him a quarter-inch of thick black coffee in the bottom of a carafe was getting thicker and blacker by the minute on the burner of a coffemaker. Filing cabinets, desks, and typewriters filled the large room. There was a murmur of activity from nearby desks, adjacent offices, the various hallways, nooks and crannies of Area Six headquarters.

Moreland put his elbows on the desk and leaned forward. "I don't really have anything more than the last time we talked. Vance Oyler called me, said he had a story, set up a meeting. We get to the meeting, Vance is dead. I told you that. This time, I wanted to talk to John."

"Why?"

"I thought he might know something about Vance's death."

"Why? One of Fisher's partners killed Vance, right? You broke the damn story yourself. Why talk to John?"

Why indeed, Moreland thought sourly. "You don't have a killer yet," he said. "It occurred to me Oyler's brother might know something, might have been in on it or something."

"Or something." Brown's lips thinned into a hard smile. "I've talked to a lot of liars in my career. You're one of the worst, you know that?"

Moreland ground his teeth silently. "All right. I wasn't sure the Fisher thing was the real story. There were a few funny things about the setup. Which even you must have thought of."

The smile disappeared. "You mean the fact that it looked like someone wanted Vance to be found? That someone stuck all those rods in him just for the effect? You mean that it looked more like a warning than just a way to shut Vance Oyler up?"

Moreland nodded. "That's what I mean."

"Well, yeah. Even we thought that was a little strange. So why the brother?"

"I'd tried to talk to him after Vance stood me up, way back at the beginning. He'd been very slippery. When somebody doesn't want to talk to the press, I figure there's a reason."

Brown's eyes left Moreland's for just a moment, then locked

back on. "So what's with the boyfriend? This guy MacLeish again."

Moreland sighed. "Oyler had refused to talk to me, so I took MacLeish along. I hoped Oyler might talk to him."

"Why the hell would Oyler talk to him?"

Moreland hesitated, blinked into the detective's baleful sleepy-eyed stare, and went on. "MacLeish was going to impersonate an acquaintance of Vance's. We had a cover story worked up, and he was going to try to find out what John knew about Vance's death."

Brown had his head tilted a little to one side, as if hearing something he couldn't quite believe. "You know, there's one thing I wish about reporters," he said. "I wish to God they wouldn't try to be so god damn smart all the time." Moreland glared, trying not to blush. "Why didn't you contact me if you thought John Oyler knew something? I'm trying to investigate this god damn case." The detective had a booming voice, a good strong hall-filling public speaking voice, and Moreland sensed heads turning.

He shrugged. "It was only a theory."

Brown shook his head, looking like a man near the end of his patience. "Well, I'm like you. I figure if somebody doesn't want to talk to me there's a reason."

"I had nothing to tell you. I had a hunch about Oyler, that's all."

Brown stared for a moment, tensing the pencil in the fingers of his big brown right hand as if debating just how to break it. "Tell me exactly what you saw in Oyler's apartment last night," he said finally.

"I never went in. MacLeish went up and found the body."

"Now see," said Brown, leaning forward, placing the pencil carefully back on the desk, his brow furrowed, "that's what makes a homicide dick sit right up and take notice. A guy like that, two guys like you, Mutt and Jeff, just happening—just *happening* to find a couple of fresh bodies like that. That just piques my curiosity all to hell. That makes me sit up nights wondering. Now can you explain why, can you give me any kind of an explanation for the . . . remarkable coincidence of you finding two bodies in two weeks? Right after they're killed?"

Moreland assumed his most innocent look. "I guess I was right on top of the story," he said.

■ ■ ■

"He was polite," said Cooper into the phone. "My guy was polite."

"With you, they would be," said Moreland. "With me, they get the charcoal going, to heat up the irons. What did he ask you about?"

"About what happened. About finding Vance and John. And about my relationship with you. Which I must say is starting to get embarrassing."

"Just burn my letters and you got nothing to worry about. Did he seem to follow any particular line of questioning?"

"Yeah. He seemed very interested in whether I'd gone inside. He kept trying to get me to say what I'd seen in there, what I'd touched. Was the window in the front room open, that kind of thing. I had to keep telling him I never stepped in the door."

"Yeah. Brown did the same thing. He wanted me to say I'd been up there, kept trying to get me to admit it."

"Huh."

"Yeah. You know what I think?"

"What?"

"I think they found something interesting up there and wanted to know if we'd seen it."

Cooper leaned on the window frame, watching the pale sun go down over the rooftops. "Or else they didn't find something up there and wanted to know if we took it."

"Yeah, that could be." For a few seconds there was silence on the line. "Shit. I'm never going to get word one out of a cop's mouth ever again."

"Well, look on the bright side. They're not ready to arrest us yet."

"No, they won't do that. But they'll harass us from here to Sunday, you can bet. When Brown was done bleeding me today, I called Guscas, the cop down in Oak Lawn. Now there is a discourteous son of a bitch. He acted like I had broken several federal, state, and local statutes just by calling him. I reminded him that I was a reporter after all and asked him for a few facts, but he just played dumb. No, they didn't get any footprints because the walk was shoveled. No, there's no indication the door was forced. No, they have no other witnesses. Nothing. We are going to get nothing at all from the cops from here on out."

"There's that pronoun again, Mel."

"But that's OK. I'm not through yet. I didn't tell Brown quite everything today."

"Hey, Mel."

"I didn't tell him I found out where Vance did his drinking. I'm hoping there's someone there that can tell me interesting things. Want to come along?"

"You're not listening to me, Mel."

"All right, stay home if you want. Me, I'm going out to rake up some muck."

"That's great. I'll be watching for the story."

"This isn't like you, MacLeish. Where's your sense of adventure?"

"I left it at the top of those stairs last night. It'll be frozen all the way through by now."

■ ■ ■

Moreland steered his rusting Toyota west along 35th Street through the deepening night, past the gigantic mass of the new Sox Park, through the long viaduct under the railroad tracks and into Bridgeport. Bridgeport for Moreland was the mystic heart of the city—Daleyland, the mysterious remote fastness of Irish clout, working-class resentment, Catholic fervor, White Sox fanaticism, and white belligerence. Bridgeport had fascinated him since the day in December 1976 when Moreland, a freshly hired and thoroughly green reporter for the City News Bureau, had been sent flying to South Lowe Street on the heels of the first breathlessly propagated reports of the unthinkable, the sudden death of Hizzoner Richard the First.

Bridgeport now was surprisingly Mexican and even a little black around the edges, though street names like Parnell and Emerald still evoked a distant green island. Moreland rolled past taquerías and discount department stores, braking as he passed the police station at Lowe, looking for the bar.

He nearly missed it because there was no sign, only the big glass window painted over with a decorative border framing the neon beer logo. *Mike's Place* was painted in modest letters between crudely rendered cocktail glasses. In the twilight inside it was much as he'd expected: a long wooden bar that shone from generations of spills and polish, Budweiser beer mats and ashtrays the size of hubcaps, the smell of yesterday's beer. There was a TV going in a corner high above the bar, but nobody seemed to be watching it. On the jukebox Tony Bennett strained to be heard. In the rear was a small pool table with a hanging lamp illuminating the bright green felt. Perhaps half the barstools were occupied. Men outnumbered women here but not by much; Moreland fit right in agewise, but his jacket and tie were a bit out of place. He drew some looks, not of hostility but of distancing; statements of territoriality. This was where people came to drink after work and not be bothered by people in ties.

Moreland took a stool at the end of the bar. The bartender spotted him and came slowly toward him, a tall heavy man with silver waves of hair and wire-rimmed glasses. Moreland asked for a draft and plotted tactics while he watched the man draw it expertly from the tap.

When the bartender brought back the beer, Moreland thanked him, tossed a five on the bar, and said, "Did you know a man named Vance Oyler? I'm told he was a regular here."

The bartender gave him a brief distant look and turned to pace back to the cash register. Moreland had the impression that at least two conversations along the bar had abruptly halted. The barkeep made change and brought it back, not meeting Moreland's eyes. "Who are you?" he said.

From the pocket inside his jacket Moreland pulled out his press card and handed it over. The bartender frowned at the card. "What the hell can I tell you? I'm not running a hotel here."

"But you knew him."

"What if I did?"

"Then you could maybe tell me who knew him better."

The bartender handed the card back. "Why are you interested?"

"Because he's dead."

The bartender raised his eyebrows and gave a little shake of the head, as if he were getting out of his depth. Moreland sensed heads swiveling. To his right a man said, "Well, you're no cop. You must be a reporter." The man wore an army fatigue jacket and a baseball cap low over his eyes. On the cap was an American flag and below it the words *Try and burn this one*. He clutched the handle of a beer stein as if it were the grip of a forty-four. "Who you reporting to?" he said.

Moreland smiled and gave the name of the paper. "I'm told Vance Oyler used to drink here quite a bit."

"He used to drink quite a bit here, anyway."

Moreland said, "People he used to work with told me he was a regular here."

The man pushed the cap back on his forehead. He was a spry-looking bantamweight with a rugged handsome Irish face and blue eyes that would not lose their mischief for another several beers. "I didn't know that guy ever held a job," he said.

"Apparently he did."

"So what the hell do you want? It's already been in the paper. I read about it."

"Like I said, I want to know why he was killed."

"I thought they knew why he was killed. He blew the whistle on those guys in Streets and San."

"The cops aren't so sure now."

There was a pause and the bartender, who had stayed in earshot, said, "So what the hell do you want in here? A guy comes in here to drink, he gets killed and all of a sudden I'm supposed to know all about him?"

"Of course not," said Moreland with a weak smile. "I'm just hoping someone can tell me something about him. Who were his friends? Who would know what he was into that might have gotten him in trouble? That type of thing."

The bartender looked at the man in the cap, who grinned. "Advertising, Mike. Think of it as advertising. We already went through this with his brother," he said to Moreland.

After a beat Moreland said, "His brother was in here?"

"Last week sometime. Same thing, asking all kinds of questions."

Moreland sat with his mouth open for a moment, just staring. "I see," he said finally.

"So I suggest you go find his brother," said the barkeep.

Moreland wondered if nobody read the paper any more. "I'm afraid that's not possible."

"How come?"

"Because the same thing happened to him last night that happened to Vance."

The faces at the bar snapped back toward Moreland. Silence reigned for several seconds. Moreland broke it by saying, "Two brothers in two weeks. The Oyler family's losing boys fast. So if you could help me out a little here, I'm sure their mother would really appreciate it."

The song on the jukebox ended and canned laughter from the TV wafted through the silence. "What the hell do you want me to tell you?" the bartender said, angrily.

"You could point me to whoever talked to John Oyler, for a start."

The bartender and the Irish bantamweight looked at each other for a moment. "Talk to Doris," they said, almost in unison.

"Who's Doris?"

"Doris," said the bantam, grinning and heeling toward Moreland, "is the best that squirrely son of a bitch could do."

"Watch your mouth," the bartender said, looking away down the bar.

"Hey, I'm just trying to help the man out." He pulled the cap low over his eyes and turned back to Moreland, his voice lower. "Vance and Doris had a little thing going. It was like watching animals in the zoo mate."

"Could you point her out to me?" said Moreland. "Discreetly?"

The Irishman leaned back from the bar until Moreland thought he must pitch onto the floor. Then he pulled himself back and leaned over to rumble in Moreland's ear. "See the one in the booth back there with the face held together with Sherwin-Williams latex? That's Doris."

From forty feet away Moreland could see the paint job. "The one in the Zsa Zsa wig?"

"That's Doris. And that's a vodka Collins in front of her. Doris don't come cheap."

Moreland picked up his beer. "Thanks."

Doris was alone in the booth and she watched Moreland come with a skeptical look, a long cigarette held aloft and fingers with bright pink nails toying with a matchbook. Moreland felt that everyone in the place was watching him as he walked the length of the bar, and he wished someone would plug another quarter in the jukebox. "Doris?" he said, halting in front of her.

"What did that bastard say about me?" Doris said. From the sound of the voice, a lot of alcohol and a lot of tobacco had gone past those red lips.

"He said you knew Vance Oyler," Moreland hazarded. "And that you had talked to his brother."

Something changed in her face; she stiffened and her fingers were still. She put the cigarette to her lips and drew hard on it, her eyes never leaving Moreland's. Watching her, Moreland thought Vance had been a desperate man; this lady had been in high school when Vance was a baby. Doris had never been pretty, but it looked as if she had always tried. The coating of make-up covered a face with pouches under the eyes and too high a ratio of nose to chin. The cheeks had started to sag and the hand holding the cigarette showed veins and spots. The eyelashes were as long and patently fake as the spun gold hair. The eyes beneath them were not trusting. This was a woman, Moreland judged, who had been oft disappointed.

"Why can't you leave me alone?" she said.

Mercifully, the jukebox sprang into action. "I could," said Moreland, sliding onto the bench opposite her, "but then I might not find out who killed Vance."

The plastic lashes blinked once. "And John?"

Moreland nodded. "You heard."

"It was on the radio. Are you a cop?" Doris said.

Moreland gave her the press card. She looked at it and then put it down on the table in front of her. Moreland took it back and stowed it.

"What do you want?"

"I want to find out why Vance died."

She digested that and said, "What can I possibly tell you?"

"Why don't you start with what you told John Oyler?"

She smoked again and Moreland recognized the stiffness of the pose and the fixity of the eyes. Doris was afraid. "I didn't tell him anything," she said.

Moreland looked at her nearly empty glass. "Let me get you another drink," he said. "Vodka Collins?"

She looked hostile for a moment and then said, "That's right."

"Sit tight. I'll be right back."

When he brought back the drink, Doris had finished the cigarette and folded her arms on the table. She wore a jangling collection of bracelets on her left forearm and on her fingers jeweled rings that Moreland thought couldn't possibly be real. "Thank you," she said quietly.

"You have to have told him something," Moreland said. "You talked with him long enough for other people to notice. And . . ."

He thought better of saying what he was going to say and drummed his fingers on the table instead. The strains of "Too-ra-loo-ra-loo-ral" filled the place.

Doris was staring at the table. "And he got killed. Right?"

"I don't know that that had anything to do with your talking to him," Moreland said.

"Then why don't you go away and leave me be?"

Moreland took a drink of beer, thought, set the glass down. "Because it might have."

There was a long pause. Doris's eyes came up from the table and held Moreland's. "So it might get me killed, too."

"More likely me, I'd say. But that's my problem." He smiled, trying to look confident. "Nobody will know you talked to me."

"Everybody seems to know I talked to the brother."

"Outside this bar, I mean. What you tell me is strictly confidential."

Her eyes went out over Moreland's shoulder, up along the bar. "I know how these things work. Those people don't like to be talked about."

"What people?"

"See? You're trying to get me to talk about it, but I won't."

Moreland frowned. After a moment, merely by way of experiment, he said, "Will you talk to the police about it?"

Her eyes were wide again. "Are you kidding me? And go to court? Have my name all over the paper? How stupid you think I am?"

"Tell me then. Your name goes nowhere. I can protect a source. Once I walk out of here I never heard of you."

"How do I know I can trust you?"

"Look, I've been a reporter for seventeen years. You can call the paper and check me out. And I wouldn't have lasted this long if I didn't know the rules. Like protect your sources."

Doris hadn't touched the fresh drink. She stared at it as if she were considering it, then looked up at Moreland. "I really don't know a thing about it."

"You wouldn't be scared if you didn't think you knew something. What was it you told John that worries you?"

Strings swelled to a crescendo. Doris wrapped long fingers around her drink. "About the mobster guy," she said.

Moreland waited. After a few seconds he said, "Tell me about the mobster guy."

She drank. "I don't know anything about him. I just saw him once, sitting at the bar with Vance. That's all. At first I thought he was Vance's father."

Moreland nodded, encouraging. "Uh-huh. Why did you think that?"

"Because I heard Vance call him Pop or something like that. I was mad at Vance because he was ignoring me, but then I figured OK, it's his dad, he wants to have a drink with his dad tonight. Except when he came by on his way to the toilet I told him to introduce his dad to me and he laughed and said his old man was dead."

"Yeah?" Moreland waited out a sip of the drink and the slow careful lighting of another menthol cigarette. "Who did Vance say he was?"

"He didn't say. He just like lowered his voice and leaned over and said whatever I did, don't stare at the guy because guys like him don't like to be stared at."

"Uh-huh."

"And I said well, he was kind of ugly and I could understand that. And Vance said don't let him hear me say that kind of thing because the guy had the kind of friends that leave people in car trunks out at O'Hare."

Moreland nodded, frowning across the table. "What then?"

"Then he went to the toilet. And I tried not to stare at the guy."

"And that was it?"

"Yeah. I figured all that was just some of Vance's bullshit. He liked to brag about tough guys he knew, things like that. That's all I thought this was." She drank again, deeper this time. "Until he got killed."

Moreland nodded. "That was all Vance said? That he had friends who left people in car trunks?"

"What more do you want?"

Moreland shrugged. "What did the guy look like?"

"I don't know. I hardly noticed him."

"Even after Vance told you not to stare at him? That would make me stare at the guy."

"I really didn't. I was talking to some other people. All I can tell you is he was an older man, gray hair, nothing special. And that's all I can tell you. Vance and him were still talking when I left."

"Nothing distinguishing? No hat, no gold chains or pinky ring or anything?"

"I don't remember. All I saw was a guy sitting on a barstool."

Moreland polished off his beer. "What did you say Vance called him?"

"Poppa or something. That's why I thought he was his father, see? He called him Pop or something like that."

"Would you recognize him from a photograph?"

"Absolutely not."

"If you saw him again?"

Doris hesitated just a moment and said, "No. I wouldn't recognize him. That's what I told Vance's brother, too. I wouldn't know the guy from Adam."

Moreland watched her as she drank, watched as she sucked the life out of the cigarette, avoiding his eyes now. His heart was racing a little.

"OK, Doris, thanks for talking to me."

"I never talked to you." Doris was waving at the bartender. Raising the foghorn voice she called, "Mike? Would you please ask this gentleman to stop bothering me?"

Once again Moreland felt all eyes on him, felt the freeze. He looked over his shoulder to see the big bartender straighten up from where he was leaning, a look of exhausted patience on his face. Moreland snapped a look back at Doris, angered, before understanding. He slid off the bench and stood up. "Thank you," he said. To the bartender and the hostile faces along the bar he waved and said, "Love to stay, folks, but I can't. Nice place you got here."

He made tracks for the door, a beatific smile fixed in place. "Too-ra-loo-ra-loo-ral," sang the jukebox.

■ ■ ■

"Fingerprints," said Moreland. "We're starting to find fingerprints." He eased back onto the immaculate white sofa, ice cubes clacking gently against the side of his glass.

"On what?" said Cleo, perched at the other end of the sofa in a blue silk robe, lightly made up, hair springing free in all its glory. "I thought they didn't find a weapon."

"That's just a figure of speech. I mean all over this case. 'The kind of people who leave bodies in car trunks out at O'Hare.' What does that suggest to you?"

"That suggests a really forgetful person to me."

Moreland laughed, loudly. "Yeah. Damn, now what'd I do with that stiff? Really, though. Who do you think of?"

Cleo shrugged. "Who?"

"The Outfit," said Moreland. "That's the way they like to do it. No fuss, no muss. Just make sure the car can't be traced to you."

"Ick."

"You said it. So Vance was hanging out with that type of person before he was killed. That's a fingerprint. That makes me sit up and take notice."

"That makes me scared. You'll be careful, won't you?"

"Oh hell yes, I'll be careful. I'm no hero. I'm just the guy that asks enough of the right questions of the right people to be able to put the story together. And once it's together and in print it's not worth killing me. It's too late."

Cleo held her head on one side, frowning. "I hope you have that figured right."

Moreland grinned. "So do I." He drained his drink and heaved himself off the couch. Striding toward the kitchenette, he said over his shoulder, "This is it, Cleo. This is the reputation maker. This is the one that makes my name." He grabbed the bottle of White Label from the countertop. "Seventeen years I've been a reporter in this town, and you know what the most important story I ever broke was?"

"What?"

"That alderman who had his grandmother evicted."

"I remember that."

"Well, it wasn't exactly snapped up by the wire services." Moreland came back toward the couch, waving a fresh drink. "In seventeen years I've written about everything—suburban lifestyle trends, church conventions, food festivals, school board meetings, high-society fund-raisers, opening day at the ballpark. I've written stories that put *me* to sleep. I've covered ethnic parades, petty crimes, funerals, traffic jams, fires, snowstorms, aldermanic temper tantrums, bankruptcies, weeping madonnas, weeping mayors, press conferences where everybody was lying and everybody else knew it, city council meetings where half the aldermen were asleep and nobody could tell. I did a feature on Hare Krishnas at the airport once. I've been a general assignment reporter, an education reporter, a business reporter, and a court reporter. I was sent on foreign assignment once—to Milwaukee. I've done everything in the newspaper business in Chicago except one." Moreland had halted in front of Cleo. He leaned forward slightly and pointed his free index finger at her. "I've never broken a really important story."

She was staring up at him, rapt. Moreland looked into his glass, musing. "I've never written a story that meant a god damn thing to the course of life in this city." He took a quick swill of scotch and looked at Cleo from under lowered brows. "And this may be the one, because somebody wants it stepped on, fast and hard. So I'm going to be careful. But I'm going to be tenacious, too. I'm going to be thorough and I'm going to be ruthless. And you can bet your sweet ass I'm going to get that story."

Cleo's lips were parted slightly; her impossibly blue eyes were fixed on Moreland's face and he could have sworn they were misty, just a little. She seemed to be breathing quickly. There was a moment of suspense and then Cleo shifted, the skirts of the robe parting to reveal her slim white legs as she slid to the edge of the couch and stood up, reaching for him. She put her arms around Moreland's neck and raised her lips to his. They were parted just enough that he could feel her warm breath. He stared helplessly into those blue eyes as she whispered, "You're a very brave man." The next instant her tongue was in his mouth and Moreland sloshed a little bit of scotch on the rug as he staggered, clutched her waist with his free hand, and scrambled to respond.

"Take me," she breathed, tearing at the belt of her robe as Moreland twisted to search desperately for a place to set the glass. She pursued him, clinging, as he spun wildly toward the glass-topped coffee table, and he just managed to put the glass down upright, in passing, as he overbalanced and toppled onto the rug. He landed on a hip and rolled onto his back, wide-eyed, as Cleo was upon him, the robe parted to reveal the stunning landscape of her body, pink nipples, genuinely blond hair and all. "Take me," she sighed, wrestling with his tie.

"Mm, oh, ah," said Moreland, before words failed him entirely.

7 COOPER CAME INTO THE living room and shook Dominic by a foot until he awoke. "Phone," said Cooper. "It's your grandma."

"Huh?" Dominic's eyes weren't quite ready for the morning light; he sat up, the blanket falling away to reveal his purple T-shirt and white long johns, but Cooper could see he was going to need some help. He took the receiver from the phone at the end of the sofa and handed it to the boy. Then he went back to the dining room and sat across from Diana, returning to his coffee and newspaper.

Dominic's end of the conversation was just audible, a petulant undertone. After a minute the phone was slammed down. At length there were sounds in the bathroom. When the boy came back to the dining room, dressed but shoeless, he didn't wait for greetings but said immediately, "How'd she know I was here?"

"I called her last night after you crashed," said Cooper without looking up.

"She's got you on her payroll, does she?" Dominic made for the kitchen. Diana and Cooper traded a look, and Diana gathered her papers and retreated up the hall to the front. When Dominic reappeared with coffee and sat at the table, Cooper said, "Call her and tell her to go to hell if you have to, but do her the courtesy of letting her know when you're going to stay out all night."

The boy fished sullenly through the sections of the paper. "Why don't you let me worry about her?"

Cooper mused. "Why don't you move out if you have so much trouble with her? You're a big boy now." A stony silence followed, which Cooper broke by saying, "Let me guess. She's got your inheritance all tied up and you'd have to get a job to support yourself if you moved out."

Dominic gave him a sharp look then. "I could support myself, easy."

"Prove it."

"I don't see you going off to work every day."

Cooper blinked at him. "I'm between jobs. When you've held

a few, you can be between jobs. You've never had a job to be between."

"Looks to me like you're just living off Diana."

Cooper laughed. "You're going to have to work a littler harder to piss me off."

"I'm not trying to piss you off. I'm just calling it like I see it."

"What I'm living off of is my savings, and I don't recommend it. Look, I'll make you a bet. Twenty bucks says I get a job before you do."

Dominic turned a page and said, "I'm going back to school in the spring anyway."

"That's what you said last fall."

"It didn't work out, OK? They wanted to put me back a year. I ought to be a senior. Shit, I could probably go to college now."

"So give it a shot. Find a place that will take you. Do something besides wasting your allowance and giving your grandmother grief."

"Jesus." Dominic shoved the paper away. "Twenty bucks, you said? You got a bet, chump." The boy took a last gulp of coffee and pushed away from the table. He disappeared up the hall and Cooper smiled, hearing him throw on his coat, taking leave of Diana. When the door slammed he heard her footsteps coming back to the dining room.

She stood in the doorway and said, "Sounds like this is one you might lose."

"Well, it'll do him some good."

Diana made no reply, walking into the kitchen. Cooper heard her lighting the gas on the stove, putting the kettle on. He pretended to read the paper for a minute and then raised his voice so she could hear him.

"Emilio knows a guy at a garage down on Broadway who's looking for a part-time mechanic. I was going to go talk to him today." There was no response, but Cooper knew what she would say: you can do better than that.

■ ■ ■

Moreland found Vince Gallo at lunch. Gallo was seldom in the city room at the newspaper, but old hands knew where he could be found at certain times; there were only three Loop restaurants where he would eat lunch.

This one was on North Wabash and featured booths thickly upholstered in leather tacked down with brass studs, heavy quasi-Italian food, and white-jacketed waiters with black bow ties. Vince Gallo sat by himself in a booth facing the door; the old hands at the paper joked that he had acquired the nervous habits of the milieu he had covered for forty years. Moreland had heard that Gallo had covered Capone's funeral, but he suspected the story was apocryphal. Gallo was not that old, he thought. Not quite. Gallo looked up at him as he approached and nodded, working on a mouthful of what could have been Veal Marsala from the looks of his plate.

"Can I bother you for a minute, Vince?"

Gallo shrugged and waved at the bench opposite him. "Plant yourself."

The host approached but Moreland waved off the menu. "I ate already. I just wanted to take advantage of your encyclopedic knowledge for a moment if I could."

"Encyclopedic." Gallo finished chewing and hoisted a glass of dark gold wine to his lips. He had gray hair above a seamed forehead, shrewd black eyes, and a long thin nose that came to a point above a wide expanse of cleanly shaven upper lip. He wore a natty blue blazer and a crimson silk tie. "You mean you want me to tell you the capital of Bolivia or something."

"Not that encyclopedia. The one you carry around in your vest pocket there. What I really need is a little dope on your Italian friends."

The jaws were working again, and Moreland had to wait, smiling into the little black eyes. Finally Gallo said, "I presume you mean what we delicately refer to as 'organized crime figures.' "

"That's right. Not the ones in Washington, the local ones."

"Then you oughta know they're not all Italian," said Gallo, one iron-gray eyebrow raised.

"Gee, Vince, I've done it again." Moreland shook his head. "I've offended your ethnic sensibilities. You know, it's the God-father movies. That's what did it. This Coppola fellow just makes up this myth of Italian organized crime out of whole cloth and now that's all people think of."

Gallo smiled a wicked little smile. "I'll read that as an apology. What do you want to know?"

"I was wondering if you knew of a . . . an organized crime figure, older guy, with a nickname something like Pop. Pop, poppa, some variation of that."

Gallo wiped his mouth with a starched white napkin and leaned back in the booth. "I might," he said after a moment.

"You might."

Gallo shrugged. "I'd have to think about it. There's a lot of people that might be considered organized crime figures."

"I understand. There's a lot of crime and a lot of it is fairly well organized, right?"

"That's right. Might I ask you what this is in relation to?"

Moreland swallowed hard. "You might. It's in relation to a guy who got himself killed. The word is that just before it happened he was bragging a little about his association with this Poppa fellow, who he said had the kind of friends who left people in car trunks in long-term parking out at O'Hare. I'm not sure why, but that suggested to me that you might have heard of him."

Gallo shook his head. "I've *heard* of a hell of a lot of people, yeah. But if all you have is that this guy had friends, that doesn't mean a thing. A lot of losers brag about having friends."

"Well, sure. It may mean nothing. In this case it was someone else claiming the guy had friends. That's a little different."

"Maybe."

"I just wondered if the nickname rang a bell."

"Poppa."

"Something like that. The source wasn't sure. It was something that suggested fatherhood."

Gallo shrugged again. "Who knows? That's not real definite."

"No, it isn't. But I thought it might jog something loose up there in that encyclopedic brain of yours."

Gallo smiled, white teeth glinting beneath the wide clean upper lip. "I'll let you know if it does."

Moreland frowned. "Look, Vince. I know information control is very important in your uh . . . your end of the profession. I'm discreet, you know that. I wouldn't ask if I didn't really need to know. And if you didn't owe me a favor or two."

The eyebrow was raised again as the wineglass halted on its way to the mouth. "Oh?"

"There have been a few Vince Gallo stories in the paper that weren't actually written by Vince Gallo, if you recall."

Gallo shrugged. "I'm a reporter. I go out and get the stories. I'm not the only guy that phones 'em in."

"And I'm not the only one who's ever rewritten your stories. But I've done quite a few of them."

Gallo conceded him a gracious nod. "I don't forget, Marvin."

"Melvin."

"What I meant to say." Gallo raised the glass, tossed off the last of the wine, and laid the napkin on the table. "Don't worry. I'll give it some thought, get back to you."

"Fairly soon?"

"Catch me tomorrow. I'll be around."

"Fair enough." Moreland scooted off the seat and stood above Gallo. "That was a hell of an interesting story you did on the Casalegno thing," he said.

Gallo eased a cigarette out of the pack. He put it in the corner of his mouth and smiled. "One of my best."

■ ■ ■

Diana closed the *Diccionario ideológico de la lengua española* and set it back on the table with a thump. She frowned at the thin volume of poetry open on the table before her, head supported on her hand, wondering if "untamed prickly pear tree" was really the best rendering of *arisca chumbera*. "Untamed fig-tree" was better but possibly inaccurate. What the hell was a prickly pear anyway?

She dropped the pencil and closed her eyes and stretched. The apartment was quiet, the radiators temporarily at rest, no traffic moving on the street outside. The sun beat in through the south-facing windows and made the bare wood floor shine. Diana was warm and comfortable and busy, and consequently happy. *Feliz* or *contenta*, she thought reflexively, or both?

Los dos, she decided. It occurred to her suddenly that there was a book up in the living room that might help her, an encyclopedia of plants that Cooper had acquired along the way and failed to cull in his periodic library-cleaning sweeps. She pushed away from the table, rose and walked up the long hallway to the living room. It took her a moment to find the book among the atlases, dictionaries, and odd lots of art books on the shelf, but she located it and headed back down the hallway to the dining room, narrowing her eyes a bit against the glare of the polished floor.

The hallway stretched the length of the place and from the living room she could see all the way through the dining room and kitchen to the back door. It was not until she saw the head and shoulders at the window in the back door that she consciously registered the footsteps she had heard laboring up the back stairway moments before. The person at the door was backlit and only a silhouette; the face was close to the glass, looking in. Diana slowed a bit, not alarmed but curious and faintly on guard like all urban residents when strangers come to the door.

The landlord? she thought as she made out the hazy outline around the head; the elderly German who had rented them the place wore such a hooded parka, she thought. The silhouette would resolve itself into a face with a few more steps. It occurred to Diana that the natural thing for the man to do would be to ring the buzzer; the button was set into the frame by the door. The thought made her slow a little more; the figure had not moved.

It moved as she entered the dining room, close enough to begin to make out features; just as she got an impression of a dark face framed by the hood, the face disappeared. The figure vanished and there was only the sound of footsteps on the porch and a clear view across the alley to the snow-covered roofs beyond.

Diana set the plant book on the dining room table and moved slowly into the kitchen, listening to the footsteps going down the stairs. When she reached the back door she looked out, but she could see no one. The footsteps reached the bottom of the stairs, but instead of proceeding out into the little concrete yard behind the building, where the man would emerge into view, they faded away up the gangway in the direction of the street. Diana stayed at the door for a moment, her faint frown gradually easing. She shrugged and returned to the dining room, wondering why she had never noticed that the landlord limped.

▪ ▪ ▪

Moreland spotted Cleo immediately in the tumult of the brass-railed, wood-paneled bar. That explosion of blond hair was like a beacon. As he moved through the crush of people toward her, Moreland felt that little kick in the chest; out of all the men in the place, younger men, taller men, men with more hair and less weight, men with square jaws and steely eyes and fat wallets, out of all these men it was he, Melvin Moreland, that Cleo was waiting for. He began to grin even before she saw him. When her eyes lit on him and she smiled and gave that silly wiggle of the fingers that passed for a wave, the grin widened and he could barely contain himself.

He nearly knocked a cocktail waitress off her rails in his haste to get to the booth. When he bent to kiss Cleo he could taste liquor and lipstick and something else, that warm fleshy taste of passion. Two weeks almost and the gut-deep excitement was still there.

"I'm late," he said. "I hope you didn't have to slap too many faces." He stripped off his coat and tossed it in a corner of the booth and sat beside Cleo, throwing a proprietary arm around her shoulders.

"Where have you been? I had to turn down a bunch of free drinks."

Moreland heaved a great sigh. "I've been out on the West Side, talking to some Catholics who don't want the Archdiocese to close their church even though they get about six people in there for Sunday Mass. It's the kind of story I've built my career on. Momentous."

"They closed the church my grandma went to. It was terrible. She kind of went downhill after that."

"What do you want 'em to do? They've got this big drafty relic of a church out in the ghetto there that nobody goes to any more. Not for Mass anyway. Maybe to shoot up in the basement stairwell. It looks like St. Paul's after the blitz standing out there."

Cleo looked blank for a second. "You mean like a linebacker just hit it?"

"Ah . . . not that blitz. The one in London. Never mind. What the hell's that you're drinking?"

"A peach sling. Want to try it?"

Moreland waved it away, teeth bared. "Cocktails should never come in pastel colors. Never. An honest cocktail looks like something you'd pump into the tank of a race car. And it doesn't have dollhouse furniture floating in it."

"That's so stupid. Where do you get these rules?"

"The same place I acquired the rest of my gentleman's code of honor. Out behind the gym in high school."

"Well, I like these."

"I'm sure they do wonders for your complexion. I'll buy you five more if you want." Fleetingly Moreland estimated the cost of elaborate cocktails in a place like this, and then his smiled broadened as he thought how base it was to stint on entertaining someone who looked like Cleo. He snagged the waitress and shouted an order for a replacement peach sling and a vodka martini for himself. The din of jukebox and high-volume conversation, the press of young and well-dressed and good-looking people cutting loose in cocktail-hour liberation, most of all the warmth of Cleo's flank next to his exhilarated him. Moreland realized that for a change he was living life exactly as he wanted to live it.

He gave Cleo's shoulder a squeeze. "How'd things go for you today?"

She shrugged. "Dull as usual. I got yelled at for leaving someone on hold too long. Like it's easy to keep track when seventeen people call at once, you know?"

"Hell with 'em. Just plug in the Muzak and let 'em wait," said Moreland, whom nothing irritated more than being put on hold. "How's Rumpelstiltskin?"

"He's OK. We were trying to figure out if he's got a new rug. It looks a little darker and it's longer in back this week."

"I would think a man as wealthy as King Van Houten could afford a hair transplant."

"Maybe he's saving up for a new glass eye, one that follows the real one. I swear to God, I never know which eye to look at. It's like watching a tennis match, just having a conversation with him."

Moreland laughed, louder and longer than the line warranted. "The bionic dwarf. Is any other part of him artificial?"

"Well, we do wonder. Oh hey, King's throwing a party tomorrow in the new suite. They were saying today the mayor might be there. Want to come?"

Moreland's face lit up. "Hell, yes. With King Van Houten's crowd? I'll wear a body mike and get material for the definitive work on clout and corruption in Chicago."

"Corruption? You think King's crooked?"

Moreland looked into the wide blue eyes, the man of the world explaining the facts of life. "Let's just say you have to know a lot of angles to get a skyscraper built in this town, and King's gotten a lot of them built."

Cleo shrugged and poked at her drink with a plastic swizzle stick. "I guess I don't really understand these things."

"It's pretty simple, really. It's all about trading favors. I let you cut into the lunch line if you pass me the answers to the test."

"So they're all crooks? King and everybody else?"

"Not all of them, no. Enough of them to keep muckraking reporters in business." Moreland drummed fingers on the table, mouth set firmly. "Most of the time, nobody gets hurt. That's why I want to get at this Oyler thing. Somebody's up to some very serious shit here."

"What kind of shit?"

"I don't know yet." Moreland glanced around for dramatic effect and pulled Cleo even closer. "I talked to Vince Gallo today. He's going to try to run down this mobster figure for me. That's the only lead I have right now. The cops know the Fisher thing was just a blind now, so they'll be rooting around the Oyler clan as well. I'm hoping I'm a step ahead of them with this Poppa character."

He felt Cleo shudder next to him. "The mob. That's kind of scary."

Moreland's chest swelled. "Nah. People don't kill reporters. Where the hell are those drinks?"

"Look, she's up there at the waitress station, probably getting them now. Give her a break."

Moreland looked, and saw the waitress standing near the cash register, loading a tray. Above her he could see a television set, playing the evening news in mute isolation. The anchorwoman's blond head stopped talking, her eyes shifted from the camera, and the picture changed. Moreland found himself looking at the yellow brick two-flat where John Oyler's body had been found.

"I'll be god damned," he said.

"What?"

"Son of a bitch." In front of the yellow brick building, holding a microphone, stood a woman with aquiline features and straight black hair just touched with gray. Her lips moved silently.

"What is it?" Cleo was trying to follow Moreland's gaze.

Moreland had taken his arm from her shoulders and was starting to move. "On the TV. It's that woman. Christine Pappadakis."

"Oh her. She needs a nose job. Where are you going?"

Moreland was on his feet. "I've got to hear what she's saying. That's my god damn story."

When he was halfway to the bar the face of the big Oak Lawn police detective filled the screen, talking into the microphone with the usual knowing solemnity. Moreland muttered excuses as he went, shouldering his way toward the TV screen. He fought through to the bar and fetched up next to the waitress, who was lowering a giant peach sling carefully onto the tray.

"I'm on my way," the waitress said frostily.

Moreland was shouting at the bartender to turn up the volume, but nobody was paying attention. Christine Pappadakis was on the screen again, in front of the Oak Lawn police station, intoning grimly into the mike as the wind whipped her shoulder-length hair about her face.

Moreland turned to the waitress, jostling the tray just enough to bring a gasp. "I need a pay phone," he said.

She pointed him to it with her chin and said to his back, "What you need is a leash."

When Moreland got back to the booth Cleo had nearly finished the second peach sling. She looked at him and said, "What happened?"

Moreland sank onto the seat. His gaze was unfocused and his hand trembled just a bit as he reached for his drink. "I called the desk at the paper," he said.

"Why? What's going on?"

"To find out what the hell that woman said on TV."

"And what was it?"

Moreland put his arm around Cleo again but without enthusiasm. "They found some tapes."

There was a two-second pause. "Who? Who found some tapes? Where?"

"The cops found a box full of tapes in John Oyler's place. Cassette tapes, recorded conversations."

Cleo blinked at him. "What conversations? Who's talking?"

"They're not saying. Apparently there's a lot of them. They're going through them all now. But it does seem they might have a bearing on the case. Shit."

"Mel, baby. What's the big deal?" Cleo took his face in her long-nailed hand and turned it to hers.

"That was Christine Pappadakis."

"So?"

"She's the best, Cleo. She's the best investigative reporter in the whole fucking city. She's caused more red faces at City Hall than flatulence."

"I know who she is. She's the one who got that alderman to resign, right? The one who had two wives?"

"She's the one. If she's on the story it's over, it's fucking over."

"You mean because she might get the story before you do?"

"She already has, it looks like. The best story of my life maybe, and the cops give it to Christine Pappadakis."

"Did she say who killed all these people?"

Moreland frowned and then focused on her at last. "No. According to the guy on the desk they don't have any more actual leads, no new physical evidence or anything."

"Well then, it's not over, is it?"

Moreland tapped a finger impatiently on the table. "I gotta get access to those tapes."

Cleo slumped a bit, turning her face away from Moreland's and reaching for her drink. "Tonight?" she said.

Moreland, alerted, squeezed her shoulders. "No. Not tonight. I'm not sure there's anything I could do about it tonight. But first thing tomorrow." He balled his fleshy hand into a fist. "I'm not going to let them screw me out of this. I got some cards up my sleeve yet."

Cleo smiled again. "That's my tiger."

"I got angles they haven't thought of."

"I'll bet you're twice the reporter Christine Pappadakis is."

"She's good, and she's got the sources. But I can beat her."

"TV's so superficial anyway, I think," said Cleo.

"JAY, IT'S A MAJOR STORY. There's dirt here. Deep, rich dirt. It's going to need sustained work. Undistracted work." Moreland leaned across the desk toward Macy, who watched him warily as if he were a tree about to fall.

"Fine. You can be undistracted as soon as you give me that feature. Then you have two days." Macy's eyes darted away, out across the newsroom.

"It needs more than two days. It's going to take some patient digging. Jesus, Jay, you're an old reporter. Can't you recognize a story when you see one?"

Macy's voice dropped to a level undertone. "Listen, Melvin. I'm already doing you a favor by not giving the story to Vince. To me it looks like it might be his kind of story. I'm giving you a break because it was yours to start with. But I can't spare a good general assignment reporter for more than a couple of days."

Moreland's head drooped suddenly and he stared at the desktop. "Fine. Two days."

"Look at it this way," said Macy. "It looks as if things are happening fast on this one. With the developments that came out yesterday, it might just be a pickup job by six o'clock tonight."

Moreland straightened up with great dignity. "In other words, you've written the story off. You think Pappadakis will sew it up and there will be nothing left for me."

Macy's eyes lit for an instant on Moreland's face and darted away again. "I've given you two days. As soon as you finish the Meigs Field thing. It's your story. Now go get it." He reached for the phone, dismissing him.

Moreland forced a smile, a wide beaming insincere smile. "Thank you, massa," he said.

■ ■ ■

When the doorbell woke Cooper he made no move to get up; he figured Diana would get it. When it rang a second time he remembered suddenly that Diana was out this morning, off to the copy center to process documents for her applications. Cooper rolled out of bed and threw on jeans and a T-shirt.

He buzzed the downstairs door and stood on the landing hearing two sets of footsteps coming up. When the visitors hove into view it took Cooper a couple of seconds to place the woman who was in the lead; when she made eye contact he realized he'd seen her on TV.

She reached the landing and fixed an appraising look on him. "Mr. MacLeish?"

"Yeah."

She stuck out a hand. "I'm Christine Pappadakis." She added the station's call letters and gave his hand a firm shake.

Still groggy, Cooper shook back. The TV didn't lie; Christine Pappadakis was much as she appeared on the tube, a handsome if slightly severe-looking woman making a graceful transition into the forties. The slightly graying hair fell straight to her shoulders, curling under in orderly fashion; the long curved nose ended at a firm mouth, and the eyes were a steady watchful gray. She wore a gray jacket over a tight black sweater and gray slacks that hugged a good figure. "This is my associate, Rob Riley," she said, presenting the man behind her. Cooper nodded at him, taking in a quick impression of considerable height and watchfulness behind rimless glasses. "We'd like to ask you some questions about your involvement in the Oyler case," said Christine Pappadakis.

Cooper had started backing inside. "Sure," he said. "If I can get some coffee in me first." He led them back to the dining room and waved them to chairs as he went into the kitchen to fire up the percolator. Fumbling with the coffee can, he heard them settle themselves at the table and then fall silent. "Where are the cameras?" he said.

"Back at the studio," Christine Pappadakis called from the other room. "We don't talk to a camera until we've got something to say."

Cooper got the coffee going and leaned against the doorframe with his arms folded. She had placed a stenographer's notebook on the table in front of her and the tall man sat at the far end of the table, apparently absorbed in the preparation of a small cassette recorder. "You want to know all about the bodies, don't you?" Cooper said.

"That's a good place to start," Christine Pappadakis said, a jaunty smile on her face.

"I've been through all this already. With the police. If you want to get the whole story, you ought to talk to a guy named Melvin Moreland."

"Your reporter friend."

"That's right. He's working on the story. He can tell you all you want to know."

The two people at the table exchanged a look. "Somehow," said Christine Pappadakis, "I doubt he would."

Cooper shrugged. "How do you take your coffee?"

When they were all provided for, Cooper sat across the table from the woman and said, "All I did was find 'em."

"So I hear. Tell me about it."

Cooper told her. She took a few notes, at what seemed random points. The tall man tended the recorder. When Cooper finished talking, Pappadakis tapped the butt end of her pen on the table a few times and said, "Now tell me what you didn't tell the police. Strictly anonymously, of course."

Cooper gave her a pained look and took a sip of coffee. He set down the mug and stared at the tabletop. Finally he looked up at her. "What makes you think I know anything more than that? And what makes you think I'd tell you if I did?"

The gray eyes narrowed. "Let's take the second question first. You might tell me if you decided you weren't going to let your reporter friend drag you down with him. Obstructing an investigation is something that tends to make policemen very unhappy, and I don't think they're very happy with you two now."

"We didn't obstruct anything. We're the ones that called the police."

"So they say." There was a faint look of amusement on her face.

"So why would I tell you what I won't tell the cops?"

"We could get you a pretty good lawyer. Better than you could afford yourself, probably."

Cooper smiled, barely. "OK, how about the first question?"

"I'd think that was obvious," Christine Pappadakis said. "People don't just happen to come across two murders in a row. Coincidences happen, but not that kind."

"The first one wasn't a coincidence. We were meant to find it."

She appeared to chew on the idea for a second. "And the second one?"

"The second one I think was a race to find John Oyler. And we lost."

"I see. And who do you think killed him?"

"How the hell would I know? All I do is find the bodies."

She exchanged a look with the tall man, a look just long enough to blink and touch base. "OK," she said. "You told the police you didn't go inside the apartment."

"That's right. I didn't."

"Why did you open the door when you got no answer to your knock?"

Cooper's face was settling into a frown. "If you know that much, I'm sure you also know the answer I gave the cops."

"Can't I hear it from you?"

"Why waste our time? You're not here just to get me to repeat what I said to the cops."

Her lips firmed in a thin tight line and the gray eyes gleamed. "What am I really here for, then?"

Cooper thought carefully before answering, listening to the hiss of the radiators. "I'd guess you're here to find out how much it would take to pry whatever I took from John Oyler's apartment out of me."

The amused look vanished. She stiffened as if someone had run a current through her. "And how much would it take?" she said quietly.

"Probably not very much," said Cooper. "But I didn't take anything. What I told the cops was the gospel truth."

She sagged back on her chair, just perceptibly, and her look became just a shade hostile. She looked at Cooper for a long moment, then at her partner, then back. "You want me to name a figure?"

"No. I was just trying to figure out what brings you here. I didn't take anything."

She tapped the pen impatiently on the table. "The cops could be pretty rough on you if they found out you had something you weren't sharing with them."

"And if I don't share it with you, they just might find out, is that it?"

"It doesn't have to be that way."

Cooper shrugged. "I told you the truth. I never went in, I never took anything. You're looking for somebody else."

From the look on her face it could have been the woman who was making the hissing noises. After a moment she said, "I may be looking for somebody else. But I have a feeling I'm going to remember you."

■ ■ ■

Vince Gallo had on a double-breasted gray pin-striped suit with a maroon silk handkerchief peeping out of the breast pocket. He exuded a faint aroma of cologne as he strolled into the newsroom, smiling greetings right and left. He drifted to a halt in front of the desk where Moreland sat swearing at a computer terminal.

"Hey, kid. What's the news?"

Moreland looked up at him, startled, then frowned. "Reporter goes berserk, slays ten in newsroom. Editor had it coming, suspect says. I'm working on it right now." He shoved a stray chair toward Gallo and looked at him a little mistrustfully. "What do you have?"

Gallo inspected the chair for vermin and dry rot and then sat on it, elegantly crossing one leg over the other and folding his hands on the uppermost thigh. He smiled, the expanse of clean upper lip widening smoothly across his face. "I heard a rumor about you," he said.

"It's a lie," said Moreland. "She's at least eighteen and it was entirely consensual."

"Not that kind of rumor. I mean I heard you almost had yourself a hell of a story."

Moreland stared, trying hard to give nothing away. "Which story are you almost referring to?"

"The one that that little girl from Channel Five got last night."

"Ah. You mean the tapes the cops found in that dead guy's apartment."

"Yeah. The dead guy that you found, I heard."

Moreland shrugged. "I almost found him. What about it?"

"It's too bad you didn't find out about the tapes."

"Isn't it. I must be a really bad reporter, I guess. I don't suppose you've managed to find out what was on those tapes, have you? I was down in Oak Lawn first thing this morning, but they had the Out to Lunch sign up already. The only person I could get to talk to me was under strict orders to give an impression of total stupidity. That chief of theirs down there is guarding those tapes like they were his daughter's honor. He knows dynamite when it falls in his lap. And I got as much clout over at Eleventh and State as the fucking janitor. Probably less. I guess I'll just have to watch TV tonight like everyone else."

Gallo's smile had faded. "Well, Pappadakis may have heard the tapes, but I think you're still in the running."

Moreland's eyes narrowed. "What do you have, Vince?"

"Well, I may have your Poppa." Gallo smiled.

Moreland cast a glance out over the room and leaned closer to Gallo. "Tell me about Poppa."

"It's Pappy, actually."

"Pappy."

"That's right. Michael Papini. Known to his friends as Pappy. A sweetheart of a guy."

"How do you know he's the guy I'm looking for?"

"I don't know for sure. But it would make sense if this has anything to do with the dead guy you almost found."

"Tell me, Vince. Talk to me. Who is the guy?"

"Nobody, now. Now he's just an ex-con. Ex by just a few weeks, actually. He was down in Marion till recently, doing some time for some uncivil things he did back in the seventies."

"And he was?"

Gallo's smile widened again. "He was associated with that crowd of people that used to run things over on South Ashland."

Moreland smiled. "That old Teamster gang, you mean."

"Yeah, that bunch. Those Italians, you know."

"Except they weren't all Italians, were they?"

"No, sir."

Moreland nodded, intent. "One of them was named Oyler, wasn't he?"

"That sounds right. Say, that sounds kind of familiar somehow. I think I've heard that name recently. Like on TV, yeah."

"You wouldn't happen to know where I could find this Pappy fellow, would you?"

"That's a funny thing, Mel. Several other people seem to be asking that same question."

"Talk to me, Vince."

"Well, I hear that when Pappy got out of jail last month his old friends weren't real eager to help him out. It seems he'd done a little talking to the people that put him in Marion, so he wouldn't have to be there quite so long. What I hear is that Pappy couldn't find anyone to take him in, not even family. He had a sister or someone like that who wouldn't even talk to him. She was kind of religious, they say."

"You do get all the gossip, don't you, Vince?"

"An awful lot of it. Anyway, Pappy had to set up in some flop-house over on Clybourn or someplace like that and go around with his hat in his hand. Sad."

"I'm moved. What happened?"

"Nothing, except nobody would do him any favors."

"So where is he now?"

"Nobody knows."

"What do you mean?"

"I mean nobody knows where he is."

Moreland stared. "Who's been looking for him?"

Gallo uncrossed his legs, recrossed them the other way, and placed a manicured hand on the desk. "Arlo Spivak," he said.

"Who the hell is Arlo Spivak?"

"Arlo Spivak is a guy that works for Walter Neumann."

Moreland gave a quick shake of the head, as if to clear it. "Walter Neumann the alderman?"

"Walter J. Neumann the alderman, that's correct. Spivak is Neumann's gofer. When Neumann wants something done, Spivak does it."

Moreland blinked five times rapidly. "Why the hell would an alderman from the Northwest Side be looking for a Teamster ex-con?"

Gallo made a ceremony of rising from the chair. "Well, kid, there you got me. That's where my sources run dry. All I can tell you is that Pappy walked out of the flophouse on Christmas Eve and hasn't been seen there or anywhere else since."

"Sounds like something might have happened to spoil his Christmas."

"It's a tough time of year for people without friends, they say."

"Mm. A little over two weeks ago."

"And Arlo Spivak has been pestering a lot of Pappy's old friends, which they really do not appreciate."

"I'll be damned."

Gallo smoothed his jacket. "Not if you're careful."

"Thanks Vince, I owe you."

Gallo's smile was gracious. "Don't worry about it, Mel. I'll be seeing you around." He nodded at the computer. "You'll have to show me how to use one of these things someday."

■ ■ ■

There was an ad in the paper for a sales position with a manufacturer of quality hand tools. Cooper had sold things before; it wasn't his favorite kind of work but the ad said some travel involved, some German a plus but not necessary, and he said what the hell. He'd forgotten most of the German he'd known but it had to be recoverable, and the idea of going to Europe on business intrigued him. He called and made an appointment, without high hopes but in a spirit of adventure. He even put on a tie, thinking gloomily of Kress and the limousine job.

The company was located in a gussied-up warehouse on Franklin near the Merchandise Mart, and the manager was an untidy but amiable man who looked less like a businessman than a slightly distracted professor, which it turned out he had been.

"I was a professor of engineering for fifteen years," he said, peering earnestly at Cooper through thick black-rimmed glasses. "Until I finally decided that business was what really made the world go around."

"More money in it too, I guess," said Cooper.

"Not necessarily. I'm not going to be retiring to the south of France for a while. But it's never boring. And if we get into Europe I might be able to afford a new car."

"No regrets, huh?"

"No. I've had fun so far and I've found business people to be straight shooters. With one exception."

"Oh?"

"Real estate. Real estate people are the scum of the earth."

Cooper smiled politely and they talked about the job. The company was young, the product of excellent quality but specialized appeal, and Europe still a distant dream. Cooper admitted he probably wasn't really qualified. "I've sold insurance and managed a restaurant. And I have used tools. I've lived in Germany but my German is mostly history. All I've got going for me is that I work hard and learn fast."

"A quick study, eh?"

"I like to think so."

The ex-professor smiled and looked down at the resumé again. He nodded at it as if it were a mildly amusing poem. "That's not a bad recommendation. But I have to tell you I've talked to some pretty sharp sales people, a couple with the language down pretty well."

Cooper's shrug and smile were gracious. "I thought I'd give it a shot."

"Thanks for coming in." The manager slipped the resumé into a desk drawer and gave Cooper a keen look through the glasses. "You've got the right idea, you know, for a man changing horses in midstream. You seem to have ability in the abstract, like Conrad's Lord Jim. If you've got brains and energy, there's always money to be made. I'd keep looking for a young company willing to take a chance on a man like you."

"Let's hope I don't have to go as far as Malaya," said Cooper.

The ex-professor seemed to enjoy the joke; he was still grinning as he saw Cooper to the door.

Outside, it was cold and getting colder. Cooper stood under the El tracks with a train rumbling and creaking by overhead and scanned for a phone. He had tried to call Moreland four times without success, and since he was near the newspaper building he thought he would try once more.

He found a phone two blocks away. This time the reporter answered. "Moreland."

"Mel, Cooper here."

"Coop, I'm on my way out, in a rush. What's up?"

"I talked to your competition this morning. She woke me up at the crack of dawn."

Moreland missed a beat and then said, "Pappadakis?"

"Live and in color. She had lots of questions."

There were three seconds of silence and Moreland said, "Where are you?"

"Not too far from you. You working?"

"Yeah, and I'm late. Can you wait around an hour or two? Or no, shit. Are you presentable?"

"Mel, you wouldn't know me. I've been talking to a prospective employer."

"Terrific. If you look OK I can sneak you in. I'm combining business and pleasure anyway. Meet me at 300 North Michigan. Pronto, we're late."

"What's happening?"

"I'm covering the inaugural shindig at King Van Houten's new offices in the Michigan Tower. Where Cleo works. She tipped me off last night and I wangled the assignment from Jay. It's fluff, gossip column stuff, but there'll be food, beautiful people, and drinks galore. Even if you're underdressed I can pass you off as a photographer or something."

"I forgot my Hassleblad."

"Fuck it, we'll get you in. Just get moving. You know the place?"

"Yeah. Main lobby?"

"Sure. Ten minutes?"

"I'll be there."

The Michigan Tower was a Regis Swanson building, perhaps the jewel in his crown. It had been completed in the depths of glut and recession, hailed as artistic triumph and economic folly, and only partially redeemed by attracting a few of the town's haughtier office tenants. It stood on Michigan north of the river like a column of ice, fifty-five stories of glass with a neo-classical crown.

The main lobby was vast, echoing and dead, like the heart of an iceberg. Architects could kill a street a lot faster than a depression, Cooper reflected, crossing it toward the impatient figure of Moreland, who was pacing by the elevators.

"Let's go. They're eating up all the hors d'oeuvres." Moreland stabbed at the elevator button as Cooper pulled up beside him.

"What's the hurry? Your editor get mad if you miss the opening drink or something?"

Moreland grinned, stepping into the elevator. "I told Cleo I'd be there at five. Like I say, I'm combining business with pleasure."

As the high-powered elevator shot upwards, Cooper frowned across the mirrored cabin at Moreland. "You interested in what Pappadakis had to say or not?"

Moreland was suddenly down to earth. "Of course I'm interested. I just have to do a little reportorial work, then we'll find a corner and get down to brass tacks. You look like a schoolteacher, you know that?"

"I'll take that as a compliment."

"I mean, the tie, the tweed jacket. Aren't you cold walking around like that?"

"The bomber jacket doesn't go with the tweed. When I'm dressing up I leave it in the car."

Moreland shook his head. "Somebody needs to take you shopping."

The elevator slowed and eased to a halt and the doors opened onto a scene of splendor. Cooper wondered briefly what was holding the building up; everywhere he looked was glass. Opposite the elevator, black Roman letters were apparently suspended in mid-air, spelling out *Van Houten and Riggs*. At either end of the slightly curving hall was a patch of sky with distant cityscape below. Through the glass partition in front of him Cooper could see a gray divider with a vacant desk in front of it and a slice of office suite beyond. There were people milling about near the desk and in the suite, provisioned with drinks.

Moreland gave his tie a tug and led Cooper through the open double glass doors into the mild hubbub of the party. A well-groomed man in a maroon blazer with a crest on the breast pocket was stationed just inside the door, and he smiled at them in a way that conveyed they'd better have an invitation. Moreland gave his name and the name of the paper and cocked his head at Cooper. "My associate, Mr. MacLeish." The man's eyes lingered on Cooper, but he thanked them and kept smiling. Moreland nodded at people hovering near the desk as he strode toward the temporary coat racks set up to the left of the entrance. People nodded back without interrupting their conversations. Hanging up his coat, Moreland jutted his chin at the desk and said, "That's where Cleo sets up during working hours. Now she'll be back there somewhere, fetching drinks and batting her eyelashes." He led Cooper into the office proper. Beyond the divider was sudden vertigo: an entire wall of large glass squares, giving a view of Navy Pier and the limitless sheet of water beyond. The space was a quarter-circle, with a radius of perhaps fifty feet. They had come in along one side of the wedge; the windows lined the arc, and the other straight edge was pierced with doorways that gave onto halls and offices. The spectacular anteroom was provided with low and mysteriously shaped items of furniture, in subdued colors that suggested the lake on a cloudy day. In amongst the furniture were men in suits and just a scattering of women, in suits or serious dresses.

"Ah, there's the bar." Moreland pointed at a linen-draped table set up along the opposite wall, where two Mexicans in white jackets worked briskly. "Listen, I really do have to do a little work—move around, take names, kiss some ass, and get a quote or two about the magnificence of the premises. Get yourself a drink and we'll talk in a minute."

"Go ahead. Sounds like your kind of story."

Moreland froze, looking at Cooper like a man who has just been jostled by a stranger. "What the hell does that mean?" he said.

"I thought you had the story of your life with this Oyler thing," Cooper said. "You haven't even asked me what Pappadakis had to say."

Moreland stared for a moment and said, "I presume she just asked you a whole bunch of questions."

"Yes. But they were revealing."

Moreland shifted, facing Cooper now. "So tell me."

Cooper smiled. "Go find Cleo. And do your work. I won't leave."

Moreland's plump face was a mask of warring impulses: protest, accede, pester Cooper for details. Finally he closed his mouth and said, "OK. I won't be long. You're a devious bastard, you know that?"

Cooper made his way to the bar, hands in the pockets of his khaki work pants. He was underdressed but he didn't much care. He hoped people would assume that if he were here he had money, and people with money can dress as they please. Cooper decided he would be an eccentric millionaire. He got a vodka and tonic at the bar, just to get into the role, and when he turned he saw Cleo making her way through the crowd toward him, the hundred-watt smile on.

She waved, a wiggle of the fingers. She was dressed in a bright yellow double-breasted jacket with padded shoulders and a matching skirt that hugged her legs and ended just above the knees, and she walked like a woman who knew what a walk could do. The lipstick and nails were muted today but the hair was still there, a shock of gold in a world that needed color. Cooper revised his estimate; if this woman was tawdry, at least she had money to work with.

"Hiiii." It was an ordinary face but a face with humor and appetite, and Cooper would have been hard pressed to find a combination better suited to attracting men. "Mel sent me over. He said you needed company."

"Hi," Cooper said. "He's afraid I'll bolt, I guess."

"Oh, he just has to do his reporter thing for a while. There was a rumor going around that the mayor might be here. It shouldn't take Mel too long. Look at him. He's cornered King already." Together they looked at Moreland, near the windows, notebook in hand, beaming as King Van Houten spoke rapidly into his ear, a hand on Moreland's arm.

"Looks to me like Van Houten's cornered him," said Cooper.

"King's bragging about the new offices. He's like a kid with a new toy and he wants everyone to know about it. They are pretty amazing, aren't they?"

"Spectacular. How do you get any work done with that view to distract you?"

Cleo made a face. "I'm stuck out there at the desk where I can't see anything. I'm like the lowest of the low, you know? Answer the phone, make coffee, stuff like that. It's the lawyers who have all the fun."

"Ain't that the truth."

"You should see King's office. It's like Star Trek or something. I'd show you, but I think there's another bunch of people in there now. It's like open house tonight. King loves to show off."

"I'll wait." Cooper's eyes moved over the crowd. "Who's the burly white-haired guy with the red face over there at the end of the snack table? I've seen him before."

"The one holding the beer? That's Chesty O'Donnell. He's Mr. Swanson's right-hand man."

"That's where I saw him. Up at Swanson's house, that night you and Mel met."

"Yeah. Chesty's always around, even at these fancy things. He drives Regis everywhere, runs errands for him, things like that."

"He doesn't look very comfortable in that suit."

"Yeah, Chesty used to be a truck driver or something. Regis calls him, Mr. Swanson I mean, calls him his interpreter. I think he means for talking to the unions and stuff."

"Chesty looks like my kind of guy."

"I'll introduce you if you want."

"That's OK. Is his boss here?"

"Yeah, over there, see?" Cleo pointed out Regis Swanson on a couch, one long leg crossed over the other, lounging as only a rich man can lounge.

"He looks comfortable."

"Regis is always comfortable."

Cooper smiled. He was, he realized, enjoying himself. "There's somebody else I know, the old bald-headed lawyer. What's his name?"

"Mr. Slazenger? Oh yes, he was at the restaurant that night, wasn't he?"

"I'm starting to feel like I'm part of a family here. Do all these people always hang out together?"

"Pretty much, I guess. They're all in the same line of work, more or less. Law and real estate."

Cooper smiled. "Real estate. Profitable business, huh?"

Cleo lowered her voice a touch, just into conspiratorial range. "You'd be surprised. From things I've picked up around the office, a lot of people got hurt by the savings and loan thing."

"Yeah, the market kind of went south, didn't it? Swanson doesn't seem to be hurting too much, though."

"He's in debt, like everyone else. Maybe I shouldn't say that."

Cooper shrugged. "It's probably common knowledge. I don't follow business that closely."

"Oh, I don't either. I just pass on the gossip."

"Hm. OK, who's the guy over there picking crumbs out of his beard? He was with Slazenger that night, but I forget his name, too."

"Milt Sellers you mean?"

"Yeah. The honcho guy with the city, you said."

Cleo laughed. "Except I was wrong, I found out. He works for somebody on the county board. I think he's King's contact over there or something. I don't know. I can't keep track of all the connections around here sometimes."

"Pretty Byzantine, huh?"

Cleo looked blank for a moment and said, "I guess so. Hey, it looks like the tour group is through with King's office. Now might be a good time to go see it."

"I'm right behind you."

Cleo led Cooper past the bar and into one of the passageways off the anteroom. The hall was painted white and hung with large and luminous watercolors. They went down to a door on the left which was standing open, and Cleo turned on her heel and waved him in with a smile, like a model at a trade display.

The office was large and decorated in subdued marine hues, blues, greens, and grays. Here the ceiling was lower but the wall was still glass; the office occupied the curved southeast corner of the building and offered a view of the lake, the Loop, and the distant south. The sun had set and the city was glittering in the deepening winter evening. A large curving desk of some jet-black material dominated the room, facing the view; set into its top was an array of buttons and phone receivers. Lining one of the solid walls were bookshelves with the standard uniform rank of law books; in the other a sliding door had been opened to reveal a bank of electronic equipment: a TV, a computer with keyboard, indeterminate displays of lights and switches. Next to this was a miniature bar with bottles glowing in the subdued lighting. Another panel was closed, and Cooper noted what looked like a sturdy lock. In the curve of the window was a sectional sofa and two armchairs around a long low irregularly shaped table that looked as if it had been carved out of a large piece of driftwood. Three men with drinks in hand sat around the table, laughing.

"See what I mean?" said Cleo, indicating the desk.

Cooper nodded. "Beam us aboard, Scotty."

Cleo laughed. The men were looking at her. "Good evening, gentlemen."

"Well," said a thick middle-aged man in a red tie. "Sunshine. Come over and join us."

Cleo looked almost demure, hands clasped at her waist. "Thanks, but I'm afraid I can't right now. Maybe later, OK?"

The man looked at Cooper, head to toe, and his thoughts were patent. "Don't forget," he said.

"I won't." Cleo turned to Cooper, cutting the men out cold, and said, "King really splurged on this room. He said he's always wanted an office to suit his name."

"Looks like he's got it." Cooper took a drink and said, "He's a zoning lawyer, is that right?"

"The best. They say that if anyone ever wants to put a McDonald's in the Vatican, King can get it zoned."

"Clout, huh?"

"Well, he does know the mayor. He knew the old Mayor Daley, too. He's always known everybody who counts. And he knows the law. That's what they say, anyway. I don't know."

There were footsteps behind them and then Cleo turned, looked a little startled, and said, "Here he is."

"Here's who?" King Van Houten stood in the doorway, smiling. He had a drink in his hand, a toupee on his head, and two eyes that never seemed to be looking at the same thing. He was about five-six, light as a bird, and ugly. King Van Houten looked like an unnaturally aged child. He wore a silk double-breasted suit, rings on his fingers, and a gold tie pin. Just behind him in the hallway were Regis Swanson and Milt Sellers.

"Cleo my dear, have you been selling all my secrets?" said Van Houten.

She gave him her best smile. "I've just been showing this gentleman your pride and joy."

"And this is?" Van Houten held his hand out to Cooper, who gave the hand a firm shake and said his name. Van Houten smiled just coyly enough to put Cooper in mind of Moreland's remark about his Marlboro Man looks. "Welcome." He moved aside to admit Swanson and Sellers to the circle. "Do you know my illustrious client, Regis Swanson? Goodness, client and now landlord."

"We've met," said Swanson, extending his hand. He looked faintly puzzled, as if he couldn't remember where.

"Briefly," said Cooper.

"And this is Milton Sellers, who is not my client but is illustrious in his own way."

Sellers merely nodded and firmed his lips in a perfunctory smile, seeming preoccupied with a careful inspection of the men on the couch. He had hair like a Brillo pad and the iron-gray beard, now crumb-free; his black eyebrows met above his eyes.

"You're with Moreland, aren't you?" said Swanson to Cooper.

"Oh, are you a writer, too?" said Van Houten.

Cooper opened his mouth and nothing came out. He grinned, shifted gears, and said, "Actually I'm doing research." As lies went, he figured, it was fairly innocuous.

"Oh, how interesting. On me?" said Van Houten.

"On the profession of journalism," said Cooper, hoping to change the subject. He looked guiltily for Cleo but she had effaced herself. Van Houten and Swanson were staring at him, the former with a broad smile and the latter with a distant, skeptical one. "Hoping to get a sizable project out of it," Cooper finished lamely.

"A book, really? How fascinating."

Cooper shrugged vaguely, looking for an exit.

Van Houten provided one. "Well, I'm very proud of my little eyrie. Did you see my control panel here? From this desk I can push buttons that will connect me with mayors or get me some Chinese food sent up for lunch."

"Which one launches the missiles?" said Cooper.

"That one," said Van Houten, pointing. "And this one activates the trapdoor. For occasions when I tire of people like those coarse types on the couch."

General laughter greeted this remark, and Van Houten, looking like a child on Christmas morning, sat at the desk and started pressing buttons. Cooper smiled politely at the joke and started to edge away. He moved around Swanson to reach the door; just beyond him he ran into Milt Sellers, who had apparently finished with the occupants of the couch and was now looking at Cooper with interest. Cooper nodded and waited for him to move out of the doorway.

"I'll bet you have to be a good listener in your trade," Sellers said quietly.

"It helps," said Cooper, caught off guard.

Sellers's eyes were a pale blue under the black brows. "I'm sure it does."

There was a gentle buzz from somewhere on the desk and Van Houten flapped his arms. "Oh my God, what have I done?"

"Nothing," said Swanson. "Your phone's ringing."

Van Houten picked up one of the receivers, said hello, punched a button, said hello again, and laughed. "Yes. Oh hello, Frank." He sat back in his chair, enjoying himself. His eyes widened and he said, "Thank you, Frank. Good of you to call. They're expecting you downstairs. Fifteen minutes. We'll be ready. Bye-bye." Van Houten hung up and clapped his hands once. "We are about to be honored by a visit from His Honor the mayor," he announced. "Or should I say . . . 'Da Mare'!"

"Richie's coming?" said one of the men on the couch.

"He certainly is. I insisted. That's all right, Milton, we'll let you stay."

At Cooper's elbow Sellers smiled. "Hey, I'm on good terms with the mayor," he said. "Even Mackey's on good terms with the mayor."

"Well, we'll see how long that lasts, won't we, Regis?"

The three men looked at Cooper and he was suddenly aware that he was an outsider. Sellers gave him a cold smile. Cooper said, "I'll go warn Moreland to get his pencil sharpened."

In the anteroom the party was at a pleasant hum. Cooper caught sight of Cleo's yellow suit in the crowd; next to her was Moreland, who had acquired something to drink and put away his notebook. He was talking rapidly, leaning slightly toward her. Cooper went to the bar and replenished his drink. He stood at the end of the table and watched people; he noted the faces he had put a name to, watched lips move, hands fly. Slazenger was still seated; Chesty O'Donnell had disappeared.

Suddenly Moreland was at his elbow. "OK, let's talk." Moreland steered him toward the windows, now dark and reflecting the party dimly. Standing a foot from the glass, Cooper could make out lights far below. "What did she say?" Moreland's expression was intense now.

"Who?"

"Aw, quit it, MacLeish. You made your point."

Cooper smiled. "They're looking for a tape," he said. "One of the tapes is missing."

Moreland peered at him. "How do you know?" he said, his voice low and taut.

"Pappadakis practically admitted it. She was ready to offer me money for it. And I don't think she believed me when I said I didn't take it."

"But she never actually said it was a tape they were looking for?"

"No. But what else would it be? That's the story. That's what brought her into it. It's got to be a tape."

Moreland moved back a step. "That son of a bitch. That backstabbing, double-crossing bastard."

"Who?"

"That big ape of a cop down in Oak Lawn, the dick that showed up when we found Oyler." He leaned in again and lowered his voice. "I finally got to talk to the guy this afternoon. And he plays like he's the best friend the press ever had. He even apologizes for holding us the other night. And then he tells me all about the tapes."

"Yeah?"

"Yeah. He says they're very interesting if you like listening to poor recordings of FM radio."

"Huh?"

"That's all they are. All but two of them. The tapes were there, but Oyler had apparently been systematically erasing them by recording over them. The cop says you can hear the radio, the TV sometimes, you can hear somebody moving around, coughing, stuff like that. From what you can hear of the radio, this was all happening over the last week or so."

"I'll be damned."

"He'd gotten to all but two."

"And what's on those two?"

"Well, that's where he dried up on me. He said he listened to them once but the sound was bad and all he could make out was talk about money."

Cooper's eyebrows rose. "My, that's vague."

"Yes, he was very vague on that point."

"Does he know who made them?"

Moreland shook his head, mouth full of vodka. "He said no, but I wouldn't take it as gospel."

"Does he still have them?"

"Nope. He turned them over to somebody from Eleventh and State. He said it's a Chicago case anyway. This morning I thought he wanted to keep them to himself, but now I think he couldn't wait to get rid of them. He doesn't need the complications in that nice quiet little town of his. He sure as hell didn't say anything about any of them being missing, the bastard. I wonder what Pappadakis had to do to get that out of him."

"Hang on a second."

"What?"

"How would he know one was missing?"

"Well, he did tell me the cassettes were numbered. There could have been gaps in the numbers."

"Uh-huh." Cooper tapped a finger on the rim of his glass. "The numbers have to mean there's a list."

"You're thinking, MacLeish. Yeah, a catalogue. I asked him about it and he said they found a piece of paper with the tapes, but they didn't know what it meant. And then he shut up and hustled me out. That's all I got from him and I was glad to get it. The son of a bitch. Now I have to watch the Channel Five news to find out what's going on with my own story. If she's got anything, they'll run it at six. They gotta have a TV here somewhere."

"Well, hell. Sounds like you're doing OK, Mel."

"OK? My top secret story has been busted wide open and hijacked. Oyler's a household word and the Pappadakis female has the inside track to whatever they find on those tapes. I'm bringing up the tail end of the parade with my little shovel again."

"She can listen to all the tapes she wants, and she still won't have that missing one. Your story may not be top secret any more, but it sure as hell ain't written yet."

"True." Moreland knocked back another mouthful. "It ain't," said Moreland. "And I've got another card she doesn't have, too. If I can just get a goddamn alderman to return my phone calls."

"What's that all about?"

Moreland cast a glance sideways. "I don't want to discuss it here, but Vince Gallo came through for me. I'll tell you about it later."

Cooper watched his friend cast a steely eyed look out over the room and take another drink. He said, "You're having fun, aren't you, Mel?"

Moreland looked at him, surprised. "I guess I am, yeah."

"Well here's to you." They clinked glasses.

"You know something, MacLeish?" said Moreland, the glass halfway to his mouth.

"What?"

"You're good for this old boy's morale."

"Just one of the many services we provide," said Cooper.

∎ ∎ ∎

The job sucked, Wilfredo had decided. It sucked bad, big time. Wilfredo had had some supremely fucked-up jobs in his time, but this one was close to the worst. He gave the space heater another kick. The coils were glowing red but the motherfucker was putting out about as much heat as a light bulb, maybe a forty-watt bulb.

Headlights played across the cracked and distorting pane of plastic that served as a window in the little shack. A car eased into the lot and Wilfredo cursed out loud and shivered as he slid off the stool. He kicked the door open and stepped out into the chill, pulling the little pad of parking slips from the pocket of his jacket. The car was a Cadillac, a long boxy battleship of a car. Wilfredo waved it to a halt and the driver's side window slid down, a hand emerging to take the ticket Wilfredo tore off the pad. "Get it stamped inside," said Wilfredo between chattering teeth, ignoring the murmured greeting from the driver. "Park it over there by the fence." As the Caddy pulled away, Wilfredo hurried back inside the shack.

I'm fuckin' crazy to live in a place like this, Wilfredo thought, jerking the ill-fitting door shut, trying to seal out the darting wind. Any place that's too cold for the fuckin' birds is too cold for me. He turned to the miniature TV set on the shelf; there was another commercial on. Every time he turned his head they ran another fuckin' commercial. Fuckin' Channel Nine for you—they put on a decent movie and then they cut the fucker every three minutes for ten minutes of commercials.

Maybe it was time to take Amalia and the rug rats and go south, someplace warm. Not the island; Davey had come back from San Juan the year before saying don't even think about it; unless you got connections down there you'll be worse off than here. You won't even feel at home, Davey had said, not after spending your whole life here. Get used to it, *chamaco,* this is your home.

Miami maybe, thought Wilfredo as the party from the Cadillac walked past the shack, heading inside to get warm and put down a fifty-dollar meal. He could see their dark shapes through the window and hear them laughing, on top of the fuckin' world.

Miami was a fuckin' zoo, but it was warm and there was shit to do if you hustled a little. Wilfredo wondered if there was a place you could live in Miami where your kids could grow up safe; he wanted to get his boy Rafael out of Humboldt Park before the gangs got their hooks in him. What it had cost Wilfredo to get out and stay out of the Kings he was not going to put his boy through.

The cracked plastic lit up again as another car swung off the street. Wilfredo pushed the zipper of his jacket up to his chin, already feeling the fingers of chill air that would go for his throat the second he stepped out the door. Fuck me, he thought. I ain't made for this weather.

This one was a dark blue Mercedes, and it almost cruised on past him. Wilfredo yelled whoa and the guy braked and the window came down. "What the hell, I gotta pay to park?" said the driver, a white guy with a fat round face.

"You gotta have a ticket," said Wilfredo, handing him one. "Get it stamped inside. Put 'er over there by the Caddy."

"You're gonna watch it for me while I'm in there then, right?" the guy said. "Anything happens to this car, I'm coming to talk to you."

"I'll be here," said Wilfredo over his shoulder.

Chuck Norris was back on the screen of the little TV; Wilfredo didn't bother to turn up the sound because all that was happening was dialogue, and the last thing you watched a Chuck Norris movie for was the dialogue. Wilfredo kicked the space heater again and peered out through the plastic; he couldn't actually see a whole lot, but he could hear if anybody was fucking with a car; there wasn't really any need to go out there to keep an eye on things. Nobody was going to try to steal a car from a well-lighted lot on Harlem Avenue anyway. On the TV things had heated up; Chuck Norris sent an Oriental guy in a black suit flying over a balcony rail with a roundhouse kick. Wilfredo turned up the volume so he could hear the sound effects, punches that sounded like the crack of a whip. He shook his head watching it, seeing guys flying right and left with those dubbed-in cracks and thuds.

He heard the guy from the Mercedes come past the booth on his way to the door and turned the sound down a little guiltily. The guy was walking funny; it sounded like he had a limp, a little shuffle and then the other foot coming down solid. The fuckin' guy sounded like the mummy or something, walking like that. Shuffle, thump all the way past him toward the restaurant entrance. After the sound was gone, Wilfredo turned his head to the window; he had been sure there were two people in the Mercedes, but the limp was the only set of footsteps he'd heard go past. He looked out the window for a couple of seconds but didn't see anything moving and he shrugged and turned back to the TV in time to see Chuck Norris beating some Chink's head like a drum. Fuck, thought Wilfredo, reaching for the volume. This guy's never been in a real fight in his life.

Half an hour and a dozen cars later, there was a knock on the door of the shack. Wilfredo pushed it open and scowled out into the cold. A middle-aged lady in a fur coat was standing there, freezing her ass off. "Yeah?" said Wilfredo, fearing suddenly he'd fucked up somehow, let somebody's car get ripped off while he was in here watching this stupid movie.

"Excuse me," said the lady. "I think somebody's ill in one of those cars over there."

"Huh?" said Wilfredo. "Ill?"

"Yes. My daughter and I noticed him as we were getting into our car. He's just sitting there, not moving."

"He's probably waiting for somebody."

"I don't think so. His head's kind of over on one side, as if he were asleep. I just thought it didn't look right. Perhaps you should take a look."

Fuck me, thought Wilfredo. Some drunk passes out in his car, and she wants me to do something about it. "OK," he said. "I'll take care of it. Where's the car?"

"Over there by the fence. My daughter says it's a Mercedes."

"All right." Wilfredo was tugging at his zipper again, cursing the cold and cursing his fate. The lady got in her car and drove off. Wilfredo crossed the parking lot and went down the row of cars by the fence until he found the dark Mercedes. He stepped to the driver's side and looked in and there the motherfucker was, leaning over to one side. It looked like the round-faced man, and Wilfredo said "Shit" out loud, because the lady was right, it didn't look good.

He tried the door but it was locked. He stood shivering for a moment and then went around to the other side of the car and tried the passenger door. The door opened and Wilfredo leaned in as the overhead light came on. He took a good look, the odor of gunfire still hanging in the air, and then backed out in a hurry, banging his head on the roof of the car, because even Wilfredo had a little trouble taking the sight of a man bleeding from a hole punched in the side of his head.

9

THE POLICE SPOKESWOMAN WAS a small person with tight red curls and a brisk manner. "The superintendent is waiting for me," she said.

"Two minutes," said Moreland. The spokeswoman checked her watch. Moreland sat on the chair in front of her broad and cluttered desk and said, "How many tapes are there?"

"I went through this with your police reporter already."

"I know. And I missed connections with him just now. So as long as I'm here, why don't I just quickly get it from the source. How many tapes are there?"

The spokeswoman gave in with a grim look. "Twenty-seven. All but two of them containing nothing but radio or TV or ambient noise."

"Have the people on the two intact tapes been identified?"

"No."

"Not even vaguely? Male, female, white, black?"

With a practiced blankness she said, "I understand no identification was possible."

"OK. Can you tell me what the subject of the recorded conversations was?"

"One of the conversations appears to be a discussion of some sort of illegal payment. The other is mostly small talk with no apparent direction. The sound quality is poor and sometimes it's hard to decipher."

Moreland grunted. "I understand the tapes were numbered." The woman gave a single wary nod. "And I was led to believe there was a list, a catalogue of some sort."

"There is. It appears to be in some kind of code. It consists of nicknames, initials, that kind of thing."

"And they can't identify the folks on the surviving tapes, even with the list as a clue?"

"No."

"Are the tapes numbered consecutively?"

"Yes."

"None missing?"

The spokeswoman looked Moreland up and down as if evaluating his clothes. "One tape is missing from the sequence, yes."

"There was no indication in Oyler's apartment of what might have happened to the missing tape? The garbage was searched and so on?"

"I believe the Oak Lawn police know what they're doing."

"I'm sure they do. Are they still working on the case? Or is it all in your hands now?"

"It's a Chicago case. At this point all the files have been turned over to us."

"I see. Is Detective Brown still in charge?"

"You'd have to ask the Chief of Detectives. I know he has a number of people working on it. Now if you'll excuse me, I really am expected upstairs." The small woman pushed away from her desk.

"One more question. A quick one."

"One more."

"What was the coded entry for the missing tape?"

"I have no idea. I haven't seen the list."

Moreland nodded, lips clamped tight. "OK, thanks," he said, rising. "I appreciate your patience."

"Patience is my middle name," said the woman, gathering papers from the desk.

■ ■ ■

Detective M. Garvey Brown was not by nature a patient man, and chronic fatigue did nothing to improve his disposition. Celebrity, however, even minor celebrity, holds a certain sway, and the familiar face across the desk from him commanded enough deference to cause him to give polite and considered responses.

"So you've got all the car thieves," said Christine Pappadakis.

"We think so," said Brown. He sat with one leg crossed over the other, rotating gently back and forth on his swivel chair.

"And none of them killed Vance Oyler?"

"We're not ready to say that. A couple of them have alibis we're still working on. But we're not ready to make an arrest, either."

"How big was the ring?"

"Small. Besides the two guys who paid off Fisher there were two others who did the boosting and one body man who did the chopping. We think that's it."

"Can I have their names?"

Brown fished a paper out of the litter on the desktop and read from it. "Lawrence Gill and Steven Micsza, that's M-I-C-S-Z-A, they swiped the cars, and an old guy named Peter Poteet, who's been doing this kind of thing for thirty years, did the mechanical end of things inside the garage."

"Are they all in custody?"

"They're out on bail. Walking around exercising their constitutional rights."

"Are any of these men linked to organized crime?"

"You need a certain amount of organization to run an operation like that, yes."

"That's not what I mean. That's not what organized crime commonly means." The newswoman softened the challenge with a smile.

Brown shrugged. "Give me a definition and I'll try and tell you if this fits it."

"Let me put it this way. Does this indicate any significant criminal presence in Streets and San linked to outside criminal organizations?"

"No." Brown gave her the look, the blank sleepy look he had mastered long ago.

After a moment she looked down at her notes and said, "What about the other killing? Have you gotten anywhere with the man you identified on tape number three?"

"We sent somebody to talk with him down in Marion. But he claims he doesn't remember ever having a conversation like the one on the tape. In any event we can't really figure out what they're talking about, except that somebody took a bribe. That's the trouble with the tapes, the two that are left, anyway. They're useless without knowing the context. They might be proof of something if we had something to prove, but we don't."

The woman nodded. "Do you think there's a connection between the two murders?"

"Of course there's a connection," said Brown. "We just don't know what it is yet."

"But they seem to be two different cases." The lady was intent, frowning across the littered desktop at him, black eyes glittering.

"Except that the victims were brothers and the same people just happened to find them both times."

"So you're still looking at my colleague in the print media and his friend?"

"I didn't say that. I don't think they did anything more than find them. But the fact that they did means there's a connection. The reporter was following a story, that's all. And the story got the Oyler brothers killed. There's got to be one story."

"So what's the connection between a scandal in Streets and San and a bunch of conversations recorded by an old Teamster boss?"

"I don't know," said Brown. "That's what's keeping me awake at night lately."

The TV woman gave a thin smile. "When you find out, will you sit down with me first, talk to me in front of a camera?"

Detective M. Garvey Brown uncrossed his legs and squared himself at the desk. "One thing you should learn about the way I work," he said. "I don't ever make promises. To anybody."

● ● ●

Moreland found Charlie Duncan in the lugubrious brown-painted stairwell between the second and third floors. The police reporter was coming down from the third floor in the company of a white-shirted police lieutenant. The two men were laughing and Moreland felt a deep pang of envy at Charlie Duncan's intimacy with the police. Charlie Duncan had been on the police beat for a couple of decades and had unparalleled, legendary access to police sources. Moreland felt like a schoolboy importuning the headmaster as he waited on the landing to accost the two men.

"Charlie, can I talk to you a second?"

"Hey, Mel. What's cooking?" Charlie Duncan was a thin, slightly stooped man who looked as if he had been dried out in the sun and then rehydrated. His skin hung loosely and his hair was thin on the ground and pure white. He stepped onto the landing and raised his eyebrows at Moreland.

Moreland cast a glance at the lieutenant, who gave him one of those cold cop looks that Moreland hated and went on down the stairs. "I need your expertise," said Moreland.

"Such as it is."

"Beats mine, for sure," said Moreland, watching as the cop pushed through the door to the second floor. "What I really need is your connections," he said.

"Oh?" said Duncan.

"I need a look at the list that came with the Oyler tapes."

Duncan was leaning toward the stairs. He said, "Why don't you ask the Chief of Detectives?"

"I can't even get in to talk to the Chief of Detectives. And I can't wait around here all day. I thought if you could work it in you could maybe get me a copy."

"That would be tough. I don't know."

"Or a look. What I really need is to know who or what was on the missing tape."

Duncan gave a whiff of laughter. "That's the sixty-four dollar question. But from what I hear the list won't help you."

"I know, it's in code. I'd still like to see it."

Duncan had started down the stairs, Moreland at his elbow, a step behind. "I'll see what I can do," said Duncan.

"You'll make me a very happy boy, Charlie."

Duncan paused at the bottom of the steps. "You don't get along real well with coppers, do you, Mel?"

Moreland spread his hands in appeal. "Me? I love cops. As long as I don't have to talk to them."

* * *

If the man would only look you in the eyes, thought Moreland, he might have a few friends. Jay Macy stood in front of Moreland's desk, resplendent in red suspenders, clutching a sheaf of papers, the eyes darting like panicked flies about the desktop, alighting everywhere but Moreland's face. "You see the news last night?" Macy said.

"I saw it. She hasn't got a thing I hadn't already guessed."

Macy focused on him, just for a second. "You knew all that about Oyler's father?"

"Like I said, I guessed. Who else could have made the tapes? Who else would John have been covering up for?"

Macy swayed on his bowed legs, as if thinking about leaving, then settled again, leaning a little closer. "Did you also guess that everybody they can identify on those tapes is dead or in jail?"

"No. That I didn't know. But it doesn't surprise me. They've pretty well cleaned house over there at the Teamsters since Gerald Oyler's day."

"Then if the tapes are pretty much worthless to anybody, who killed Oyler? And why?"

Moreland shrugged. "They're still working on the damaged tapes. They may find something worth killing for yet."

"Unless somebody took it."

"Yeah. There's always that."

"It wouldn't have been you, would it?"

Moreland looked up to meet Macy's eyes, but they were away again. "Not you, too. The cops already put me through all this."

"Well, did you take any tapes? You gotta tell me if you did."

"I never went in the fucking building, Jay. And neither did my partner. If I had a tape, you can bet your ass I'd be waving a transcript in your face. I'd have had a story for you the morning after the killing. Right? Even the cops know I didn't take anything by now."

"Ok, just trying to keep on top of things. How are you following up on it?"

"I'm ingratiating myself with every policeman from here to Joliet. I'm working my contacts over at the Teamsters. I'll have a story for you, Jay, things Christine Pappadakis never dreamed of."

"All right, you don't need to sound so hostile. Listen, the sheriff's giving a press conference at ten about the shenanigans down at the jail and you're up."

Moreland wanted to thrash, moan, throw things. "Jay, you said I had two days."

"Look, we got caught short. It'll be quick. The other thing will keep for an hour or so."

"Come on, Jay. Send Becker or somebody. Becker's the one who's been following all that."

"Becker's out on the Northwest Side for that hit on the alderman's guy."

Moreland froze. "What hit? What guy?"

"The hit in the parking lot. Guy named Spivak, worked for Neumann the alderman. Found him dead in the parking lot of one of those Italian places on Harlem last night."

"You're shitting me."

This time Macy focused on him, for a full two seconds. "What's the matter? You know the guy?"

Moreland blinked at him, feeling blood draining from his face, starting to calculate. "Yeah. Yeah, I knew the guy. Why do you say it's a hit? What happened?"

Macy flapped the papers at him in exasperation. "I don't know, Mel. He got killed. Becker's out there following up on it. Look, I'm sorry. But I gotta have somebody down there in twenty minutes. Now get moving."

"I'm going, I'm going." Moreland was rising, reaching for his jacket. "When Becker gets back tell him I want to see him, would you?"

"Sure." Macy wisely squeezed against a desk as Moreland went by, flailing his way into the jacket. "Can I talk to you a little more later about this Oyler story?"

Over his shoulder Moreland said, "If you're so worried about it, talk to the lady at Channel Five."

■ ■ ■

"Look at that asshole," Cooper said to Boyle across the table.

Boyle twisted to look out the plate glass window across Sheridan Road. "Which one?" he said.

"The guy in the red Buick. Parked at the corner there."

"Yeah, why is he an asshole?"

Cooper shook his head in wonder. "He just pulled a U-turn in the middle of Sheridan Road, just so he could move from a spot up the block there to where he has a better view of the window here."

Boyle turned back and peered across the table at Cooper. "Paranoid today, are we?"

"Well, this is the second time today I've seen the same guy pull a dumbass stunt with the car just to stay near me. I'm not shitting you."

Boyle was large and pony-tailed and surly and had seen it all.

He twisted to look again, turned back and shrugged. "Maybe it's me he's following," he said. "I was in Dallas that day, you know."

"I'm serious. I really think the guy's following me. I saw him outside the Laundromat two hours ago. Doing just like he's doing now, sitting there looking in my direction."

Boyle peered at him, the afternoon sun coming in through the window highlighting the gold in his walrus moustache. "Why you?"

Cooper drained his coffee cup. "You got me. But I'm starting to get a little curious."

"It's your move. Decide what to do with that bishop before you go brace him."

"The bishop? It's the knight that's in trouble."

Boyle sighed. "You can't play chess and watch the street at the same time. Look at that queen side there and tell me what you see."

Cooper looked. After a few seconds he said, "All right. So I go down a piece either way. Look, I'll concede this one. Set it up again while I go talk to this guy."

Boyle gave him a critical look. "Hold on. What'll you do if he just takes off?"

"I don't know. Try to get the license number, I guess."

"Sit down." Boyle pushed away from the table, his chair creaking beneath his weight. "Don't do anything until he gets out of the car." Boyle reached for his fatigue jacket, smiling.

Cooper watched from inside the door of the café while Boyle waited for a green light and then ambled across the road, newspaper under his arm. He made his way to the corner where the red Buick Sky Hawk was parked and, looking up the street as if watching for a bus, halted by the car and leaned his two hundred and fifty pounds against the right front fender, unfurling the paper. The car sagged a little under his weight.

Cooper grinned as he saw the driver look for second or two, incredulous. Then the horn sounded. Boyle turned his head slowly, looked at the driver for three seconds, and turned back to the paper. Cooper pushed open the door of the café, figuring it wouldn't be long.

The driver came out of the car while Cooper was waiting for a break in the traffic, and by the time Cooper was in earshot things were getting heated. "It's no fatter'n the rest of me," Boyle was saying. "And I'll put it where I god damn please."

"If you don't get it off my car I'm gonna beat it for you." The driver was a tightly wound young man in a black leather jacket, with closely trimmed black hair and a thin face dominated by wide blue eyes. He was getting seriously into Boyle's face. Cooper had crossed so as to come up behind the car; Boyle was doing his immovable object act, holding the man's attention with his sheer bulk, not looking at Cooper. "I think you'd do better to show some manners," Boyle was saying.

Cooper had the door open and was going for the ignition keys before the man heard him and spun with a shout. Boyle grabbed a handful of black leather to keep him from going anywhere and Cooper was out of the car with the keys in hand by the time the man had thrashed himself out of Boyle's grip.

"You wanna live, you better gimme those fuckin' keys," the man said. The eyes were bright and the index finger shook.

"You'll get 'em back when you tell me who you are and why you're watching me," Cooper said.

"I'll get 'em back now, or you'll wind up on the ground, Jack."

Cooper watched his hands, waiting for a move inside the jacket. "Let's scrape this piece of shit off our shoes," he said to Boyle, and slipped the keys into his jacket pocket, turning away.

The man's lunge was cut short by Boyle's hand on his collar. He twisted and flailed, but Boyle's arms were longer than his. Cooper had stepped onto the sidewalk by now, laughing. Boyle put the man on the pavement, arms and legs flying, and moved to join him. A car horn wailed by at forty miles per hour, the car swerving in alarm.

When the man made it to the sidewalk like a shipwrecked sailor climbing out of the sea, he saw he was whipped. He looked from Cooper to Boyle and back again, panting a little. "I want my keys," he said, in a low flat tone.

"Why are you watching me?" Cooper said.

"I'm not. You're out of your fucking mind."

"You're no damn good at it, you know. I spotted you down on Devon Avenue two hours ago."

It was a blow to the chin, but the man regained his footing. "You're dreaming."

"And you're losing. Tell me who you're working for and you can have your keys back."

"I'm not working for anybody."

"Let's go," said Cooper to Boyle, turning away.

"My keys, Jack."

"Come and get 'em," Cooper said over his shoulder.

"All right." From the man's tone of voice Cooper knew he'd won. "You want to see a license?"

Cooper halted. "That would be a start."

The man tore a wallet from his hip pocket and held it at eye level, advancing. Judging from his face he was having trouble keeping the lid on; panic was running a close second to anger. Cooper took the wallet and looked at the card in the plastic window. *Eagle Investigations* it said, over an official-looking seal. The name *Randy G. Liffick* was typed in at the bottom.

"This isn't even an official license," Boyle said at Cooper's shoulder. "This came out of a bubble gum machine."

The man drew breath over sharp white teeth. "I do surveillance for Eagle. My license is pending."

"Pending," said Boyle with a snort. "Like your lower lip right now." The man rocked back on his heels, a second away from taking a swing.

"Who hired your firm?" Cooper said, handing back the wallet.

"I don't know. They give me an assignment, they don't tell me the client's business." He was having trouble getting the words out of a tight throat.

Cooper nodded and pulled the keys from his pocket. "Here you go. I'm going to save you some work. I'm going to play another game of chess with my partner here, and then I'm going to go have lunch in the Korean place down on Morse Avenue there, near the El. After that I'll probably go home. I won't call your boss and tell him how bad you are as long as you don't bother me."

"Fuck you guys," Randy G. Liffick said, and spun on his heel. He stalked back to the car, tore open the door, and gunned the engine. Cooper and Boyle watched as he pulled deftly into the path of a bus, drawing a squeal of brakes and a blast on the horn, and then sped away south. Boyle waved.

"That boy's going to go far," Cooper said.

"That boy's gonna be lucky to live till nightfall," said Boyle. They walked back toward the café. "Well, you were right."

"I told you."

"Yeah. Any idea why?"

Cooper shrugged. "I'm having that kind of month, I guess."

■ ■ ■

Moreland found a message waiting for him: *Call Duncan,* with a phone number. He dialed the number.

"Duncan," a voice said in his ear.

"Charlie, Mel here. What you got?"

"I got what you asked for, that's what. And a thorny job it was, too."

"You got the list."

"No, but I got a look at it. And you got any idea how many people I had to sweet-talk down here, how many promises I had to make just to get that?"

"It'll be worth it, I swear on my sainted mother's grave."

"They're holding that piece of paper damn close to the vest."

"But they let you sneak a peek."

"A little one, yeah. No copies. And it better not hit the paper tomorrow, you hear me?"

"I hear you. What the hell did you see?"

"Elizabeth Leland."

"What?"

"Elizabeth Leland. That's who's on the missing tape."

"Who the hell is Elizabeth Leland?"

"Beats me all to hell. There's a bunch of Lelands in the phone book, but none of 'em's Elizabeth."

"Wait a minute. I thought all the names on the list were in code."

"Except this one and one other. George Raft."

"George Raft?"

"Yeah, like the actor. All the others were nicknames, place names, stuff like that. Grumpy, Butterfingers. Inchon."

"Inchon?"

"Yeah, like the Korean War battle. Another one was Lace Curtains. Weird things like that."

"And Elizabeth Leland."

"Yeah."

"L-E-L-A-N-D?"

"That's it."

"And they can't break this code by looking at the people they managed to identify on the two good tapes?"

"Well, Clarinet they decided was old Frankie Piccolo. Get it? But there doesn't seem to be any pattern to it. I think he was just free-associating, putting down the first thing that came into his head that suggested the real name. Or else some of them are nicknames that only a few people know. That's what the dicks are working on now."

"Elizabeth Leland. I'll be damned."

"Kick it around a bit. Something will come to you. I got other things to do."

"Charlie, thanks. I owe you."

"I'll get my pound of flesh, don't you worry."

"Flesh I got lots of. Call me."

▪ ▪ ▪

Ralph Becker started when Moreland grabbed his arm at the door to the city room. "Hey. What's up, Mel?"

"I gotta talk to you."

"Talk fast. I got a story to write." Becker was making for his desk.

"Tell me about Spivak."

"You know the guy?"

"Kind of. What happened to him?"

Becker slid behind the desk, shucking off his jacket. "Somebody shot him."

"Shot him. Not stabbed?"

Becker paused to look at him through thick lenses. "Shot, like I told you. Why?"

Moreland shook his head impatiently. "Nothing. I heard at first he was stabbed. They have any idea who did it?"

"Not yet. He was shot with a .38, that's all they know. Right through the head. His wallet was still there so they don't think it's a robbery."

"No witnesses?"

"Nobody. The parking attendant found him, sitting in the car dead. Nobody heard a shot. The attendant was watching TV in a booth and Spivak was shot inside a closed car at the other end of the lot. They think it happened about ten last night and the attendant thinks there were two guys in the car when it drove in."

"No description?"

"The attendant said he thinks the second guy might have had a limp."

"A limp."

"Yeah. What, was this Spivak a friend of yours?"

"Not really. Did you talk to Neumann?"

"Of course I talked to him. He says it's a senseless crime and if the mayor would just put enough cops on the street this kind of thing wouldn't happen and the usual horseshit."

"Where'd you talk to Neumann? Over at City Hall?"

Becker looked up from the keyboard. "Yeah, but he was on his way out. What the hell's it to you?"

Moreland was staring out the window, glaring at the blind façades across the river. "Nothing. I just may want to talk to him myself, that's all. I knew the guy, like I said."

"Yeah, well, that's too bad, I'm sorry. Neumann seemed kind of upset about it, I'll tell you."

"I bet he was," said Moreland, making tracks.

■ ■ ■

Diana answered the phone and her eyebrows rose as she listened. She said, "Just a minute, please," and held the phone out for Cooper, her face inscrutable again. "It's for you. It's the TV lady."

Cooper took the phone, smiling. "Yeah."

"Mr. MacLeish. This is Christine Pappadakis. I understand you tried to contact me earlier."

"I did."

The woman was brisk. "I can meet you somewhere, or I can be up at your place in half an hour."

"I think we can handle this over the phone, to tell the truth."

"As you wish. Do you mind if I tape your call?"

"Hit the button. I just have one question for you."

There was an instant's pause. "What's that?"

"Did you hire a detective agency called Eagle to follow me around?"

The silence lasted for perhaps five seconds. Finally Christine Pappadakis said, "I'll try your line out on you, Mr. MacLeish. If I did, what makes you think I would tell you?"

"I guess you wouldn't. Just in case you did, I have to tell you, they don't use the brightest people. This guy they had on me today was like a red dress at a funeral. He kind of stood out."

"I see."

"I know your station probably has deep pockets, but even so I wouldn't want you to pay all that money just to have some guy watch me read the newspaper every day."

"It's good of you to be concerned."

"Don't mention it." Cooper was grinning at Diana, who was directing a quizzical look over the top of her paperback.

"I suppose there's only one thing to do, isn't there?" Christine Pappadakis said.

"What's that?"

"We're just going to have to get somebody better, aren't we?"

"I guess so," said Cooper.

10 MORELAND TOOK THE KENNEDY out toward O'Hare, into the Northwest Side, where the streets are clean and quiet and the only qualification for owning property, besides wangling a mortgage, is a skin tone somewhere to the lighter side of Ricardo Montalban's. Walter Neumann's 44th ward had survived the 1992 remap largely intact; it had a forest preserve, two hospitals, a business college, a vast cemetery, a few strip malls, block after block of hundred-thousand-dollar homes, and a minority population of around four percent. Walter Neumann had been reelected three times with the implicit understanding that he would do his utmost to keep things pretty much the same.

The Regular Democratic Organization for the ward had its office on Foster Avenue, in a modest storefront between a Mandarin Chinese restaurant and a real estate agency with shuttered Venetian blinds in the window. A second-floor window above the ward office bore gold lettering that spelled out *Walter J. Neumann, Attorney-at-Law.* Moreland parked at a meter fifty feet beyond the Chinese restaurant and hiked back to the ward office, shoulders hunched against the wind. *Working for You,* said red letters painted on the glass, below the big block capitals of *Organization* and above a hand-lettered sign propped in the window that said *Support Our Senior Citizen's.* Through the big plate glass window Moreland could see a radiator, a counter, and three or four wooden chairs, two of them occupied.

Moreland pushed into the office, causing a bell attached to the door to tinkle madly above his head. The office was lighted with fluorescent tubes, giving the men on the chairs an unhealthy cast of skin. One of them sat with legs stretched out and crossed, thumbs hooked in the waistband of his tan polyester slacks, a royal blue windbreaker with the emblem of a labor union Moreland had never heard of stretched over a round belly. He was past fifty and had eyebrows that were growing wildly out of control. The other man was younger, shorter, and thicker; he had muscles but was just starting to bloat as men do in the middle thirties if they don't cut back on the drinking. He had neat light brown hair and a moustache and a broad unwelcoming face.

The men just watched as Moreland shut the door and leaned on it, sealing out the wind. The way they watched him did not give Moreland the impression that his arrival brightened their day. "How you doing?" he said, nodding at each of them.

"OK except when someone opens that door," the older man said.

Moreland smiled blandly, unzipped his parka, and turned to look at the door. "Well, see, it has hinges on it. There's your problem right there."

"I guess we'll have to do something about that," said the man. His eyes were not particularly friendly as he delivered the remark.

"Shouldn't be too hard to fix. Is the alderman in?"

"That depends on who you are." The man smiled for the first time, just with the lips.

"Melvin Moreland, from the paper you got sitting on the chair there. I just missed Neumann at City Hall and they told me he was heading this way."

The man took his thumbs out of his waistband, uncrossed his legs, and sat up with a very slight grunt. "A reporter, huh?"

"For a great metropolitan newspaper. Need to see some credentials?"

The man rose to his feet with a creaking of joints. He fixed gray appraising eyes on Moreland's face for a moment. "Save 'em. What did you want to know? Maybe I can help you."

"I need to talk to Neumann about Arlo Spivak's murder."

One thick eyebrow went up a quarter-inch or so. "I don't think he's going to want to talk about that much more today."

Moreland's smile was perfunctory. "You never know. You can ask him, can't you?"

The man shrugged slightly, mostly with his eyebrows. "I'll see if he's back there." He went slowly around the end of the counter and disappeared through a curtained doorway behind it.

Moreland stood next to the radiator listening to the wind rattle the big plate glass window. The younger man sat studying a fingernail, careful not to look at Moreland. He had on brand-new white basketball shoes, crisp new blue jeans, and the standard windbreaker, in black, open and revealing a plaid flannel shirt. The windbreaker failed to hide the revolver and star at his waistband, and Moreland wondered if it was S.O.P. for Neumann to have an armed cop on the premises, or only on days when important aides were shot.

From the look on the old man's face when he returned, Moreland knew what the answer was going to be. "I'm afraid the alderman's not in right now," the man said. "I think he got tired of talking to reporters and went home."

"He's not in for anybody, or not in just for me?" said Moreland.

The man shrugged and made for the chair. "He's not in. What do you want me to tell you? He ain't in, he ain't in."

"All right." Moreland dug inside the parka and pulled out a notebook and pen. "Before you get settled again, do me a favor. Take a note back there to where the alderman ain't and put it where he could read it, if he was here. OK?" After another shrug the man watched Moreland with no particular expression while he scrawled a few words on the pad and tore off the sheet. "Here you go. I appreciate it."

The man looked at the message and then at Moreland. He shook his head and made for the door behind the counter. This time the younger man appeared to be studying Moreland instead of his fingernail. Moreland stared back at him for a second or two and then turned to look out at the trash scuttling along the street outside. A couple of minutes went by; Moreland imagined he heard muffled voices somewhere in the rear.

He turned when he heard steps behind him. A policeman had emerged from behind the curtain and was coming around the end of the counter. The cop was putting the gold-banded cap of a commander on his head and looking at Moreland. He had a long pitted face with slitted, almost Oriental eyes. The look he was giving Moreland was a look to strike terror in men's hearts, a cold predatory cop's look. He nodded at the younger man on the chair and pulled the door open. By the time Moreland thought to look for the tag on his jacket to read his name, he was gone.

In the curtained doorway the older man jerked his head toward the back and said, "Come on." Moreland skirted the counter and followed him down a short hallway partitioned off with flimsy wallboard. The man rapped on a door at the end of the hall. A voice beyond it said, "Yeah," and the man opened it, waved Moreland in, and shut it behind him.

Walter Neumann sat at a gray steel desk, in his shirtsleeves with a loosened necktie. The trademark tight white curls were slightly less spectacular in person than under the TV lights, but Neumann would always stand out in a crowd. He was a short compact man with a boyish face at odds with the white hair, and in public appearances he often gave an impression of suppressed mirth, a feature which added to his charm and electability. Now, however, it looked as if the only thing he was suppressing was a few choice swear words. He looked tired, sullen, and hostile. There was a glass on the desk in front of him. In the glass was a half-inch or so of what Moreland presumed was Early Times, judging by the bottle that stood beside it. There was a second glass, empty, on the corner of the desk.

"What the hell does this mean?" said Walter Neumann, holding Moreland's note between index and middle finger.

"It means what it says. It means did Arlo Spivak find Michael Papini before he died."

Neumann stared at Moreland for a moment longer and then let the note fall to the surface of the desk, next to his glass. He reached for the bottle and carefully poured another half-inch of bourbon into his glass while he thought. He took a drink, made the bourbon drinker's grimace as the whiskey went down his throat, and said, "I don't know you."

Moreland pulled his press card out of his inside pocket and tossed it on the desk. "You've met me," he said. "Two or three times. But I wouldn't expect you to remember every reporter you've ever talked to. Can I sit down?"

Neumann made no move to pick up the card. He glanced at it and looked back at Moreland. "Sit down," he said.

There was a chair at the corner of the desk to Neumann's left, where someone would sit if he were drinking out of the second glass. Moreland dragged the chair to a position directly opposite Neumann and sat down. He picked up the press card and put it back in his pocket. "So did he?"

Neumann looked at Moreland with a faint authoritative frown on his face. It was the look Moreland remembered seeing him wear at a press conference in 1983 when explaining why he, a Democratic heavyweight, was supporting the Republican candidate against the black man who had won the Democratic primary. "What do you know about Michael Papini?" said Neumann.

"Damn near nothing. Except that Arlo Spivak was looking for him."

"And how the hell do you know that?"

"Sources. Sources I have to protect. You can understand that, I'm sure."

Neumann acknowledged the point with a small nod and a sour look. For a moment the look went up over Moreland's shoulder and far away. When he was through thinking he came back to Moreland and said, "We're off the record here. As of right now you never walked into this office. Agreed?"

Moreland raised his hands. "We're so far off the record we'll have to hitch a ride to get back."

Neumann nodded, his mouth a tense fine line. "So how much do you have?"

Moreland opened his mouth and drew breath, then closed it again. On the second try he said, "Depends on what you're talking about."

"I'm talking about what brought you in here. What do you know?"

"About Papini?"

"About Wilson Throop."

Moreland stared at him, just stared. After a few seconds his brow wrinkled and his eyes went to the bottle on the desk. "You got an extra glass?" he said.

Neumann looked startled and then smiled. He reached for the glass on the corner of the desk and slid it across to Moreland. "I don't think the commander has any bad diseases," he said, pushing the bottle toward him.

Moreland poured himself a shot and downed it. He looked into the empty glass, making the grimace, and then set it down. "About Wilson Throop," he said.

"Wilson Throop. What do you know?" Neumann had leaned back in his chair. His look was absolutely blank.

Moreland said, "I know he's running for mayor. I know you might support him if he was running against Saddam Hussein."

Neumann smiled, coldly. "You don't know shit," he said.

"I know two people have been killed who were looking for Michael Papini. And one who found him."

"Who found him?"

"Vance Oyler," said Moreland.

Neumann peered at him, eyes narrowed, then looked at the wall behind him again. "Hm," he said after a moment.

Moreland felt his heart pounding underneath the parka. "I think we have two different pieces of the puzzle," he said.

Neumann picked up his glass. "Maybe," he said over the rim.

"Suppose we put them together. Will you give me an exclusive?"

Neumann stared at him for several seconds and then smiled a faint grim smile. "That would depend," he said.

"Oh what?"

"On how it was handled."

Moreland frowned. "I don't handle news. I report it. If you want somebody to handle things carefully you're talking to the wrong guy."

Neumann smiled. "How long have you been in the news business, pal? News gets better handling than fine china in this town. Or any other."

Moreland sat there with his heart pounding and thought about climbing into bed with the devil. After a moment he said, "Let's see what we have before we worry about handling it."

Neumann nodded, like a teacher talking to a slow pupil. "OK."

"So what are we talking about?"

Neumann took a drink, set the glass down, and let out a long slow breath. "I don't have any proof," he said.

"Of what?"

"Of anything. I'm not sure I have anything you could write up yet."

"You've got something."

Neumann nodded. "Something."

"About Wilson Throop."

"Maybe."

"Are we going to dance around much longer? My feet are getting sore."

"Why don't we start with Papini? That's what you came for. We'll see where it leads us."

"OK, did Spivak find Papini?"

"I don't know," Neumann said. "The last time I talked to Arlo was yesterday morning. He hadn't found him then, and I don't think he expected to."

"Why do you say that?"

Neumann took his time answering. "Because he thought Papini was dead," he said finally.

Moreland frowned again. "And why did he think that?"

"Because Papini stopped coming home at night to a room paid up for a month in advance."

"I see. That would indicate something a little unusual, I guess."

Neumann smiled. "That might indicate a little problem, yes."

"And Spivak hadn't found any leads?"

Neumann looked down at his glass but didn't pick it up. "He had been talking to some of Papini's friends."

"So I hear."

"That's how you came into this?"

"Yup. I understand they were a little peeved with Mr. Papini."

"So they were. But Arlo didn't think that was what got Papini killed."

"What did he think did?"

Neumann smiled his cold little smile again. "That's where I think Wilson Throop comes in."

"I'm listening."

Neumann drained his glass and refilled it with slow careful motions. He offered the bottle to Moreland, who declined. Neumann took a sip, set down the glass, and sat back in his chair. "Couple, three weeks ago, a guy walked into the office here and wouldn't budge until I got back from downtown and agreed to see him. He wouldn't tell my people here a damn thing. He just did the same thing you did—asked them to give me a note. The note said something like, 'If you want a guarantee that the good guy will win in '95, talk to me.' You get all kinds of lunatics walking into the office, but I said what the hell and brought him back here. He sat right where you're sitting and told me he could guarantee that Daley won't have any trouble in the next primary election. Which is, of course, the real election."

"Of course. And this gentleman's name?"

"You've heard of him. Vance Oyler."

Moreland nodded. "Can you remember the exact day?" he said.

"Maybe. It was a Wednesday, because I had my regular committee meeting that morning." Neumann pulled a desktop calendar toward him and flipped through the pages. The office was silent except for the whisk of the pages turning. Finally Neumann fixed on a page and said, "December twenty-second, it was."

Moreland nodded. "What did he have?"

"The son of a bitch wouldn't say."

"I've heard that term used a lot in reference to Vance Oyler."

"I can understand it. First he tells me he's got something that will guarantee the mayor's reelection. I say OK, I'm all ears, and he says I can have it for fifty thousand dollars."

"Fifty thousand?"

"Yeah. As if I had that kind of money to throw around. I threw him out of the office."

"And he never said what it was?"

Neumann picked up his glass and swirled the whiskey gently, as if trying to read his fortune in it. "He dropped a hint, just before he mentioned the fifty thousand dollars."

"And the hint involved Wilson Throop."

Neumann took a quick nip. "He said he had something that would send that smart black boy who was talking about running for mayor back to the ghetto. Those were his words."

Moreland gave a little shake of the head. "And that didn't pique your curiosity?"

"Sure it did. But I still threw him out. The price was ridiculous. And, of course, it would be unethical." The cold little smile was back.

"But you started Spivak looking into it."

"After Oyler turned up dead, yeah."

Moreland picked up his glass and finished off the whiskey. Looking into the empty glass he said, "So Oyler had something on Throop he thought you would pay big money for." He set the glass down. "Why you?"

"I guess because I haven't exactly made a secret of my opposition to Wilson Throop."

Moreland frowned. "Where does Papini come in?"

"I don't know. He may not come in anywhere. If Arlo had found him, he would have been able to ask him."

"Why was Arlo looking for him?"

"Just a hunch. An educated guess. See, after we heard about Oyler getting killed we put our heads together. That really got our attention."

"I guess it would."

"It was Arlo that came up with the connection. He knew Oyler's old man had been part of that Teamster bunch back in the old days, and he figured if the kid had something, it had to be from the Teamster angle. So he went fishing for a connection between Wilson Throop and the Teamsters."

"And what did he catch?"

"Nothing real solid. Just some paths crossing, you know. First of all, since Throop's decided he wants to be mayor he's been fluttering eyelashes at just about anybody he thinks might swing to him, including every labor union in town. Word has it he's got some buddies in that new crowd over on South Ashland, and he's been just as friendly as can be with that bunch. That made Arlo think, but he never put his finger on anything. So he started looking into Throop's career and turned up a thing or two way back when." Neumann paused, impassive eyes on Moreland's face, head slightly tilted. "You know how Wilson Throop started out in this town?"

"No."

"He was an Assistant State's Attorney back in the late seventies. A pretty good one, they say."

"He's been good at everything he's done. They say."

"Yeah. Well, he didn't win 'em all. He helped prosecute a case once that got away from the State's Attorney in a big way. Some Teamster gorilla found himself on the business end of a murder indictment after a guy turned up dead outside a bar in Cicero. A love triangle, they said. Anyway, the prosecution's main witness got up on the stand and just rolled over and played dead. Couldn't remember a fucking thing. The Teamster guy walked and everyone said they'd wired it, but nobody ever proved anything."

"I remember that, vaguely. What's the insinuation, that Throop knew about it or something? He was the prosecutor, you said."

"There's no insinuation, we're just looking for connections. Throop helped prepare the prosecution's case, that's all."

"OK, so what?"

"So nothing, maybe. Then Arlo took a look at the year when Throop was one of those bright young minority lawyers Jake Slazenger loves to hire to stay in good with the liberals. Well, remember when old Jake was appointed to overhaul some of the city's major union contracts, among them the Teamster one, after all that nonsense about snowplows and things? Well, our boy Wilson was apparently in the middle of all that. No hanky-panky alleged, just a possible connection."

Moreland raised an eyebrow. "Connections."

"That's what makes the world go round."

"So where does Papini come in?"

"Well, Arlo took a look at who was still around from the old gang, and what with senility and forced retirement and death from natural and unnatural causes, Michael Papini was just about the only guy left who might have known about both of those things, the guy that walked and the Teamsters surviving Jake Slazenger's pruning shears. And lo and behold, Papini just got out of jail."

Moreland nodded. "So Arlo went looking for him."

"Just to ask a few questions."

Moreland looked longingly at the bottle of bourbon. "So what do you think?"

"Hell, what do you think?"

"I think you've got nothing so far except suspicions."

"That's what I told you up front. But doesn't anything, you know, leap out at you?"

"You want me to say Wilson Throop had Papini and the Oylers and Spivak killed because they had something on him?"

"I don't want you to say anything but the truth."

"Well, we're on the same page then."

"But to answer your question, no. I don't think Throop had 'em killed. But I'd take a long hard look at Throop's godfather if I were you."

Moreland blinked at him for a moment and then said, "Hairston?"

"Give the man a cigar. Mackey Hairston."

"That's quite an accusation."

"That's not an accusation at all. I never said it. It just came to you in your sleep one night."

Moreland gave the slightest of nods, lips firmed. "What now?"

Neumann shrugged. "Now you dig it all up. You turn over the rock and watch 'em run for cover."

Moreland tugged at his tie and looked at Neumann, wanting to ask him about other rocks. After a moment he said, "OK. Can I have access to whatever notes Spivak made? Whatever evidence he dug up?"

"Arlo didn't make notes. He went and talked to people and carried it all around in his head. But you can trust everything I told you. You want to document it, that's your job. I've given you the lead, you write the god damn story. And don't quote me."

Moreland nodded. "Who else have you told about this?"

"Not a living soul."

"You must have told the cops."

Neumann looked as blank as a conscious human being can look. "I didn't indulge in any speculation with the cops."

"Your right-hand man just got killed and you didn't tell the cops who you think was responsible?"

"Like I say, I didn't waste time on things I have no proof for."

Moreland frowned. "How about that impressive-looking specimen that just walked out of here? What did you tell him?"

For a moment Neumann's look went very hard; then it softened. "Spike's a friend. He comes by, we toss off a drink for old times' sake. Once in a while he's useful for liaison purposes with the Police Department. Don't worry about Spike." Neumann's chin went up a few degrees and his eyebrows rose. The look said, any further questions?

"Why are you telling me all this?"

Neumann smiled. "All what? I haven't told you anything. We've just been kind of speculating. I can't speculate with the cops. They need facts. With the cops, everything's on the record."

Moreland nodded. He looked at the wall behind Neumann and considered. He said, "Does the name Elizabeth Leland mean anything to you?"

"No. Should it?"

"It's just a name that came up in connection with Gerald Oyler, Vance and John's old man. I wondered if Spivak had mentioned it to you."

"No, but if I run into a lady by that name, I'll let you know."

"Thanks. Can I get back to you if I need to?"

"Hey," said Neumann, leaning forward to cap the whiskey bottle. "I'm a public official. Accessible is my middle name." He put the bottle in a desk drawer as Moreland stood up. "Just remember."

"Yeah?"

"I still don't know you. I've just been sitting in here talking to myself."

Moreland smiled a feeble smile. "Bourbon's been known to do that to a man."

11 THE POOL HALL WAS EMPTY in the early afternoon, cool and dim with the only light coming from the distant front windows and the shaded lamp over the table. "Rudiments," said Cooper. "This is one of the rudiments. This goes in your bag of tricks." Dominic watched, standing with his cue like a shepherd leaning on his staff, as Cooper bent over the bright green felt, positioning the balls with deft practiced movements. "Any time you have two balls frozen against each other like this . . ." Cooper placed the five against the nine, just touching, three feet from a corner pocket. "Now we do a little geometry. Imagine a line connecting the centers of the two balls. See it? Now, the line perpendicular to that one and passing between the two balls is tangent to both of them, right?"

The boy shrugged. "I guess."

"Well hell, that's just eighth-grade geometry. Trust me, it's a tangent. Now, follow that tangent. Where does it lead you?"

"Looks like it goes to the pocket."

"Straight and true. Now, you know what the beauty of this setup is?"

"What?"

"You hit either of those balls, no matter where, and it goes straight into the pocket."

"No matter where?"

"As long as you hit it solid. Watch." Cooper spotted the cue ball, leaned over the table, and potted the five with an easy practiced stroke. "Set it up again, you try it. You've got a lot of room for error. All you have to do is hit the ball nearest you, practically anywhere. It'll follow that tangent. If the tangent goes into a pocket, you've got a made shot."

Dominic tried it a couple of times and was convinced. "That's cool," he said.

"It can help you." Cooper grinned. "You know, you work on your game a little more, you'll be ready to play me for money and I'll be able to win my twenty bucks back."

The boy smiled. "Didn't think I could do it, huh?"

"How much they pay you for pouring coffee up there?"

"Hey, there's more to it than pouring coffee. There's an art to making a good espresso."

"How many years before they let you make a cappuccino all by yourself?"

"Jesus. Chill, will you?" Dominic hefted the cue ball, frowning, then set it back on the table. "Where'd you learn to play pool, anyway?"

Cooper chalked his cue. "The proverbial misspent youth. In the Army, mainly." He grinned. "The Army's about as misspent as a youth can get."

Dominic laughed and took an idle swipe at the cue ball, sending it rocketing around the table. He watched it hit six or seven rails, losing energy slowly. "So how come you're always on my case?"

Cooper set down the chalk, studied the tip of the cue, blew off the excess chalk. "Because I've got a college degree sitting in a drawer at home. You're a high school dropout."

Dominic stiffened, watching the ball. "Hey, I read like constantly. I know a lot more than most of these imbeciles who come out of the public schools."

Cooper watched with him as the cue ball came to rest. "Sure. You know a lot about Eastern religion, pop psychology and certain fashionable novelists. But as far as I've been able to tell, you know nothing about mathematics or hard science."

"Aw, don't gimme . . . Come on, Cooper. The world needs more than . . . engineers and corporate robots."

"I'm not finished. Your knowledge of history is at the comic-strip level. What you know about economics is mainly myth. You're close to innumerate. You have a foundation of basic knowledge and skills that should allow you to educate yourself, but your in-

tellect right now is just a tangle of fashionable prejudices. You
have no practical skills that I can discern, zero. Right now you
have all the skills you need for a long career drawing espressos in
a hip coffeehouse. You're the bourgeois equivalent of the ghetto
kid looking forward to a career at McDonald's. I hope you'll be
happy. Rack 'em up?"

Dominic stood immobile, looking at Cooper with shock through
the dangling forelock. "Don't start with the lectures and shit,
OK?"

"I'm your father. That's what I'm supposed to do. I'm supposed
to give you lectures."

The boy subsided onto his heels, hands clenching the pool cue.
It was very quiet in the pool hall. "Sure, you're my father," he
said. "You got your rocks off with my mother and knocked her
up. Big fuckin' deal. You never even knew I existed till she was
dead. Where the hell were you when I needed a father? When
that other asshole was killing my mother?"

Cooper laid his cue on the table and leaned on the rail with both
hands, fixing the boy in the eye. "Look, the deal's always been
that I'm just as much of a father as you want me to be. I make no
claims, never have. I consider that you have certain claims on me
by virtue of that act of getting my rocks off, but that's your option.
You want to be my son, you're my son. You don't, you're not. Fair
enough?"

The boy cleared the forelock out of his eyes with a toss of the
head. "Sure. Well, today I don't feel like being your boy. Adios."
Dominic tossed his cue on the table and stalked away. Cooper
watched him disappear out the door into the afternoon light.

He replaced Dominic's cue on the wall carefully, racked the balls,
and scattered them with a savage stroke. He watched a couple of
balls drop and then his head drooped. He laughed at the green
felt. He straightened up slowly and looked out the front window
into the light. He shook his head and gathered the balls into the
tray. He could see Derrick watching him from behind the counter.

"What's with the kid?" Derrick said when Cooper laid the balls
on the counter.

"He's a wastrel," Cooper said, handing his pet cue across to
Derrick. "Kid needs a better role model, I guess."

■ ■ ■

"You'll excuse me if I eat while we talk, I hope," said the lawyer. "This really is the only time I can give you." The lawyer was in her forties, with dull brown hair in a halo around a face that had never driven men wild but with eyes that made them quiver if their own lawyers were not tip-top. The eyes were sharp and penetrating, with dark circles below them that suggested stress, lack of rest, and obsessive attention to work.

Moreland smiled an expansive smile and held up a deferential hand as he sank onto the well-padded leather chair opposite the desk. "Please, dig in. I'm sorry to intrude on your lunch hour. It's very good of you to see me."

The lawyer extracted a massive submarine sandwich from a Styrofoam container and shot Moreland a mistrustful look as if she suspected him of packing a hidden camera. "I'm not entirely clear on why you're here," she said before taking the first great tearing bite, squinting with the effort. She leaned forward to keep sandwich debris from falling on her expensive brown suit.

Moreland averted his eyes, looking out the window over the scattered landscape of the South Loop. "I'm here because I have a question or two about Jake Slazenger's firm."

Chewing, the lawyer said out of a corner of her mouth, "Why don't you ask Jake Slazenger?"

Moreland smiled. "I tried. He's a very busy man, apparently, or else I'm not on his approved list of journalists to talk to."

"OK, why me?"

"My colleague Ned Dickerson did a story on the firm a couple of years ago. He said for the story on Jake Slazenger, Gay Brooks was the one to talk to."

Between bites, Gay Brooks said, "Ned Dickerson. He did that feature on S, G and W while I was still over there."

"That's right."

"OK, I'll ask you again. Why me?"

Moreland smiled again. "I'm just following an old journalistic principle. If you want to get the real story on someone, don't ask their friends."

The lawyer chewed methodically, forcefully, while Moreland's smile faded. She swallowed and said, "What makes you think I have anything against Jake Slazenger?"

"The impression Ned gave me was you had not parted amicably."

"What does he know? He talked to me for about five minutes, three years ago, as I recall."

"Maybe he talked to Jake Slazenger longer."

The lawyer nodded and took another bite of the sandwich. She chewed and said, "If you want gossip or dirt, you've come to the wrong person."

"Neither one. I'm not looking for someone to smear Slazenger. I'm looking for an impartial source. Given the choice of Slazenger himself or a former associate who no longer has any reason to be loyal to him, I chose you. I figured you'd have no reason to trash him, but were more likely to be impartial. And, I hope, informed."

Moreland got a good dose of the look that had cowed better men than he. "So what are you fishing for?" the lawyer said.

"I'm not fishing. I have a couple of very specific questions."

The lawyer shrugged. "Shoot." She tore into the sandwich again, coming away with lettuce threads and lunch meat hanging. Moreland looked out the window again.

"Number one. Did Wilson Throop work with you at S, G and W?"

The chewing stopped. After a second it resumed, but the lawyer was on guard; Moreland could see that. "Yes," the lawyer said. "Why?"

"I'm wondering if he was involved in the matter I'm interested in."

"What matter would that be?"

Moreland shifted on his chair, getting comfortable. "Eight years ago Jake Slazenger was hired by the city to review their contract with the Teamsters Union, who represent a goodly number of city workers in various fields. Correct?"

"Correct." The lawyer had abandoned the sandwich and was dabbing absently at her lips with a paper napkin, peering at Moreland.

"And my research indicates that there was some dissatisfaction, some noise that the city was left with pretty much the same restrictive work rules that they had complained about earlier."

The lawyer nodded. "There was some noise."

"People wondered why such a clever lawyer as Jake Slazenger had not been able to come up with a better deal."

"Politics."

"I beg your pardon?"

"Politics." Brooks had finished wiping her mouth and now leaned back in her chair, hands resting on the arms. "He came up with the best deal he could given the political constraints. What's the big deal?"

"No big deal. Was Wilson Throop involved in the Teamster negotiations?"

The look came back; Moreland was unpleasantly reminded of his ex-wife's divorce lawyer. "It's a little early for this, isn't it?" said the lawyer.

"For what?"

"For the smears. The election's more than a year off. Save it for when you really need it."

Moreland opened his mouth, closed it, opened it again and drew breath. "I think you have the wrong impression about why I'm here."

"You're not really here to ask about Jake. You're here to find dirt on Wilson Throop. Aren't you?"

Moreland considered, giving her the same firm look he'd always tried to maintain with his wife's lawyer. "Somebody else already has dirt on Wilson Throop," he finally said. "I'm just trying to find out what it is."

The lawyer's eyebrows went up. "I see."

"I didn't initiate the contact that led to this and I'm way behind the curve. But if the dirt's there, wouldn't you rather see it swept out now?"

"Why would I?"

Moreland hesitated. "If you're planning to support Throop."

"What makes you think I am?"

"Just a wild guess. Slazenger's a Daley man, you split with Slazenger and took umbrage when I asked about Throop."

"You think I split with Jake Slazenger for political reasons?"

Moreland shrugged. "I heard whispers about ethical differences no one will talk about. But I figure it's all tied up with politics in the end."

"Whispers." She smiled. "Well, since you didn't come here for gossip, you wouldn't be interested in that. As for the politics, you're right, I'm certainly not a . . . Daley man. And I think Wilson Throop is moderate, principled, and committed to reform. Besides being electable. So by your criterion I'm not likely to give you what you call the real story on Wilson Throop, am I?" For the first time the lawyer smiled, icily.

Moreland returned it. "But you wouldn't lie about him."

"I'm not inclined to say anything about him until I have more than your assertion that somebody has dirt on him."

"Of course," Moreland said. He had to consider again, frowning out the window. "All right, I have a source who claims that a man has been killed to prevent him making public information that implicates Throop in wrongdoing. The source claims that the wrongdoing is linked to the Teamsters Union. I'm trying to find the link. Hence my question."

The look that Gay Brooks gave Moreland this time was unreadable. After a couple of seconds she picked up the sandwich again and took another bite, smaller this time. While she chewed, looking at the wall behind Moreland, he could see her thinking hard about all the killings she'd read of in the last week or two. Moreland thought she looked a little shaken. She swallowed and said, "That's ridiculous."

"Maybe. I'll ask again. Was Throop involved in that Teamster business?"

"No."

Moreland waited, but there was no further elaboration. "He had no dealings with the Teamsters while he was working for Jake Slazenger?

"He was not involved in the negotiations you referred to. I don't know about every case he worked on while he was at S, G and W. You'll have to go elsewhere to find your dirt."

Moreland nodded, his lips tensed in the pose of a thoughtful, serious journalist. Inside, he was clenched tight, wondering sickeningly if he'd just given away the store. "All right," he said. "I guess I will." He stood up abruptly. "Thanks for your time."

The lawyer sat looking at the sandwich as if it were a mess to be cleaned up. "I suppose," she said, "you have the utmost confidence in your source? You wouldn't allow yourself to be . . . manipulated by anyone, would you?"

Moreland rose to his full height. "I won't take that as an insult," he said, as doubt settled like cold heavy silt inside him. "I'll assume it wasn't intended that way."

"Take it any way you like," said the lawyer, fixing him with the look again. "Just do your work honestly."

"Of course," said Moreland. He stood still for a moment, meeting her look. "One more question," he said.

"All right. One more."

"Does the name Elizabeth Leland mean anything to you?"

"Elizabeth Leland?" She took another bite and chewed it. "No. Should it?"

"Not necessarily." Moreland made for the door. "Just fishing."

■ ■ ■

This one's a little better, thought Cooper, looking in the rearview mirror. He was heading north on Clark Street, hissing through slush, nudging through tentative traffic. Cooper had never believed it was as easy either to tail someone or to detect a competent tail as the movies made it look. He was aware that he never would have spotted the old pale green Buick Skylark behind him if he had not been alerted the day before. It had taken a conscious effort to catalogue what he saw in the mirror throughout a morning's driving, to make him finally notice the car, anywhere from half a block to a couple of stoplights behind him.

They're dressing down, he thought, signaling and sliding into the left-turn lane. From late-model bright reds to junkyard refugees. The Buick Skylark was at least fifteen years old, he judged. He made the turn as the light went yellow and thought that here was the best test yet of how good the man in the Buick Skylark was. Cooper went halfway down the block and turned right into an alley running north. A glance in the mirror showed him the Buick Skylark had not yet reached the corner behind him. He'll have to be more than good, Cooper thought. He'll have to be lucky. Fifty feet up the alley was a little yard behind a Lebanese restaurant that fronted on Clark Street. Cooper pulled up beside a battered Ford and sat in the car, not really expecting the Buick Skylark to come down the alley but curious. After a couple of minutes he got out of the car and made for the back door of the restaurant.

This will only make her more curious, Cooper thought.

Inside, Cooper nodded at the usual handful of Lebanese men around a table at the back of the restaurant, waiting out their exile in a cloud of cigarette smoke. He took a seat by the front window.

The place was not crowded and the service was prompt. Cooper ordered hummus and a shawarma sandwich and spread the jobs section of the paper at his elbow.

He had driven down to the near North Side on a wild-goose chase. Boyle had a friend who needed a new manager for a struggling bar on Division Street; Cooper had gone to talk to the man and been struck both by an immediate dislike for the premises and by his ignorance of the economics of running a bar. The interview had been short.

His lunch arrived; Cooper skimmed the ads and found nothing of interest. Over coffee, he looked out at the street and thought of his son, his lover, his life that was drifting downriver with the current. He drained the coffee and picked up his bill. There was nobody at the cash register and he wandered toward the back, looking for the owner. There was a commotion, he became aware: a couple of the men who had been at the rear table were in the hallway that led past the restrooms to the back door. Cooper could not see through to the door, but it sounded as if it were open and someone was shouting in the alley.

He waited, and in a minute or so the men came shambling back to the table, chuckling listlessly and murmuring in rapid impenetrable Arabic. The back door slammed and the owner, a dark little man in a white shirt, came back up the hallway looking peeved. He said something to his audience and they erupted with laughter. Cooper waved the check at him and he hustled up to the register.

"People have no respect," the owner said with a heavy trill of the *r*. "I ask him to move, he tell me bad words."

"What happened?" Cooper said, taking his change.

The owner's hands flew with Levantine eloquence. "He just sitting back there in the car, just sitting. I ask if he waiting for someone, he say no. I ask if he a customer, he tell me go to hell. So I get mad. For you is OK, you are my customer. But only to sit back there waiting in the car, no good. I tell him, 'This for the customers only, can't park here.' He say me bad things. So I tell him OK, I call the police, you can say to them bad words. Then he leave. Stupid man."

Cooper smiled. He was turning away when a thought struck him. "What kind of car was it?"

The owner shrugged, coming away from the register. "Old car, very old. Big, like before the oil crisis, you know?" He grinned.

"What color?"

The owner paused, the grin fading. "Green, green like . . ."

"Light green or dark green?"

"Light green, yes. Light."

"And he was just sitting back there waiting?"

"You know him?" The look now was suspicious.

Cooper shook his head. "No, I don't think so."

Cooper stood at the back door and looked out into the alley. The Valiant and the Ford were still there, but there were no other cars in sight. Cooper walked to the middle of the alley and looked north and south, but saw nothing. He got in the Valiant and drove home, watching the mirrors. He didn't see the light green Buick Skylark any more, and after a while he stopped wondering.

■ ■ ■

Moreland was working the phone like a demon, a spider in the center of his web, connections everywhere. "Buck, what's up?"

"Hey, Mel. I thought I'd be hearing from you. You people been all over us since those god damn tapes turned up."

"I'll bet you've been having fun with it."

"If this is fun, give me tedium. You want the spiel?"

"About how everyone on the tapes is dead or in jail and it's all irrelevant to the new improved Teamsters? I heard it already. On TV. You looked good."

"Yeah, I think I hit all the channels. My kids think their old man's a celebrity now. I work my ass off to keep 'em fed, they treat me like the hired help. I'm on TV for ten seconds and suddenly I'm God. Kids are screwed up these days, I'm telling you. The video generation."

"Speaking of which, I hear you had the Greek lady snooping around over there."

"Christine Pappadakis? I heard she was here one day. She didn't talk to me, though. I'd a told her where to take her sweet ass."

"She's got a reputation for digging out the dirty stuff."

"What dirty stuff? You guys are all fixated on this Teamster mythology."

"So what do you think got the Oyler boys killed?"

"You really want to know? I'll tell you what got 'em killed."

"My pencil is poised."

"Vance got himself killed, like I told you, fucking around with the bad boys. And then John got killed because he knew who did it and was preparing to fix his ass."

"What do you mean, like getting revenge?"

"You bet. Teamster families stick close, my friend. John's death was a preemptive strike."

"So what do the tapes have to do with it?"

"Not a fucking thing. John found them in his daddy's attic or something and was going through them out of curiosity. It was like finding your dad's old *Playboys* down in the basement, and you never knew the old devil went in for that kind of thing."

"That's the official Teamster line, is it?"

"That's the truth, and you're gonna see. The cops have written this tape bullshit off already, I'm telling you. When they get that bunch that was stashing the cars over at Streets and San they'll have the killer."

"Well, maybe so. What I'm calling about is actually something completely different."

"You tired of this Oyler thing already, huh?"

"They just gave it to better people. You know me. I'm the guy that does the school council reports. If a story starts to look interesting, the word goes out: 'Keep Moreland off it.' "

"You're too modest. So what do you want to know today?"

"I want to know what kind of dealings you people have had with Wilson Throop."

Silence. Moreland was starting to think the line had gone dead when Buck said, "What? What the hell do you mean, what kind of dealings?"

"I mean I'm hearing rumors that Throop has good friends over there."

"What do you mean good friends? I've never met the man. He's never been over here, to my knowledge."

"I mean I hear that Throop is cultivating contacts over there in case he becomes mayor."

"Cultivating contacts? Hell, you mean he's kissed somebody's ass over a hundred-dollar dinner. What else is new? That's what people planning to run for mayor do."

"Let me put it this way. Is there any significant support over on South Ashland for Wilson Throop's candidacy?"

A sound that might have been a laugh came over the wire. "Wilson Throop has no constituency here."

"OK, tell me this. When you people had your slugfest with the city back in the eighties, was Throop involved in the negotiations?"

"Man, you're all over the map today. I think I'm starting to see a pattern, though. All I can tell you on that one is, not that I know of. I'll tell you again—as far as I know, Wilson Throop has about as many friends over here as Bill Clinton does in the Pentagon. I'm not saying he hasn't made some advances, but advances are a dime a dozen. He's not scoring yet."

"OK, Buck, you would know. And I'm sure you would tell me straight."

"Damn right I would. For a pal like you? Hey, you want to see the Flyers when they come in town? Lindros and company? Couple of weeks from now."

"Can't say now. I'll let you know. Hey, one more question."

"Let 'er rip."

"Who the hell is Elizabeth Leland?"

"Aw Christ, not you too."

"Somebody else been asking about her?"

"Only the cops. And the broad from Channel Five, or so I heard. Since then Elizabeth Leland is kind of a joke around here. Nobody's ever heard of her. So I'll tell you the same thing I told the cops. I went to grammar school with a Becky Leland, but she didn't have any sisters. You're all barking up the wrong tree."

"Ok, well thanks, Buck. I appreciate your time."

"Any time. And don't believe the bullshit. Believe me. See you."

Moreland hung up and sat with his hand on the phone, scowling across the room. After a minute he shook himself, rose from his chair, and dodged through the maze of desks in the large room with creditable agility for a man of his shape. He went out of the news room and down a hallway to the open door of a small office. He stuck his head around the doorframe and rapped on it with a knuckle. The man inside was on the phone; he waved Moreland in and held up a finger in a just-a-second gesture.

While Moreland waited for the man to finish off his conversation, he looked at the things a long-time political columnist accumulates on his walls: photos of the columnist with four different mayors and assorted famous faces, many signed "to Jack," a calendar the size of a bath towel covered with trails of illegible writing, a cork board shaggy with thumbtacked notes, books jumbled haphazardly on metal shelves, and a handful of framed award certificates, including one that seemed to start with a *P*. The desk at which the columnist sat looked as if a Hefty bag had ruptured on it. Most impressive of all was a window with a view of the river, a metallic gray-green shimmer below.

"Let me know," said the columnist, and hung up. "Mel," he said. "What can I do you for?" Jack Puckett was a small solid man with a round bald head, round face, and round belly. His eyes were not round; they were narrow slits under heavy lids that gave him a shrewd look. An iron-gray moustache just missed being dashing.

"Tell me about Wilson Throop," said Moreland.

Puckett's eyebrows rose, briefly. "What about him?"

Moreland sank onto a chair opposite him. "Who's supporting him? Who stands to gain and lose if he wins? That kind of thing. The real dope, I mean. I know the superficial stuff 'cause I do occasionally find time to read the paper."

Puckett smiled. "You want the clout map."

"I guess so."

Puckett leaned back in his chair and clasped his hands behind his head, revealing sweat stains in his armpits. He smiled again, revealing a glint of metal somewhere back in his molars, and Moreland knew he was watching a man who enjoyed his work. In all Chicago there was no more thoroughly political animal, outside of City Hall itself, than Jack Puckett.

"Well," he said. "The clout map could go the way of all those maps of the USSR, if Wilson gets himself elected."

"Aha. Does he have a chance?"

"Sure he has a chance. It'll be interesting."

"So who wants him to win? Besides the black electorate, I mean."

"Well, it's mainly them, though not all of them. Richie's done OK by a lot of blacks. But yeah, Wilson Throop is undoubtedly the strongest black candidate since old Harold himself. Right now there's nobody else on the horizon who could unseat Richie. To do that you need a black, of course, but not a firebrand. Wilson's a moderate, he's never gone in for that plantation rhetoric, the _____ive stuff. He's pro-affirmative action, but then so's everybody else, publicly anyway. He's strong on crime, being a former pros-ecutor, he's not seen as anti-business, he's made the right noises about taxes and privatization and all. He's been a decent alderman. He's a hell of a candidate."

"Would he make a good mayor?"

Puckett shrugged. "What's a good mayor? He'd probably run an ordinarily efficient administration. Beyond that, whether you think he'd be a good mayor depends on whether you can get through to him on the phone. He's not perceptibly different from Richie on any major point of political philosophy. Sure, he's got different ideas about who to screw to build an airport and that kind of thing. But that's just tactics. He's not going to revolutionize the city, and that's not what blacks want, most of them anyway. They just want a black Richie. And that's pretty much what Wilson Throop would be."

"Speaks volumes for the level of political debate in this town, doesn't it?"

Puckett smiled a wise, fatherly smile. "Two-thirds of the voters will vote straight skin color. That's a given. Here and any place else there's a skin color equivalent. Try and get Serbs to elect a Croat, or Tamils to elect a Sinhalese, or Ukrainians to elect a Russian, or you name it. See, that's the fun thing about politics." Puckett leaned forward now, elbows on the desk, recondite black eyes gleaming. "It has very little to do with the rights of man and sound economic policy and all that stuff that put you and me to sleep in college. What politics has to do with mainly is the same thing that quickens your pulse in a poker game—drawing the right cards, betting intelligently, keeping that poker face. The smoke-filled room, the bottle at the elbow, the quick calculation of odds, the stare-down. Occasionally the odd ace up the sleeve. That's what makes politics fun." Puckett sat back smiling and Moreland wondered if he'd just been treated to a rehearsal of a paragraph from Jack Puckett's memoirs.

"So who are the players here? Winners and losers if Wilson Throop is the next mayor."

Puckett shrugged. "Winners? The black mandarins. The black bureaucrats, the black bourgeoisie. The independents, the reform bunch, because Throop at least makes sympathetic noises and will draw from them to fill all those empty offices up on the fifth floor. But nothing radical." Puckett frowned at the ceiling. "Losers? The governor—Throop will twang the poverty string till Springfield squeezes more blood out of the stone for welfare. Developers— Richie loves developers and Throop's a little more skeptical. The casino people will lose, not because Wilson will keep them out like he says, but because his price is higher. Those white aldermen in their bunkers out on the Northwest Side will be losers. Siminowicz and Neumann and those guys." Puckett waved a hand, vaguely. "Assorted others. For most people things will be just about the same."

"The unions?"

"Hard to say. No reason to believe Throop would change anything."

Moreland nodded, slowly. "Let's get down to individuals. The clout map. Winners and losers."

Puckett smiled. "You have the look of a man after a story," he said.

"Background, Jack. I'm just looking for background. Who's behind Throop?"

"Mackey Hairston, of course. Mackey's been grooming Wilson for a long time. Ever since he was a bright young student-athlete at Leo High School down on 79th Street. With Wilson on the fifth floor, Mackey's empire will be complete."

"Hm," said Moreland. "Who's backing him outside the black mandarins?"

"Nothing but rumors so far. The election's still a long way off. Anybody who thinks they can get a better deal from him than from Richie, probably. That's where the poker playing starts."

"OK, who would shoot his grandmother to keep Wilson Throop from becoming mayor? Who loses clout?"

"Besides Richie? Let me think."

"Who does Richie like that Wilson doesn't?"

Puckett considered for a moment. "King Van Houten, that's who. Throop's been hard on him in the Council, all those zoning fights. Wilson loves to rail at influence peddlers and the people who buy it."

"Mm. What about Jake Slazenger?"

"Jake?" Puckett looked surprised, then cocked his head to one side, thinking. "Jake's what they call a Daley intimate, you know that. But then Wilson used to work over there, didn't he? I don't think Jake would necessarily lose that much city business in a Throop administration. I suspect Jake's going to await the election results fairly philosophically. Why?"

Moreland shrugged. "I was just hearing about him, that's all. Any other thoughts come to mind?"

"A few, but unless you have more names to throw at me, I don't know how specific I can be. Nobody really knows how the fault lines are going to form yet. Right now it's all happening in smoke-filled rooms." The grin appeared again, spreading the moustache across the round face.

"Yeah." Moreland frowned out the window. "One more thing. Does the name Elizabeth Leland mean anything to you?"

Puckett looked blank. "No. Should it?"

"I guess not." Moreland put his hands on his knees and pushed, rising to his feet. He was suddenly very tired. "Thanks, Jack. If I have any more specific questions I'll drop by again, OK?"

"Any time. You want to talk baseball, you go see Maury. You want to talk politics, come to me."

Moreland paused in the doorway. "I'll ask you about politics what I asked Maury about baseball once. Do you ever get tired of watching it?"

Puckett was leaning back in his chair again, smiling. "Once every couple or three years, for an hour or two."

Moreland shook his head. "That's about what Maury said, too."

▪ ▪ ▪

Cooper found himself looking out the window, lights out, trying to make out shapes of cars in the street below. The snow glowed an evil yellow under the sodium vapor lamps. Cooper's range of vision was too limited to see whether an old Buick Skylark was parked on the block.

Cautious, he thought, heading for the back door. Time to be a little cautious, that's all. The restaurateur's tale had unsettled him just enough to make him wary. He let himself out the back, into the cold night air which bore the sounds of distant traffic over from the big north-south arteries to the quiet tree-lined streets west of Broadway. Cooper went down the back steps slowly.

He followed the alley to a side street, crossed it and went a full block down to circle around to where he'd left the Valiant. If somebody was watching his front door, they'd miss him. The Valiant started a little uncertainly; Cooper knew the old charger was going to have to be replaced soon. Next winter would be one too many.

He saw nothing disturbing on the street as he rolled up the block. He made a left on Devon and then took Glenwood north. He found a place to park not too far from Burk's, under the high El embankment. He sat in the car looking out at the street for a moment: there was broken glass in a doorway and garbage frozen into the snowbanks in the gutter. The old neighborhood was looking tired and decrepit, like an old man who has finally lost the will to shave in the morning.

Where am I going to go? thought Cooper. Us. The two of us. Where would we go?

He felt better once he got inside Burk's, his second living room for nigh on a decade. He nodded to half a dozen faces, chalked his name on the board for the pool table, smiled at Lisa, his favorite barkeep, hired a dark German beer, and put his elbows on the bar, waiting for solace. The Christmas lights still framed the mirror; the jukebox was playing "Honky Tonk Women"; the aroma of smoke and spilled beer settled slowly into him. The sign above the antique cash register said that in order to be served, you had to have been born on this date or later in the year Cooper got out of the Army. Cooper shook his head, thinking that had been a fast twenty-one years indeed.

Is this where you want to be twenty-one years from now? he asked the melancholy face in the mirror. Ten? Five? Next year?

Why not, he decided, and reached for the beer.

"You lie to me again, *bitch*, I'll kill you." Somebody was shouting over the noise of the jukebox. Cooper set down the beer. Six feet down the bar to his right, a man was in a woman's face, seriously in her face. The man was broad through the shoulders and bullet-headed, black browed and unshaven, straining at the leash. He had one hand on the bar and one in her face, index an inch from her nose. The woman was on a stool with her back to the bar, pinned against it. She wore tight jeans and a sweatshirt and had red hair piled up in a topknot. She sat as still as ice, trying to glare back at him, but her eyes were too wide to bring off the defiant look. Her arms were folded tightly at her breast. "You think I don't talk to people?" the man screamed. "You think I'm *stupid*? Is that it, huh?"

Stay clear of this, Cooper told himself. Nobody ever thanks you.

The woman said something Cooper couldn't hear, her lips moving rapidly. Cooper saw that Lisa was aware; she had come down the bar to just within earshot and halted, watching. Cooper made eye contact with her briefly; she gave just the slightest shake of the head, looking wary but not panicked.

The man clutched the woman's hair at the base of the topknot, pulling her head sideways. Her face contorted in pain and her hands went to his chest, pushing. He was shaking her head, screaming into her face. "You dumb cunt, you think people don't talk?"

Lisa had seen it all before; she stepped swiftly away to reach under the bar and in a second the jukebox died in mid-chord and the loudest sound in the place was the woman's soft whimper as the man twisted her hair. The man was oblivious; in the sudden quiet his bellow was enough to rattle windows. "Your name's on every bathroom wall in the whole fucking city!" He gave her head a violent shake; her eyes were squeezed shut and she had two handfuls of shirtfront, but she was not going anywhere.

Heads were turning and Lisa was speaking softly and rapidly into the phone. Cooper was sliding off his stool because private or not, there were some things he couldn't sit and watch. "Let go of her," he said.

Cooper had seen eyes like the ones under those black brows before. Eyes like those meant a person was way beyond polite talk and china was going to break. Cooper was already thinking of ways to minimize damage, mostly to himself. "You stay the fuck out of this," the man with the eyes said, slowly and clearly, the index pointing at Cooper now.

"Sorry, Jack. I'm in it. I was in it the minute you grabbed her. I don't give a fuck about your problems, but if you don't let go of her you got a problem with me." Cooper had taken a step or two, halting just outside closing distance.

"Blow, motherfucker. Turn around and motor."

Cooper smiled. The smile was partly tactical and partly a response to a sudden surge of adrenaline, the sublimest, wickedest drug he knew. "There's more room out in the street and no furniture to break. You want to be a man, try beating on me instead of her."

Cooper was ready for the move because he knew the look in the eyes; when the hand in his face went to his chest and grabbed cloth, he twisted left, knocking the hand away with a hard swipe of his right forearm that hyperextended the man's elbow. The man let out a quick yelp of pain; he had let go of the woman's hair, but he had no chance to bring the big sweeping right around because Cooper was already uncoiling, coming back with the left hook. It caught the man on the mouth and sent him back against the pinball machine with a crash, the eyes suddenly unfocused; he bounced off and landed on the floor on his back.

Cooper had the sole of his boot on the man's chest before he could rally. "Don't," he said. "Don't get up." He waited for the eyes to focus on him before he went on. "You had a chance to avoid it. Next time think." The man spat blood from a split lip; he was focused on Cooper, but the mad-dog look was gone; now he was surprised.

That was the last thing Cooper noticed before somebody behind him yelled his name. He ducked by reflex and a freight train hit him in the back of the skull. He fell forward, flashbulbs going off everywhere, grabbed at the cigarette machine and missed, and slid to his knees in the corner beneath the wall phone. Someone was screaming at him, a woman. Cooper closed his eyes and waited for his brains to settle.

When he started to make sense of things again, they had him propped up on a chair, somebody on either side of him, ice inside a towel to the back of his head. "What the fuck," he said.

"She cold-cocked you with a pitcher, man," a voice to his right said. "You ducked just enough to make her graze you."

A voice to his left said, "Them pitchers are solid. If it'd a broke, you'd be in worse trouble. You got a lump back there, but nothing cut." The voices sounded like his conscience in stereo.

"Who the fuck hit me?" said Cooper.

The right channel said, "The lady. She didn't like the way you laid out her old man. She led him out of here like a mama with her three-year-old."

Cooper looked down at his left hand. The knuckles were bleeding. "Love is a wonderful thing," he said.

Left said, "You don't never want to mess in a lovers' quarrel. I learned that a long time ago."

"Never pays," said Right sagaciously. "Best thing to do is let 'em slug it out. Woman gets tired of that kind of thing, she can always walk."

"How you doing, Coop? The bells still ringing?"

Cooper steadied himself on the chair, pushing his helpers away gently. "I'll live," he said.

The man on his right handed him the ice pack. "Not if you keep trying to help people."

"Nobody ever thanks you," said Cooper.

"All you get is a headache." The jukebox kicked in again, proving the point. Cooper stood up, reeling just a little. Lisa watched him anxiously from behind the bar; he looked at her and shook his head, making it hurt.

Standing outside the door of the bar, Cooper looked up and down the empty street and felt the back of his head gingerly. The knot was sizable, but he'd had lumps on his head before. Fuck these people, he thought. All of 'em.

It's a big planet, Cooper thought, walking back to the car. And no place on the whole damn thing for me.

12 MORELAND HAD ALWAYS HAD mixed feelings about the Cook County Criminal Court Building rising massively out of a nondescript neighborhood at 26th and California, conveniently next to the County Jail; on the one hand, it was a place where things happened, where a reporter could see the drama of life unfolding, see judges and cops and prosecutors and defenders and evil-doers and mere hapless chumps engaged in their endlessly absorbing dance; on the other hand, it was a sump of institutional failure and human misery, the grimmest place on earth.

Moreland found the man he wanted in the back row of a courtroom on the third floor where a young black man in a beige jumpsuit with "D.O.C." stenciled on the back stood as impassive as a statue while his lawyer, a diminutive white woman, spoke to the judge in tones inaudible at the back of the room.

Moreland slid onto the battered wooden bench next to his man. "Afternoon, Counselor," he said.

The man was elderly, spare of figure and loose of limb, draped in a black suit with white stripes, and sporting a striped bow tie. His hair was iron-gray and cut short enough to stand up in a style that had been out of fashion for twenty-five years until it had finally come back in. The old man's face was long and equine, mobile, seamed and intelligent, his eyes blue and full of humor. He smiled in response to Moreland's greeting and said, "Haven't seen you around in a while."

"Well, they have me covering a higher class of story now. I get to go to City Hall and functions at the Chicago Club and places like that."

"And I bet you miss it like hell."

"That's right, like hell."

At the front of the room something was happening; a corrections officer was leading the defendant through a door at the right while the lawyer stuffed papers into a folder and a handful of cops milled, grinning. On a bench several rows in front of Moreland, six black people waved at the defendant. "We love you, LeVon," a woman called. The defendant cast a single bewildered glance behind before he disappeared through the doorway.

The old man turned to Moreland in the lull between cases. "Well, son, all I can say is, you're missing the best show in town down here. Pathos, rage, deliverance, and damnation, you'll see it all."

"It's an education, I'm sure."

The blue eyes crinkled with the smile. "It was, fifty years ago. Now it's just entertainment."

A gavel sounded and the hum began to die. A fresh cast of characters was shuffling onstage at the front of the courtroom. Moreland leaned closer and said, "Counselor, can I interrupt your entertainment to pick your brains for a few minutes?"

"If it's not as painful as it sounds."

"I'll be gentle."

"Sure. There's a young firebrand of a lawyer I wanted to see here, but I don't think he's up for a while." The old man unfolded himself from the bench with careful agility and they made for the door.

Out in the echoing hallway they stood face to face near a wall as dazed and rudderless people drifted past. The old man stood with his arms folded, head slightly forward and slightly turned, as if favoring a good ear. He was a tall man and Moreland felt mysteriously much younger looking up at him.

"I wanted to tap that memory of yours again. I was hoping you might recall something about a case back in 1978."

"Well, that depends on whether it had anything particularly memorable to snag it in this memory of mine."

"It had its remarkable aspects. I looked it up in our files back at the paper, but there wasn't a whole lot of comment on it at the time. I was hoping you could tell me more. Do you remember the Pete Clay case?"

Moreland had expected a certain amount of squinting and head scratching; instead the old man nodded immediately and said, "Oh, yes. Pete Clay." He smiled a quick taut smile. "I remember that one."

"He was a Teamster official accused of murder, right?"

"That's right. He supposedly shot a gentleman named Joey Stubbs in the parking lot of a restaurant in Cicero."

"In the parking lot of a restaurant?"

"That's right. Shot through the head."

"Huh." Moreland blinked at him and went on. "As I understand it the main prosecution witness lost his memory on the stand and the guy walked. Apparently there was a good deal of speculation that it was wired but nothing proved."

"That's about what happened."

"Tell me about the witness."

"Well, he seemed like a pretty good one. A young kid who had just parked his own car saw a man climbing out of Joey Stubbs's car and striding rapidly away. The kid noticed a second man in the driver's seat of the car, slumped over, saw he had been shot, and called the police. The police asked a few questions and found out Stubbs had quarreled with Pete Clay inside the restaurant. Over a young lady, it was said. So they pulled in Pete Clay. The witness identified him without hesitation and it went to trial."

"Open and shut, huh?"

"A strong case, let's say."

"And what happened?"

"The young man got on the stand and presto, he wasn't sure of anything. The light was bad, he was too far away, he could have been mistaken, yes, he had identified Pete Clay but he had slept on it and changed his mind—you know how it goes."

"Yeah."

"So the case was dismissed. Pete Clay went back to work and

the young man went back to whatever he had been doing and Joey Stubbs, since he didn't have any particularly powerful friends, just got buried."

"And nobody raised a stink?"

"Well, of course, there was a certain amount of stink raised, you could say, but what could anybody do? The case rested on the testimony of the witness, who was adamant. Of course everyone assumed that they had gotten to him, with threats or with money or with both. Carrot and stick, you see."

"Yeah."

"Always an effective combination. As I recall the young man refused to talk to the papers and it all faded out of the public view fairly rapidly. Things do down here, you know. There's so much that's new every day."

"I'm sure. Do you by any chance recall the witness's name?"

"No, but it wouldn't help you if I did, I'm afraid."

"Why not?"

"Because I do recall hearing about his death in a traffic accident about six months after the trial. That caused a few murmurs around the building, but nothing more."

Moreland nodded slowly. "I see. What happened to Pete Clay?"

The old man's eyes twinkled a little, as if he were preparing to recite a joke. "Pete Clay went the way of all flesh in about 1982 or so. Somebody waited for him in his driveway one morning and discharged a shotgun in his face. That one they got a conviction on."

Moreland grinned perfunctorily, appreciating the joke. "I understand Wilson Throop was an Assistant State's Attorney back in '78 and worked on the Clay case."

The old man nodded once, slowly. "He was. I remember hearing about him. I had just left the State's Attorney's office, but I still kept in pretty close touch. He was one of their young hard-charging types."

"Do you remember hearing anything about him in connection with the Clay case?"

There was a suggestion of caution in the old man's bearing suddenly. He drew back the long horse's face and his eyes went away down the hall. After a moment he said, "I recall hearing that our Mr. Throop took it pretty hard when the witness went stupid. You see, he had been assigned to baby-sit him."

"Baby-sit him?"

"You know, prepare him, watch over him. The State's Attorney likes to take care of his star witnesses. Some kind of attempt on the witness was not totally unexpected, of course. The prosecutors have been around the block a couple of times, after all. When it seemed like it had happened in spite of all their best efforts, I think young Throop was a little upset. But I didn't hear of anyone trying to blame him for it. They were up against a tough smart crowd in that Teamster bunch."

Moreland listened to the shuffle and murmur around him in the hall, thinking. Deep in his guts something ran cold. "Did you ever hear of a man named Michael Papini?" he said.

"Michael Papini," the old man enunciated. "The one they called Pappy?"

"That's the guy. You know him?"

"I know who he is, or was. He was another one of that Teamster crowd."

"That old Teamster gang of mine. What do you know about him?"

"I know he's in jail. Or maybe he's out now, I'm not sure. That all happened up at the Federal Building. Not my turf. But they finally put him away. He was muscle, just a tough guy. They don't have as much use for guys like him any more."

"What about a man named Gerald Oyler?"

"The name rings a bell. I think maybe he was one of them, too. But I don't know much about him."

"Was either Papini or Oyler involved in that Pete Clay thing?"

The old man frowned. "Could have been. That was the type of thing guys like Papini did for them, allegedly anyway. But as I said, nobody ever was able to say who did what in that case. That was one they just had to write off. Another story to swap over drinks when the crowd thins out at the bar."

Moreland nodded and looked distracted for a few seconds, and then reached for the old man's hand. "Thanks, Counselor. One more thing. You ever hear of a lady named Elizabeth Leland?"

The old lawyer held his head to one side, as if listening for a distant sound. "No, I don't believe so. Why?"

"Just a hunch. I appreciate your time. I might want to check back with you on this, OK?"

"You know where to find me." Moreland was starting to move

away, but the old man stopped him with a finger on the arm. "You want to hear something funny?"

"Sure."

"You're not the first guy who's come around recently asking about Wilson Throop's tenure in the State's Attorney's office."

"No kidding."

"Nope. An old friend I have over there was telling me the other day somebody else was interested in the same thing."

Moreland stared for a moment and said, "Was it a guy named Arlo Spivak?"

"I believe that was the name," the old man said gravely. "But that's not all that's interesting."

"What else?"

"Another guy came around asking about Spivak after that. He seemed kind of concerned about Spivak, my friend said."

Moreland waited and then said, "Was it somebody I should know?"

The old man stuck out his lower lip, considering. "Maybe. It was a guy named Pegleg Haynes."

■ ■ ■

The employment counselor was a trim, smart, sharp-looking woman in her middle thirties in a long black skirt and a gray jacket, with the kind of haircut Oxbridge undergrads of the thirties used to sport. "This is a very interesting resumé," she said.

Cooper shifted on the chair opposite her, shamefaced, feeling like the lonely man at his first singles mixer, defeated and desperate. "That's a very kind word for it," he said.

Her smile was brief but not unkind. "You've done a good many things in your time."

"I've quit a lot of jobs, yeah."

He could see her framing the question tactfully. "Why is that, would you say? Why so little staying power?"

Cooper considered honestly, staring out the window behind her into the pale gray sky. "Partly a low tolerance for authority. Partly a low threshold of boredom. And partly a fear that if I sat still for too long something might catch up with me."

"Anything in particular?" she asked with a faint look of alarm.

"The same thing that worried Satchel Paige, I guess." He smiled but the allusion had gone over her head. She looked down at the paper again.

"And yet you've driven a taxi for almost ten years now."

"Yeah, I've been pretty happy at it."

"So why change now?"

"I don't want to get shot."

"I see." The employment counselor ran the eraser end of a pencil down the margin of the resumé. "You do have some skills, it would appear. You were in the food business for a while, you did some sales work. And you do have that degree."

"I'm not quite sure what it certifies. Except that I can read and write."

She smiled. "That gives you a leg up on a lot of people I see in here," she said. "What about your military experience here? What kinds of skills did you acquire in the Army?"

"Mostly how to shoot people." She looked up to see if he was joking. Cooper said blandly, "How to handle a variety of small arms and explosive devices. How to lay out an ambush, mark a landing zone with smoke grenades, dig holes in the ground, sleep sitting up in a rainstorm. Things like that. Skills that are really in demand in today's high-tech job market."

She smiled again, warily. "No electronics, no computer skills, nothing like that?"

"I did use the radio once, to call in a medevac after the RTO got shot."

She nodded slowly. "I see."

Cooper laughed softly. "I'm the toughest case you'll ever see. You find me a job, they'll put you in the career counselors' hall of fame."

"I'll tell you what you should do," she said, straight-faced.

"What's that?"

"You could always hang out a shingle as a career counselor."

■ ■ ■

"What do you know about a guy named Pegleg Haynes?" Moreland said, leaning so close into Charlie Duncan's face that the man recoiled.

"Watch the suit." Duncan looked down at Moreland's hand wrapped around his arm.

Moreland released his grip. "I'm in a rush, Charlie. Tell me about Pegleg Haynes."

Moreland had collared the police reporter in the lobby at Eleventh and State, near the wall displaying the stars of dead Chicago cops. "What about him?" said Duncan.

184 · SAM REAVES

"Who is he? I know he used to be a cop and that's about all I know. My informant says he doesn't think he's still with the department."

"Hasn't been for three or four years. What the hell's all this about?"

"I don't know. His name came up in connection with a trail I'm following. Tell me about him and I might figure out what it's all about."

"Where do I start? He was a cop."

"Why do they call him Pegleg?"

Duncan smiled, fishing a cigarette out of a pack. "They don't. Not to his face. To his face they call him Mr. Haynes, mostly. But everyone knows the nickname."

"Why Pegleg?"

"Because of the leg." Duncan shrugged and lit the cigarette with a cheap plastic lighter. "He left part of his right leg in Vietnam."

"And he got on the police department?"

"By special dispensation. He had friends downtown, he had a chestful of medals, they needed black officers and he was an incredible specimen even on an artificial leg. They let it pass. He limped a little, but he could still spread-eagle you and get the cuffs on you before you could say uncle. There's a whole Pegleg Haynes legend in the department."

"What'd he do, retire?"

Duncan blew smoke and looked out across the lobby, eyes narrowed. "No. He resigned and threatened to file a discrimination suit against the department. He claimed he'd been passed over for lieutenant unfairly. Down here most people agreed it was more likely because of the occasional lapses in judgment."

"Oh? Such as?"

"Such as beating a dope dealer nearly to death out on the West Side. Or shooting a pimp in the head in circumstances where it was not real clear at first whether the pimp had a gun, too."

"At first."

Duncan shrugged again. "The investigation determined he had. I'll tell you, stuff like that never hurt Haynes in those neighborhoods. The man was a hero to a lot of people. I saw him once at a murder scene out on West Jackson. He was practically signing autographs. It's too damn bad things went sour for him around here. A lot of people got upset about that."

Moreland took a deep breath. "What's he doing now?"

"Now?" Duncan scratched behind his ear, the cigarette held between two fingers. "Now I think he's working for Mackey Hairston."

■ ■ ■

Cooper poured black steaming coffee into his mug and, because he felt it was late enough in the day and he had been drinking with commendable moderation recently, allowed himself to add a dollop of bourbon from the bottle that sat on top of the refrigerator. It was a reward for his ordeal with the employment counselor, he told himself. He carried the mug through the dining room, up the long hallway and into the living room, which was growing dim and gloomy as the light died outside.

He set the mug on the coffee table, remembered Diana's scoldings and found a newspaper to put under it, and sat on the sofa. He reached for the switch on the lamp beside him but paused, looking out the front window at the translucent western sky. He sat in the shadows for a moment, wondering where the sudden melancholy had come from. He had his coffee and bourbon and a fresh copy of *The Economist* to work through. He had the house to himself, a steak and all the other makings of a good bachelor dinner in the refrigerator, and a pool date at Burk's with Emilio at nine. It was just like the old days.

Except for two things, he thought. One, you haven't done a lick of work in weeks. Two, you don't really have the house to yourself and you never really will again.

For a moment Cooper wanted the old days again, badly. Stickups and lonely evenings and all. When that mood passed Cooper sat looking at himself, a middle-aged failure drinking secretly in a dark room, with just enough education to deceive himself, not enough ambition to get more, and no idea what to do with himself.

Diana rescued him again, the thought of her faith in him and her reviving influence, and he switched on the light. He took a drink of spiked coffee, toasted the cheerful room decorated with Diana's quiet touch, and stiffened his resolve. The employment lady was going to come through for him, anyway. Soon. He set down the mug and reached for the magazine.

When the lights went out he was absorbed in the economic perils of Tajikistan. He sat in the dark for a moment, startled, looked out the window to see night fallen, and tossed the magazine aside. He could see lights on across the street; it was not a general outage.

He stood up and felt his way down the dark hall. He flicked the dining room switch uselessly, walked slowly through to the kitchen, and looked out the back window. Across the alley lights shone as well.

Circuit breakers, Cooper thought. Somebody stuck one plug too many in an outlet and blew the building. The whole building? No. Each apartment had its own circuits. Somebody was installing an appliance and had thrown the wrong switch, blacking him out instead of the intended apartment.

Whatever it was, he would have to go down and look. Cooper found the basement key by feel on the nail in the pantry where he and Diana kept it. He didn't bother with a coat since it was a quick trip down three flights of stairs. A flaw in their household planning became evident; there was no flashlight in the apartment. Cooper's car was a block away and he didn't feel like going after the one he kept there. He would hope the lights in the basement worked.

He stepped out onto the porch, locked his door behind him, and descended. The wind whipped his breath away into the night. The light bulbs on every landing were shining feebly as always. His downstairs neighbors' lights were on, too, he noticed.

He came down into the yard at the rear of the building. The basement door was at the foot of the stairs in a well sunk four feet into the ground. Cooper stepped down into it; it was very dark under the stairs. He raised his eyes, straining to see the light bulb over the door; as he stepped closer he could see it was intact but not burning. Cooper raised his hand to the bulb. It was warm to the touch. Cooper hesitated, suddenly wary, then gave it two quick clockwise turns and the light came on.

Cooper looked at the basement door. The frame was splintered where someone had driven a chisel or a crowbar into it at the level of the bolt. Where the latchplate had been there was a jagged gap in the wood. The door was very slightly open, the room beyond it dark.

Cooper wanted to believe it was kids, looking for washing machines to jimmy open for quarters. He had heard nothing, but there was no telling when the entry had been made. The warm light bulb bothered him, though.

He listened, growing cold. Nothing stirred in the dark basement just beyond the door. He heard cars go by; he heard music coming faintly from behind closed windows.

This is a door I'm not going through, not even with a flashlight, he thought. He went back up the steps at a trot, let himself into his dark apartment and leaned on the door. He knew he should go to the phone and call somebody, the police maybe, but he didn't want to leave the door. After a moment he said hell with the cold and softly opened the door. He stood inside the screen, shivering in the wind that came through, listening.

He thought he heard a door creak, far below. When the footsteps came they were so soft that he was unsure for a moment that he was not imagining them. Then the sound registered, just audible over the distant hum of traffic and the sighing of the wind: a quiet shuffle and then a padding sound as the other foot went down, a soft asymmetrical step Cooper had heard before.

He stood as the sound went into the gangway and began to fade toward the front, then suddenly was out on the porch and taking the steps as quietly as he could two at a time. He paused at the bottom, hearing nothing, and considered the wisdom of turning up the gangway after that limp. A look, he told himself; get a look.

Cooper stepped quietly to the corner of the building and looked toward the street; there was no silhouette in the gangway. He began to run, no longer trying to be quiet, wanting only a look at the man who walked with that sound. He slipped on a patch of ice and had to put a hand on the rough brick to steady himself; he regained his balance and shot out from the gangway onto the sidewalk.

The block was deserted. Cooper looked north, then south; he scanned the opposite sidewalk and listened for car doors slamming; he ducked to look for dark heads and shoulders in parked cars. He thought of the gangways on either side and knew he was not going down them. Finally he thought that he was making a pretty good target.

Cooper went back down the gangway and down the steps to the basement door. He reached in and felt for the light switch; it worked. He went into the lighted basement and found the circuit breaker board. The two switches for 3S had been thrown; they were the only ones disturbed. Cooper threw them back and hurried up the stairs.

Inside again, the door locked and the lights on, the still-warm bourbon and coffee starting to take away the chill, Cooper wondered briefly if his imagination was at fault.

No, he decided; I heard it. And the circuit breakers were not my imagination. He called the janitor and reported the break-in and then sat by the phone trying to decide what to do. Call the police, call Diana at work, move out, leave town.

A couple of phone calls first, he told himself, and then think. It's time for some serious thinking, at last.

He called the restaurant and left a message for Diana to meet him at Burk's after she got off, instead of going home. Then he gathered overnight things and a change of clothes for himself and Diana and stuffed them into a bag. Finally he put on his jacket and left by the back door, guessing that he'd survived the only attempt that was going to be made that night, hoping he could spot it coming if he was wrong. He took the alley again, this time going north, watching shadows.

He walked all the way to Morse Avenue, slipping through alleys, stopping to watch behind. There was a restaurant on Morse that had a nice quiet phone in back. He dialed Moreland's place, getting no answer. From directory assistance he got a number for a C. Mix at what sounded like the right address and dialed that. When Cleo answered he asked for Moreland and a few seconds later heard the reporter on the line, with a note of surprise in his voice.

"MacLeish. What's shaking?"

"You got a minute to talk?"

"Yeah, I got a minute. What's up?"

"I want to hear about the case. Everything."

There was a silence and then Moreland said, "Well, old buddy, you called the right place. I'm close, Coop. I'm real close. I think I got things kind of figured out."

"Fill me in, Mel. You just might save my life."

■ ■ ■

Diana didn't want anything to drink; she didn't even take off her coat. She stared at him, her face a foot from his, her deep dark eyes growing desolate as he told her about the man with the limp. "I picked up some things for you," he said when he was finished. "I called in a favor and found us a place to stay. Kelly's not living behind the shop any more. He says we can crash there in the loft as long as we need to. I went over and got a key already."

In the soft, warm light from the Christmas bulbs around the mirror, Diana's gaze grew slowly harder. "You're a very hard man to live with," she said.

Cooper had expected the reaction but nonetheless felt things sinking inside, falling a long way. "You're not chained to me," he said, aware of the brutality of the words.

Diana's look was faintly shocked for a moment and then hard again. She said, "All I want to know is how long it's going to be this time."

"As long as it takes to catch him. Mel thinks he knows who it is. In a day or two he'll have enough to take to the cops and they'll reel the bastard in."

Diana nodded, the slightest tilt of the head. She took a deep breath and exhaled. "I'm not made for this kind of thing, Cooper."

"You think I enjoy it?"

"I wonder sometimes," she said, her eyes going far away.

13

COOPER LAY LISTENING TO Diana's breathing; it had only just settled into a deep regular pattern. He was warm and comfortable in the loft, with little night sounds around him: the hiss and clang of radiators, the ticking of a distant clock, at long intervals the muffled passage of a car outside along the narrow street, under the high wall of the El embankment. He could not sleep.

Cooper had lain thinking of all that he had seen and heard and all that Moreland had told him. Some of it made sense to him and some did not. None of it reassured him. Cooper had not liked being marked. If someone had traced him to his home, there were questions to answer that could not wait until morning.

Cooper turned over onto his side, slowly, trying not to wake Diana. He tugged at the blanket, tried to settle himself comfortably, and thought. Two questions, he thought—two questions neither Mel nor I asked tonight; two questions that need answers.

After a time, the ticking of the clock put him to sleep.

■ ■ ■

"Can I go home at all?" Diana emerged from the tiny curtained cubicle in the corner that served as bathroom, gathering her hair to pin it in place.

Cooper looked up from lacing his boots. "That's a tough call. It's me he wants, not you. If he's still watching, he sees you go in, what's he going to think? Is there any reason he'll associate you with me? You could be a neighbor."

"I need my work clothes. I need my books."

Cooper nodded slowly, calculating. "All right, here's what you do. You'll find Boyle over at the coffee house on Sheridan. He's always there in the morning. Tell him what's up, ask him to come with you. You should be all right with him. But don't stay long. And keep your eyes open."

She gave him a bitter thin-lipped look. "What will you be doing while I'm getting an armed escort into my own house?"

Cooper gave his bootlaces a final tug. "I called Moreland while you were still asleep. We're going to have breakfast and figure this damn thing out."

■ ■ ■

Moreland had agreed to meet Cooper at a coffee shop at Irving and Sheridan, not too far from his apartment on the border between dismal Uptown and fashionable Wrigleyville. Cooper took the El because he figured the Valiant was marked and he wanted to be sure his back was clear for a while. Moreland was waiting in a booth by the front window when Cooper came in, sucking on a cup of coffee, one city paper spread out before him and the other at his elbow.

"MacLeish. Still breathing, I see." He set down the coffee cup and shoved the papers aside.

"No thanks to you." Cooper slid into the booth.

"Now that's an unkind remark. Especially for a man taking time out from his busy workday to meet with you."

Cooper just stared at him. "Mel," he said. "There is a man out there in a pale green Buick Skylark who tried to kill me last night. Because of you and your muckraking. Wipe that silly motherfucking grin off your face and check in with the rest of us for a minute.

Remember when I said I didn't think you were scared enough? Well, you're still not. I look at you and I see a man who's having the time of his life while people are dying around him."

The grin had vanished. "Coop, it's just my manner. I know it's serious. I'm trying to put a stop to it, for Christ's sake."

"Maybe you need to find a corpse, see some fresh blood, see that never-never look they have in the eyes. Maybe then you'll be scared."

"Jesus, look, I'm sorry. I'm not trying to make light of it."

"Your cat didn't impress you, fine. The Oyler boys, who needs 'em? The alderman's guy, a name in the paper. OK, this is me now. Your pal, Cooper. Somebody wants to ram that thing up into my brain now. I've got to take it personally."

"Coop, I'm sorry. I'm a jerk. I'm a fucking buffoon. What's the point?"

"The point is, you could be next. Number one."

Moreland nodded, lips compressed. "And number two?"

"Number two, it's time to think clearly."

Moreland's eyebrows lowered. The sun came in through the window and made him look slightly mad, thinning hair standing up from his round pate. "OK. Let's think."

"I mean it's time to start at square one. Clear the slate."

"OK. Clean slate. What are you getting at?"

"Two questions, Mel."

"Shoot."

"Why me?"

"Huh?"

"Why me? Why would the guy come after me?"

Moreland stared until the waitress arrived. For a minute they were distracted with ordering. When the waitress left, Moreland stirred cream and sugar into his refilled coffee and said, "I give up. Why?"

"Think about it. You're the one who's digging up the story. All I did was find the bodies. I'm just playing Tonto to your Lone Ranger. What the hell do I know that poses a danger to anybody?"

Moreland set the spoon down on the saucer and frowned into the light brown liquid. "I'll have to think about that."

"Do that. Question number two."

Moreland looked up. "OK, two. What is it?"

"How did he find me?"

The waitress returned with coffee for Cooper while Moreland drank and stared out the window. Cooper let the fumes from the rank black coffee rise into his face. Moreland looked at him and said, "Damn. That's a good question. I don't know."

"My name never came out in the news. Pappadakis only knew about me because she talked to the cops. I suppose they could have thrown my name around to a few other people, but I doubt it. How about you? Have you been going around broadcasting my name and address?"

"No." Moreland's brow furrowed as he thought. "Macy knows about you, because I keep him on top of the story. But that's about it. And I don't think he's loose-lipping it all over town, either."

"Then how did this guy Haynes, if it is him, know where to find me?"

"I don't know."

"I do," said Cooper. He watched Moreland's round soft face go through the changes: incomprehension to alarm to suspicion.

"What are you saying, MacLeish?"

Cooper made a production of doctoring his coffee, less for dramatic effect than from a sudden reluctance to proceed. Stirring the coffee, he said, "You tell Cleo all about this?"

Moreland froze, and then his look gradually hardened. "Horseshit," he said after a long pause.

"Well, do you? You keep her up to date every night?"

Moreland's silence answered the question, but Cooper could see him retreating farther and farther behind the narrowed eyes. "Give me a fucking break," he said.

"Mel." Cooper set his spoon down gently. "How come we just happened to be there when the Oylers got killed? The first time, it was a setup. We were supposed to be there. The second time, coincidence. Right? We just happened to be right on the guy's heels. Right?"

Moreland was no longer looking at him; he was looking at something far-off and disturbing. "Sure," he said, without conviction.

Cooper took a sip of coffee. "Who knew we were driving down there?"

Moreland's eyes snapped back. Quietly but crisply he said, "You are out of your god damn Hoosier mind. Are you seriously trying to tell me Cleo's involved?"

"It's a hypothesis. Try and falsify it."

"So how did this happen? Who knows we're together, for one thing? Who would try to get at me through her? Who the fuck is she working for?"

"Well, she gets a paycheck from King Van Houten." The name hung in the air for a few seconds. Back in the kitchen pots clanged and somebody laughed.

Suddenly Moreland relaxed, subsiding perceptibly, exhaling. He smiled. "Well, there you go then, Sherlock. It's all wrong. Van Houten wouldn't be trying to cover up something Throop had done; he'd want it to come out. He loses big if Throop becomes mayor. Throop's got him in his sights."

"Well, Van Houten's buddy Milt Sellers works for Mackey Hairston. Factor that in."

Moreland looked like a suspicious housewife listening to a vacuum cleaner salesman. "No. That's ridiculous."

"OK, pick somebody else. There were a lot of people at that party."

Moreland's expression hardened again. "Wait a second. I think I'm starting to capture your drift. You think it was all bogus from the start. You think somebody sicked her on me. She's been faking it all along."

"I'd hate to think it was true. I'm just looking at the way the chips have fallen."

"My, my. Subtle this morning, aren't we? And vicious, too."

"Mel, you still haven't shown me why it couldn't be Cleo who's telegraphing your moves. And she's the only person who could have, number one, told the killer we were going to see John Oyler and number two, told him who I was."

"What you've shown me is that hearing footsteps has made you paranoid. There's a million ways your name could have gotten to the wrong people. Somebody talked. Macy let it slip or something, and it got picked up by someone who's in with Hairston and Throop."

"There aren't a million ways. We're talking about a fairly limited group of people here. And there sure as hell aren't a million ways the guy could have known when we were heading down to look up John Oyler."

"He was going to hit Oyler anyway. We were just on top of the story, like you said."

"Too much coincidence. For the cops, and for me."

"It's horseshit, MacLeish. You had a close shave and your judgment's been clouded."

"Yours, of course, is crystal clear on this point."

Moreland opened his mouth to say something and thought better of it. He looked hostile for the first time. "You're not going to drive a wedge there, Coop. I know what you think of her, but that doesn't give you the right to try and sabotage us like this."

Patiently, Cooper said, "It's not personal. It's just logic, Mel. Cool off a bit and think about it."

Moreland stabbed a finger across the table at him. "You cool off. Get out of town if you're worried about your hide. Go someplace and go fishing and talk to me in a week or two."

Cooper persevered, grim-faced. "Did you tell Cleo where you're going to be today?"

Moreland drew a deep patient breath and said, "Would you please knock it off?"

"Did you tell her?"

"No. I don't know exactly where I'm going to be today."

"Good. You heading to work now?"

Moreland stared, sullen and immobile. "Yeah, after I drop off some laundry at my place."

"The laundry will keep. Where do you park your car when you go to the paper?"

"In the lot, like everybody else."

"Good security?"

Moreland blinked. "Sure."

"Don't park it there. Leave it somewhere else and take a cab to the office. Don't do anything predictable today. If a guy wants to hit you he has to know where you're going to be."

Moreland looked at Cooper the way a man looks at a senile parent. "MacLeish. It's under control."

"You staying at Cleo's tonight?"

Moreland just looked at him for a beat. "No. I was going to check in at home."

"Cleo's idea or yours?"

"Aw, for Christ's sake."

"Well, which was it? Did she ask for a night to herself?"

"We've been spending a night or two apart every week. We're not married, for Christ's sake."

"But did she suggest tonight?"

Moreland stared at Cooper just keenly enough and just long enough to show he was thinking about it, but he finally said, "I'm not worried about it, Coop. This is bullshit."

"Let's try an experiment."

"What the hell are you talking about?"

"Give me the keys to your place. Don't go home. Stay in a motel tonight."

Moreland blinked, a sullen and irritable look on his face. After a moment he said, "You're nuts."

"OK, I'm nuts. Give me the keys. Try the Holiday Inn. It's cheap."

"What are you going to do?"

"I don't know. Maybe nothing. But you're a damn fool if you go home tonight. Cleo or no Cleo. Think about it."

The food arrived, and they ate in silence, trading occasional distant glances. Finally Moreland washed down a mouthful of corned beef hash and said, "Well, you did it. You wiped that silly motherfucking grin right off my face."

"That's a start," said Cooper. "Do I get the keys?"

Moreland ate for another minute, scowling at the plate, before he set down his fork, fished out his key ring, and detached two keys. He slid them across the table.

"Front *and* back," said Cooper. "I want some flexibility."

Moreland scowled and pulled off a third key. "I'll put money on it. One thousand dollars says Cleo has nothing to do with it."

"Keep the money. You're already betting something you can't afford to lose on her."

"What's that?"

Cooper slipped the keys into his shirt pocket. "Your life."

■ ■ ■

Moreland cooled his heels on a couch in a room that had been decorated by a colorblind person: three walls were white, the wood-work was black, and the rug and the furniture were gray. The dark green rubbery plants were an obvious afterthought. The fourth wall was of glass, and immediately beyond it, so immediate that Moreland had caught his breath upon entering the suite, was the meteorological *magnum opus* that is a Chicago winter sky above the lake. Today the sky went well with the room; on a sunny day it would spoil the harmony.

A plain young woman in a startlingly red dress issued from a passageway and said, "Mr. Stilwell will see you now." Moreland followed her down the passage to a gray door and smiled at her as he edged past her into the office. The man who rose to shake hands with him across the desk was trim, middle-aged, moustachioed, and quite bald. He appeared entirely unperturbed by the fact, which disconcerted Moreland. The man shook his hand perfunctorily and pointed him to a chair. "Sorry to make you wait," he said, smiling.

"That's OK. I got lost in the view," said Moreland.

"It does kind of grab you, doesn't it?" Stilwell sat back down and crossed his legs. He wore a crisp navy blue suit with a muted red tie.

"It's nicer than the view from 26th and California, that's for sure."

"Mm." Stilwell nodded, a bit warily. "I understand you've been talking to old Jack Wister."

"The Counselor, we newspaper types call him."

"I've heard that." A smile came and went quickly. "I'm surprised he's still haunting the courthouse."

"I think he wants to die there. The way old ball fans dream of dying at Wrigley Field."

"Well then, I hope he gets his wish." Stilwell paused and then said briskly, "Just what was it Jack thought I could do for you?"

Moreland shifted on the chair, settling his broad haunches into the upholstery and mustering his thoughts. "He said you worked with him in the State's Attorney's office, lo these many years ago."

"I did."

"He said you worked on the Pete Clay case."

Moreland had seen that wary look before; all reporters knew it. "I did that, too," Stilwell said.

"The Counselor said he thought if anybody could tell me what happened to that case, you could."

The wary look vanished. Moreland thought he could read what replaced it; the new look said: ancient history; can't hurt me. Stilwell smiled. "How they wired it, you mean?"

"Yes. How they wired it. How did they?"

Stilwell shrugged. "The way they always do. They got to the witness."

"Do you remember the witness's name?"

"Sure. Young guy named George Chappas. He practically saw

Clay do it. He knew Clay and there was no doubt whatsoever about the ID."

"He knew Clay?"

"By reputation. This was a neighborhood place, out in Cicero someplace. People knew each other. Pete Clay was a local big shot. A bully and a drunk. With a mean temper."

Moreland nodded. "Would you hazard a guess as to who got to him and how?"

Stilwell shrugged. "A guess? Not much hazarding about it. Pete Clay's friends and associates."

"At the Teamsters."

"Yeah. As for how, it would have been easy. All they had to do was have a little talk with the kid. They dispatched somebody to take him aside and explain the meaning of life to him. He testifies, life gets very hard. He loses his memory, nice things happen. Simple."

"This kind of approach must have been anticipated."

"Sure it was anticipated. It happens all the time."

"Were any measures taken to protect the kid?"

"Like spiriting him away and giving him a new identity? Who has the money? We tried to keep his name out of the papers. But like I say, they all knew each other out there. They knew who they had to reach. We just had to count on his integrity, and most people's integrity can only stand up to so much."

"Was somebody assigned to baby-sit him?"

"Baby-sit him?"

"You know, coach him, warn him against the dangers, that kind of thing?"

"Sure. We had somebody working pretty closely with him."

"Somebody incorruptible?"

Now Stilwell froze, wary again, and his chin rose. "Of course," he said.

Moreland delivered the next question with his gravest look. "Has it ever happened that a State's Attorney has found out about an attempt to get at a witness and been bribed himself, to keep quiet about it?"

"What, just to let things run their course, you mean?"

"Yeah. A totally passive role. Just look the other way."

Stilwell gave him a hard stare. "I won't say it's never happened. But I'll stand up for the State's Attorney's Department any day

We may not have been untouchable, but we were pretty damn clean. It was a good department, still is."

"Was there any hint of that kind of thing in the Pete Clay case?"

Stilwell frowned down at his hands, a deep vertical furrow appearing between his eyebrows. "You have a reason for asking that question, don't you?" he said.

"Sure. But I really don't know the answer. I'm just hoping for an honest one."

Stilwell looked up at him. "OK, here's an honest answer. When something like that happens, people always wonder, just a little. But if somebody's corrupt, it shows after a while. The wondering gets confirmed, one way or another. A guy starts living beyond his salary, whatever. And in this case, nobody went that way. I have absolutely no reason to believe the person you seem to be asking about did anything at all untoward or neglected his duty in any way in that case."

Moreland affected an innocent and bewildered look. "Who do I seem to be asking about?"

Stilwell looked at him, the hard look softening a little. "Knock it off. You've had my honest answer. Any other questions?"

Moreland blinked and looked down at his blank notebook. "I guess not. Thanks for your time."

As Moreland rose from the chair Stilwell said, "I'd be damn careful if I were you."

"About what?"

"About an allegation like that. If you don't have rock-solid proof, I'd advise you to not even whisper it."

Moreland nodded. "You're not the first person who's told me that."

* * *

Boyle looked up from a comic book as Cooper approached his table. There were flecks of steamed milk in the big man's moustache. "Diana's not real happy with you right now," he said.

Cooper sank onto a creaking chair opposite him. "I know. How'd it go?"

Boyle shrugged. "Nobody shot at us. She said to call her at work if there's any more bad news."

"Thanks. What are you doing this evening?"

Boyle set the comic book aside. "Make me an offer."

"I want to get a look at this guy. Want to help?"

"All you want is a look?"

"A look. A confirmed sighting. The man is armed and dangerous. All I'm trying to do is flush him."

Boyle smiled. "Hell, why don't you just stay home tonight? He may come for you again."

"Because I got a hunch it's somebody else's turn. It's a long story. What I want you to do is come watch a place with me."

"Whose place?"

"The reporter's. He won't be there, but I'm hoping the word gets out that he will be."

Boyle frowned and the moustache twitched. "It'll be a mighty cold night to sit and watch."

"We'll take your van. One of us will be in the van, the other inside, where it's warm."

The walrus moustache spread out in a smile. "Inside. Waiting for the guy to come through the window, huh?"

"Waiting for anything. The doorbell, footsteps on the porch, I don't know. I don't know what he'll try this time. But whatever it is, we'll have it covered."

"You hope."

It was Cooper's turn to smile. "With you and me both, what can go wrong?"

Boyle slowly picked up an empty cup and looked into it, seeking the answer. "Nothing, I guess." He set down the cup. "But then that's what Hitler said to Tojo."

14 THE LADY WAS MIDDLE-AGED, short and plump, with skin of a rich brown hue and hair straightened and carefully styled in a demure matronly way. She wore rimless glasses, a royal blue dress, and shoes that went right past sensible on into virtuous. She had a large black patent leather handbag, which she held close to her midsection as she came along the lunch counter, looking uncertainly at the people on the stools.

Watching her come, Moreland remembered what his colleague Ross Delpino had told him about the lady. "She's religious," Delpino had said. "And you can play on that like a fiddle. But she's my very best source over there, and I swear to God if you do anything to blow her, I'll have your nuts."

The lady paused when she saw Moreland, alone at the end of the counter. "Ms. Hopkins?" said Moreland, raising a hand, the stool creaking beneath him as he spun away from the counter. The woman nodded once and stopped in front of him, her eyes narrowing as she inspected him. She had a face composed of soft curves, from the full lips to the broad cheeks to the heavy eyelids that gave her a look of sadness.

"Mr. Moreland?" she said softly.

"That's me." Moreland flashed her a wide smile and slid off the stool. "Are you sure you wouldn't prefer to sit in a booth?"

"No, I'll sit here. I always sit here." Lucretia Hopkins brushed past Moreland with a look of determination, set her purse on the counter, and perched herself on the end stool as if she owned it.

"That's fine by me," said Moreland, sitting next to her. "I appreciate your taking the time to talk to me."

She gave him a sidelong glance while reaching for the menu. "I hope you understand that I could lose my job," she said quietly. "And I can't afford to lose my job." She spoke with precise correct diction, with the phantom *r* and just a shade of a drawl on the accented vowels. To Moreland it made her sound genteel and Southern. "I have three grandchildren I have to support and at my age I'm not going to find another job very easily. You understand that, don't you?"

"I do," said Moreland, with gravity. "I'm aware of the risk you're taking."

"Mr. Delpino promised complete anonymity."

"Absolutely. We protect our sources. You can put that in the bank."

A waitress came and stood in front of them, brandishing an order pad, and they ordered, Moreland in a distracted flurry and the woman with terse efficiency. "They do their pork chops fairly well here," she said, replacing the menu.

"Well, I'm watching the waistline this week," Moreland said, smiling. He had ordered a salad.

Lucretia Hopkins disconcerted him by actually giving the waistline in question a critical look. Then she said, "I want you to understand another thing."

"OK," said Moreland warily.

"I'm only talking to you because I believe in what's right. I'm not talking to you because I want to bring down Mr. Hairston."

Moreland nodded. "Ross said you were a woman of strong principle."

"I'm not talking to you because I want to do any harm to black people or the way they're represented in this city."

"Of course not."

"Mr. Hairston has been a good leader and for the most part honest. About as honest as the rest of them, anyway. I talked to Mr. Delpino about that shady business last summer because I thought it was wrong, and I was glad to see Mr. Hairston pay the price for it when it came out. But I don't want to see anybody throwing dirt just to be throwing dirt or just to bring down a black man because they think he's got too much power."

Moreland gaped at her. "Ah . . . certainly not. You can . . . you can rely on me. I'll be fair."

"I hope so. Now what did you want to know?"

Moreland took a deep breath. "I wanted to ask about Earl Haynes."

She looked at him, eyes narrowed for three or four seconds, and then she looked straight over the counter at the desserts stacked above the icemaker. "I can't tell you anything about him. I don't work with him."

"But you know who he is."

"Of course I know who he is."

"Do you have any knowledge of what he does for Mr. Hairston, or could you direct me to someone who does?"

The desserts absorbed Lucretia Hopkins's attention for another few seconds, and then she said, "Mr. Hairston and Mr. Haynes don't discuss their business with anyone else."

Moreland drummed his fingers on the counter. "Would you say Mr. Haynes handles security matters for Mr. Hairston?"

"I don't really know what he does." Her tone was growing distant.

"Who would know?"

"Mr. Hairston. But I doubt he'd tell you."

"Why not? Are some of the things Mr. Haynes does illegal?"

"I didn't say that."

"I know you didn't." Moreland looked at the cards he had in

his hand and tried to calculate chances. "What I've heard is that people have been checking up on something that happened while Wilson Throop was in the State's Attorney's office nearly fifteen years ago, and that Mr. Haynes has been trying to make sure it doesn't get out. Would you know anything about that?"

She turned her head enough to look at him. "So it's really Mr. Throop you're after."

"I'm not after anybody," said Moreland with less than total conviction. "I'm just after the truth. I hear reports of shady business, I try to follow them up. What I'm hearing now is that Mr. Hairston is very concerned about something in Wilson Throop's past and that Mr. Haynes is in charge of bottling it up. If that's false, OK, set me straight. If you've heard something about it, well, it's up to you and your conscience, I guess. You don't have to tell me a thing. Although if there's anything to it, it might be better if it came out now instead of later, when the mayoral campaign is really underway." Moreland clasped his hands to keep from drumming on the counter and joined Lucretia Hopkins in her perusal of a pecan pie, an apple pie, and what looked like it might have been lemon meringue. A half minute or so passed.

"They had a meeting the week before last," the lady said finally in her soft careful way. "The three of them. Mr. Hairston, Mr. Throop, and Mr. Haynes, in Mr. Hairston's office. In the middle of the day. It came up very suddenly, like it was an emergency or something. And I don't think Mr. Hairston was very happy with Mr. Throop. That's the impression I got. But I never found out what it was about."

Moreland nodded, his head bobbing slowly up and down for a few seconds. "You've heard no allusions to the meeting since then, no references to what might have been going on?"

Lucretia Hopkins reached out to align the fork more perfectly next to the knife on the napkin at her place, then replaced her hand in her lap. "I haven't heard a thing," she said.

"Would you have any idea what Mr. Haynes was doing two nights ago?"

"Now how would I know something like that?" she said. She was looking down the counter toward the kitchen, as if impatient for her pork chops.

Moreland was drumming on the countertop again, unable to

contain himself. "I guess you wouldn't." He had tentatively opened his mouth to phrase another question when the lady abruptly turned toward him.

"May I ask you something?" she said.

"Sure."

"May I have your word of honor that you will treat Mr. Throop fairly?" The look in the deep brown eyes was utterly earnest over the underlying sadness, and Moreland had a sudden impression that he was looking into the eyes of the last completely guileless adult on the face of the planet.

"Of course," said Moreland. "Oh, absolutely. You have my word of honor."

The deep brown eyes held his as she said, "The Lord hears you when you say things like that, you know."

"I'm sure He does," said Moreland. "I try to keep that in mind."

■ ■ ■

"OK," said Cooper. "You want to kill the guy, how do you do it?"

Boyle sipped coffee from a Styrofoam cup and tossed his head in a shrug. "Depends on how patient I was."

"Pretty patient. But getting less so. I think it's getting urgent for him. He's gotten in here once, but Moreland put up some bars, so he may not be able to do it again."

Boyle exhaled, breath steaming out in the cab of the van. Outside, the street lamps had come on, shining on parked cars in the late afternoon dusk. "Well, then I'd probably do just what we're doing. Sit and watch for the guy."

"And hit him at the door."

"I guess so. What's he got?"

"The first two times, he used an icepick or something like that. The third time, he'd picked up a gun. When he came for me, I think he was planning to try the icepick again. I think if he can get the drop he prefers it 'cause it's quiet."

Boyle nodded, slowly, his short ponytail bobbing in silhouette. "I don't mess with firearms any more. Had enough of that shit."

"Well, that makes two of us. All I want is a confirmed sighting. Race and maybe a license number."

"Race?"

"Moreland's got a suspect. He thinks the guy's black."

"OK. What's he driving?"

"I think he's in a light green Buick Skylark, one of the old ones, late seventies I think."

"Well, he'll have trouble parking that thing along the block. I think we got the last spot."

"So we'll see him cruising. You want first shift up in the apartment?"

"Nah, go ahead. Switch off in an hour?"

"Sounds good. Remember to check the alley every once in a while. The guy seems to like the back door approach."

"Got it. You have any trouble, haul up those shades. I'll come running."

Cooper nodded and slipped out of the van. He slammed the door and eased around the rear, watching. Moreland lived on a quiet side street off Broadway in a section of Uptown that had been partly gentrified; the buildings were mainly three-flats, solid and well-tended. There was an abundance of dark gangways. Cooper was very conscious of them as he crossed the street and went up Moreland's front steps.

He made it upstairs and into Moreland's apartment without incident. There were no lights on. Cooper stood with his back against the door and listened. He heard the slow drip of a leaking faucet and a distant rumble of footsteps in an apartment above. A faint odor of cat excrement still hung in the air.

Cooper moved cautiously into the living room and made for the front windows; the last of the light outside was going. He lowered the shades. The code to Boyle was one shade up for call me, let's talk; two up was come running. When the shades were down he found a lamp and turned it on.

Cooper recognized the style. His own apartment, pre-Diana, had had the same mixture of worn mismatched furniture, abandoned garments, and scattered reading matter. There was a television but it was not prominent; there were a few books but many more magazines, spilling from shelves, chairs, end tables. On the walls was a grab bag of posters and prints: Magritte's train coming out of the fireplace, a garish movie poster advertising *Jason and the Argonauts,* an original oil seascape in a clumsy, overbright style.

Cooper moved softly into the hall and made his way to the kitchen, turning on lights. In the kitchen he inspected the back door, seeing the lock intact and the freshly installed burglar bars set solidly into the door and window frames. He went into the pantry and selected a cast-iron frying pan from Moreland's sparse complement of utensils. Carrying it with him, he found the bedroom, with its unmade double bed, chest of drawers painted green, and closet with dirty laundry.

The bathroom was reasonably clean, and nobody was lurking behind the shower curtain. The small second bedroom that Moreland used as a study was cluttered with books and contained a word processor that was covered with a light coating of dust. The closet held coats, boots, old magazines, an ancient baseball glove.

Cooper returned to the living room, nerves easing a bit. He laid the frying pan on an end table and sank onto the couch. It was not even six o'clock.

■ ■ ■

Moreland sat at the end of the bar and tried to pace himself. He picked up the glass, brought it to his lips, set it down without drinking. He looked again at the pay phone in the corridor to the restroom. She'll be home by now, he thought. He stared into his glass, rehearsed approaches, questions, reproaches. It's horseshit, he thought again.

To distract himself he pulled the notebook out of the breast pocket of his jacket and flipped through pages slowly, going over it all again, wondering if there was anything more he ought to do this evening, his frown deepening with the doubts but fading again as he reconsidered, feeling he had to be right. One page held his attention. On it was written the name Elizabeth Leland and below it a tangle of other words: names of other queens of England, anagrams of Leland. Andell, Mary Andell. Victoria Landel. Most of the names were crossed out. Moreland scowled and flipped the notebook shut and replaced it in his pocket. He looked out the door of the bar at the creep of traffic in the slush-clogged street; night had fallen.

Somewhere out there in the city, he thought, echoing MacLeish, a man is trying to kill me. The thought gave him a momentary unpleasantness in the entrails, but nothing more. Moreland was no longer scared.

"I'm smack in the middle of it, he thought, and I'm not scared any more. I'm through being scared. He drained his drink, made up his mind, and looked at the phone again. A woman in a bright green dress and Reeboks was talking into it. Moreland scowled and ordered another drink.

▪ ▪ ▪

When the phone rang Cooper figured it was Boyle asking for a shift change; it had been an hour and Boyle had to be even more bored in the van than he was up here, not to mention cold. "Yeah," he said into the receiver.

"Comfortable?" said Boyle.

"You bet. Guess what I found in his refrigerator."

"Whatever it is, kill it quick. Your Skylark just pulled over at the end of the block."

Cooper's feet hit the floor with a thump. "I'll be right down. What's he doing, just sitting there?"

"So far. I didn't even try and see, I just got out when I saw him in the mirror and came up to the liquor store to call. Look, if you want, just sit tight and I'll mosey on down and ask him for a light or something."

"No. I want to see the son of a bitch if I can. Which end?"

"East. Go out the back and come around behind him to get the number. I'll walk down and keep his attention to the front."

"Hey, don't take any chances."

"Don't worry. I'll ask him for the time or something. What's he going to do?"

"I don't know, but be ready. Give me one minute."

Cooper fumbled a bit with the back door lock. His heart was pounding. The cold had deepened since nightfall, but Cooper was too intent to notice; he pulled the watch cap down over his ears and headed down the steps at a trot. The footing in the alley was treacherous; it was potholed and cracked and ice had frozen in hard jagged ridges. When he got to the end Cooper slowed; he didn't want to attract attention by hurrying and he wasn't going to walk into anything he hadn't scouted.

He saw the Skylark immediately when he rounded the corner. It had pulled over next to a hydrant, the only spot left on the block. The long boxy shape was unmistakable; the color was indistinguishable but pale under the sodium vapor lamps. Cooper could see a dark hooded figure behind the wheel. He ran cold inside for a moment, certain.

A car passed in the street between him and the Skylark, going up the block toward the lights of Broadway. Cooper looked up toward the yellow illuminated sign above the liquor store, looking for Boyle on the sidewalk but not finding him. He paused, not wanting to press it. He moved closer to the corner of the building, into the shadows. He looked for Boyle again; now he thought he could see him, under the yellow sign.

The engine of the Skylark roared, and the lights came on. Cooper watched as the big machine rocked out of the parking place and started to roll. Its tires spun on the ice and then caught, and it was heading up the block. After an initial burst of speed it slowed and crept at a steady ten miles an hour, red tail lights growing smaller. Cooper had come out of the shadows, wondering. He looked up toward Broadway and at the end of the block, in front of the liquor store, saw tail lights and white reverse lights going into a parking place.

And suddenly the penny dropped; he knew that car that had come past. Cooper was running now, in the middle of the street, cursing desperately and seeing it all unfold; the Skylark would be even with the little brown Toyota by the time it finished parking. "Boyle!" he shouted.

The Skylark had slowed to a crawl; the Toyota was in the parking space in front of the liquor store and Boyle was coming fast down the sidewalk. "The Toyota!" shouted Cooper.

Boyle halted, spinning around; the tail lights on the Toyota died and Cooper knew it was too late. The Skylark was in perfect position, fifty feet behind the Toyota and creeping, ready to nail Moreland when he stepped out of the car.

Cooper ran, legs heavy and breath short and too, too far away. He was no longer looking for Boyle; he was watching the Skylark close with Moreland, the door on the Toyota opening now, and saving his breath for a last-chance shout.

The brake lights on the Skylark went on; Cooper could see Moreland's round head coming out of the Toyota. He drew breath for the shout but it never came out, because just then Boyle flew into the street like a bull coming out of the chute and jumped onto the back of the Skylark. Cooper heard him roar, saw the Skylark bounce on its springs as the big man sprawled against the back window and scrambled for footing, saw Moreland rigid with surprise watching the spectacle in front of him, saw Boyle leap to the top of the Skylark and stomp with both feet, screaming like a madman.

Then it was tires screaming, and Boyle was flying, suspended for an instant in midair, weightless, tumbling slowly through the lamplight toward the unforgiving pavement, arms and legs flying. He hit the street with a sound like a solid right to the gut.

Cooper covered the last twenty feet as the Skylark squealed around the corner, heading north on Broadway. "Jesus, Boyle." Boyle rolled onto his back, eyes screwed tight, hands flopping to the pavement.

"Shit," he said through clenched teeth.

Cooper grabbed one of the hands. "Talk to me," he said.

"Collarbone," said Boyle.

"Easy. Can you stand up?"

"Give me a fucking minute, will you?" said Boyle, and Cooper knew he was going to be all right. He looked up at Moreland, who was still standing in the open door of the Toyota, looking like a gaffed fish.

Cooper let go of Boyle's hand and stalked the six feet to the Toyota. He grabbed Moreland by the front of his Michelin Man coat. "What the *fuck* are you *doing* here?" Cooper blew out all the anxiety with the shout as he shoved Moreland back against his car. Moreland's face was blank for a moment and then as he regained his balance it hardened.

"I fucking live here," he said. He put a hand to Cooper's chest and shoved back.

"You damn near died here," said Cooper. He shot a look toward the corner where the Skylark had disappeared.

"Who the hell is this guy?" said Moreland.

"This guy just saved your life, asshole. Help me get him back to the van."

Boyle was trying to rise; Cooper hauled him to his feet and pulled him toward the sidewalk, Moreland trailing behind after locking his car. People had appeared at the door of the liquor store, watching. "I can walk," said Boyle, pulling free of Cooper. He lurched down the sidewalk with his left arm pressed to his side.

"Got a hospital preference?" said Cooper. "There's a couple of them right around here."

"Let's just clear the fuck out of here before he gets back around the block." Boyle began to jog, wincing, holding his arm to his side with the good hand. Cooper kept pace.

Moreland pulled abreast and said, "OK, I'm catching on. Look, I was gonna call from the liquor store to see what was up."

"Why didn't you do what I told you?" said Cooper. "I told you to stay the hell away."

" 'Cause I'm tired of being kept out of things." Moreland's voice rose.

"Don't worry, Mel. You're in 'em. You're in neck deep. The only reason you're still alive is that God protects the stupid."

They reached the van and Cooper took the keys Boyle hauled painfully out of a pocket. He got Boyle inside, in the back, and motioned Moreland into the passenger seat. "Get in."

Moreland stood fast. "Hey, fuck you, MacLeish. I don't need abuse from you."

Cooper wheeled to face him. "You going to go sit up there and wait for him to come back? Lead him around in your car a while longer? Get your ass in." Cooper went on around and hopped in the driver's seat, casting a quick anxious glance behind for the wide headlights of the Skylark. By the time he had the engine started, Moreland was climbing in. As soon as the door was shut Cooper wheeled out of the parking space and tore up the block.

Moreland stared grimly ahead. Cooper could feel the steam building. He wheeled the van out onto Broadway, going south. Beside him Moreland pounded the dash, hard. "If I'm so damn stupid, why is this maniac after me in the first place?" He was shouting. "I've put this story together from scratch."

Cooper steered smoothly, watching the mirrors. "OK, I take back the stupid part. But about people trying to kill you you're a babe in the woods. That's why I told you to keep clear."

For a moment there was heavy breathing all around. Cooper made a left on Irving. "How you doing back there, Boyle?" he said.

"Nurses. I want blond nurses in crisply starched white uniforms," came the voice from the darkness.

Cooper laughed, reaction setting in. "You'll be lucky to get an overworked resident who hasn't slept in forty-eight hours." He eased to a stop at a red light.

"So who the hell was that in that car?" said Moreland, sounding merely terse now.

"You saw him, I didn't," said Cooper.

"I didn't see him. I was watching your friend here." After a moment and an exasperated sigh Moreland twisted to speak to Boyle in the back. "I guess I owe you a word of thanks, pal."

"Hey," said Boyle from the darkness, his voice fading. "My pleasure. Any time."

■ ■ ■

"Convinced?" said Cooper, standing close to Moreland, his voice low. They stood in a chilly foyer looking out into a parking lot. Through glass doors behind them were the tedium and misery of a brightly lit big-city emergency room on a moderately busy night.

"Convinced of what?" said Moreland. "That somebody wants to kill me? OK, I'm convinced. That it has anything to do with Cleo? Not by a long shot. The guy already knew where I lived."

"And he's been mounting a continual watch on the place, huh? Just waiting for you to come home? When he's not killing other people, I mean."

Moreland's lips were set tight. "That makes more sense than your hypothesis."

Cooper stared, shook his head. "OK. When are you going to the police with this?"

Moreland folded his arms. "When I have proof. There's no proof. I'm even starting to think I might be on the wrong track entirely. There's one big missing piece. The woman, Elizabeth Leland. The woman on the tape has to have something to do with Throop and the Pete Clay case, but there's no woman in the Pete Clay case. We've got a *cherchez la femme* situation and no *femme* in sight."

Cooper looked at his friend's profile and shook his head. "You still haven't figured that out, huh?"

15 THE WIND HAD DIED and the temperature had crept to within hailing distance of freezing. From the end of the pier Cooper could just see the distant downtown skyline, ghostly under the heavy sky. Out past the blocks of ice that choked the shore, the water was a sheet of iron. Cooper stood rigid in the cold, the watch cap pulled low over his ears. He was determined to stand at the end of the pier until he knew the answer.

He was right about Cleo, had to be. He knew how; he still didn't know why.

Figure out why, he thought, and you'll know who.

His eye came back up the shoreline past distant harbors and colorless stretches of park and files of high-rise condos. He scanned the park, looking for hostiles. The snow on the beach was still nearly virgin; few people shared Cooper's taste for a solitary ramble. He was not the first to hike out to the end of the pier, however; several sets of feet had trampled the drifted snow at the base of the light tower.

Cooper stared at the snow and then turned and looked far out over the cold still waters; after a minute he knew why someone wanted to kill him.

■ ■ ■

Moreland found a message waiting in his mailbox in the newsroom; it said *Call Walter Neumann* followed by a phone number. He sat down without removing his parka and punched out the number. While the phone rang at the other end he frowned at the message, holding it between thumb and forefinger and flicking it back and forth with the third.

Somebody picked up the phone and informed him that he had reached Walter Neumann's office. Moreland gave his name and in a moment he was speaking to the alderman. "I got your message," he said.

"You alone?" said Neumann. "Can you talk?"

"As alone as I ever am in the middle of a big room full of people. Nobody's listening, if that's what you mean."

"All right then, just listen. I presume you're working on the matter we discussed the other day?"

"You presume right."

"Well, I don't know what you've got, but step carefully. My source has done a little work and set off a couple of alarms."

"Whose alarms? The, uh, godfather we mentioned?"

"That's right. Hairston's on alert now. So watch your step."

"Always do. Say, can we meet and talk about this in less constrained circumstances, maybe?"

"No. Just listen. Don't waste your time with Pegleg Haynes."

Moreland's mouth opened and shut a couple of times. "How do you know about Pegleg Haynes?"

"Well, he was the obvious suspect, wasn't he? He's Mackey's ace in the hole. But don't waste your time."

"Why not?"

"Because he's got an alibi. Cast-iron tight. He was at a community meeting in Englewood with Mackey when Arlo got killed. Only about three dozen people can put him there. Whoever did Arlo, it wasn't Pegleg."

"Ah," said Moreland. "I see."

"Of course, that doesn't mean Hairston's not behind it. It just means he's too careful to compromise Pegleg. Look for somebody else."

Moreland leaned forward, resting his forehead on his hand. "I take it this is all gospel?"

"You can put it in the bank."

"That . . . specimen I saw in your office has been working overtime, has he?"

"Don't worry about how I know. I know. You just keep digging."

"Listen," said Moreland, frowning, and then there was a click in his ear.

After he hung up Moreland stared across the room for a minute or two, oblivious to the hum and banter. He was in yesterday's clothing, unshaven and poorly rested after a night at the Days Inn on Lake Shore Drive, and he was starting to think he didn't understand a thing. Not a god damn thing. Finally he regrouped and punched a different number into the phone. After one ring Cleo's voice purred, "Van Houten and Riggs, can you hold, please?"

"It's me, Mel."

There was a pause of only a second and Cleo said, "Please hold."

Moreland waited through an eternity of Muzak and then Cleo was back, speaking in a low voice. "Sorry, baby. Things are kind of hectic here."

"I need to talk to you."

"Sure. What's going on?"

"I mean talk. Can we have lunch?"

Another pause, another long second. "Is everything all right?"

Moreland rubbed his eyes, clenching the phone. "Everything's fine. I just need to talk to you."

"OK, let's have lunch." Cleo sounded careful. "Where?"

"Name a place."

After three or four seconds, she said, "How about that seafood place on Hubbard where we ate last week?"

"Fine. What time they let you out of the cage up there?"

"I can get away as early as eleven-thirty if you want me to."

"Terrific. Don't be late."

"Mel, you don't sound right. Are you like . . . mad at me or something?"

Moreland glared out across the news room, a man struggling with a question he could not answer. After a moment he said, "No, I'm not. Really. I just had a rough night and I need to talk to a friendly face."

"Poor baby," said Cleo.

■ ■ ■

Cooper found Kelly with the entrails of a grandfather clock spread out on his workbench. Kelly looked up and said, "Diana left. She said she'd be working at the library up at Northwestern and she'll go on to work from there. She had what you'd call a frosty demeanor."

"Can't blame her. Can I use the phone?"

"Help yourself."

Cooper looked up the number for Area Six Violent Crimes and punched it in.

■ ■ ■

"But you don't have any proof," said Macy. His eyes were all over the map today.

Moreland closed his eyes briefly, slumped on a chair opposite Macy. "No, I don't have any proof. I thought I already said that."

"You don't really have a thing we can print right now, in fact."

"Not now, no. Except speculation."

"Well, how much longer do I give you before I put a little more experienced bloodhound on this? Vince has been in here asking about it, Charley too. Word's getting around. The Pappadakis woman's dropping hints all over the map, I hear."

"If she had anything more than I do she'd be on TV with it. Look, we know Wilson Throop did something and the proof is on that tape. We don't have the tape because it was probably stolen when John Oyler was killed and then destroyed. We don't have a smoking gun, we don't have anything more than clever deductions. Yet. The thing to concentrate on now is the coverup, the murders. These are outright political killings and that's rare even in Chicago. This is big fuckin' news, Jay."

Macy leaned back in his chair, scanning the ceiling. "I can't print unsupported allegations about somebody like Mackey Hairston."

Moreland was out of his chair with a burst of energy. "God damn it, I know that, Jay. Look, I'm working on it. You want to put Charley on it and send me back to the dogcatcher beat, you're the boss. But you'll have to find me first." Moreland swept out of the office and back to the news room, heading for his desk, expecting a shot in the back. He had just grabbed his parka off the back of his chair when the copy clerk called his name across the room. "Pick up your phone."

Moreland picked it up and heard Cleo's voice.

"Hi, baby. I'm glad I caught you."

"You damn near didn't. What's up?"

"Could you like do me a favor on your way?"

"Sure."

"I've got this like killer headache and I'm out of aspirin. There's no drugstore between me and the restaurant, but I think there's one on the corner right where you go down the stairs to Hubbard, you know?"

"Yeah."

"Could you get me some aspirin or something on your way? I'm like seeing double here."

"Sure thing. See you in a minute."

"Thanks, baby."

Three minutes later Moreland was out in the cold again. It was a quick walk over uncertain footing from the newspaper building to Hubbard, which ran on true ground level below the raised grid of streets that came across the bridges from the Loop. Moreland turned toward the stairs that led down to Hubbard and then swerved, remembering his commission. He went on across the overpass to the drugstore, found a box of Tylenol and paid for it, and headed for the top of a stairway that plunged to the lower level. Moreland reached the top of the steps and stopped, looking down at the street in the shadows below and remembering what Cooper had said. *If a guy wants to hit you, he has to know where you're going to be.*

He stood looking down the steps and remembering what Cleo had told him over the phone. Moreland was suddenly keenly aware that in the normal course of things he would have taken the first staircase, the one on the south side of the street. He stood clutching the rail and directing every muttered curse he could summon at Cooper, for planting that one tiny poisonous seed of doubt. He could see the neon winking in the window of the restaurant, across the street and two hundred feet ahead. He could see cars parked at the curb below him. "Fuck you, MacLeish," he said, just audibly enough to alarm an elderly woman who was passing by. He went down two steps and stopped, replaying the phone conversation with Cleo, hearing Cooper's voice and seeing his eyes, those skeptical eyes.

Suddenly Moreland was sweating, from the rapid walk in the warm parka perhaps. He stood frozen on the steps, waiting for enlightenment. A young man in an expensive overcoat appeared at the bottom of the steps and mounted them. He came slowly up and looked at Moreland, who stared back at him. The man altered course just a little so as to avoid him and averted his eyes. Moreland stood frozen until he had gone past. *He's got to know where you're going to be*, he thought.

Abruptly Moreland turned and skipped back up the steps. He called Cooper the worst name he could think of, because Cooper had won. Moreland knew it was bullshit, but still it bothered him that Cleo had asked him to do something that made him cross the street and go down a different stairway. Moreland thought about what he was doing, what he was conceding by crossing the street, and said "God damn it." A young couple passing gave him a worried look.

He went down the steps on the other side, composing himself. It was a silly precaution but he had taken it; Cleo need never know. He scanned the street, looking across to the foot of the steps he would have come down. There were cars parked there, but he saw no one loitering, nobody watching. Moreland laughed to himself and said softly, "MacLeish, you're a jerk."

There were cars parked on this side as well, and as Moreland skipped off the last step he looked up and saw the light green Buick Skylark, big as a battleship and right in front of him, and remembered something else Cooper had said. He took three steps and stopped, recognition kicking in. Somebody was sitting in the Skylark, on the passenger side, and through the windshield Moreland could see a figure in a hood, looking at him.

Now that's a hell of a coincidence, he thought, watching the window roll down. He was six feet away and could just make out features ringed by the fur on the hood, and when the man said, "Hey, buddy," Moreland went cold all through. He forgot about Cleo and his doubts and everything except Cooper's man in the green Skylark, and as the hand came up Moreland was moving, turning tail. He was walking, not convinced enough to run, heading for the foot of the stairs, but when he looked over his shoulder and saw the muzzle of the gun coming out of the window, he broke into a run. The stairway was not the most intelligent choice but it was there, like Everest, and Moreland started to climb. He had made it up three steps when the bang came and he yelped because something had whacked him on the butt, a hard kick and a burning pain, and he was hauling himself up the steps and yelling "Jesus God," and then tires were squealing below and Moreland was flat on his ample belly on the steps, cheek against the hard steel, hearing the pale green Buick tearing off into the shadows east on Hubbard.

Moreland tried to get up and couldn't. "Oh dear God," he said. "No, no, no, no, no."

▪ ▪ ▪

Cooper sat across the desk from Detective M. Garvey Brown in the big second-floor room at Area Six and organized his thoughts. "It didn't click in until this morning," he said. "When I was looking at the snow, out in the park."

"Just looking at the snow." Brown looked sleepier than ever. Cooper thought perhaps he genuinely was; he never seemed to be off duty.

"At the footprints, actually. And suddenly I remembered More-land telling me that the cops down in Oak Lawn hadn't gotten any footprints because the walk was shoveled. I didn't think about it when he said it, because I hadn't really noticed. But I thought back today, and it wasn't shoveled, not when I walked down it."

Brown made what might have been a grunt. "You sure?"

"Positive. I followed footprints around to the back. Nobody had shoveled. There was less snow in the gangway, because it was sheltered. But at the front and the back there was enough to show prints. I remember seeing them. And then I understood why the killer was coming after me."

"Oh?" Brown was listing very slightly, perhaps about to subside into sleep and plunge off the chair. "Why?"

"Because I can identify him."

"What, from his footprints?"

"No. I've seen him. I looked him right in the eye."

Brown woke up; his eyebrows went up and he looked almost interested. "When was that?"

"About five minutes after he killed John Oyler, I'd estimate. He was coming out of the gangway of the house next door, with a snow shovel he'd swiped. He knew he had to get that walk cleared."

Brown was leaning forward now. "Why?"

"Because there was something distinctive about the trail he'd left in the snow. Something to do with the limp, probably."

Brown smiled, just barely. "Did you see the trail?"

"I must have, but it didn't register. All I can swear to is that the walk wasn't shoveled. I'm wondering if the guy doesn't use a cane or something. That idea could come from some subconscious image I retained of marks in the snow, or maybe I just made it up. I don't know. But I'd swear that was the guy."

"And he knew you saw him."

"He was interested in me. He saw where I'd come from and he had to know I'd work out who he was eventually."

"So give me a description."

"Fifty to sixty years old I'd guess, thick black eyebrows, big nose. Solidly built. Can't say much about the hair because he had his hood up. He's got an intense pair of eyes, I can tell you that. I've been seeing that look he gave me ever since I tumbled to who he was."

"Did you see him move?"

"No, but I had a distinct impression at the time he was using the shovel for support."

Brown nodded. "If it's the guy I'm thinking of, he had both knees broken with a ball peen hammer a few years back. One healed better than the other, they say."

"That would do it. He moves pretty well for an old guy with a bad leg, though. I've heard him make tracks a couple of times."

"He's not that old, really. And he's reputed to be pretty tough."

"I can believe it."

"You know who I'm talking about?"

218 • SAM REAVES

"I think I have a pretty good idea."

"You wouldn't happen to have any idea where he might be, would you?"

Cooper smiled. "I drove my car down here. He just might be sitting right outside."

■ ■ ■

Cooper didn't hear about Moreland until he was back at the shop. Brown had taken him seriously enough to walk him back to his car, then thanked him for coming in and told him to watch his step. Cooper had driven away thankful that Brown hadn't yet thought to ask about how the man with the limp had found him, because he wasn't quite sure about all the rest of it.

When he overheard the report, faintly, on the radio Kelly listened to while he was working up front, Moreland's name jumped out at him. Cooper came hustling out of the back room. "What was that about the reporter?"

Kelly looked up from a tangle of gears. "Huh?"

"The reporter who got shot. I only heard part of it."

Kelly stared blankly at the radio. The announcer was talking about a gas leak on the West Side. "Oh. Somebody shot him, somewhere downtown. He's in the hospital."

"Christ. How bad?"

"Good condition, they said. You know the guy?"

"Yeah. I know him. What hospital, did they say?"

"Northwestern Memorial. I think." Kelly watched as Cooper reached under the counter for the phone book and started flicking pages. "Uh, Cooper. Does this have something to do with why you and Diana are staying here?"

"Everything," said Cooper.

Kelly was still staring. "Are we like, going to have hit men descending on us here?"

"No," said Cooper, running a finger down the columns. "I'm going to find this son of a bitch and kill him myself if I have to."

■ ■ ■

Moreland was in a double room, but the other occupant, if there was one, was hidden behind a drawn curtain. Moreland was lying on his stomach, looking forlorn, like a confused whale on a New England beach. Someone had decorously closed the hospital garment over his backside. He watched as Cooper walked into the room, straining to raise his head. Whatever mix of emotions

Cooper thought he discerned in Moreland's eyes seemed to be dominated by shame. The reporter watched without a word as Cooper walked to the window, looked out for a moment, and sat down in an armchair. "Still breathing, I see," said Cooper.

Moreland let his head sag onto the pillow. "No thanks to you." His eyes closed.

"Tell me about it."

A television was droning in a room somewhere nearby; Cooper sat and listened to a round of commercials before Moreland's eyes opened. "She hasn't come. She hasn't even called," he said.

Cooper shrugged. "Maybe she hasn't heard."

"Maybe. Or maybe you were right about her. I don't understand a god damn thing right now. All I know is my ass hurts."

Cooper let the smile spread into a grin and then rupture into a laugh. He sat shaking, trying to suppress it, managing to keep it fairly quiet. After half a minute or so he wiped tears from the corners of his eyes. Moreland was glaring at him.

"Yeah, it's a fuckin' riot, ain't it?" he said.

Cooper shook his head. "When I called, they said you had come out of surgery. I had visions of you with tubes sticking out, in a coma."

Suddenly Moreland was making hissing noises into his pillow, shaking. He raised his face, screwed tight with pain and hilarity battling, pain losing. He let out a couple of peals of outright laughter and said, "God damn you, MacLeish."

They were already settling down when a nurse stuck an outraged face in the door. Cooper waved at her and she went away. Moreland's face was wet. "Shit," he said. "You're wrong, you son of a bitch. You're all wrong."

"Could be," said Cooper. "Tell me what happened."

Moreland composed himself, wriggling a bit, grimacing. "I've been thinking about it all afternoon. I called her and said let's have lunch. She named the place. But she asked me to pick up some aspirin for her on the way. And that meant I had to cross the street. There's two stairways you can take to get down to Hubbard. Crossing the street meant I'd be more likely to use the one on the north side. But just as I was about to go down, I remembered what you said, and thought about Cleo asking me to cross the street and damn you, you'd made just enough of an impression for me to walk back across the street and take the one

I was going to use, feeling guilty about not trusting Cleo but thinking you just might know what you were talking about. And I walked right into it. Right smack into it. It was like that old story about the guy who goes out of town to get away from the reaper, only the reaper is waiting in the next town over. If I'd done what Cleo said I would have walked by the guy on the other side of the street. So tell me. If Cleo set me up, how come she told me to get the aspirin? Why didn't she let me walk into it?"

Cooper shrugged. "I don't know. How did the guy know you were going to come down those stairs, except through Cleo?"

"Somebody in the office heard me talking to her. Somebody was listening on the phone. That's all I can figure."

"Somebody in the office? Another reporter is in on the cover-up?"

"Or somebody who was tapping the phone. There's powerful people in on this, Coop."

Cooper frowned. "You talked to the cops, I take it?"

"Yeah, Brown was just in here."

"That was fast. What'd you tell him?"

"I didn't tell him about Cleo, if that's what you're hoping. I said I was going to lunch by myself."

"How long are you going to keep lying to him?"

"I'm not telling him what I have until I have the whole story. And I'll tell you another thing. We were wrong about Pegleg Haynes. He's got an alibi. And the guy who shot at me wasn't black."

"I know. He was a white guy about fifty years old, with heavy black eyebrows and a big nose."

Moreland stared for a moment and then his head sagged again, onto the pillow. "God damn it, how do you know these things? How do you always know more than I do?"

"I had a nice long talk with Brown earlier. He's had his suspicions for a while."

"So who the hell is it?"

"Who's the missing player? Who hasn't shown up yet?"

"I can't handle riddles right now. Spell it out."

Cooper shrugged. "The guy who started it all. Michael Papini."

After a moment Moreland said, "I'll be damed. What does Brown know?"

"Not a lot. He got on to Papini the same way your alderman

did. He started asking about Gerald Oyler's friends and bingo, here's one who just got out of jail but nobody can find him. And he fits the description. Papini walks with a cane because somebody in Marion took a hammer to his knees about a week after he checked in there. A message from the people he'd talked about, apparently."

"Christ. Does Brown know about Throop?"

Cooper smiled a thin smile. "No. That's your edge. But the competition's right on your tail. I asked Brown something I've been wondering about—if he knew yet how Vance Oyler got the keys to the garage where he was killed. He just smiled and said I could probably find that out on the Channel Five news before too long."

"Shit. She's going to beat me to it. She's going to wrap the fuckin' story up while I'm in here trying to figure out how to use the bedpan."

"Nobody's going to wrap it up until they get that tape."

"Hell, the tape's long gone by now."

"Maybe not."

Straining to follow Cooper's drift toward the window, Moreland said, "What do you mean? Isn't that why Papini killed John Oyler? To get the tape, destroy it, smother the Throop thing?"

"Smother it, for sure. But destroy the tape? I don't think so. I don't even think John had the Throop tape up there.'

"Why not?"

"What was Vance peddling? If he had the goods, it had to have been something more than a rumor. I think Vance had the tape and Papini took it from him when he killed him. John got killed just because he knew about it. I'd bet John confiscated the rest of the tapes from his mother's house after Vance took the one with Throop on it. That's about as far as I've gotten."

Moreland's neck gave out and he let his head fall with a sigh. "So what the fuck is going on? Cleo's working for Michael Papini? Sort me out here, Cooper."

"You know who Cleo's working for. The gnome up in the tower there."

"And I told you, he's got the opposite motive. He's opposed to Throop, for Christ's sake. Anything he could get his hands on to discredit Throop, he'd have it on the news before sundown."

"Nah, he's smarter than that."

"What do you mean?"

"Come on, Mel. You've been around the block. Van Houten wouldn't get his hands dirty like that. All he wants is an airtight guarantee that Throop treats him right if he gets in."

Moreland lay silent, his eyes closed. "Tell me something," he said finally. "Is everybody smarter than me, or is it just you?"

Cooper turned from the window. "It's just a guess. But I haven't heard any better ones. I didn't tell Brown all of my night thoughts. I kept your secrets, but you have to level with him soon, pal. Your story won't do you any damn good if you're dead."

"All right, I'll talk to him."

Cooper strolled to the hall door, looked out, and came back to the bed. "They going to put a cop outside your door? On the radio it said you're in good condition. I don't think that's how the guy wanted to leave you."

"Brown's moving me. He's sending people to shift me to another hospital. Inside an hour, he said."

"That's good. Security in most hospitals can be summed up in four words. 'None to speak of.' "

"You always find a way to make me feel better, don't you?"

Cooper stood and listened for a moment; the TV was still going and somewhere a young woman laughed. "There's an explanation for what happened today, you know," he said.

"What?"

"Cleo was told to set you up. But she didn't want to do it. So she told you to get the aspirin."

The silence stretched on into minutes after that. Moreland lay still; outside the light was going. Cooper slapped Moreland on the shoulder. "I got things to do. You get your rest. Just whatever you do, don't roll over."

"My mama always said I'd come to a bad end. What are you going to do now?"

"Me?" said Cooper. "Why should I do anything?"

"I don't know. I just know that look on your face. That's not your heading-home-for-a-beer look."

Cooper stood looking down at his friend and after a moment he smiled. "I guess I need to work on my poker face."

16 ON HIS WAY TO THE ELEVATOR Cooper saw a hospital
security man, perhaps placed on the floor by
Brown. He was festooned with cuffs and stick and
all the trappings of police work except for a firearm,
and he was hovering at the nurses' station. He appeared more interested in the nurses than in anybody's security,
and Cooper hoped Moreland would be gone before too long.

He stood with his hands in his pockets waiting for the elevator,
staring at the wall and running over all the reasons he had to go
someplace safe and just wait until he could talk to Brown again.
When the door slid open he stepped into the empty car, turned,
punched the button and saw a man in the hall hurrying to catch
the elevator. He reached to hold open the doors and then regretted
it; it took him a second to place the tall man who hopped in to
join him, but he'd seen him before.

"Mr. MacLeish," said the man, nodding. There was no pretense
at coincidence; Cooper knew immediately the man had been waiting for him to leave Moreland's room. "Rob Riley. We met the
other day."

The doors slid shut. "Not bad," said Cooper. "The worried
relative communing with his coffee at the end of the hall. I saw
you but didn't notice you."

Christine Pappadakis's right hand man smiled. "The trick is not
to hover around any one room, so everybody thinks it's the guy
next door you're there to see."

Cooper nodded. "And to make the coffee last."

"That's right. Christine would like to talk to you."

Cooper scowled at the descending numbers above the door.
"Why doesn't she come to talk to Moreland? He's the one who
got shot."

The quick smile came again. "I guess she doesn't think he'd be
too communicative."

"But I would, huh?"

Riley shrugged. "You're not a rival. You're just a private citizen,
right?"

"Sure. Why should I talk to her?"

"Why shouldn't you? A reporter asks you questions, there's no law says you have to answer, but if you don't we wonder."

Cooper rocked on his heels, looking up into the tall man's face. Information, he thought. It's all about information. The elevator settled gently and the doors opened. "OK," he said. "Take me to your leader."

It was dark outside and with the going of the sun a hard chill had settled onto the city. Cooper agreed to follow Riley to the TV building and they walked to the hospital parking garage together. When Cooper got the Valiant out onto the street he spotted Riley's black Infiniti waiting for him just ahead and flashed his brights. The Infiniti pulled away from the curb. Cooper followed the tail lights, calculating what he ought to say and ought not and why.

The network had built a fancy skyscraper on the river; the network logo shone in color from the top of the neo-deco tower. Cooper was cleared by Riley past a security booth into an underground parking lot and they took an elevator to the fifth floor. The halls were carpeted and quiet. They were buzzed through a glass door that bore the station's call letters and the logo. A security guard nodded at Riley and looked Cooper up and down. Cooper saw no cameras, no monitors, no famous faces. He followed Riley down more hallways to an office where Riley knocked once and pushed the door open.

Christine Pappadakis sat behind a desk that bore a computer terminal, a telephone, a coffee cup, and the aftermath of a hurricane. Papers, disks, stray pens and pencils, directories, almanacs, and more papers had washed up from the storm on the top of the desk. Behind the desk was a window with a view east into the blackness over the lake. Christine Pappadakis leaned back in her chair, smiled, and said, "Well, well. Look what the cat dragged in." She was dressed in purple this evening, a purple jacket with a shawl collar and the inevitable padded shoulders setting off the squarish lines of her hair and features.

"No dragging necessary," said Riley. "The man's here of his own free will."

Pappadakis nodded. "Of course." She pointed him to a chair.

"I'll tell you one thing," said Cooper. "The man's not here out of a desire to be on TV, or to help you scoop the papers."

"OK." Pappadakis leaned an elbow on one arm of her chair,

clicking fingernails on the other. She looked hard, shrewd, and at the moment slightly amused. "Why are you here?"

"Because people are getting killed. And the quicker those of us who have parts of the picture put them all together, the quicker the killing stops."

Pappadakis shot a glance at Riley, who had settled into a chair in a corner behind Cooper. "You mean you tell us what you know, we tell you what we know?"

"Seems to me that would get the job done fastest."

The thin smile widened and then disappeared. "And where does Mr. Moreland come into all this?"

"Mr. Moreland does not come into any of this. He's lucky to be alive tonight and he's on the sidelines for the rest of the game. I don't work for his paper and I don't represent him."

"And whatever you might learn in here stays in here, right?"

"Unless I think the police ought to hear it."

Christine Pappadakis shook her head, a woman who had heard it all. "You're just a public servant, are you?"

Cooper stared her down; cynicism was something he understood but didn't particularly care for. "No," he said. "It's mainly my own ass I'm concerned about. But I'm willing to deal if that's the only way you understand things."

"Oh? And what currency are we dealing in?"

Cooper took his time, sending a long level gaze across the desk, hearing Moreland screaming protests the whole while. Finally he said, "I can tell you who Elizabeth Leland is."

Cooper had seen that look before; the look that transformed Christine Pappadakis's face was the look of the hustler when the mark says sure, the look of the drunk when they open up the bar. "Really," she said.

"Really. But it'll cost you."

Her eyes went to Riley and back to Cooper. "Who else knows?"

"Moreland. His source, who won't be talking. Elizabeth herself. That's about it."

Pappadakis took a breath, her chin rising a few degrees, looking down the long nose at Cooper. "What do you want for it?"

"Everything. Every fucking thing you've got."

"You're not serious."

"The hell I'm not. I don't care who breaks the story first. I'm not going to do it. I'll talk to Brown when I figure out what's going on, nobody else. Like I say, it's my ass I'm worried about. I want everything I need to know to get a killer off my back."

Her eyes went briefly to Riley again, but Cooper could tell that was *pro forma*. The decision was hers, and she was straining to make it. She picked up the gold-plated pen from the desk, examined it for a few seconds, and said in a tightly controlled voice, "What do you want me to tell you?"

"Where's Michael Papini?"

She gave him the compliment of a raised eyebrow. "We don't know. Nobody can find him. He might be dead."

"He's not dead. If you're in tune with Brown, you know that. Don't bullshit me."

She shrugged. "OK, we don't think he'd dead, but he's sure as hell out of sight. And all his old friends are getting tired of being asked about him."

"I believe it. Who's he working for?"

"Your mysterious Elizabeth Leland, I suppose. She's the one who would want the tape squelched, isn't she?"

"You're going to have to come a little cleaner with me. Look, I know you can figure as well as I can. Papini's not working for Elizabeth Leland."

"She told you so, did she?"

"I'm making the kind of educated guesses I'm sure you've made. Papini's the trigger in this, has to be. He gets out of jail and bang, people start dying. That's no coincidence. It's not a simple coverup, with Papini keeping things quiet for some old pal in the Teamsters. Papini has no old pals in the Teamsters at this point."

Pappadakis nodded. "Gold star for you. Keep talking, let's see how you read it."

"OK. The thing broke now because Papini broke it. He needed money, he knew the tape was worth a fortune. He got Vance to get it out of his father's collection for him, then killed Vance when he couldn't keep a secret. John would have kept the secret, but John also figured out who killed his brother, so he had to go."

"Bravo." The condescending look had started to fade. "And so?"

"So what do you do with a secret like that? One, you take it to the papers and destroy someone for political or personal motives. Two, you sell it. Three, you keep it to try to blackmail someone.

Vance tried number one, but Papini talked him out of it before he spilled the beans. So then he wised up and tried number two, and Papini killed him, because he wanted to sell it himself. I don't think Papini would keep it to try the blackmail himself, because that's dangerous. It's better to sell it to someone a lot more powerful than you, who can pull off the blackmail without fearing too much for his own well-being. Then, of course, you only have one thing to worry about. For the secret to have market value, it has to stay a secret. You have to keep it quiet. When aldermen or newspaper reporters start trying to sniff it out, you have to kill them."

"You've been around this town a while, haven't you?" said Pappadakis.

"It's not just this town. They were working deals like this when contracts for the Pyramids went out."

"Yes. So who did Papini sell the secret to?"

"You tell me. That's what I'll trade you the secret for. Elizabeth Leland's real name and what she has to hide for your end of it."

"Well, that may be a fair trade, but I'm afraid you're asking more than I have. I don't know who has the tape, and that's the real story. Without the tape as proof, there really isn't a story, is there?"

"I guess not. But you've been working on this for a while now. You've got to have some ideas."

"Ideas, sure. Facts, not too many. We've run all of Gerald Oyler's old friends to earth, the ones who are still alive, and none of them knew he was making tapes of all his deals. What they do say is that Papini might have known, because he was Gerald's right-hand man. Rob even flew down to Florida the other day to talk to his widow. She's still in shock and all she would say was that Gerald never told her anything about business. Nobody's heard of Elizabeth Leland."

"OK, let's try a different tack. Who had keys to the garage where Vance Oyler was killed?"

The glance at Riley meant something this time. Cooper's heart thumped a little faster. Pappadakis looked back at him, impassive, and said, "Yes, that would seem to be important, wouldn't it?"

"Yeah, it's important. And you're going to tell me if you want what I've got. Who had keys?"

Pappadakis subsided, just perceptibly, into her chair. She smiled. "You should be in my line of work."

"I should be at home with a good book. Now who had the keys?"

Pappadakis looked at Riley again, the smile fading, then back at Cooper. "The car thieves, of course, but their security was tighter than the CIA's. They had one set and it never left the head guy's pocket. I think we can believe him on that, because if he'd lent them out or something, he'd know who to suspect of selling him out, and he'd tell us."

"Maybe. That leaves the Streets and San guy, then."

"Fisher, yes. I finally had a talk with him yesterday, with a very nervous lawyer listening in. Fisher told Brown the same thing the thieves did, that he had no idea who could have gotten the keys or how, but he told me yesterday he's had time to think it all over and there are a few people who could have gotten access to the keys and made copies. He's not a professional criminal and his security was more like a congressional committee's. This is a very remorseful man we're talking about. I think he's going to have a good cry in front of the judge and they won't be too hard on him."

"Anyway."

"So anyway. He's narrowed it down to three people. Three people who were enemies he'd made in the course of a couple of decades in city employ, and who had access or could have gained access through allies. He gave us three names."

"And they are?"

"My Lord, you're relentless."

"Only when people are trying to kill me. The envelope, please."

"I believe you're enjoying this," said Pappadakis with a grudging smile. "All right, the names are Lowell Montgomery, Chester O'Donnell, and Stanley Dybzinski. Mean anything to you?"

Cooper looked out the window into the night and exhaled. He opened his mouth to ask another question, then shut it again. "None of them rings a bell," he said. "But I'll keep my ears open."

He could tell she didn't believe him, but he watched her run through options and decide not to press it. "OK, your turn," she said. "Drum roll, edge of the seat. Who in the hell is Elizabeth Leland?"

Cooper rose slowly from his chair, trying to suppress a smile. Pappadakis watched him with a look growing slowly murderous. Cooper stood in front of the desk and said, "You've got to have a street map around here somewhere, right?"

"A streep map."

"That's right. That's what the code is."

"What?"

"Street names. That's what I heard when I heard Elizabeth Leland. I'm a taxi driver. I know lots of streets."

She shot a panicked look at Riley. "Where's that map?"

"Here's what you do," said Cooper. "You find Leland Avenue up on the North Side, and you go a block south. Then you find Elizabeth Street down on the South Side, and trace a block west. And it'll all be clear."

"Wait," she said, rooting frantically in a drawer, but Cooper was gone. He went slowly down the hall, and by the time he reached the security desk he heard Christine Pappadakis's distant voice raised in triumph. "Wilson," she said, and Cooper knew it wouldn't be long before she found Elizabeth Street and its westward neighbor, Throop.

■ ■ ■

Cooper had to thrash about in the Near North traffic for a while before he found an electronics store on Huron that was still open. He bought a single 60-minute cassette tape and took it back to the car, where he stripped off the plastic wrap and used his car key to break out the tab in back. He slipped the cassette into his jacket pocket and looked for a phone.

He found one in a drugstore and punched in Cleo's number. He was hoping a mere receptionist wouldn't work the excessive hours lawyers were known for and would have had time to reach home by early evening. He leaned on the wall by the phone, hearing it ring and hoping he knew how to play it.

"Hello." The greeting sounded distant and peremptory.

"Cleo. It's Cooper."

Cooper waited to hear what note she would strike. Surprise? Alarm? "Cooper," she said after a moment, with what sounded like an attempt at brightness. "What's going on?"

"Did you hear about Mel?"

There was another pause. "The bastard stood me up at lunch today. What are you talking about?"

"He's in the hospital. Somebody shot him."

"Oh my God." It all sounded genuine: the intake of breath, the hurried words. "Oh, my God, is it bad?" The very slight quaver, the hint of a break in the voice. She was good; either that or he was all wrong.

"No," he said. "They shot him where he sits. He's going to be standing a lot for a month or so. But he's all right."

"Oh my God. What happened?"

"I don't know the details. I just heard about it. Listen, I got something for Mel, and I don't want to hold on to it. Can I leave it with you?"

Silence. Cooper waited, fearing suddenly that it was all transparent. Finally Cleo said, "What is it?"

"It's what Mel's been looking for, a copy of the missing tape. Vance made a copy and left it with a lawyer he knew. I just tracked the guy down today and pried it out of him. He hadn't come forward because he was going to try to use it himself. I don't want to keep it any longer than I have to, 'cause the guy could change his mind and come after me, or send someone. I can't find Mel 'cause they've moved him from the hospital. That's why I thought of you. Nobody knows about you. You can keep it for Mel till he's back on his feet."

It was mighty thin, thought Cooper; the wind whistled right through it. But it didn't have to be airtight to work; they'd have to check it out.

"I don't know," said Cleo.

"Please. You're the best bet. I'll come and drop it off. Nobody knows but you and me. Look, Mel will contact you before he does me. This is the fastest way to get it to him."

"It sounds dangerous."

"Only if they know you have it. They won't."

"Jesus, I don't know."

"All right, shit. I'll have to hang on to it."

"No, wait. It's not that I don't want to help, I just . . . They won't like, come after me?"

"They don't even know you exist. You'll be all right. Just for Christ's sake help us out."

"All right. When will you be here?"

"Give me twenty minutes," said Cooper. He hung up the phone and shook his head, then turned to grin at a lady who was coming through the door. "They ought to give me an Oscar," he said to her.

∎ ∎ ∎

Cooper couldn't park within three blocks of Cleo's place. If all he had wanted to do was to drop off the tape he would have double-parked, but he had other plans. He cruised the narrow Lincoln Park streets, cursing. Finally he left the Valiant too close to a hydrant and marched back to the narrow gangway that led to the coach house.

The gangway was clear of snow and lighted by a spot high on the wall of the apartment building. The gate at the end was shut but there was a bell labeled *C. Mix* and an intercom speaker. Cooper buzzed and when Cleo's voice came from the speaker he said his name. The lock clicked; he pushed open the gate and went across the little yard to her door. He knocked and it opened immediately, and Cleo was there, backlit by the subdued track lighting from the living room, in black tights under an oversized sweater in rustic-looking wool. Her hair was subdued by some contrivance in back but she was still made up, and Cooper had to admit suddenly he envied Moreland just a bit for the ride he'd had.

"I called the paper," she said, shutting the door behind him. "They told me what happened. He was shot on the way to lunch with me. I'm like . . . freaked out."

"He'll make it," Cooper said. "I've seen men with worse injuries than his walk two miles to a dust-off."

"Oh God, I feel like it's my fault or something."

"Forget it," Cooper said. "Here's the tape."

She stared at the cassette in his hand. "You're sure nobody else knows about this?" she said.

"Right now it's just you and me. You keep this safe and Moreland has the story of the decade."

She took it and slowly closed her fingers over it. "I'll keep it safe."

"Do that. I'm going to try to track down Moreland and tell him you've got it. Just put that in with the rest of your tapes and don't look at it too much. They put it through a scrambler or something, so there's nothing to listen to until the electronics guys have a crack at it. But it's the real thing, or I'll have that shyster's ass." Cooper was pulling the door open, a man in a hurry.

"Cooper, thank you. For everything you've done for Mel." She put a hand on his arm, and her face was suddenly illumined, open, inviting, the picture of feminine gratitude. Cooper stared for a moment; it was a face and a gesture that begged for an embrace or a quick kiss.

She's a pro, he thought. "Take care," he said, and left.

When the door shut behind him he took one look up at the rear of the house before him, checking the windows, and moved fast across the dimly lit yard. He was suddenly aware of the truck-sized hole in the plan; if she was quick off the mark, she could have gotten somebody here before him, somebody who would be waiting in the shadows.

She won't have it done on her doorstep, he told himself, and I'm not going much further. Cooper reached the gate to the gangway, pulled it open, looked over his shoulder to make sure he was out of view of windows or peepholes, and then let the gate swing shut with a clang. He stood immobile for a few seconds, uncomfortably visible in the light from the spot, before moving silently back along the wall to the rear of the house.

Here there were steps up to the enclosed back porch. Cooper waited another five seconds, scanning shadows, windows, the narrow stretch of alley he could see through the back fence at the side of the coach house. He was fairly sure nobody was going to pot him here in the yard; if there was anybody it would be on the way to the car. Even so, he had that rush, that sharpening of the senses and quickening of the heart. He mounted the steps.

They creaked just a bit but he took his time and got the flimsy door open. He had checked on his way in that there was no lock on it; the lock would be on the back door of the house. He eased the door shut behind him and stood in the dark listening. From outside he had seen that the only light showing was on the second floor. Here he could see light coming feebly around curtains from a kitchen just beyond the door to his right. He let his eyes grow used to the dark, making out stacked lawn chairs and half-empty bags of charcoal briquets, the detritus of summer. After a minute he went softly toward the windows overlooking the yard, careful to avoid kicking things.

Below him he could see the narrow shoveled path in the snow leading to Cleo's door. The curtains in the coach house were drawn, with light showing behind them. Cooper figured he'd taken no more than a minute to reach his post, probably enough time for Cleo to call whomever she was going to call.

Cooper shifted quietly from one foot to another, wishing he had a place to sit, trying not to make noise. He'd stood a lot of sentry duty in his day but he'd lost the edge. It wasn't going to be a pleasant wait in the cold, though he was sheltered from the wind. He spread his feet, relaxed tense stomach muscles, settled in.

He thought he could predict who was going to come down that gangway and across the yard to Cleo's door; he had it all now, he thought, everything he needed. There were details lacking but a confirmed sighting would give him plenty to take to Brown.

Moreland could come later. Cooper wasn't worried about Pappadakis stealing his friend's thunder; she had it all except one piece, and it was that piece Cooper would take to Moreland after he laid the whole thing out for Brown. Cooper figured that with luck he might even be able to take Diana home that night.

The waiting came more easily than he expected. From the house at his back he heard distant muffled sounds: music, an occasional faint voice. From the avenues not too far away, Fullerton and Halsted with their ceaseless traffic, he heard the mumble of engines, honks, sirens. Cooper checked his watch from time to time, out of a sense of orderly record-keeping. The third time he checked, it was nearly eight o'clock, twenty minutes after he had left Cleo's. He had just pulled down his sleeve again when the clang of the gate outside stiffened him like cold water down his back. He moved closer to the window.

Footsteps came deliberately across the yard into view. The yard was lit only by what light made it in from the lamps in the alley and the spot in the gangway, but it didn't take much light to show up the fine white head of hair. Cooper smiled.

Chesty O'Donnell thumped once on Cleo's door with a gloved hand. The door came open and he slipped quickly inside. When the door shut Cooper started to move; he wanted to get closer to the door, for a better, absolutely unmistakable look. He made a bit of noise, but he wasn't too worried; if somebody chased him off he could wait for O'Donnell on the street. It was all over.

Cooper stood by the door, in shadow, placed where O'Donnell would have to walk just below him. After maybe five minutes Cleo's door came open; she was silhouetted briefly with O'Donnell; then the door closed and the head of white hair shone as it came back toward the gangway. Cooper smiled again, seeing the florid face pass by him, features contracted against the cold, unmistakable. O'Donnell disappeared up the gangway.

His footsteps faded and Cooper stayed where he was. Part of

him wanted to rush the coach house, batter down the door, grab Cleo by the hair and drag her bodily through the snow to Belmont and Western. The anger was less on Moreland's behalf than his own; if she'd played Moreland for a fool, it had been with his eager collaboration, and she had at least tried to spare his life. Cooper's anger was stoked rather by the thought that Cleo had to be the one who had set Papini on his trail. Cooper was neither a misogynist nor a particularly violent man, but he thought briefly with great pleasure of the ringing smack to the face that would send Cleo across the room and put fear in those bright blue eyes, maybe even knock one of the contacts out.

He still, however, needed to get her to Belmont and Western, and he wanted her to go willingly. He was considering tactics when he heard someone come limping around the corner of the house.

17

COOPER WATCHED THROUGH the window in the door as the figure in the hooded parka labored into view, leaning on the cane with every step, making painful but brisk progress across the yard. One leg seemed to be worse than the other; the limp was jolting, asymmetrical, inefficient, but charged with an energy that was disturbing to watch. The man angled across the yard like a schooner making leeway across a bay, making for Cleo's door.

Cooper watched him go. He had long ago learned that when you're outgunned you just watch, head down and trying not to breathe too loudly. The man fetched up at Cleo's doorstep and knocked. There was a delay of half a minute and then the door came open a crack; Cooper could see Cleo's head in silhouette again. She didn't immediately move to let him in; the door was on the chain. Cooper couldn't hear what was being said, but he could see the man in the hooded parka leaning on the doorjamb, gesturing with the hand that held the cane. Whatever was spoken, the door closed abruptly and then came open again, enough to let the man slide inside before it was closed again.

And Cooper felt the rage again; this woman had broken bread

with him, taken him into her confidence, tried to work her charms on him. And now she was in conference with the man she had sent to kill him.

The quickest solution was merely to turn to the door behind him, knock, ask to use the phone. Amateur hour was over and it was time to get some law over here and stick a gaff in Michael Papini. Cooper was framing his speech to the householder when it finally occurred to him that there had been no clang of the gate after O'Donnell had left. Papini had come in on the sly, with O'Donnell's help.

And suddenly Cooper had a bad feeling that there was only one thing that anybody would send Papini to do. He came down off the porch into the yard and made warily for the window by the door of the coach house. The curtains were pulled but there was a gap at the edge. Cooper crunched across the snow, seeing as he drew closer that the gap wasn't big enough to show him anything but a corner of the room, thinking of windows at the side, windows on the alley in back.

He heard the scream loud and clear, muffled though it was by the well-insulated walls of the coach house. It was a good healthy scream, but it trailed off into a rasping wail of despair, and Cooper knew there was no time. He had seen the door pushed solidly shut and knew it would have locked automatically; it was a waste of time even to look at it.

Which left the window. Cooper spun to look around the yard and saw snow-draped garden furniture, a round table made of iron with four chairs stacked beside it. The top chair made a racket coming off the stack; Cooper still had the scream ringing in his ears and needed nothing more to propel him back toward the window with the chair coming up above his head. He heaved it dead center with the force of his run behind it.

The window caved in with a noise to wake children in the next county and the curtains were kicked apart in a shower of glass. The instant before they fell back showed Cooper a tableau frozen in the soft lighting inside: the man in the parka, swaying in the middle of the room on uncertain legs, and the woman on her knees, straining to free her hair from the grip of the hand buried in its roots. Cooper knew he'd given her only a temporary reprieve unless he got in there fast. There were shards sticking in the window frame, but Cooper knocked them clear with a gloved fist and had a leg over the sill when another scream came, a straining angry cry that told him it wasn't over yet.

By the time Cooper was all the way in and fighting clear of the curtains Cleo had saved her own life by rolling onto her side and unloading a wicked kick at the frail knees. The man went down, letting go of her hair; now Cooper could see the long evil skewer in the man's right hand, glistening in the light. Cleo was rolling free; as Cooper came charging away from the window he tripped over the lawn chair, sprawling headlong into the room.

By the time he had made it up to a clumsy sprinter's stance, ready to keep charging, Cleo was clawing her way up the room toward him and the man with the familiar face was sitting up. He had dropped the skewer and had his hand inside the parka. Cooper knew what he was going to bring out and went for the only weapon he had at hand. He picked up the lawn chair again and heaved it the length of the room. It went sailing over the man's head and bounced off the bank of stereo equipment with a thousand-dollar crash. Two strides took Cooper to Cleo and he grabbed her high on the arm and hauled her past him, throwing her toward the door.

The man had recovered and Cooper saw the revolver coming up again, so he had to keep going. The heavy glass coffee table was the next thing in his path and he grabbed the end and heaved. The table went end over end onto the man just as he fired; the glass spiderwebbed as the round came through it and then the table came down on him and Cooper was sprinting for the door, wondering briefly if he was hit, seeing Cleo scrabbling at the locks, wondering how it could take so long to run the length of a twenty-foot room.

Cleo had the door open and was looking back past him; her widening eyes made Cooper duck and pitch to the left, toward the kitchenette, just as another shot came. Cleo screamed again but then she was gone, out through the foot-wide gap into the night. Cooper hit the kitchen counter and grabbed it; he looked back to see the man pitch sideways onto the floor, grimacing; he had overbalanced in making the last shot.

Cooper grabbed the big knife from the cutting board on the counter, jumped clear of the counter and wound up. He had never thrown a knife with intent to maim and he knew it was pure theater, but the man would have to pay attention. Cooper let fly and saw the man curl into a ball, arms over his head with the revolver pointing at the ceiling as the blade spun flashing through the soft light toward him, a hard mean throw.

Cooper didn't wait. He heard a snarl as the knife hit something but he was gone, out the door and into the snow. He made for the gate in the gangway barely under control, seeing Cleo's heels disappearing. He reached the gate before it swung shut and was through, glancing off the frame and careening up the gangway.

Cleo was fast. She made a left at the sidewalk, slipping just a bit, and went north, arms pumping and feet flying. Cooper had to strain to catch her, and he was shod. Cleo had lost both of her house slippers at some point and started to slow perceptibly as her socks took a beating on the ice. Cooper drew even and collared her halfway up the block. He grabbed an arm and nearly took them both down before they hit a cleared patch of sidewalk and steadied. Cleo tried to wrench free, gasping, but Cooper hung on.

"Cleo. Give it up. They sold you out."

"Let go. Let go of my arm." There was panic in her eyes. Her fingers dug at Cooper's grip on her arm.

"It's all over. Time to talk." Cooper knew he had to keep moving; there was no guarantee he'd put anybody out of action back in the coach house and they hadn't come far.

"Let me go," said Cleo, louder, pulling away.

"Hey!" somebody shouted. Cooper had been aware of figures on the opposite sidewalk as he ran; now they were here, coming across the street. "Do you need help, miss?" somebody said.

Cooper let go of Cleo's arm and turned to face the posse. There were three men, very young and very robust. They bracketed him quickly, full of concern and hostility, ready for a good stomping. One of them grabbed his arm. Cooper ignored him and looked at Cleo, who was backing conveniently into the arms of another.

"What about it? You need help?" Cooper said.

He could see Cleo getting a hold of herself; she focused on him, then the rescuers, detaching herself from the man behind her. Her eyes narrowed and she took a quick look down the block past Cooper, toward the gangway.

"It's over, Cleo," said Cooper. "You come with me to my car or the cops come looking for you before morning. Make a decision and make it fast."

For a long second they stared at each other, panting, their breath streaming away in the cold. "Don't let him intimidate you," said the boy with his hands on Cooper's arm.

Cleo looked the boy in the eyes. "Fuck off," she said. To Cooper she said, "Where's your car?"

Cooper shook free. "The way you were going." He looked at the boy, whose face bore a look of deep and honest shock. "Nobody ever thanks you, kid," Cooper said.

He and Cleo moved up the block at a brisk trot. Cleo appeared not to be hampered by her lack of shoes or coat, but by the time they reached the end of the block her panting had a ragged throaty tone to it and her eyes were bugging. Cooper was about to offer to carry her when a black Buick Park Avenue came up the block from behind them, squealed around the corner, and stopped on a dime directly in front of them, blocking the crosswalk. The driver's window was down and a black man with a black X-cap looked out at them and said, "Whoa there. Get in back."

Their momentum had carried them almost to the car. Cooper hauled on Cleo's arm and prepared to spring in a different direction, but the black man was suddenly flashing a star in a wallet and saying, "Git in the back of the fuckin' car."

The star decided Cooper and he got the back door open and shoved Cleo in. Back down the block he could see the three good citizens drifting slowly back across the street, looking in their direction. There was no sign of the man with the limp.

When they were in, the Buick peeled away from the curb and accelerated toward the lights of Halsted Street. The power window slid up with a hum and it was warm and quiet. "Y'all made quite a bit of noise back there," said the driver.

For response all he got was panting from the backseat until he hit Halsted and turned north, going at a leisurely pace. "Who are you?" said Cooper finally.

"I'm what you call an interested observer," said the black man. Cooper was directly behind him and could see only his eyes in the rearview mirror. The eyes appeared to be smiling.

Cooper thought hard as they cruised north under the bright lights. "You're Pegleg Haynes, aren't you?" he said after a minute.

The eyes in the mirror were harder. "And you're a very well informed man," the driver said. "That's Mister Haynes to you, by the way."

"My apologies." Cooper wasn't sure where he stood, but he didn't want to lose the initiative. "You're not really supposed to have that star any more, are you?" he said.

The eyes were smiling again. "That's all right, it's not a real one."

"Huh. Well, thanks for the ride."

"My pleasure. The only thing we need now is some footwear and a wrap for the lady."

"Can I ask where we're going?" said Cooper.

"That all depends on you," said Pegleg Haynes, drawing out the word "all."

"You know this guy?" Cleo said, suddenly rejoining the conversation.

"By reputation only," said Cooper. "But I have a feeling we're about to become acquainted."

Haynes laughed. "You don't rattle easy, do you, fella?"

"Don't push it. Who were you watching, me or her?"

"Neither one. I was watching the TV people. When they brought you in to talk, I got interested in you."

Cooper nodded in the dark, trying to keep up. "OK," he said. "Start talking."

"Uh-uh," said Haynes, accelerating smoothly through a yellow light. "You first. Who were all the visitors and who got shot back there?"

Cooper took a deep breath and avoided looking at Cleo. "The visitors were a guy named Chesty O'Donnell, who works for Regis Swanson, and a guy named Michael Papini, who you probably have heard of. The shooting didn't amount to much. It was Papini's gun, but he missed."

"All that noise and nobody got hurt?"

"I might have nicked him. I threw a knife at him."

"Shit, I'm sorry I missed it. You know, I thought that looked like Pappy under that hood. He don't get around as well as he used to, does he?"

"Well enough to kill people."

"No shit. That what he was at the lady's for?"

"That's it. And I think it was an eye-opener for the lady." Cooper looked sidelong at Cleo, huddled against the opposite door, shivering.

"You're not a cop," she said. "And I'm out of here at the next traffic light."

240 • SAM REAVES

"Whoa now," said Haynes.

"Cleo," said Cooper, shifting toward her and stabbing a finger at her. "Give it the fuck up. Swanson has sold you down the river. The man just tried to have you killed."

She stared at him, frowning, and Cooper thought she was having trouble registering; she looked as if she were listening to somebody insisting the world was flat. After a moment she said simply, "Yeah." Her eyes went away out the window, intent on something in the street.

"So it's talking time. You fingered me, didn't you?"

She looked at him sharply. "I didn't finger you. They asked me your name and I told them."

"And you didn't know they were going to kill me."

"I don't have to take this shit."

"The hell you don't. You're going to talk to Mister Haynes here and then you're going to talk to the police."

"Well now, I don't know about the second part of that," said Haynes from the front.

Cooper leaned forward to speak just behind Haynes's ear. "What are you going to do, kill us? You can't kill everybody who knows about this. It's too late. The best you can hope for now is to get a hold of the proof before anyone else does."

Haynes held up a hand. "I didn't say nothing about killing. You're a little shook 'cause of all that noise just now, I can see that. Just slow down a minute and let's talk about that proof you mentioned."

Cooper flopped back on the seat. "OK. Regis Swanson has it. I don't know what it'll take to get it out of him, but I'm hoping Cleo here can help us."

"Well, well. How do you know Swanson has it?"

"That's who O'Donnell works for, and O'Donnell's been running this whole show. O'Donnell set Vance Oyler up to be killed and he set Cleo up just now. Swanson needs the tape because it would give him a hold on Wilson Throop like nobody's had on a mayor of Chicago for a long time. Now, I don't give a shit about Wilson Throop. What I want out of this whole deal is Michael Papini off my back. So I'm willing to look the other way while you work on getting the tape back, but after that she's mine, and she's going to tell the cops whatever they need to know to stick Papini and O'Donnell and Swanson too, if he gave the kill orders. You got a problem with that?"

Haynes chuckled. "Well now, I can't say yet, can I? I got to find out the female point of view here. What about that, sister?"

Cleo's eyes flitted from Cooper to Haynes and back, light from the street passing across her pale face. "You mean can I get the tape back for you?"

"That's about the size of it."

Cleo was still shivering, arms clasped tightly, but her eyes showed every sign of control, and calculation as well. They went back and forth a few times, and then she said, "If you can get me a coat and a pair of shoes, I can give it a shot."

"What's your shoe size?" said Haynes.

■ ■ ■

Haynes took them up Halsted almost to Irving Park. He pulled over at the curb in front of a bar with a roughly paneled, nondescript façade. Cooper recognized the place; from the people he had taken there in his cab over the years he had gained a fairly clear idea of the sexual orientation of the clientele. Haynes turned to look over the back of the seat. In the half-light all Cooper could tell about his face was that it was broad and dark and had a moustache and very experienced eyes under the bill of the cap. "The lady comes in with me," he said. "You ain't goin' nowhere, are you?" he said to Cooper.

"Not without her."

"That's what I figured. We won't be long."

Haynes shepherded Cleo into the bar, a gentlemanly hand on her elbow. He limped just perceptibly, a powerful man in the black cap and leather jacket. Cooper sat in the back seat and thought seriously about the consequences of staying in the car or disappearing into the night.

Ten minutes later they reappeared, Cleo in black pumps and a leopard skin jacket that screamed fake. She appeared to have combed her hair. Haynes held the back door open for Cleo and got in the front. "What would that be, Winnetka?" he was saying.

"Glencoe, I think," said Cleo. "Just drive, I'll show you the house."

"Did I miss something?" said Cooper.

"We're going to see Regis," said Cleo.

Haynes started the car. "She got right on the phone as soon as my friends in there got her fixed up. It was kind of noisy with the music and all and I couldn't hear what she was saying, but I have to figure she's playing it straight. She don't really have much of a choice, does she?" He put the Buick in gear.

"Not as far as I can see," said Cooper.

On the long drive north they were mostly silent. Cooper watched the shabby city neighborhoods give way to the big solid houses of the north lakeshore and went over it all again, hoping he had it figured right.

He remembered the entrance to the driveway, a narrow gap in the brush that was easy to miss, and the long tree-lined drive up to the house on its bluff above the lake. The night of the party the house had been blazing, but tonight only a few lights shone behind curtains on the ground floor. "My, my," said Haynes, wheeling up the curved drive. "How many slaves you suppose this man owns?"

"One less than he used to," said Cleo.

Haynes chuckled. "Sounds like we've had a little attitude adjustment back there."

There was a light blue Chevy van parked in front of the broad porch, shining in the glare from the floodlight on the corner of the house. Haynes pulled up behind the van and braked gently. He switched off the ignition.

"Company. Anybody recognize the van?" Neither Cooper nor Cleo answered. "Is he expecting all of us?" Haynes said, looking at Cleo.

"No. When I talk to Regis, I talk to him alone."

"Whoa, now. I'm not sure I could go for that."

Cleo leaned forward. "Listen, if I'm going to get that tape back I'm going to have to use some leverage. And Regis is not going to stand for strangers listening in on my leverage. You get it?"

Haynes grunted, or maybe laughed, and shook his head. "Yeah, I think so." He twisted further around to look at Cooper. "I sure as hell am glad I ain't married to her."

Cooper looked at Cleo. "One question. Where's O'Donnell likely to be right now?"

"I don't know. He's got a room around back, but he's off at night and he's not always here. Could be anywhere."

"Let's assume he's here. Will he be inside, reporting to Swanson? Around back in his room? In the bushes over there drawing a bead on us?"

"Don't ask me. But I don't think it's O'Donnell you have to worry about."

Cooper looked at Haynes. "I'm not sitting in the car. How about you?"

"Me neither. I think we need to come in with you, Blondie. Just to show the flag, you know?"

"Regis won't talk with you there."

"Well, shit," said Haynes. "A place like this, there's got to be a little parlor somewhere we could wait. Maybe with a bar. He got a butler could serve us some drinks? We promise not to put our feet up on the table."

Cleo squinted at the front of the house. "There's a couple that cook and stuff, but they might be off by now. I think Regis'll be alone. Unless Chesty's there."

"Well, I'll take my chances. These places have doorbells?"

They got out of the car and went up on the flagstone porch, where Haynes was pleased to find a doorbell. "Just like on my grandma's house in Yazoo City, Mississippi," he said, pushing it with a wide flat thumb.

They waited, Cleo huddled in the remarkable coat and Haynes smiling and rocking on the balls of his feet like a tourist in line for Disneyland. The porch light gave Cooper a better look at Haynes: this was a solid muscular man of past forty who had kept in shape. Leg or no leg, this man was not going to lose a fight quickly.

After nearly a minute noises came from behind the thick door and it was pulled open. Regis Swanson stood in the doorway blinking. He wore a cabled wool sweater that was coming unraveled at one cuff and faded blue jeans. He looked more like a college art professor than a millionaire. He looked at Cleo and said, "You didn't tell me you were bringing a committee."

"We're just the hired help, boss," said Haynes.

"They insisted," said Cleo, pushing past Swanson as if she lived there. "Make 'em wait in the kitchen or something." She was already heading down the hall toward an open doorway spilling light.

Swanson glared at Haynes as the black man put his foot over the doorstep. " 'Preciate it," said Haynes.

Cooper followed. His eyes met Swanson's and he nodded very

slightly. Swanson returned the nod, and recognition showed in his face. He pushed the door shut behind Cooper. Cleo had disappeared through the lighted doorway. Haynes was dawdling in the hall at the foot of the main stairway, looking up into the shadows on the first landing. Dead ahead the room with the spectacular lake view was entirely dark.

"Why don't we put you gentlemen in the parlor?" said Swanson, walking past them with a preoccupied look.

"What'd I tell you?" Haynes said to Cooper. He was smiling broadly.

They followed Swanson through several rooms, their host flicking on lights as he went. Cooper recognized rooms from the party, orienting himself. As he'd suspected, they wound up in the room with the bar and the fireplace. Swanson turned on a lamp with a marble base sitting on a table in the corner. "Help yourself to drinks," he said, and left the room without looking back, like a man who had just chained two dogs to a post.

Haynes did a circuit of the room with his slightly crooked gait, looking at the furniture and the paneling, shaking his head. "Damn," he said. "I forgot to wipe my feet."

Cooper unzipped his jacket and walked slowly to the bar. He pulled out a stool, sat on it, and leaned back with his elbows on the bar. "Let's talk," he said.

Haynes stopped his wandering and turned to face Cooper. He eased the cap back on his head about an inch, spread his legs, put his hands on his hips and said, "OK, who the fuck are you?"

"I'm a friend of the reporter who got shot. The only reason I'm in this is because he convinced me in a weak moment to come along for the ride. I found a couple of Papini's bodies and I can identify him. He's tried to hit me and he'll try again. I want him dead or in jail so I can go home again. That's all."

Haynes nodded. He opened his mouth to say something but nothing came out because just then they both heard the distant sound of tires on gravel. Somewhere outside a car drew to a halt and the engine died. Seconds passed and Haynes said, "More company."

A car door slammed, faintly. Cooper and Haynes looked at each other for a moment, and then each looked into the shadows in a different part of room while they listened to the doorbell, and soft footsteps in the hallway, and voices too low to distinguish. The door slammed, the footsteps faded, another door closed with a distant, final click. Haynes and Cooper traded looks, and Haynes said, "House like this, they must have more than one parlor."

"You were saying," said Cooper, feeling suddenly that things were getting urgent.

"I was saying, what does your reporter buddy know?"

"Just about all of it. He knows Wilson Throop's on a tape somewhere selling his soul to the devil, but he's never heard the tape. I'd say if you can get your hands on that tape nobody's ever going to prove a thing. I doubt if they'll even dare to mention it, libel laws being what they are. All the witnesses are dead."

"Except one."

Cooper thought for a beat and said, "Papini was there, huh?"

Haynes chuckled. "Now don't expect me to go telling you things you got no business knowing. Here's my point." Haynes came over to the bar and hoisted himself up on to a stool. He put an elbow on the bar and leaned closer. In the soft light from the single lamp his skin glowed like mahogany. "Sounds to me like it's too bad you didn't kill Papini back there at the lady's place."

"If I'd had a way, I would have."

"And then we'd both have pretty much what we wanted, right?"

Cooper looked into the dark eyes in the dark face. "I guess I would," he said.

"And I guess I would, too. So then there wouldn't be no need for the young lady to talk to the police, now would there?" Haynes pronounced 'police' in the classic black manner, with the accent on the first syllable.

"I guess not," said Cooper quietly. "You volunteering to do it?"

"Shit." Haynes shook his head, drawing back a bit. He looked disgusted. "I'm a former officer of the law, boy. Who the fuck you think you're talking to?"

"OK, forget I said it. As long as we're just speculating, can I speculate that I would be safe if something happened to Papini? Can I trust you to let things lie after that?"

"As much as I can trust you. Just that much."

Cooper nodded. "OK. So what happens now?"

"Well, now we work on getting two things—the tape and the fuck out of here. Once the lady brings us the tape we leave, and you go home and forget all about tonight. You forget about the lady and the cops and everything else. If your reporter friend asks you what happened, you tell him anything except what happened."

"And what if she doesn't bring us the tape?"

Haynes grinned. "Well, now in that case it sounds like we just might have to shoot our way out."

Cooper shook his head. "Sounds to me like we ought to be keeping track of what's going on in other parts of this house."

Haynes slid off the stool. "That's just what I'm fixin' to find out."

Cooper folowed him toward the door. "Let me take the point. I've been here before."

Haynes gave him a sharp look and then smiled. "Suits me fine. Ever since I took that one wrong step outside of Duc Pho I let anybody that wants it go first."

Cooper went slowly through the rooms they had traversed, listening. An obscure instinct made him turn out lights as he went. restoring the house to darkness. He could hear nothing but house noises: the hum and creak of a large house in the winter cold. In the distance he thought he could hear the deep-throated rumble of the lake. Every once in a while he heard Haynes's soft step somewhere behind him, not too close. Haynes was going to let him flush whatever there was to flush.

When he reached the entrance hall Cooper stopped. Now he could hear distant voices. He listened but could make out no words. People were speaking softly, and they were separated from him by doors. He wasn't even sure of the direction; the voices came, he thought, from the rear of the house. A different voice sounded, indistinct; Cooper thought it was female. And it sounded closer at hand.

It's a surprise party, thought Cooper. He moved into the hall. The light by the front door was still on; he located the switch and turned it off. He stood in the darkness reconstructing his memories of the house; he recalled a study from his wanderings at the party, down the hall and off a perpendicular hall to the right. His guess was that that was where Swanson and at least some of his visitors were. He remembered also that the study could be approached from two directions; the hall connected at the far end with a room Cooper had noted because it had a full-sized pool table. The billiard room in turn connected via a sitting room with the living room that had the high arched window.

Instinct told Cooper that it would be best to approach by the roundabout route. If anyone was on guard, they would most likely expect people from the direction of the front door. In addition, taking that route would provide reconnaissance; Cooper always liked having a clear sense of the terrain.

He went slowly down the hall toward the main living room. He could just make out the high arched window, black in the eerie near-darkness of the white-walled room. There was some light here, but not much, coming from a hallway through a door on the left; Cooper thought the kitchens were back that way, as well as the solarium. To the right was the series of rooms that led to the study by the back way.

Cooper navigated carefully around the shoals of furniture in the living room. The voices had faded; here the noise of the lake was louder. Cooper brushed a lampshade with his shoulder and put out a hand to steady the lamp; he wished his breathing were quieter. He wished he were home with Diana; he wished he had never set foot in Regis Swanson's house. He wished he hadn't had any bright ideas. He wished he had told Moreland to go to hell.

While he was standing there he heard the footsteps. They were coming down the hall behind him from the solarium, softly and slowly, fifty feet away but closing. There was the scrape of the dragging foot, the planting of the sole, the slight creak of the cane.

Cooper wheeled and looked toward the doorway. For a moment he was frozen, as helpless as a deer in the headlights. Then he remembered rule number one and looked for cover. There was plenty of it in the dark room; Cooper went to hands and knees behind a sofa, ready to move. He could not see the doorway now but he could see the entrance to the hall through which he had come. The footsteps were close; they were on the threshold of the room. To Cooper it sounded as if there were more than one person; there were too many footsteps for just one man with a cane.

The footsteps were muted now on the thick carpet and Cooper was afraid his breathing, his heart, the brushing of his arm against the sofa back would give him away. For a bad moment he thought the party was coming across the room toward him but then he saw them, backlit from the rear hall, making for the front door.

And Cooper strained to see through the darkness, unable to credit his senses, as he saw Melvin Moreland, on crutches, making his painful way across the room, escorted by Jay Macy and Regis Swanson.

18

COOPER STAYED ON HIS HANDS and knees, listening as the three men made their way up the hall to the front door. After they had passed out of the room he had doubted, a cold suspicion of illness or madness passing through him for a moment, but Cooper was a realist and he knew it had been no hallucination. Now he just watched and listened, not even trying to think. The light by the entrance went on again, casting light back into the living room, and Regis Swanson spoke, too softly to distinguish words. Cooper heard a murmur from Macy and then a single hoarse whisper, quickly stifled, that sounded like Moreland. The front door opened, steps faded away, the door closed, the light in the hall clicked off, and Regis Swanson's tread came away from the door and turned down the side hall toward the study. Outside, a car engine started.

Cooper rose to his feet. The sofa was right there and he sank onto it and sat for a minute or so, elbows on his knees, hearing the car drive off, hearing the lake outside, and wondering just where he had lost track of things.

He wondered where Haynes was. The temptation was very strong to just leave. There would be a door at the back, down that lighted hallway. Maybe it was check-out time. Cooper considered how likely it was Haynes would let him stroll, how likely it was he could stop him. He considered options once he was outside the house, in the snow with no car. And he decided that if he left he would still not have Michael Papini off his back. All the choices were bad, so Cooper took the closest to hand.

He rose and swept the room with a look; if Haynes was anywhere near he was damn good. Cooper shook his head and set out for the sitting room. His eyes were used to the dark and he had no more trouble with furniture, but he went slowly. Inside the sitting room, he stopped to orient himself; the house had more furniture and gadgets than a whole floor at Field's. He could make out the gigantic square of an oversized TV screen in the corner. This room was darker, and he went with great caution. He could hear the voices again, and he could see a corner of the pool table in the next room, light from the hallway shining on the solid oak rail.

Cooper went a little faster now that he could see better, moving silently on the thick carpet. He crossed the room and paused on the threshold of the game room; something said be careful. He looked past the table to the heavy curtains on the front windows, the mini-bar on the left-hand wall; he had the impression someone was near.

His attention was misdirected; when the warning step, the touch of steel and the soft voice came, it was from behind.

"Don't move, dickhead," someone said.

Cooper's heart had nearly failed him and his mouth was suddenly parchment; for a second he couldn't have moved if he'd wanted to. What he had at the base of the skull was nobody's finger; it felt like the double muzzle of a sizable shotgun.

"Lie down," said the man behind him.

Cooper obeyed, sinking to his knees and then onto his stomach with great deliberation. Cooper had a thing about shotguns; in his day he'd stopped rounds from military assault rifles and handguns and deeply regretted both, but nothing had ever scared him quite so much as seeing what a shotgun could do to a human being at close range.

"You move a finger, Regis is gonna have to get his rug cleaned," said the voice.

Cooper lay on his belly on the carpet, just inside the game room, head turned to the right. The muzzle of the gun rested lightly on his neck. He could see the butt ends of pool cues in the rack on the wall. He wondered where Haynes was. Most fervently of all his present wishes, he wished that Haynes wouldn't try anything too hasty. Feet straddled him and a rough hand patted him down, starting at the ankles and moving up the inside of the thighs. The hand lingered at the waistband, then moved on to the ribs and armpits. "Roll over," said the voice.

When Cooper obeyed, the first thing he saw was the gun; an over-under shotgun with an engraved barrel. He looked right up along the rib to the fleshy face and white hair of Chesty O'Donnell. There was just enough light to make out the expression of careful concentration on O'Donnell's face as he patted down Cooper's front with his left hand, holding the shotgun to his cheek with the right. Cooper couldn't decide whether to close his eyes or not; he didn't want to miss anything, but the foreshortened perspective of the shotgun barrel was not a pretty sight.

O'Donnell straightened up and put his left hand on the fore-end of the shotgun. He took a step back, the double muzzle still trained on Cooper's face.

"Freeze," said Haynes quietly from the darkness. "You make a real nice silhouette there, just like on the practice range."

There was no change in O'Donnell's face, none at all. The shotgun was still trained on Cooper's face. Years went by, and Haynes said, "Lay down the gun, sloooow and careful." Now O'Donnell's lips tensed in an expression of disgust. He and Cooper were looking into each other's eyes. Cooper thought he saw regret in the florid face and then O'Donnell moved, slowly stepping back another pace, raising the muzzle of the shotgun and carefully lowering the butt to the floor. Cooper breathed.

As O'Donnell bent to lay the gun on the carpet, Cooper sat up. He could see nothing of Haynes in the darkness behind O'Donnell, but he heard him. "Get the gun," the black man said. Cooper reached for the muzzle of the gun and pulled it to him. He stood up and pointed it at O'Donnell, who had put his hands in the air. Cooper found the double trigger with his index, and suddenly he felt a whole lot better.

"Take us to your leader," said Haynes, and Cooper saw him for the first time, a flash of white teeth and the silver X on the cap ten feet behind O'Donnell in the dark room. Cooper moved aside to let O'Donnell pass. O'Donnell came slowly through the door-way, hands at shoulder height, looking bored. Cooper kept well out of snatching range, backing against the pool table and sliding along the rail.

O'Donnell made for the lighted hall. Haynes appeared in the doorway and motioned with a large revolver for Cooper to pre-cede him. Cooper nodded and trained the shotgun on O'Donnell's back.

The hallway was lit by a lamp in a sconce on the wall. Behind a door somewhere ahead a woman was talking. She did not sound happy. There were doors on either side of the passage; O'Donnell paused at the second door on the left. He turned and looked at Cooper, then past him to Haynes. There was a slightly strained look of contempt on his face under the silver waves of hair.

Through the door they could hear the woman's voice. It was raised now. Distinctly, Cooper heard her say, "If anybody can beat you, it's me, and you damn well know it. There is no way in hell you will get away with this." A silence followed, while Cooper tried hard to place the voice, and then Regis Swanson's voice could be heard, too low to make out words. O'Donnell was staring at the door, hands still in the air.

Just behind Cooper's shoulder Haynes said to O'Donnell, "Get in there." O'Donnell cast him one dubious look and reached for the doorknob. To Cooper Haynes whispered, "Help him."

As soon as O'Donnell had the door open Cooper was behind him. He obeyed Haynes, kicking O'Donnell in the small of the back and sending him across the rug to stumble against Regis Swanson's desk. Cooper went into the study with the shotgun at his shoulder, sweeping the room, freezing the people in it.

A broad wooden desk was opposite the door; Swanson sat behind it with both hands on it, blinking. At one corner of the desk stood Astrid Huber in an unzipped purple ski jacket, her mouth open. And Cleo sat on a Chesterfield on the right-hand wall beneath loaded bookshelves. She too was motionless, but she looked almost casual with her legs crossed and one hand resting on the seat of the sofa, the other holding a cigarette. Cooper moved quickly to the side of the room opposite her, commanding the entire study with the gun. Everyone watched him except O'Donnell, who had regained his balance and was looking at the door.

Haynes came into the room slowly, the big blue steel revolver out front. He took in the room at a glance. " 'Scuse us," he said. "We found this riff-raff prowling around your living room. Thought you might like to know." He smiled at Swanson.

Swanson nodded. He looked alert but far from panicked. After a couple of seconds he said, "You mind putting away the guns?"

"I'm afraid we can't do that," Haynes said. "Not until we get what we came for."

"Who the hell are you?" said Astrid Huber. She was white and trembling, hanging on to a corner of the desk.

"We're the garbage collectors, come for the trash. What you got sitting on the desk there."

For the first time Cooper noticed the tape, on the green blotter on the desktop, between Swanson's hands. It was a black cassette with a white file label stuck onto it. Cooper could not read what was on the label. Near Swanson's left hand was a cheap-looking portable tape player of Japanese manufacture.

"You can't have it," said Swanson.

"I wouldn't bet on it," said Haynes. "Put it in the recorder there and let's have a listen."

Swanson looked long and level into Haynes's face and made the only possible decision. He picked up the cassette and slipped it into the recorder. "Rewind it?" he said politely. "We were sort of in the middle."

"Don't bother. Just play it."

Cooper's arms were tired from holding up the shotgun, but he didn't want to relax anything. He had been calculating since he walked in the door and he figured his best chance of walking out again was keeping the big gun ready.

Swanson punched the play button and the tape kicked in with a hiss. There was the hollow murmur of background noise and then a voice on the tape, blurred by distortion and static, said, "*You're a young man. You got a bright future.*"

"*Not if I go for this kind of shit,*" said Wilson Throop's distinctive bass.

"That's enough," said Haynes. "You can shut it off."

Swanson obeyed. He smiled at Haynes and said, "I take it they persuaded him?"

"Don't ask me, I wasn't there. Take out the tape and toss it over here in front of me, real easy."

Swanson removed the tape, took a last rueful look at the label, and with a flick of the wrist sent it spinning across the study. Haynes let it hit the rug at his feet without moving, watching the group clustered at the desk. Then he slowly and precariously went to one knee to pick it up, keeping the revolver trained on Swanson.

Timing, thought Cooper, timing is everything. "Don't move," he said, swinging the shotgun to aim at Haynes's head. "Don't," he repeated, as the revolver wiggled a little, jerking just a few degrees in his direction.

Haynes's face set into a frown. He looked at Cooper and shook his head, just perceptibly. "I'm disappointed in you," he said.

"Drop everything," said Cooper. "The gun and the tape. And go sit on the couch next to Cleo. Do it now. You make a real fine target right there."

Haynes laid the revolver on the rug. He, too, took a last look at the tape before tossing it down next to the pistol. He put a hand to the floor to steady himself as he got up, and Cooper sighted down the barrel of the shotgun, his finger on the front trigger, ready to shoot if the hand made a move for the revolver. But Haynes just stood up and went to the couch, shaking his head. "You're making a mistake, friend," he said.

"Maybe so," said Cooper. "But I'd be making a bigger mistake if I let you have things your way." He swung the gun toward the party at the desk and took three strides across the room to where the gun and the tape lay together. He moved the gun back to Haynes, holding it one-handed, and knelt just as Haynes had. He felt for the revolver, put it in his left-hand jacket pocket, and then found the tape. He reached inside his jacket to slip it into his shirt pocket.

It was snap judgment time. Cleo was smoking her cigarette; Haynes was shaking his head. Astrid Huber was trembling at the corner of the desk and Chesty O'Donnell looked like a man waiting for a pit bull to jump. Regis Swanson sat behind his desk with his hands in sight and a thoughtful frown on his handsome features. There was a telephone a foot from Swanson's right hand and Cooper gave it a look, but the prospect of using it without dropping his guard and then holding five people at gunpoint for an indefinite time was one that lacked appeal. Cooper stood up and looked at Astrid.

"You got a car outside?"

She flinched as if he had hit her and her lips worked a little. "Yes," she said finally, without much breath behind it.

"Then you're driving," Cooper said. Nobody moved. "Let's go," he said. "I'm with the good guys."

Two seconds ticked off and Astrid came to life. She took one slow step away from the desk, then two fast ones, and by the time she made the door she was running. Cooper stood aside to let her pass, covering the room with the shotgun. Everyone seemed to be wide-eyed and open-mouthed. Regis Swanson was rising slowly from his chair, eyes blazing, daring Cooper to shoot him. "You're making a mistake," he said.

"Says you," said Cooper. "Nobody comes after us." He backed out, leaving the door open. Astrid was already at the end of the hall, looking back. Cooper put the shotgun at port arms and ran. Astrid had the front door open by the time he got there and they went out into the cold. The van was gone. Astrid led him at a trot to a Mercedes sedan parked behind Haynes's Buick and fumbled with keys while Cooper watched the doorway. A curtain in a front window moved, catching his eye, and he swung the shotgun toward it. The curtain fell back. Cooper stepped to the rear of Haynes's car, pointed the shotgun at a tire, and pulled the trigger. The double explosion of the gun and the tire rent the night and the Buick settled onto the rim of the wheel.

Astrid had the doors of the Mercedes open and Cooper got in on the passenger side, handling the shotgun carefully with the muzzle toward the ceiling. The car started with a roar, jerked into reverse, spun its tires, and clawed its way around the circular drive to the lane leading downward. Astrid wrestled with the wheel a bit but steadied the car. Snowbanks and black trees flashed past. Over his shoulder Cooper saw Swanson and O'Donnell emerging onto the brightly lit porch.

"Who are you?" said Astrid.

"Nobody you know. Just get us back into the city." They were approaching the end of the drive and Astrid slowed. "How do you get this window down?" said Cooper. Astrid did something with a switch and the window hummed open. Cooper hoisted the shotgun out the window muzzle first and pitched it into a snowbank as the car slewed around the last curve in the lane.

There was no traffic in sight on Sheridan Road. Left was south into the city, but Astrid spun the wheel to the right and the Mercedes squealed into the northbound lane.

"What are you doing?" said Cooper.

"They're expecting us to go south," she said. "Chesty and Regis both have cars around back." Astrid Huber's voice was a little tight but steady now, and she drove like she knew what she was doing. A car came around a curve ahead and its light swept over them. Two hundred feet on, just above where the ravine bottomed out, was another driveway. *Private Road—No Outlet* said a sign. Astrid braked smoothly and whipped the Mercedes around an acute angle into the lane. It was blacktopped and clear of snow. On either side steep banks rose to a tangle of bare branches. Astrid went a hundred feet up into the trees, around a curve and onto a level stretch, leaving the lights on the road behind. She cut the lights, stopped, and threw the gear lever into park. It was very dark. Cooper heard her reach for a switch and the overhead light went on. In the dim yellow light she was shifted partly toward him, peering at him. The tousled frosted hair topped a face with well-tended skin that was dominated by dark eyes with long lashes. She was, Cooper was struck again, a beautiful woman. "All right," she said, "I don't know you, fair enough. But you can tell me what you know."

Cooper scowled at her. "I know your husband wants Wilson Throop in his pocket if he gets elected mayor. I'm guessing a guy named Michael Papini approached him through Chesty O'Donnell to sell the tape, probably because he knew O'Donnell from the Teamsters a long time ago. I know Papini's been killing people to keep the story quiet, probably on O'Donnell's orders, and I figure your husband had to know. How's that?"

Astrid nodded. "I think you've got it right. Regis is the ultimate dealer. This is the kind of thing that bastard loves. I don't think he's a killer, but he'd tell Chesty to get the job done, whatever it took."

"How did you find out about it?"

Astrid pursed her lips and blinked at him for a few seconds before answering. "Cleo told me."

"I see," said Cooper.

"All right," said Astrid. "So what are you going to do with the tape?"

"Get it into the hands of an eager reporter."

"Got one in mind?"

"I did."

There was a silence and then Astrid said, "Macy's lap dog? What's his name, Moreland?"

"You know him."

"Regis has Macy on a leash. You give it to Moreland, it'll never see the light of day."

"OK, I'll give it to the competition." Cooper was very tired suddenly, tired of the sour sick smell of corruption.

"Let's think about this," said Astrid.

"Don't tell me you have an angle, too."

"No. But I've got a lot of things to consider. I've got legal aspects to consider," she said.

Cooper felt for the tape through his jacket. "There's only one legal aspect to consider. Air out the laundry. As long as there's something to cover up, people are in danger. What the hell were you going to do with it?"

She shrugged. "I was hoping to leverage the tape out of Regis and then make it public. But there are different ways of doing that. There are ways it could help me, and there are ways it could hurt me. It was going to take some thought."

"Well, you don't have to worry about that now. I've got it. The tape hits the papers tomorrow and if that's not the most politically convenient thing for you, you have my sincere regrets."

She peered at him for a moment longer and then smiled, the shrewd expression softening. She shook her head and a small sigh escaped her. "An honest man, huh?"

"I try."

The smile faded. "All right then. That's a bottom line I can respect. Just one thing. I've jumped into a car with a gun-toting madman who's commandeered the hottest political potato to come along in twenty years. People are going to ask me a lot of questions."

Cooper was getting irritated. "If you don't want to be involved, you can tell people I took you at gunpoint."

"I'd just as soon skip the whole thing. I don't think anyone back there's going to the papers. And I'm late for dinner."

Cooper blinked. After a moment he said, "OK, don't let me take you out of your way. I think I can fend for myself from here."

She just looked at him for a second or two and then smiled. "That's very gallant of you." She switched off the overhead light and reached for the gear lever. "You can try hitchhiking or walk a mile or so west and catch the train. But as far as I'm concerned we're just strangers in the night, agreed?"

"You got it. Thanks for the ride." Cooper had the door open already.

"It's been interesting," said Astrid. As soon as Cooper was out of the car and standing clear, she put it in reverse, switched on her lights, and backed slowly down the lane toward Sheridan Road. Cooper watched her disappear around the curve. Then he started walking slowly down the lane.

He didn't hear the Skylark until it was almost on him. It had come drifting down the lane in neutral, lights off, steering between the faintly luminous banks of snow; the hiss of the tires warned Cooper when the big car was about fifty feet behind him and closing fast. Cooper turned to see it coming out of the dark like a bat out of a cave. He had no time to think of anything except climbing the snowbank on his right. He leapt, scrambled, slipping in the snow, knowing he could never climb high enough; it was last stand time.

The engine roared to life; Cooper flopped on his belly onto the snow, sliding sideways down to the edge of the lane, clawing at the hardened lumps of ice to keep from going right into the path of the car slewing wickedly toward him. Cooper stopped his slide; for a bad moment he thought the car was going to catch him and drive him deep into the snowbank. It swerved and went by him, the brakes locked and squealing now, the right rear fender just brushing Cooper where he crouched. Then abruptly it stopped, ten feet further on. The engine died.

The door on the driver's side opened and in the silence Cooper heard the driver heave himself out, panting, grunting as the stiff legs hit the ground. Cooper listened as the man hauled himself along the side of the car, limping, leaning on the car, forgetting the cane. There was just enough light for Cooper to see the familiar hooded silhouette come around the back of the car, the bandaged hand holding the gun, lurching, wheezing, looking for the kill.

Cooper shot him with Pegleg Haynes's revolver. He shot him once in the center of the torso just to stand him up, then steadied his aim and shot him three more times a little higher, hoping for the heart. When Papini toppled over backwards and hit the ground with a thump, Cooper rose and walked to where he lay, kicked the revolver away from his hand, and shot him once in the face. Then, stupidly, for sheer relief, he put one last round into the forehead above the thick black eyebrows. Finally Cooper leaned on the car, the revolver hanging at his side.

He stood that way until he heard the faint voices from the bottom of the lane, against the sound of idling engines; one of the voices was a woman's and Cooper could do sums quickly enough to know why he'd been brought up the lane. He started jogging, thinking the quickest way to find out all the things he didn't understand was to throw her against the car and ask her with the revolver in her well-tended face.

When he rounded the curve he saw headlights, two sets of them, both pointing uphill. At the rear of the Mercedes was another car which had come into the lane and blocked it. The door of the Mercedes stood open and Astrid was at the driver's window of the second car, talking to the driver in a tone that was less than polite.

Something made Cooper stop and watch; he wanted to know who was in the other car before he charged onto the scene. Astrid had had enough, it seemed; she straightened, flung out an arm in a gesture of rage, and turned to stalk back to her car.

She had made two steps when the door of the rear car opened and Chesty O'Donnell stepped out, white hair shining in the light from the Sheridan Road lamps. Cooper started running when he saw O'Donnell pull the shotgun off the seat. Whatever Astrid had done, Cooper wasn't going to stand and watch another murder.

He yelled a hey at the top of his lungs; Astrid stopped in her tracks and Chesty wavered for a second. Cooper yelled "Behind you!" and Astrid turned. She saw the shotgun and had time to scream a single no and then Chesty shot her. Chesty's headlights showed her as she went onto the snowbank at the side of the lane, all arms and legs and not much face. Cooper had stopped, appalled, and whether he was out of ammo or just out of ideas, Chesty paid him no more attention. He just threw the gun in the car, jumped in after it, and started backing out in a hurry. As he went, his lights swept over something in a purple ski jacket that lay in a spray of crimson on the snow. As Cooper came on down the hill, horror rising in his throat, a van turned into the mouth of the lane and collided with the reversing car with a loud bang.

The door of the car was torn open and O'Donnell got out with the shotgun. "Move outta my fucking way!" he screamed. The engine of the van had died at impact and now it ground uselessly for a second or two, not catching. O'Donnell pointed the shotgun at the windshield of the van and Cooper heard Jay Macy scream "No!"

"O'Donnell!" Cooper had almost reached the Mercedes now and at the sound of his voice O'Donnell wheeled and brought the shotgun to bear on him. Cooper dived for the snow and waited, but no shot came; instead he saw O'Donnell turn again and pull open the door of the van.

O'Donnell reached in and pulled Macy out onto the asphalt with a mighty heave; Macy hit like a sack of potatoes and lay still, his hands covering his head. O'Donnell was climbing into the van and Cooper was on his feet again. He made his way around the Mercedes, stepping over Astrid's body, as the engine turned over and the van jerked into reverse. It wheeled out onto the road, drawing a honk and a swerve from a passing car. The van rocked as O'Donnell braked and shifted gears, and then it headed south. Macy was just rolling over, dazed, his hands coming away from his head. "Melvin," he said.

"Huh?" Cooper pulled him upright by the arm. "What?"

Macy looked up at him with wide staring eyes. "Moreland's in the back of the van."

"Shit," said Cooper, and took off running. He came out of the lane in time to see the van slow down, wander across the center line and run up on the opposite shoulder, where it stopped, its rear end sticking out into the road. Cooper ran for it like Carl Lewis; the fifty yards looked like a mile.

The door came open when he was still too far away and O'Donnell slid out under a rain of blows from an aluminum crutch that seemed to be coming from behind the driver's seat. The shotgun came with him and O'Donnell got his balance and pointed it back into the van. Cooper screamed his name and O'Donnell wheeled, the gun coming around with him. Cooper skidded to a halt ten yards from O'Donnell and leveled the revolver at him.

"The shotgun's empty," he said. "I fired once, you fired once. It's all over. Give it up."

O'Donnell froze for a moment and then, with no change in expression, brought the shotgun to his shoulder and sighted along the rib. Cooper looked into the double muzzle and it suddenly occurred to him that there was no reason in the wide world why Chesty O'Donnell could not have reloaded the shotgun.

Not here, thought Cooper, not in the cold in the middle of the road, not now.

Moreland lunged over the back of the driver's seat and drove the saddle of the crutch into O'Donnell's neck, ramming his head against the open door. The shotgun went off with a sound to end history and shot went past Cooper's head like the breath of the Devil himself. Cooper stood in the roadway, frozen, while O'Donnell turned and in fury swung the now empty shotgun at Moreland, instead hitting the doorframe and denting the side of the van. The shotgun flew out of his hands and fell on the pavement. He staggered a little and came away from the van and saw Cooper standing there with the revolver still pointing at him.

Chesty O'Donnell saw the look in Cooper's eyes and was afraid. He put his hands in the air and said, "All right, all right. I'm through. Don't shoot that thing." Cooper walked slowly toward him, still running cold inside. He backed O'Donnell against the hood of the van, standing six feet away with the revolver pointing at his chest, and looked into his eyes for what seemed a long time. Headlights washed over them; cars were honking.

"Guess what?" said Cooper. O'Donnell tried to say something but only a wheeze came out. "Mine's empty too," said Cooper, and pulled the trigger. The hammer rose and fell and the gun clicked and Chesty O'Donnell jerked as if somebody had plugged him into a 120-volt circuit. Cooper closed with him, the gun slipping out of his fingers, and when O'Donnell rallied and shoved off the hood, Cooper met him with a right he'd been saving for a long time. The blow rocked O'Donnell's head back and Cooper felt teeth break. He hit O'Donnell again, in the gut this time, with fury. The punch hurt him but there was a lot of gut there, and Cooper hit him again in the same place and then grabbed a handful of white hair to steady the target and hit him with a final right that put Chesty on the gravel at the side of the road with eyes that weren't seeing anything and blood coming from both nose and mouth.

Cooper flexed his hand, hoping he hadn't broken it, and stepped to the door of the van. He looked in and saw Moreland hanging on to the back of the seat, wide-eyed and sweating. "I thought you were dead," gasped Moreland. "Twice."

Cooper shook his head. "Man, I hope you can explain all this."

◾ ◾ ◾

"Talk fast," said Cooper, watching the door. "I think we got about three minutes before they get enough reinforcements in to send somebody back here to baby-sit us."

Moreland lay face-down on a flowered sofa in the room with the bar and the fireplace. His trousers were down around his ankles and blood was seeping through the half-acre of gauze that covered his right buttock. He was pale and his face was drawn with pain, but there was intensity in his eyes. "Why Astrid?" he said.

"It was a snap judgment," said Cooper. "I heard her telling Swanson he couldn't get away with it, and since I had him pegged as the bad guy I figured she was with the angels." Cooper sagged back against the bar. At the moment he and Moreland were alone in the room; in another room nearby, a small-town police chief was carefully dealing with the case of his life. The monotonous flash-flash of police lights came feebly through the curtains.

"Swanson was a good guess," said Moreland. "If Jay hadn't come to see me at the hospital I might have come to the same conclusion."

"How come you never asked him about the party before?"

"It was never important until this thing with Cleo came up. When Jay told me it was Astrid who had him invite me, bells started ringing. I told him about Cleo and he went and called Swanson. He was going to come out here by himself, but I made him bring me. I had to threaten him, but he agreed. He went and got his van so I could lie down in the back and brought along a new pair of pants for me. We had to fight our way through three ranks of nurses to get me out of there."

"And what did Swanson have to say?"

"We laid out what we knew and he got this look in his eyes and said so that's what all that was about. He said Chesty had come to him with an offer from an unnamed old buddy. Lots of hints, no specifics, and a high price tag. Swanson said forget it, he didn't deal in blackmail, and then he didn't hear anything more about it. I guess that's when Chesty took it to Astrid."

"Huh. So what did Astrid stand to get out of it?"

"Jesus, you name it. A politically connected lawyer like her? She could write her own ticket with Throop in the mayor's office. Bond issues, favors to sell, brokering contracts, you name it. She'd put the money away in sacks with the clout that would give her. That would be the end of her aspirations for the legislature, for sure. She'd just stay here in town and watch it pile up. She'd be the new Jake Slazenger."

"A nice clean reformist type like her."

"She's schmoozed the reformists, but nobody's ever accused Astrid Huber of turning down an invitation to a smoke-filled room. She's been up to her elbows in politics in this town since she was Jake Slazenger's pretty young protégée."

"Huh. Did Swanson know she was having an affair with O'Donnell?"

"No. But I could see him putting two and two together when we told him what we suspected about the party. He called Astrid and told her to come over, and just after that Cleo called him. By the time you showed up with your little friends, we had almost pieced it all together. Jay kept apologizing for infringing on his privacy, but Swanson seemed willing to talk. Then when you drove up, he took us back to the solarium and asked us to wait. A few minutes later he came back and got us and told us he was hashing it all out with the interested parties and he'd call us. Jay was bowing and scraping all the way out the door, but I was god damned if I was going to miss anything and I made him pull across the road into that gully and wait. And then Astrid comes tearing down the drive and I see you toss the artillery out, and I'm thinking all these years I've known you and you can still surprise me. Then she turns up the very next driveway and O'Donnell comes screaming down the lane, brakes when he sees the gun, grabs it, jumps back in the car and goes right up the same drive, and by this time I'm thinking somebody's going to get hurt. I started telling Jay to move before we heard the shots, and it was like moving an elephant to get him to put that van in gear."

"I don't blame him. It was ugly." Cooper mused, looking into the empty fireplace. "I'm trying to reconstruct what happened. O'Donnell had to have gotten in touch with Papini right after the mess at Cleo's place. He might even have been waiting around for him."

"Yeah. Those two were in close touch all the way through. When Papini disappeared back in December I bet it was because O'Donnell stashed him somewhere. He disappeared about the time O'Donnell approached Swanson with the offer."

"That makes sense. Anyway, tonight O'Donnell probably listened to the tape I gave Cleo right away and saw it was bogus. He'd know the shit was hitting the fan and start planning to cover his tracks. I bet he got together with Astrid and they started scheming. It would get really urgent after Swanson called her on the carpet. O'Donnell must have told Papini to drive out here and wait in the lane next door just in case he was needed, and he told Astrid he was there. And he got the shotgun out, with enough shells to handle anybody that needed shooting. The son of a bitch was ready to take out the whole neighborhood if he had to."

He fell silent and they listened for a while; somewhere they could hear voices, muted but insistent. Moreland wriggled on the couch, grimacing. "Jesus. I gotta tell you, MacLeish, I wouldn't have believed a woman like Astrid Huber was capable of something like this."

Cooper rubbed his eyes. "When she was driving me up the lane, playing along with my idea about Swanson, she said she didn't think Swanson was a murderer but he'd tell O'Donnell to get the job done no matter what it took. I think she was trying to make excuses, telling me what had happened with her—she wanted the job done but didn't want to know the details. Except she knew exactly what she was doing driving me up there and turning on the light to give Papini a good look. She was desperate and that was it for her scruples. O'Donnell rubbed her nose in the details tonight, and it was too much for her. I didn't hear what she said to him just before he shot her, but I bet it was something like 'we're through.' And I think he shot her because he knew S.O.P. in these things is for the person in Astrid's position to sell out everyone below her and ride out the storm. Astrid the pillar of society bats her eyes at the prosecutor and says how the nasty man misled her, and Chesty does twenty to life in Stateville. Chesty wasn't having any of that."

Moreland gave a short dry laugh. "Well, he's going to get it for sure, now. Hard to see how he thought he could get away with it."

"Maybe he just wasn't thinking. He won't be the last man to be led astray by a woman."

Moreland scowled. "I'll ignore that."

"Here's what I want to know. Why didn't Cleo set me straight? She knew what was going on. Why didn't she tell me I had it wrong?"

Moreland gave it some thought. "Because she was working for Astrid. She'd try to protect her."

"She would have to at least suspect that Astrid sicked Papini on her."

"Maybe not. Maybe she figured it was O'Donnell's call all the way. She'd at least want to talk to Astrid, to find out what was going on. I think she and Astrid were close. Astrid gave Cleo her first job, and I don't think she ever really stopped working for her, even when she and Swanson were getting it on. From things Cleo said, I gather Astrid used her to spy on Swanson. And loyalty to the boss is one of Cleo's strong points. She'd protect Astrid as long as she could."

"Huh. What the hell happened to her and Haynes?"

"Swanson said they went off together right after you and Astrid and O'Donnell ran out. Swanson said he'd never seen a guy change a tire so fast. And who's going to turn Cleo down when she asks for a ride?"

Cooper shook his head. "Sounds like this could be the beginning of a beautiful friendship."

There was a step in the doorway. Regis Swanson stood there, hands in his pockets. He looked from Cooper to Moreland and back, an expression of deep but troubled thought on his face. After a moment he said, "The doctor says Jay's OK. It's not a heart attack."

Moreland gave an approving grunt. "I think the sight of that shotgun was a little too much for him."

Cooper said, "Well, I'm damn glad he saw it in O'Donnell's hands. Otherwise it's my word against O'Donnell's as to who shot Astrid." Cooper looked at Swanson as he said it. Explanations had been made in the first frantic minutes while waiting for the police, but Cooper wondered if Swanson believed it all.

Swanson looked back at him, giving nothing away. He made a small soft sound that might have been an expression of interest and turned to Moreland. "He says he'll come have a look at your . . . your injury there, in a minute."

"Fine," said Moreland.

Swanson turned to go but lingered in the doorway, his eyes sweeping over the room absently. He looked like a man who had just seen a bad accident and isn't quite sure how he feels. "They're not letting the TV trucks up the drive," he said. "There's quite a tie-up out there on the road."

Cooper and Moreland traded glances. "Sounds like we're going to be here a while," said Cooper.

"Yes. They've taken Chesty over to the station. The chief's on the phone to your detective friend in the city now. He says he's going to want to have a nice long talk with all of us when he gets off the phone. I've got Felicidad making some coffee and sandwiches for us."

There was an embarrassed silence. Cooper waited for Swanson's eye to meet his again. "I owe you an apology," he said.

Swanson shrugged. "I don't know. Sounds like you handled things pretty well."

Cooper wasn't sure if it was sincere or devastating sarcasm. "I was trying to save my own life," he said.

"I know," said Swanson. "I'm sorry I didn't manage to clarify the position for you there in the study."

"I should have known. From what you said to Haynes when we

listened to the tape I should have realized that was the first time you'd heard it."

Swanson nodded. "Astrid brought it over. I told her if she didn't she could forget about her career in this town."

"If I'd been on the ball, I'd have just held you all at gunpoint and called the cops, let them sort it out. I panicked."

Swanson looked as if he wanted to drop the topic. "Hey, who thinks that fast?"

■ ■ ■

Cooper came out of the study, the hard looks of policemen wearing holes in his back. He was worn out, wrung dry. The house seemed to be filled with policemen and all the lights were on, just like the night of the party. Besides policemen there were mysterious men in plain clothes, who strode down hallways or conferred in corners in hushed voices. A cop led Cooper back to the room with the fireplace, where he found Macy and a young policeman sitting in attitudes of self-absorption, as well as Moreland, who was still prone on the sofa. There was a new bandage on his rump. Moreland's jacket hung on the arm of the sofa, his parka lay on the floor, and the crutches leaned against the wall. Macy's tie was loosened and he looked as if someone had just socked him in the solar plexus. Moreland raised his head with an inquiring look.

"Well, they're not going to charge me," said Cooper. "Not tonight, anyway. They found all the guns and they've got people over in the lane right now looking at tire tracks and things. I think Brown put in a good word for me, too. I'm hoping it's going to be a justifiable homicide."

"What else could it be?" said Moreland.

"Well, the guy asked me if it was necessary to shoot him six times."

"What'd you say?"

"I said probably not, but once I got started it was kind of hard to stop."

Macy, Moreland and the young policeman all looked at Cooper for several seconds without speaking. Cooper looked at the cop and said, "Mr. Swanson offered us drinks earlier. Is it all right with you if I take him up on it now?"

The cop frowned for a moment and then shrugged. "It's his booze. I guess it's OK with me."

Cooper moved behind the bar and started checking bottles.

"Anybody else?" he asked. Macy and Moreland shook their heads, still watching him. Cooper selected a bottle of Jim Beam from the array behind the bar and then foraged under it until he found a glass and some ice in a small refrigerator. He fixed himself a drink and then moved around the end of the bar and sat on a thickly upholstered wing chair next to the end of the sofa where Moreland's head was.

"See any signs of the competition?" Moreland said.

"Not yet. I think the police have the drive pretty well defended."

"Great. Now all we need is for them to let us out of here. Any idea when that might be?" Moreland said, addressing the policeman.

"That's up to the chief," the cop said. "You're all witnesses in a murder case. If you're lucky, maybe by morning."

"I've got a story to write. Ask my editor here." Macy jerked as if startled but said nothing. The cop shrugged.

Moreland glanced at the cop, then looked at Cooper. "One thing about that."

"What?"

"Who's got the tape now?"

Cooper shrugged. "Probably the cops do, by now."

"Probably?"

"If they've found it yet. It's dark out, you know."

Moreland gaped at him, not an easy feat from his position. "I thought you had it."

"I did. But when they asked me for it just now I couldn't seem to locate it. I had it in my pocket, but it must have fallen out in the scramble. They even searched me."

Moreland's eyes widened and his jaw slackened. "Jesus Christ, MacLeish, I'll kill you myself. That tape is the story."

"Sorry, man. I had more important things on my mind."

Moreland's head sagged onto the upholstery and his eyes closed.

Footsteps approached the door of the room; the young policeman leapt to his feet. Another officer appeared in the doorway and nodded at Macy. "Mr. Macy? They want to talk to you now." Macy rose to his feet looking dazed. The two policemen watched him as he made for the door, eyes darting wildly. Cooper slipped his hand into his jacket pocket and pulled out the cassette, which he had taken from the shelf under the bar. He slipped it into the pocket of Moreland's jacket hanging on the arm of the sofa.

"I'm not feeling terrific right now," Macy was saying, his voice fading away. The young cop sat back down and yawned.

Cooper looked at Moreland and said, "You're shivering, man. You need a doctor." He set his drink on the floor and took Moreland's jacket off the arm of the sofa.

"I've seen a doctor. I'm not going to die." Moreland brushed the jacket away with an irritable swipe. Cooper persevered and laid the jacket over his back and shoulders. "You're going to be sick as a dog if you don't take care of yourself." Cooper smoothed the jacket over Moreland's back and patted it in the right place to be sure Moreland felt the cassette. "There. You'll feel better in a while."

There was a silence and then Moreland said, "I'm starting to feel a lot better already. Thanks."

"My pleasure," said Cooper. "By the way."

"Huh?"

"You saved my life tonight. I never thanked you."

"Hey, what are friends for?"

Cooper picked up his glass and took a drink of bourbon. "All kinds of things, I guess."

IT WAS A DIFFERENT BED in a different hospital but Moreland still looked like a beached whale. Cooper straddled a straight-backed chair with his arms crossed on the back and looked into his friend's eyes. "You got it written, huh?"

"It's done. I got it in the computer at ten this morning and then collapsed. They brought me here in an ambulance. I woke up about an hour ago and the doctor chewed me out for running around all night. I told him to hold the lectures and keep the drugs coming."

"The radio and TV were all over it at noon."

"They'll have that full day's lead because it broke at night, but none of them have the Throop angle yet. That's my baby."

"The cops ask you about the tape?"

"Not yet. They will when the story runs, that's for sure. I'll tell 'em I found it on the parlor floor and I'll hand it over. They won't believe me, but they won't be able to do anything, either."

Cooper nodded. "Pappadakis knows about Throop, but she doesn't have the tape. I think you're going to scoop the world on this."

"Terrific." Moreland's eyes were closed.

"You know, for a man who just broke the story of the year, you don't look real happy."

Moreland heaved a deep sigh. Cooper waited him out, watching the broad back rise and fall with the breathing. "I feel like shit," Moreland said.

"How come?"

Moreland took a few seconds to answer. "You're not going to believe this, but I keep thinking about Wilson Throop."

"Why?"

"By all accounts he's a pretty decent man. And I don't want people saying I was part of some attempt to bring down the black man or something."

"You're doing your job, Mel. You heard the tape."

"Yeah, it's all there. They bought him. There's no denying it."

"You won't be the first journalist who's ruined somebody's life."

"Thank you, that's a very comforting thought."

"The scruples do you credit. But if Throop was white, would you hesitate for a minute to break this story? For a second?"

There was a long silence. Moreland never answered the question. Instead he said, "I keep thinking about Cleo, too."

"Oh yeah, her."

"She played me like a fish, didn't she, MacLeish?"

"Don't be too hard on yourself. She's a pro."

"Yeah, she really did a job on me."

"Well, hell. Did you enjoy the ride?"

"Sure. I guess. But it's not much to brag about, is it?" Moreland sounded half asleep. "All that passion, MacLeish. How could all that roll through somebody and just be part of another day at the office?"

"I think the pros have a different attitude about that kind of thing."

Moreland gave vent to another long sigh. "You were right, Coop. It's the cheap and tawdry ones you got to watch out for."

"Remember one thing, Mel."

"What's that?"

"She tried to save your life. If it had been completely professional, she would have let them kill you."

Moreland lay so still that Cooper thought he was asleep after a while. He stood up and put the chair back where he had found it.

"Thanks, MacLeish," came a voice from the bed.

"Hey," said Cooper. "What are friends for?"

■ ■ ■

Dominic stared sullenly across the table at his father. Cooper stared back, toying with the handle of his coffee cup, catching just a glimpse of the resemblance even Diana said she could see.

Dominic shoved the book bag toward him with an elbow and picked up his coffee. Cooper pulled out the top book on the stack. "*Calculus Made Simple*," he read. "Damn. You start at the top, don't you?"

"Aim high, right?"

"Well, this is higher than I can help you with. Calculus was the end of the line for my mathematics career."

"Actually . . . I think this might be like, a little advanced for me," said the boy, pulling the book to him and riffling the pages. "I've forgotten a lot."

"I've got an old trig and analytic geometry text at home I can lend you."

Dominic shrugged. "It was just kind of like an impulse. I don't know if I'm gonna do anything with it."

Cooper opened his mouth to say something and thought better of it. Dominic looked him in the eye, waiting for it with a slightly contemptuous look. Cooper shifted gears. "I was a little hard on you the other day in the pool hall," he said. "I'm sorry."

Dominic shrugged. "That's OK. You got your role to play, like everyone else."

"I've been through a couple with you, haven't I? See, I'm making it up as I go along. We missed a lot of stages in this relationship."

"No shit."

Cooper reached for the cup again. "So. You think it's worth pursuing?"

Dominic looked away out the window of the coffee house for a while, out into the deep, gray afternoon. Snow scuttled fitfully along the sidewalk and it looked as if spring was a lifetime away. Finally he looked back at Cooper, and for once the face looked a lot older than nineteen. "I think it's too late for you to be my father. I think that other asshole really was my father. Too bad he was an asshole, but what the fuck. The world's full of them, like you always say. I think you gotta give up the Dad thing, man. I always got room for more friends, but I don't think I can take another father."

Cooper stared, then nodded slowly, feeling a great weight lift, soaring slowly up into the winter sky. "It's a deal," he said softly, and then man and boy sat carefully not looking at one another, while the early night descended.

Cooper got the newspapers at the corner store early in the morning. His breath steamed out of him and was sucked away by an Arctic wind as he walked back down the block, scanning the headlines. Cooper read the papers at the dining room table with cold winter sunlight coming in through the south window. The competition had put it on page one under the headline *Sheridan Road Shootout Still a Mystery*, but Moreland's paper had kicked out the jams: *North Shore Carnage Linked to Throop Scandal* led it off under Moreland's byline, with a sidebar under the title *Throop: No Comment* and another that promised *Swanson on Wife: Ambition Run Wild*. In the bottom right corner was a small item: *Reporter's Close Shave*. It was with distinct discomfort that Cooper read Moreland's spare account of his own doings. He closed the paper and shoved it aside, remaining with his head in his hands for a long time.

Diana found him there when she came in. She shed hat, coat, and scarf and came and stood in the doorway with her arms folded until Cooper looked up.

"I didn't think you went over there on weekdays," said Cooper.

Her gaze was placid, serious but serene; it was one of many looks that he loved. "I don't usually. But after all this I felt the need of a little reassurance from upstairs."

"Had to talk to the Man about your wayward boy, huh?"

"Something like that." She came in and kissed him on the top of the head, looked at the papers without a word and proceeded to the kitchen. When she had her own coffee she came and sat at the table and started to read. Cooper got up and wandered about the apartment. Finally he came back to the dining room and sat opposite her.

"What on earth is this?" she said. " 'An investigator retained by this newspaper.' Since when have you been retained by the newspaper?"

"I guess Mel thought it sounded better than 'this guy I asked along for a ride because I was scared.' At least he kept my name out of it."

She shook her head. "I'm glad you came clean about all this yesterday. If I'd read it for the first time here, I'd be pretty upset."

"You'd be swearing in Spanish by now."

"English, too. I'd want to make sure you understood."

Cooper laughed, then fell silent looking into her dark, dark eyes and waiting for the other shoe to fall. He watched the eyes grow serious and then finally Diana said, "You're a hard man to love sometimes."

"I'm sorry."

"If this is the best you can do, I'd rather see you back in the taxi."

"I won't be getting back in the taxi." Cooper rose, went into the kitchen and refilled his mug, and came back. "I got three job offers yesterday after you left for work."

Her face went through a couple of changés and she said, "What?"

"For real. Christine Pappadakis came by to try to persuade me to go on TV and talk about all this shit. I refused, but before she left she said her right-hand man's leaving her. He got himself a Christine Pappadakis-type job in Omaha or someplace like that, so she needs a replacement. She offered me the job."

"You're kidding."

"No. She wants an assistant. Sounds like a combination research assistant, chauffeur, and office boy. Bodyguard sometimes maybe. I'd probably have to make coffee for her too."

Diana looked as if she could not quite bring herself to look hopeful. "What'd you tell her?"

"I told her I'd think about it."

"And the other two?"

"The second was from Regis Swanson."

"No."

"Yes. He needs a replacement for O'Donnell. Driver and factotum. He said I wouldn't have to live up there as long as I could be there at seven in the morning to drive him into the city. That's a drawback—I like my mornings. He promised flexible but occasionally long hours, variety, good pay and benefits."

"Why you?"

"I don't know. I had a little talk with him the other night after the cops left and I guess he was impressed. God knows why."

Diana nodded. "And what did you tell him?"

"Same thing."

"OK, what was the third offer?"

Cooper smiled. "Boyle's decided he needs to start work again. Except this time he's going to start up his own outfit, and he wants a partner. He asked me if I wanted to come in with him."

Diana's look now was resigned. "And just what is it that Boyle does for a living?"

"He's a skip chaser. He goes after bad debts."

Diana closed her eyes briefly. "No," she said. "You can't be serious."

"Relax," said Cooper. "I told him I'd have to give it some serious thought."

■ ■ ■

Cooper stopped in Burk's just after four. The place had just opened and the only person in there was Burk himself, grizzled and surly, hunting vaguely in the darkness under the long wooden bar for something that didn't seem to be there. He interrupted his labors long enough to serve Cooper a beer and then resumed.

On the television above the bar, volume turned down, a black man was reading a statement into a bank of microphones, pausing occasionally to wipe his eyes with a finger. The destruction of Wilson Throop had begun.

"You hear about this guy?" said Burk, emerging from under the bar and reaching for the volume control.

"Yeah," said Cooper. "I heard."

"That ought to take care of his chances for mayor."

On the screen Wilson Throop was saying, "I am prepared to pay whatever price the law deems appropriate. I take full responsibility for my actions."

Cooper shook his head and hoisted his beer. "I don't know. The man just won my vote."